A.J Moore, H.I Strang

Thomson's Seasons - Autumn and Winter

with an introduction and notes for the use of candidates preparing for university

matriculation and teachers' certificates

A.J Moore, H.I Strang

Thomson's Seasons - Autumn and Winter
with an introduction and notes for the use of candidates preparing for university matriculation and teachers' certificates

ISBN/EAN: 9783337256081

Printed in Europe, USA, Canada, Australia, Japan

Cover: Foto ©Andreas Hilbeck / pixelio.de

More available books at **www.hansebooks.com**

THOMSON'S SEASONS.

AUTUMN AND WINTER,

WITH AN

INTRODUCTION AND NOTES

BY

H. I. STRANG, B.A.,

Head Master, and

A. J. MOORE, B.A.,

Mathematical Master of

GODERICH HIGH SCHOOL.

FOR THE USE OF CANDIDATES PREPARING FOR
UNIVERSITY MATRICULATION AND
TEACHERS' CERTIFICATES.

—

TORONTO:
THE COPP-CLARK COMPANY, (LIMITED), PUBLISHERS, Front Street West
1886.

PREFACE.

IN offering for school use this edition of the poetry prescribed for next year's examinations, we are not sanguine enough to expect that it will escape unfavourable criticism. We have followed our own judgment in regard to the nature and amount of the help to be furnished, and while we have neither hoped nor desired to relieve teachers from teaching, or students from studying the poems, we have honestly tried to lighten their labour in doing so.

The object of the introduction is to supply necessary information in regard to the life and character of the author, and the influences that surrounded him ; that of the notes, to help candidates to a better understanding and appreciation of the poems, and at the same time to lead them to notice, think, and investigate for themselves. In writing both we have kept in mind that the book is designed for different grades of students, and that many who are likely to use it will have but little time or opportunity to consult good works of reference.

For reasons which need not be mentioned, the work has been done more hurriedly than we should have liked, and hence some omissions or mistakes may have been overlooked. Partly for the same reasons the notes on *Winter* were written first, which will account for some of the references in the notes to *Autumn*.

Lastly, while I am set down on the title-page as joint editor with Mr. Moore, and while I accept my full share of the responsibility for the work, it is only fair to say that he deserves the credit of it. I have simply been consulting and revising editor, and, except a few slight alterations and additions here and there, both introduction and notes appear substantially as they were written by him.

H. I. STRANG.

GODERICH, *July 30th, 1887.*

LIFE OF THOMSON.

JAMES THOMSON, the author of the *Seasons* and the *Castle of Indolence*, was born at Ednam, a little village on the Tweed, in the county of Roxburgh, September, 1700. His father, who was the minister at that place, shortly after the poet's birth removed to the parish of Southdean, in the same county, a rather remote and rugged district, among the lower slopes of the Cheviots. His father was noted for piety and zeal in church work rather than for great natural endowments, but his mother seems to have been a very superior woman, possessed of every social and domestic virtue, united to a most imaginative and devotional nature. Thus of Thomson it can be said, as of many other sons of genius, that he was indebted to his mother for his chief mental excellencies.

He attended the school at Jedburgh, but while there showed no superiority to other boys; on the contrary, he experienced some difficulty in mastering the rudiments of Latin and Greek. During the last three years of his residence with the family in the Southdean manse, while he was attending Jedburgh Grammar School, his education was superintended by a Mr. Riccaltoun or Riccarton, parish minister of Hobkirk, a man of some literary taste and capacity. Mr. Riccaltoun became much attached to Thomson, and seems to have been the first to discern in him the evidences of poetic genius. Thomson, thus being fortunate in his friend, became a fair general scholar, and received a good grounding in classical literature.

By this time he had attracted some notice and made some friends among the gentry of the neighbourhood, by poetical compositions at school and other scraps of verse, most of which, however, so little pleased himself that on each New Year's day, the productions of the past year were with mock solemnity committed to the flames.

Great as Thomson's natural gifts undoubtedly were, yet the rural grace and rugged grandeur of his home among the hills must have had much to do in developing and shaping his peculiar character as a poet. Allan Cunningham describes the landscape as "lovely, with its green hills and its blooming heather, while the slender stream of the crystal Jed winding through the whole adds a look of life by its moving waters to the upland solitude." This natural loveliness, and the legends and songs in which Roxburgh is rich, proved in the case of Thomson to be meet nurses for the poetic spirit within. A fragment preserved—by accident we suppose from the periodical burnings, shows considerable powers of fancy and felicity of expression, and shows, too, the early bent of Thomson's genius towards the apostrophe and descriptions of the powers of nature, and of the Divine attributes displayed in them :

> ' Now I surveyed my native faculties,
> And traced my actions to their teeming source ;
> Now I explored the Universal frame,
> Gazed nature through, and with interior light
> Conversed with angels and embodied saints,
> That tread the courts of the Eternal King.
>
> *   *   *   *   *
>
> Ah my Lord God ! in vain a tender youth,
> Unskilled in arts of deep philosophy,
> Attempts to search the bulky mass of matter,
> To trace the rules of motion, and pursue
> The phantom Time, too subtle for his grasp.
> Yet may I from thy most apparent works
> Form some idea of their wondrous Author.

At eighteen he went as a divinity student to Edinburgh College, where his poetical reputation had preceded him and was the means of gaining for him the life-long friendship of David Mallet and of Murdoch, his biographer. At college he was not popular with the students in general, and was voted by many a dull fellow and a fair mark for ridicule. Scarcely three years had elapsed when his father suddenly died, leaving his large family—there were nine, of whom Thomson was the fourth—in straitened circumstances. His mother, who had inherited a small estate or farm from her own people, mortgaged it, and came with the family to Edinburgh, resolved by strict economy to complete James's education for the ministry.

One day, while pursuing his divinity studies, he handed in to the Professor as an exercise, a paraphrase of the 119th psalm. Johnson says " his diction was so poetically splendid that Mr. Hamilton reproved him for using language unintelligible to a popular audience." Probably advice and not reproof was given, still the incident may have had its effect in determining Thomson to forsake divinity for the muse of poetry. But Edinburgh at that time offered few inducements to the man of letters. The stern theology of Calvin had so permeated the national character that to most Scotchmen the playhouse was an abomination, and the cultivation of poetry a suspicious pursuit. So, encouraged, it is supposed, by his mother, and by the praises bestowed by others on poetry he had written at college, especially a paraphrase of the 104th psalm, Thomson took the decisive step, and in the spring of 1725 set out for London to try his fortune.

He carried with him very little money, but many letters of intro- duction to persons of consequence, either social or literary, and the yet incomplete manuscript of *Winter*. While gaping about him in the streets he had his pockets picked of most of his letters, and in this strait he sought out his old friend Mallet, then in London and tutor to the sons of the Duke of Montrose. He advised him to complete *Winter* and connect the individual scenes into a regular poem. While doing this Thomson received news of his mother's death, and it was under the burden of this affliction and amid the uncongenial labour of a tutor, that the poem was finished and made its appearance in March, 1726. With difficulty he obtained from Millan, the publisher, three guineas for the copyright, and for a while there were no buyers. But owing to the good offices of a Rev. Mr. Whatley, who by accident took it up in the shop, approved of it, and sounded its praises in the coffee houses, Thomson began to grow famous. The friendship of Aaron Hill, immortalized as one of the divers in the *Dunciad* (II. 295) secured for him an invitation and a twenty guinea present from Sir Spencer Compton, Speaker of the House, to whom *Winter* had been dedicated, although he was probably ignorant even of the poet's existence. Thomson was not above the true Grub-street servility of the literary men of that age, and the fulsome adulation offered by the poet to the poetaster (Hill) is painful and dis- gusting to read. However, the popularity of *Winter* grew apace, and before the end of the year two new editions were required. Money was still so scarce with Thomson that he was again forced to resort to teaching, this time in a private academy; but his reputation and amiability were gaining for him many friends, and we find that Duncan Forbes, who helped him to prune his style a little, Aikman the painter, Miss Drelincourt, a beauty and a wit, "who looked and taught him into reputation," Dr. Rundle, Arbuthnot, Gay, Savage, Collins and Pope came to be among his familiar acquaintances, although Pope was never very cordial.

Next year (1727) *Summer* was given to the world, and in 1728 *Spring*, dedicated to the literary dabbler, the Countess of Hertford. The poet was honoured with an invitation for the summer to her country-seat, but paying more attention to the table than to her ladyship's poetic effusions, the invitation was never repeated. Thomson's literary fame was now sufficiently established to ensure a respectful reception to his poem *Britannia* (1729), which is nothing but a fatiguing invective against the government for their slackness in the Spanish war, Thomson, with most of the men of letters, being in opposition.

A quarto edition of the *Seasons* (*Autumn* now first appearing) was issued by subscription in 1730. In the same volume appeared the poem in memory of Newton, and the work closed with that magnificent hymn which has been called Thomson's finest production. Among the subscribers, of whom there were three hundred and eighty-seven, taking four hundred and fifty-four copies, were the leading men of letters, and besides, many persons of high social rank.

Thomson's first tragedy was *Sophonisba*, acted in 1729-30; but, although its rehearsal drew together a splendid critical audience, yet when performed it evoked no enthusiasm. The story goes that one weak line:

O, Sophonisba! Sophonisba, O!

was parodied by a wag into

O, Jemmy Thomson! Jemmy Thomson, O!

This set the town a-laughing, and the play after a short time was withdrawn. Thomson wrote other plays, but their declamatory style and want of humour unfitted them for stage dialogue, and with one doubtful exception, they were all unsuccessful.

In 1731, through Dr. Rundle's influence, he became travelling companion to the son of Sir Chas. Talbot. They visited France, Switzerland and Italy, and were away about a year. Grateful and beneficial as this journey must have been to Thomson, yet the first product of it, a dreary poem entitled *Liberty*, proved a dismal failure. In September, 1733, his young fellow-traveller died, and Thomson's tribute to his memory in sincere but not very felicitous verse, was the cause of his being given by Sir Chas. Talbot, now Lord Chancellor, the post of Secretary of Briefs in Chancery, where the pay was good and the work was nothing. In consequence we find him removed to Richmond, in a cottage close to the river's edge, and with a garden attached so that he could indulge his taste for gardening. His prosperity seems to have made him indolent, but showed at the same time his kindness of heart and his natural affection. He settled a small annuity on two of his sisters, and invited his invalid brother to live with him, but the poor fellow could not endure the damp English climate and returned to Scotland only to die.

It is pretty certain too that Thomson at this time meditated matrimony with a young lady whom he celebrates in his songs as Amanda. She was a Miss Elizabeth Young of Dumfries. The course of true love did not run smooth or end happily for the poet, for Cupid's best arrows are often tipped with gold, and Amanda succumbed to a wealthier suitor. His dreams of lettered ease proved to be nearly as transient as those of love, for the old Chancellor (Talbot) died in 1737, and Thomson, too indolent or too proud to solicit the new one (Hardwicke) for reappointment, lost his place. Perforce he betook himself to work and produced the tragedy of *Agamemnon*, a classical piece, and a year afterwards *Edward and Eleanora*, dealing with early English history. This last was a greater failure than *Agamemnon*, which is saying a good deal.

Just a little before the poet had been arrested for debt, and conveyed to a sponging-house, from which he was released by the actor Quin, who out of admiration for the author of the *Seasons* visited him there, ordered in a good supper (which Thomson liked) and in the course of the evening gave him £100. Immediately after he was introduced by Lyttelton to the Prince of Wales, who being out of favour at Court and anxious for popularity, gave Thomson a pension of a hundred a year. Through these two windfalls of fortune and the sales of his published works, which now were considerable, Thomson was able to retain his suburban cottage and garden on the Thames, where he lived in a sort of rural retirement, attending to his garden and fruit trees, revising the *Seasons*, and at odd moments adding a stanza to the *Castle of Indolence*.

In 1744, his friend Littelton, being in the new Ministry as a Commissioner in the Treasury, lost no time in appointing Thomson Surveyor-General of the Leeward Islands. The emoluments, after paying a deputy to perform the active duties, amounted to about £300 a year. This to Thomson was almost affluence, and made him independent of the pension which the Prince had given him, but four years later had rather shabbily withdrawn. The snug cottage in Kew Lane was comfortably, even elegantly furnished, and became the scene of much social enjoyment with his friends. Lyttleton's seat was also a favorite resort of his in those days.

Tancred and Sigismunda, his most successful tragedy, came out in 1745, and for a while it was a public favorite. Some have thought that its popularity was due less to its intrinsic merits than to the celebrated actors, Garrick and Mrs. Cibber, who took parts in it. But that such was not wholly the case, is apparent from the fact that Johnson speaks of it in his time as still keeping its turn upon the stage.

The *Castle of Indolence*, on which he had been engaged at intervals during fifteen years, appeared in May, 1748, and must be considered as his greatest work, if judged as a work of art, though if excellence be gauged by the number of readers, the *Seasons* will easily bear away the palm. Thomson has been accused of negligence of style, perhaps with justice, but the *Castle of Indolence* shows no faults of this kind, each stanza and phrase being polished with consummate care. It is an allegory, written in the Spenserian measure, and happily conceived in the style and spirit of the *Fairy Queen*.

On such a theme as *Indolence* Thomson wrote *con amoré*, and for a picture of lazy luxury set forth in the most melodious verse, the opening stanzas of the first canto have no equal in the language.

Thomson's death resulted from a neglected cold. He had walked into town, as was usual for him to do, and in the evening feeling tired and overheated, took the boat. The night air brought on a chill. Next day he was in a high fever, and imprudently venturing out before he had fully recovered, suffered a relapse. This time medical aid was of no avail, and he died at four o'clock in the morning of Saturday, 27th August, just two weeks before completing his forty-eighth year. He was buried in the church at Richmond. His loss was severely felt by a large circle of friends. Collins, the poet, who lived near him, left Richmond and refused to return. Quin, who spoke the prologue to his last play, *Coriolanus*, was affected to tears. Millan, his publisher, marked his esteem by devoting the profits of a splendid edition of the poet's works to the erection of a monument in Westminister Abbey, where it was placed between those of Shakespeare and Rowe. Never was man more sincerely mourned. Murdoch, his old friend and biographer, speaks of him as "our old, tried, amiable, open and honest-hearted Thomson, whom we never parted from but unwillingly, and never met but with fresh transport; in whom we found ever the same delightful companion, the same faithful depository of our inmost thoughts, and the same sensible, sympathizing adviser."

In youth Thomson was thought handsome, but with age his figure became ungainly, and his countenance gross and unanimated. He was, as is said in the *Castle of Indolence*, more "fat than bard beseems." In a numerous company he was generally silent and appeared somewhat stupid, but if directly addressed and engaged in conversation his features underwent a remarkable change; his eyes lighted up with unwonted fire, and he became, as he always was with a few select friends, sprightly and entertaining in his talk. Many stories have been told of his laziness. One represented him as standing at a peach tree with his hands in his pockets, eating the fruit as it grew. But an easy and indolent good nature was more than redeemed by an unaffected simplicity of heart. His patriotism, his tenderness for the brute creation, his love for his friends, his strong affection for the members of his own family, his extensive general acquirements, and his classical learning would have made James Thomson a beloved and respected member of society, even if he had not been, as he was, one of England's greatest poets.

THE STATE OF THE LITERARY WORLD.

IN the year 1700, in which Thomson was born, Dryden died Dryden, who had been king of the literary world so long. He had been a time-server all his life; had praised Cromwell, had belauded Charles, had apostatized to please James. Although fallen on evil days, deprived of his laureateship, and forced to work for his bread in his old age, he yet conferred the chief literary ustre on William's reign. He had brought in the French tastes in literature, and as a playwright had performed a great part in corrupting the English stage. His very last work, the "Fables," showed that adversity had taught him nothing in that respect, for they are tainted with even greater licentiousness than the originals from Boccacio and Chaucer. But however we may lament his indecencies, his knowledge of English was exquisite and wonderful. He was the greatest living writer in prose or verse. Pope, his immediate successor,

> " Whom Dryden taught to join
> The varying verse, the full resounding line,
> The long majestic march, and energy divine,"

acknowledges him as his master and model in the art of versification. Pope, however, i proved on Dryden, if by improvement be meant greater smoothness and regularity ; a more polished and balanced antithesis ; a more biting sarcasm ; a more stinging and pointed wit. He brought the heroic couplet to such perfection that it has ever since remained the vehicle for those kinds of poetry in which Pope excelled, viz. : the didactic, the satiric, the argumentative. Pope was the head of what has been called the artificial, the classical, and also the correct school. By these terms the student must understand a conforming to certain rules ; a sort of poetical code for versifiers. For instance : a redundant syllable must not be admitted, except in dramatic writing ; a pause of some kind must be at the end of every couplet : a full stop must never be placed, nor a new paragraph begin in the middle of a line, etc. These terms also refer to more than the mere form. It was an age of venality and insincerity in politics, of open profligacy or thinly-veneered vice at court and among the upper classes ; of ignorance and bestiality among the lower classes ; and worst of all, the church was sunk in indifference and lost to spiritual life. The upper and educated clergy were either busy in securing preferment, or engaged in metaphysical discussions on the nature or origin of religion ; the country clergy were often equally ignorant and coarse with their parishioners. The picture Thomson has given of their habits in " Autumn," 565 9, was unfortunately too often true. Under Walpole, the policy of Government patronage, of lucrative sinecures for literary men, was entirely changed. After this the literary life became one of indigence and obscurity often a struggle for bare existence. Here begins the generation of Grub street hacks. In no other age were the

writers so beggarly and vile, so fierce and rancorous. Pope has immortal
ized some of them in his inimitable satire. There were a few exceptions to
the usual misery. Pope from the profits of his *Homer* was snug in Twickenham ; Swift got his deanery by *ratting;* Young, his pension, by flattery;
Richardson lived by his printing ; Addison was especially fortunate.

The mission of the poetry of Anne and George I. was not to delineate
external nature, but to satirize or eulogize human nature. Wordsworth
makes the rather strong statement " that, excepting a passage or two in the
'*Windsor Forest*' of Pope, and some delightful pictures in the ' Poems of
Lady Winchelsea,' the poetry of the period between the publication of
' Paradise Lost ' and the ' Seasons ' does not contain a single new image
of external nature." The whole world of letters was engaged in satirizing,
in translating, in arguing, in declaiming, in uttering maxims, in sentimental
reflecting. The poetry is a reflex of the time ; it is correct ; it is brilliant
with wit ; it perhaps convinces, but it does not stir the emotions. Sarcasm
is much oftener found than honest, passionate indignation. Comedy is a
much greater favorite than tragedy. Of polish and affectation there was
plenty ; of deep passion of any kind there was very little. From the publication of "Winter" we must go forward twenty years to find the fancy and
pathos of Collins. About twenty years more brings us to the publication of
Percy's " *Reliques,*" which is an epoch in the slowly reviving taste for
what is natural and simple and unaffected. Our older poets again began
to be studied and imitated. New subjects were chosen, a new treatment
adopted.

And here it is proper to notice that religious awakening in the middle of
the 18th century, which had such profound moral results, and which no
doubt contributed not a little to affect the form and substance of literature.
The Puritanism which had successfully resisted the tyranny of the first two
Stuarts, developed a tyranny of its own, more galling perhaps by reason of
its austerity. When in 1660 England was released from the gloomy reign of
the Saints, the great principles of morality and of religious liberty seemed
for awhile to have departed with them. But they soon reappear. The
moral force of Puritanism, its chief and abiding glory, asserts itself in the
revolution of 1688, and shows itself in the Methodist revival, which was but
a protest against the apathy of the Church. It is seen in the plea of Burke
for the Hindoo, in the philanthropy of Howard, in the work of Clarkson
and Wilberforce for the black man. It is seen in the evangelic movement
which took place within the pale of the English Church itself. The gentle
Cowper took a part with Mr. Newton, its leader, in reclaiming the irreligi-
ous of Olney. No other poem breathes a purer spirit of piety and Christian
philosophy than the " Task," and this poem is generally taken to be the
culmination and completion of that rebellion against the reign of the false
and affected, and of that return to the simple and sincere in which Thomson
had taken the first step.

POETRY, like painting, or sculpture, is imitation, and is finest and most successful when it produces on the mind the effect of the original. If the object of descriptive poetry is to create through the imaginative faculty the liveliest images of the real objects from which they are drawn, then. Thomson is the greatest of our descriptive poets. As we read him, we see the green fields, the trees covered with white blossoms, and the bees humming among them, the flowers that grow by the brook and give out their fragrance as it goes purling by. We see the shadows chasing each other over the yellow cornfields, we hear the sighing of the autumn winds and the groaning of the winter's tempest, and we seem to see before our very eyes, away out on the bleak snowy waste, the poor lost wretch plunging through the shapeless drifts.

There is no other writer that has drunk in more of the soul of his subject. "He looks on nature with the eye that nature bestows only on a poet, with a mind that comprehends the vast and attends to the minute." Nature was his first love, when he saw her in the valleys of Southdean; and years after, in the gardens of Kew, he again exclaims:

> "I care not Fortune, what you me deny;
> You cannot rob me of free Nature's grace,
> You cannot shut the windows of the sky,
> Through which Aurora shows her brightening face;
> You cannot bar my constant feet to trace
> The woods and lawns, by living streams at eve;
> Of fancy, reason, virtue, nought can me bereave."

It is common to make comparisons between Thomson and Cowper. In chasteness of language and harmony Cowper is the superior, yet it is thought the former possessed a greater share of the true spirit of poesy. Thomson loves to paint with bold sweeping strokes, and makes a grand general impress on the mind. Cowper delights us by a series of minute and delicate touches, which make his picture stand out in exquisite clearness and beauty. Thomson loves images of power and energy; Cowper those of grace and quiet —his life was passed among scenes of less rugged character. (See W. 729, n.) Thomson seems to have been fortunate in his choice of a subject, and even its very title seems a happy one. There existed in his time very little descriptive poetry worthy of the name. Spencer was forgotten, and Milton had been neglected. "From Dryden to Thomson there is scarcely a rural image drawn from life to be found in any of the English poets except Gay." Thomson's subject admitted of being treated in the digressive and desultory manner suited to his indolent temperament, and gave ample scope for diffuseness of description, as well as for gorgeous colouring and unlimited epithet.

POETICAL FORM.

The "Seasons" are written in Iambic Pentameter, or Blank Verse—that is in lines which do not rhyme—and which contain regularly ten syllables, or five iambic feet, the number of the accents being, however, of more importance than the number of the syllables. The general rule that every line shall end with some important word, Thomson has pretty strictly observed. The terminal words are nearly always nouns or verbs, occasionally a pronoun, an adjective, or an adverb, never a pure preposition or conjunction. The scansion is, generally speaking, regular and easy. A *trochee* sometimes occurs in place of an iambus, usually in the first foot, and *anapæsts* or *amphibrachs* are not uncommon, but these are the only changes necessary to make the accents of the line fall on the properly accented syllables of the words. . . . In form as well as subject the "Seasons" may be considered a new departure. The causes of Thomson's adoption of blank verse are not far to seek. His ministerial nurture and training, and on that account greater familiarity with pre-Restoration and Puritan authors, no doubt inclined him toward the verse in which Milton wrote. The form of his boyish efforts, of which a specimen is given in the Life, will show best the force of his early associations. He seems all along to have been conscious (See A. 646, and n.), not only that an entire poem in the rhyming measure of the day would weary by the regularity of its cadence, but that blank verse would better suit his theme, and would have besides the added charm of novelty.

THE RELIGIOUS ELEMENT IN THE SEASONS.

The religion of the Seasons is but that religion which nature alone might teach ; it recognizes a Supreme Architect : it has a lofty and moral tone, and has a pleasing harmony, and a disposition towards sweetness and light which Mathew Arnold might envy. But its character is very indefinite ; it has little reference to the *quality* of our beliefs, or to the real remedy for the evil tendencies of the heart, the acceptance of Christ and the influence of the Holy Spirit. In only a very few passages we discover with some difficulty any recognition of the revealed character of God. Some have thought that the speculations of the English Deists, the plausible advocates of natural religion, may have had some influence with Thomson, as we know they had with Voltaire.* The more charitable view is that the poet, not altogether wanting in that shrewdness inherent in the Scottish character,

---

* Voltaire visited England in 1726, and remained two yeurs. He thus became familiar with the writings of Shaftesbury, Bolingbroke, Collins, Tindall, Wollaston, etc. It must be remembered that only ignorance attributes atheism to Voltaire. In fact Diderot was disgusted with him for not being sufficiently advanced, and thought him a mental weakling for still adhering to the belief of God.

adapted his religious sentiments to the prevailing taste. Pope and his school then ruled the republic of letters, and this of itself may explain the repeated moral platitudes, whose wearisomeness the ornate and splendid diction cannot always conceal. In a transition period we must expect some temporizing, and this cautious treatment no doubt secured and still does secure a wider circle of readers. None but an atheist could find fault with the theology of the *Seasons*.

LOVE AND THE DOMESTIC RELATION.

SAVAGE, who was an intimate of Thomson's, says he knew no love but that of the sex. But one could hardly get such an opinion from his works— certainly not from the "Seasons." We see, indeed, that love as presented by him is not of the highest order ; is, in fact, a little prosaic ; although for every day wear, a solid, serviceable sort of article. His women have a certain robustness, a blowzy healthfulness about them, which our later poets tacitly deny to their highest types. They seem to lack that delicacy, that simple grace, that indefinable charm, with which the magic numbers of Tennyson and Coleridge invest their female creations.

We give Thomson the highest praise when we say that he is purity itself in comparison with his contemporaries. Here and there may be a line in which a little coarseness is suggested rather than expressed. Yet the "Seasons" contain no expression that need raise the blush of modesty, except in those too easily conscious, or of prurient imagination. His pictures of domestic happiness, and his estimate of the conjugal relation do him honor ; for the public conscience on these topics was not too tender. The comedy of intrigue, which Beaumont and Fletcher introduced, found congenial soil in the dissolute court of Charles II. It was still common in Thomson's time for ladies to wear masks when hearing for the first time a new play. Rowe's " Fair Penitent," whose " gay Lothario " has become a synonym for an un principled rake, was still in the full tide of its popularity. Congreve, who had defiled the splendour of his wit in the grossest dialogue, and scoffed at the sacredness of the marriage tie, lived till 1729. He had produced nothing but some miscellaneous poetry since the failure of his " Way of the World," but he and his plays were still famous. Farquhar died in 1707, while all London was roaring with delight at his *Beaux' Stratagem*, the female char- acters of which are quite as free-spoken, if not as frail as those of Wycherly or Congreve. The "Provoked Husband " of Vanbrugh, was published in the same year as "Winter," and was hardly an improvement on his last play, " The Provoked Wife," of thirty years before. Since Collier had made his vigorous assault against the immorality of the English stage, had intimi- dated Dryden and vanquished Congreve, who came to its defence, there had been a partial reformation. The essays of Steele and Addison helped to abate the nuisance, but the poison of the Restoration was active for some time longer. We see it in the novels of Fielding and Smollett ; we see it in

Laurence Sterne, the earliest of the Men of Feeling, who may have had the "finest spirit of whim," but whose works proclaim him a "refined and sickly blackguard."

CHARACTERISTICS OF HIS STYLE.

WORDSWORTH accuses Thomson of "writing a vicious style." He means that his verse should be devoid of tawdry ornament and swelling phrases, of classical allusions and of harsh inversions, all which accord but ill with the simplicity and severity of Nature. To a great extent this criticism is true. There is a good deal of classical and artificial embroidery in the "Seasons." In scores of places he imitates, even translates, Virgil. His frequent personifications are often abrupt, unexpected, and therefore not natural, as for example, those at the beginning of each "Season." His invocations to the Muse, to Spring, to Philosophy, to this, that and the other, are endless and wearying. Sometimes, too, by his dedications, and fulsome flattery, he works us into a most unchristian mood, and we almost wish that some of his patriots had died an untimely death. These faults, and they all exist, are partly of the man and partly of the imitative, non-original age, in which he wrote. It must be confessed, however, that while he is engaged in the pure contemplation of Nature, the luxuriance and redundancy of his style seem somewhat venial faults. In the moist air and rank vegetation, in the teeming and humid English climate, this excessive verbal drapery, like the flowing garb of an Oriental, lends to his descriptions a dignity and a pomp not altogether inappropriate.

But when in the same manner he describes the loves of Palemon and Lavinia, the fox hunt, the drinking-bout, the rustic revelry of the harvest home, the effect is disagreeable, sometimes even grotesque in its absurdity. It is unfortunate for Thomson that he introduces so many episodes, declamations, digressions, and dedications. But it must be remembered that he was a pioneer, and that it would be too much to expect that he could keep himself free in all things from the influence of the artificial school, especially as versifiers were swarming in London, and some of them his intimates. These parts were probably the most efficient in recommending the author to general notice, and some critics approve of them as tending to relieve the tedium of general description.

Dr. Craik characterizes Thomson as "all negligence and nature. So negligent indeed, that he pours forth his unpremeditated song without the thought ever occurring to him that he could improve it by any study or elaboration." The "Seasons" in its present state is the result of careful and repeated revision, so much so, that the latest edition as compared with the first, is almost a new work. But a tasteful and candid critic might see no harm in a little more pruning and chastening.

Let us here, in conclusion, enumerate the chief mannerisms of our author, although noticed in their place in the annotations. (1) His free use of adjectives as nouns, and nouns as adjectives. It would seem quite indifferent to Thomson whether he said "immense serene" or "serene immense." (2) His continual use of words with their Latin meaning. (3) His coining of compounds, some of them not too well formed. (4) His frequent use of absolute constructions. All these are due to his classical reading. (5) His frequent alliterations. (6) He doesn't disdain to use such tricks of phrase as "sees astonished and astonished sings," "gay care," "pleasing dread." (7) His meaningless turgidity, as "in pure effusion flow," "sound integrity." (8) His often extravagant hyperbole as in A. 527, 699. (9) His frequent use of metonymy and personification. (10) His frequent and, generally speaking, unambiguous use of adjectives for adverbs, which sometimes makes us think that English would be improved by being, in this respect, just like German.

Other points will no doubt strike the reader as worthy of note : for instance, (1) Thomson's weakness in scientific knowledge ; and (2) The almost entire absence from his pages of irony or sarcasm, humour or wit. For the last two, his cumbrous style would be like the armor of Saul to the youthful David.

QUOTATIONS AND PASSAGES FOR MEMORIZING.

THE selection, it need hardly be said, is not authoritative : but while no one is bound by it, or even expected to accept it as wholly satisfactory, it is hoped that it will be found helpful.

AUTUMN.

Ll. 122, 177 185, 201 206, 229 230, 298 306, 433 236, 602 609, 903 969, 1032 1036, 1257 1277.

WINTER.

Ll. 1 16, 66-71, 217 222, 276-321, 431 435, 545 549, 611 645, 716 751, 859 865, 894 900, 1028-1041, 1064 1069.

CHRONOLOGICAL PARALLEL.

THOMSON'S LIFE.	EVENTS, LITERARY AND GENERAL.
1701. Thomson b.	Dryden d., Congreve's " *Way of the World*," Act of Settlement.
2.	War of Spanish Succession.
3.	Wesley b., *The Fair Penitent*.
4.	Blenheim, Locke d., *Tale of a Tub*.
6.	Ramilies.
7.	Union Act, Farquhar d., *The Beaux' Stratagem*.
8.	Oudenarde.
9.	Malplaquet, *Tatler*, Johnson b.
10.	Sacheverell's Trial.
11.	*Spectator, Essay on Criticism*.
12. at Jedburgh School	Marlborough dismissed.
13.	Treaty of Utrecht, *Cato, Rape of the Lock*, Shaftesbury d., Sterne b.
14.	*Jane Shore*, Whitefield d.
15. goes to Edinburgh College	The 15, Riot Act, Rowe Laureate, Wycherley d.
16.	Septennial Act, Garrick b., Gray b.
18. his father d.	Quadruple Alliance.
19.	Addison d., *Robinson Crusoe*.
20.	South Sea Bubble.
21.	Prior d., Walpole's Ministry. *Hist. of our own Times*.
23.	Bishop Atterbury banished.
24.	*Drapier Letters*.
25. goes to London	Pope's *Iliad* and *Odyssey* completed, *The Gentle Shepherd*.
26. *Winter*	*Gulliver's Travels*.
27. *Summer*	Newton d.
28. *Spring*	Goldsmith b.
29. *Britannia, Sophonisba*	Congreve d., *The Dunciad, The Wanderer, The Methodists at Oxford*.
30. 4to edition of *Seasons. Autumn*	Colley Cibber Laureate, Burke b.
31. Continental tour, Fr. Sw. Italy	Defoe d., Cowper b.
32.	Gay d.
33. Sec. of Briefs	*Essay on Man*, Walpole's Excise Bill.
35. *Liberty*	The Wesleys accomp. Oglethorpe to Georgia.
36. In his cottage at Richmond	
37. Lost his place	Hume's *Treatise on Human Nature*.
38. *Agamemnon*	Whitefield in America.

xix.

CHRONOLOGICAL PARALLEL. *Continued.*

Thomson's Life.	Events, Literary and General.
39. *Edward and Eleanora* {	Wesley's real conversion, begins his Itinerancy, War with Spain.
40. *Masque of Alfred* .	*Pamela,* Wesley and Whitefield separate.
41. . . . . {	*The Schoolmistress, Joseph Andrews,* Hume's *Essays.*
42.	Resignation of Walpole.
43. visiting at Hagley .	Dettingen.
44. S. G. of Leeward Isles	Pope d., *The Night Thoughts.*
45. *Tancred and Sigismunda* . . }	Swift d., Walpole d., Fontenoy.
46. Auth. Version of Seasons }	*Ode on the Passions,* Culloden.
48. *Castle of Indolence* in May; died in August . . }	Roderick Random, Clarissa Harlowe, Treaty of Aix-la-Chapelle.
49. *Coriolanus* . .	*Vanity of Human Wishes, Irene.*

THE SEASONS.

AUTUMN.

CROWN'D with the sickle and the wheaten sheaf,
While Autumn, nodding o'er the yellow plain,
Comes jovial on, the Doric reed once more,
Well pleas'd, I tune.   Whate'er the wintry frost
Nitrous prepar'd—the various-blossomed Spring
Put in white promise forth—the Summer suns
Concocted strong—rush boundless now to view,
Full, perfect all, and swell my glorious theme.

Dedication.

Onslow! the muse, ambitious of thy name,
To grace, inspire, and dignify her song,   10
Would from the public voice thy gentle ear
Awhile engage.   Thy noble care she knows,
The patriot virtues that distend thy thought,
Spread on thy front, and in thy bosom glow ;
While listening senates hang upon thy tongue,
Devolving through the maze of eloquence
A roll of periods, sweeter than her song.
But she too pants for public virtue : she,
Though weak of power, yet strong in ardent will,
Whene'er her country rushes on her heart,   20
Assumes a bolder note, and fondly tries
To mix the patriot's with the poet's flame.

The Fiel's Roady for Harvest.

When the bright Virgin gives the beauteous days,
And Libra weighs in equal scales the year,

From heaven's high cope the fierce effulgence shook
Of parting Summer, a serener blue,
With golden light enliven'd, wide invests
The happy world.   Attemper'd suns arise,
Sweet-beam'd, and shedding oft, through lucid clouds,
A pleasing calm; while, broad and brown, below,   30
Extensive harvests hang the heavy head.
Rich, silent, deep, they stand; for not a gale
Rolls its light billows o'er the bending plain;
A calm of plenty! till the ruffled air
Falls from its poise, and gives the breeze to blow.
Rent is the fleecy mantle of the sky;
The clouds fly different; and the sudden sun
By fits effulgent gilds th' illumin'd field;
And black by fits the shadows sweep along.
A gaily-chequer'd, heart-expanding view,   40
Far as the circling eye can shoot around,
Unbounded tossing in a flood of corn.

Industry and its Effects.

These are thy blessings, Industry! rough power!
Whom labor still attends, and sweat, and pain;
Yet the kind source of every gentle art,
And all the soft civility of life:
Raiser of human kind! by Nature cast,
Naked, and helpless, out amid the woods
And wilds, to rude inclement elements;
With various seeds of art deep in the mind   50
Implanted—and profusely pour'd around
Materials infinite; but idle all.
Still unexerted, in the unconscious breast,
Slept the lethargic powers: corruption still,
Voracious, swallow'd what the liberal hand
Of bounty scatter'd o'er the savage year;

And still the sad barbarian, roving, mix'd
With beasts of prey ; or, for his acorn meal,
Fought the fierce tusky boar.   A shivering wretch !
Aghast and comfortless, when the bleak north,   60
With winter charg'd, let the mix'd tempest fly,
Hail, rain, and snow, and bitter-breathing frost.
Then to the shelter of the hut he fled,
And the wild season, sordid, pin'd away ;
For home he had not : home is the resort
Of love, of joy, of peace, and plenty, where,
Supporting and supported, polish'd friends
And dear relations mingle into bliss.
But this the rugged savage never felt,
Even desolate in crowds ; and thus his days   70
Roll'd heavy, dark, and unenjoy'd, along ;
A waste of time ! till Industry approach'd,
And rous'd him from his miserable sloth ;
His faculties unfolded ; pointed out
Where lavish Nature the directing hand
Of art demanded ; showed him how to raise
His feeble force by the mechanic powers ;
To dig the mineral from the vaulted earth ;
On what to turn the piercing rage of fire,
On what the torrent and the gather'd blast ;   80
Gave the tall ancient forest to his axe ;
Taught him to chip the wood and hew the stone,
Till, by degrees, the finish'd fabric rose ;
Tore from his limbs the blood-polluted fur,
And wrapt them in the woolly vestment warm,
Or bright in glossy silk, and flowing lawn :
With wholesome viands fill'd his table : pour'd
The generous glass around, inspir'd to wake
The life-refining soul of decent wit ;
Nor stopp'd at barren bare necessity ;   90

But still, advancing bolder, led him on
To pomp, to pleasure, elegance, and grace ;
And, breathing high ambition through his soul,
Set science, wisdom, glory, in his view,
And bade him be the lord of all below.
    Then gathering men their natural powers combin'd,
And form'd a public ; to the general good
Submitting, aiming, and conducting all.
For this the patriot council met, the full,
The free, and fairly represented whole.   100
For this they plann'd the holy guardian laws,
Distinguish'd orders, animated arts,
And, with joint force oppression chaining, set
Imperial justice at the helm -yet still
To them accountable ; nor slavish dream'd
That toiling millions must resign their weal,
And all the honey of their search, to such
As for themselves alone themselves have rais'd.
    Hence every form of cultivated life
In order set, protected, and inspir'd,   110
Into perfection wrought.   Uniting all,
Society grew numerous, high, polite,
And happy.   Nurse of art, the city rear'd
In beauteous pride her tower-encircled head ;
And, stretching street on street, by thousands drew,
From twining woody haunts, or the tough yew
To bows strong-straining, her aspiring sons.
    Then Commerce brought into the public walk
The busy merchant ; the big warehouse built ;
Rais'd the strong crane : chok'd up the loaded street   120
With foreign plenty ; and thy stream, O Thames,
Large, gentle, deep, majestic, king of floods !
Chose for his grand resort.   On either hand,
Like a long wintry forest, groves of masts

Shot up their spires : the bellying sheet between,
Possess'd the breezy void : the sooty hulk
Steer'd sluggish on : the splendid barge along
Row'd regular to harmony : around,
The boat, light skimming, stretch'd its oary wings ;
While deep the various voice of fervent toil   130
From bank to bank increas'd ; whence, ribb'd with oak,
To bear the British thunder, black and bold,
The roaring vessel rush'd into the main.

　　Then, too, the pillar'd dome, magnific, heav'd
Its ample roof ; and luxury within
Pour'd out her glittering stores : the canvas smooth
With glowing life protuberant, to the view
Embodied rose : the statue seem'd to breathe,
And soften into flesh, beneath the touch
Of forming art, imagination-flush'd.   140

　　All is the gift of Industry ; whate'er
Exalts, embellishes, and renders life
Delightful.   Pensive Winter, cheer'd by him,
Sits at the social fire, and happy hears
Th' excluded tempest idly rave along.
His harden'd fingers deck the gaudy Spring.
Without him, Summer were an arid waste ;
Nor to the autumnal months could thus transmit
Those full, mature, immeasurable stores,
That, waving round, recall my wandering song.   150

Reaping.

　　Soon as the morning trembles o'er the sky,
And, unperceiv'd, unfolds the spreading day,
Before the ripen'd field the reapers stand
In fair array ; each by the lass he loves,
To bear the rougher part, and mitigate
By nameless gentle offices her toil.

At once they stoop, and swell the lusty sheaves :
While through their cheerful band the rural talk,
The rural scandal, and the rural jest,
Fly harmless, to deceive the tedious time, 160
And steal unfelt the sultry hours away.
Behind, the master walks, builds up the shocks
And, conscious, glancing oft on every side
His sated eye, feels his heart heave with joy.
The gleaners spread around, and here and there,
Spike after spike, their scanty harvest pick.

Be not too narrow, husbandmen ! but fling
From the full sheaf, with charitable stealth,
The liberal handful. Think, oh grateful think !
How good the God of Harvest is to you ; 170
Who pours abundance o'er your flowing fields ;
While those unhappy partners of your kind
Wide hover round you, like the fowls of heaven,
And ask their humble dole.   The various turns
Of fortune ponder ; that your sons may want
What now, with hard reluctance, faint, ye give.

The Story of Lavinia and Palemon.

The lovely young Lavinia once had friends ;
And fortune smil'd, deceitful, on her birth ;
For, in her helpless years, depriv'd of all,
Of every stay, save innocence and Heaven, 180
She, with her widow'd mother, feeble, old,
And poor, liv'd in a cottage, far retir'd
Among the windings of a woody vale,
By solitude and deep surrounding shades,
But more by bashful modesty, conceal'd.
Together thus they shunn'd the cruel scorn
Which virtue, sunk to poverty, would meet
From giddy passion and low-minded pride ;

Almost on Nature's common bounty fed,
Like the gay birds that sung them to repose, 190
Content, and careless of to-morrow's fare.
Her form was fresher than the morning rose,
When the dew wets its leaves ; unstain'd and pure,
As is the lily, or the mountain-snow.
The modest virtues mingled in her eyes,
Still on the ground dejected, darting all
Their humid beams into the blooming flowers ;
Or, when the mournful tale her mother told,
Of what her faithless fortune promis'd once,
Thrill'd in her thought, they, like the dewy star 200
Of evening, shone in tears. A native grace
Sat fair proportion'd on her polish'd limbs,
Veil'd in a simple robe, their best attire,
Beyond the pomp of dress ; for loveliness
Needs not the foreign aid of ornament,
But is, when unadorn'd, adorn'd the most.
Thoughtless of beauty, she was beauty's self,
Recluse amid the close-embowering woods.
As, in the hollow breast of Apennine,
Beneath the shelter of encircling hills, 210
A myrtle rises, far from human eye,
And breathes its balmy fragrance o'er the wild ;
So flourish'd, blooming, and unseen by all,
The sweet Lavinia ; till, at length, compell'd
By strong necessity's supreme command,
With smiling patience in her looks, she went
To glean Palemon's fields. The pride of swains
Palemon was, the generous, and the rich,
Who led the rural life in all its joy
And elegance, such as Arcadian song 220
Transmits from ancient, uncorrupted times,
When tyrant custom had not shackled man,

But free to follow nature was the mode.
He then, his fancy with autumnal scenes
Amusing, chanc'd beside his reaper train
To walk, when poor Lavinia drew his eye.
Unconscious of her power, and turning quick
With unaffected blushes from his gaze,
He saw her charming, but he saw not half
The charms her downcast modesty conceal'd.   230
That very moment, love and chaste desire
Sprung in his bosom, to himself unknown ;
For still the world prevail'd, and its dread laugh
Which scarce the firm philosopher can scorn,
Should his heart own a gleaner in the field ;
And thus in secret to his soul he sighed :
    " What pity ! that so delicate a form,
By beauty kindled, where enlivening sense
And more than vulgar goodness seem to dwell,
Should be devoted to the rude embrace   240
Of some indecent clown ! She looks, methinks,
Of old Acasto's line ; and to my mind
Recalls that patron of my happy life,
From whom my liberal fortune took its rise ;
Now to the dust gone down ; his houses, lands,
And once fair-spreading family, dissolv'd.
'Tis said that in some lone obscure retreat,
Urg'd by remembrance sad, and decent pride,
Far from those scenes which knew their better days
His aged widow and his daughter live,   250
Whom yet my fruitless search could never find.
Romantic wish ! would this the daughter were !
    When, strict inquiring, from herself he found
She was the same, the daughter of his friend,
Of bountiful Acasto, who can speak
The mingled passions that surpris'd his heart,

And through his nerves, in shivering transport ran?
Then blaz'd his smother'd flame, avow'd and bold ;
And, as he view'd her, ardent, o'er and o'er,
Love, gratitude, and pity, wept at once.   260
Confus'd, and frighten'd, at his sudden tears,
Her rising beauties flush'd a higher bloom,
As thus Palemon, passionate and just,
Pour'd out the pious rapture of his soul :
    " And art thou then Acasto's dear remains ;
She whom my restless gratitude has sought
So long in vain ?   O yes ! the very same,
The soften'd image of my noble friend,
Alive, his every look, his every feature,
More elegantly touch'd.   Sweeter than Spring !"   270
Thou sole surviving blossom from the root
That nourish'd up my fortune !   Say, ah where,
In that sequester'd desert, hast thou drawn
The kindest aspect of delighted heaven,
Into such beauty spread, and blown so fair,
Though poverty's cold wind and crushing rain
Beat keen and heavy on thy tender years ?
Oh let me now into a richer soil,
Transplant thee safe, where vernal suns and showers
Diffuse their warmest, largest influence ;
And of my garden be the pride and joy !
It ill befits thee, oh ! it ill befits
Acasto's daughter, his whose open stores,
Though vast, were little to his ampler heart,
The father of a country, thus to pick
The very refuse of those harvest fields
Which from his bounteous friendship I enjoy.
Then throw that shameful pittance from thy hand,
But ill-applied to such a rugged task !
The fields, the master, all, my fair, are thine,   280

If to the various blessings which thy house
Has on me lavish'd, thou wilt add that bliss,
That dearest bliss, the power of blessing thee!"
    Here ceas'd the youth; yet still his speaking eye
Express'd the sacred triumph of his soul,
With conscious virtue, gratitude, and love,
Above the vulgar joy divinely rais'd.
Nor waited he reply.   Won by the charm
Of goodness irresistible, and all
In sweet disorder lost, she blush'd consent;   300
The news immediate to her mother brought,
While, pierc'd with anxious thought, she pin'd away
The lonely moments for Lavinia's fate.
Amazed, and scarce believing what she heard,
Joy seiz'd her wither'd veins: and one bright gleam
Of setting life shone on her evening hours,
Not less enraptur'd than the happy pair,
Who flourish'd long in tender bliss, and rear'd
A numerous offspring, lovely like themselves,
And good, the grace of all the country round.   310

A Storm in Harvest.

Defeating oft the labours of the year,
The sultry south collects a potent blast.
At first, the groves are scarcely seen to stir
Their trembling tops; and a still murmur runs
Along the soft-inclining fields of corn.
But as the aerial tempest fuller swells,
And in one mighty stream, invisible,
Immense, the whole excited atmosphere
Impetuous rushes o'er the sounding world,
Strained to the root, the stooping forest pours   320
A rustling shower of yet untimely leaves.
High-beat, the circling mountains eddy in,

From the bare wild, the dissipated storm,
And send it in a torrent down the vale.
Expos'd, and naked, to its utmost rage,
Through all the sea of harvest rolling round,
The billowy plain floats wide, nor can evade,
Though pliant to the blast, its seizing force ;
Or whirled in air, or into vacant chaff
Shook waste.   And, sometimes, too, a burst of rain   330
Swept from the black horizon, broad, descends
In one continuous flood.   Still over head
The mingled tempest weaves its gloom, and still
The deluge deepens, till the fields around
Lie sunk, and flatted, in the sordid wave.
Sudden, the ditches swell, the meadows swim.
Red, from the hills, innumerable streams
Tumultous roar, and high above its banks
The river lift ; before whose rushing tide,
Herds, flocks, and harvests, cottages, and swains,   340
Roll mingling down ; all that the winds had spar'd,
In one wild moment ruin'd; the big hopes
And well-earn'd treasures of the painful year.
Fled to some eminence, the husbandman
Helpless beholds the miserable wreck
Driving along : his drowning ox at once
Descending, with his labours scatter'd round,
He sees ; and instant o'er his shivering thought
Comes winter unprovided, and a train
Of clamant children dear.   Ye masters, then,   350
Be mindful of the rough laborious hand,
That sinks you soft in elegance and ease,
Be mindful of those limbs in russet clad,
Whose toil to yours is warmth, and graceful pride ;
And, oh be mindful of that sparing board,
Which covers yours with luxury profuse,

Makes your glass sparkle, and your sense rejoice ;
Nor cruelly demand what the deep rains
And all-involving winds have swept away.

Description of Shooting ; Its Cruelty.

Here the rude clamour of the sportsman's joy,   360
The gun fast-thundering, and the winded horn,
Would tempt the muse to sing the rural game :
How, in his mid-career, the spaniel, struck
Stiff, by the tainted gale, with open nose,
Outstretched, and finely sensible, draws full,
Fearful, and cautious, on the latent prey,
As in the sun the circling covey bask
Their varied plumes, and, watchful every way,
Through the rough stubble turn the secret eye.
Caught in the meshy snare, in vain they beat   370
Their idle wings, entangled more and more ;
Nor on the surges of the boundless air,
Though borne triumphant, are they safe : the gun,
Glanc'd just and sudden from the fowler's eye,
O'ertakes their sounding pinions, and again,
Immediate brings them from the towering wing,
Dead to the ground, or drives them wide-dispers'd,
Wounded, and wheeling, various down the wind.
These are not subjects for the peaceful muse,
Nor will she stain with such her spotless song,   380
Then most delighted, when she social sees
The whole mix'd animal creation round
Alive and happy.   'Tis not joy to her,
This falsely cheerful, barbarous game of death ;
This rage of pleasure, which the restless youth
Awakes, impatient, with the gleaming morn
When beasts of prey retire, that, all night long,
Urg'd by necessity, had rang'd the dark,

As if their conscious ravage shunn'd the light,
Asham'd.   Not so the steady tyrant, man,
Who, with the thoughtless insolence of power
Inflam'd, beyond the most infuriate wrath
Of the worst monster that e'er roam'd the waste,
For sport alone pursues the cruel chase,
Amid the beaming of the gentle days.
Upbraid, ye ravening tribes, our wanton rage,
For hunger kindles you, and lawless want,
But, lavish fed, in Nature's bounty roll'd,
To joy at anguish, and delight in blood,
Is what your horrid bosoms never knew.

The Chase of the Hare.

Poor is the triumph o'er the timid hare,
Scar'd from the corn, and now to some lone seat
Retir'd; the rushy fen; the ragged furze
Stretch'd o'er the stony heath; the stubble chapp'd
The thistly lawn; the thick-entangled broom;
Of the same friendly hue, the wither'd fern;
The fallow ground laid open to the sun,
Concoctive; and the nodding sandy bank,
Hung o'er the mazes of the mountain brook.
Vain is her best precaution, though she sits
Conceal'd, with folded ears, unsleeping eyes,
By Nature rais'd to take the horizon in,
And head couch'd close betwixt her hairy feet,
In act to spring away.   The scented dew
Betrays her early labyrinth; and deep,
In scatter'd, sullen openings, far behind,
With every breeze she hears the coming storm.
But nearer, and more frequent, as it loads
The sighing gale, she springs amaz'd, and all
The savage soul of game is up at once:

The pack full-opening, various ; the shrill horn
Resounded from the hills ; the neighing steed,
Wild for the chase ; and the loud hunter's shout
O'er a weak, harmless, flying creature ; all
Mix'd in mad tumult and discordant joy.

The Chase of the Stag.

The stag, too, singled from the herd, where long
He rang'd the branching monarch of the shades,
Before the tempest drives.   At first in speed
He, sprightly, puts his faith ; and, rous'd by fear,
Gives all his swift aerial soul to flight.   430
Against the breeze he darts, that way the more
To leave the lessening murderous cry behind.
Deception short ! though fleeter than the winds
Blown o'er the keen-air'd mountain by the north,
He bursts the thickets, glances through the glades,
And plunges deep into the wildest wood ;
If slow, yet sure, adhesive to the track
Hot steaming, up behind him come again
The inhuman rout, and from the shady depth
Expel him, circling through his every shift.   440
He sweeps the forest oft, and sobbing sees
The glades, mild opening to the golden day,
Where, in kind contest, with his butting friends
He wont to struggle, or his loves enjoy.
Oft in the full-descending flood he tries
To lose the scent, and lave his burning sides ;
Oft seeks the herd : the watchful herd, alarm'd,
With selfish care avoid a brother's woe.
What shall he do ?   His once so vivid nerves,
So full of buoyant spirit, now no more,   450
Inspire the course ; but fainting breathless toil,
Sick, seizes on his heart : he stands at bay,

And puts his last weak refuge in despair.
The big round tears run down his dappled face.
He groans in anguish ; while the growling pack,
Blood-happy, hang at his fair jutting chest,
And mark his beauteous chequer'd sides with gore,
    Of this enough.   But if the sylvan youth,
Whose fervent blood boils into violence,
Must have the chase, behold, despising flight,   460
The rous'd-up lion, resolute and slow,
Advancing full on the protended spear,
And coward-band that, circling, wheel aloof.
Slunk from the cavern and the troubled wood,
See the grim wolf : on him his shaggy foe
Vindictive fix, and let the ruffian die ;
Or, growling horrid, as the brindled boar
Grins fell destruction, to the monster's heart
Let the dart lighten from the nervous arm.

The Chase of the Fox.

    These Britain knows not : give, ye Britons, then,   470
Your sportive fury, pitiless, to pour
Loose on the nightly robber of the fold.
Him, from his craggy winding haunts unearth'd,
Let all the thunder of the chase pursue.
Throw the broad ditch behind you : o'er the hedge
High bound, resistless ; nor the deep morass
Refuse, but through the shaking wilderness
Pick your nice way : into the perilous flood
Bear fearless, of the raging instinct full ;
And, as you ride the torrent, to the banks,   480
Your triumph sound sonorous running round,
From rock to rock, in circling echoes toss'd.
Then scale the mountains to their woody tops ;
Rush down the dangerous steep ; and o'er the lawn,

In fancy swallowing up the space between,
Pour all your speed into the rapid game,
For happy he who tops the wheeling chase ;
Has every maze evolv'd, and every guile
Disclos'd ; who knows the merits of the pack ;
Who saw the villain seiz'd and dying hard,
Without complaint, though by an hundred mouths
Relentless torn : oh glorious he, beyond
His daring peers ! when the retreating horn
Calls them to ghostly halls of grey renown,
With woodland honours grac'd ; the fox's fur,
Depending decent from the roof ; and spread
Round the drear walls, with antic figures fierce,
The stag's large front : he then is loudest heard,
When the night staggers with severer toils,
With feats Thessalian centaurs never knew,
And their repeated wonders shake the dome.

The Fox-Hunters' Evening.

But first the fuel'd chimney blazes wide.
The tankards foam : and the strong table groans
Beneath the smoking sirloin stretch'd immense
From side to side ; in which, with desperate knife,
They deep incision make, and talk the while
Of England's glory, ne'er to be defac'd,
While hence they borrow vigour : or amain
Into the pasty plung'd, at intervals,
If stomach keen can intervals allow,
Relating all the glories of the chase.
Then sated hunger bids his brother thirst
Produce the mighty bowl : the mighty bowl
Swell'd high with fiery juice, steams liberal round
A potent gale, delicious as the breath
Of Maia to the love-sick shepherdess,

On violets diffus'd, while soft she hears
Her panting shepherd stealing to her arms.
Nor wanting is the brown October, drawn,
Mature and perfect, from his dark retreat   520
Of thirty years; and now his honest front
Flames in the light refulgent, not afraid
Even with the vineyard's best produce to vie.
To cheat the thirsty moments, whist awhile
Walks his dull round, beneath a cloud of smoke,
Wreath'd, fragrant, from the pipe; or the quick dice
In thunder leaping from the box, awake
The sounding gammon; while romp-loving miss
Is haul'd about, in gallantry robust.

At last, these puling idlenesses laid   530
Aside, frequent and full, the dry divan
Close in firm circle, and set, ardent, in
For serious drinking.   Nor evasion sly,
Nor sober shift, is to the puking wretch
Indulg'd apart; but earnest, brimming bowls
Lave every soul, the table floating round,
And pavement, faithless to the fuddled foot.
Thus, as they swim in mutual swill, the talk,
Vociferous at once from twenty tongues,
Reels fast from theme to theme; from horses, hounds,   540
To church or mistress, politics or ghost,
In endless mazes, intricate, perplex'd.
Meantime, with sudden interruption, loud,
Th' impatient catch bursts from the joyous heart.
That moment, touch'd is each congenial soul;
And, opening in a full-mouth'd cry of joy,
The laugh, the slap, the jocund curse, go round;
While, from their slumbers shook, the kennel'd hounds
Mix in the music of the day again.
As when the tempest, that has vex'd the deep   550

The dark night long, with fainter murmurs falls,
So gradual sinks their mirth.   Their feeble tongues,
Unable to take up the cumbrous word,
Lie quite dissolv'd.   Before their maudlin eyes,
Seen dim and blue, the double tapers dance,
Like the sun wading through the misty sky,
Then, sliding soft, they drop.   Confus'd above,
Glasses and bottles, pipes and gazetteers,
As if the table even itself was drunk,
Lie, a wet broken scene ; and wide, below,   560
Is heap'd the social slaughter, where astride
The lubber power in filthy triumph sits,
Slumbrous, inclining still from side to side,
And steeps them drench'd in potent sleep till morn.
Perhaps some doctor, of tremendous paunch,
Awful and deep, a black abyss of drink,
Outlives them all ; and from his buried flock,
Retiring, full of rumination sad,
Laments the weakness of these latter times.

The Evening Occupations of Women.

But if the rougher sex by this fierce sport   570
Is hurried wild, let not such horrid joy
E'er stain the bosom of the British fair.
Far be the spirit of the chase from them !
Uncomely courage, unbeseeming skill,
To spring the fence, to rein the prancing steed,
The cap, the whip, the masculine attire ;
In which they roughen to the sense, and all
The winning softness of their sex is lost.
In them 'tis graceful to dissolve at woe ;
With every motion, every word, to wave   580
Quick o'er the kindling cheek the ready blush ;
And from the smallest violence to shrink,

Unequal, then the loveliest in their fears—
And by this silent adulation, soft,
To their protection more engaging man.
Oh may their eyes no miserable sight,
Save weeping lovers, see ! a nobler game,
Through love's enchanting wiles pursued, yet fled,
In chase ambiguous.   May their tender limbs
Float in the loose simplicity of dress,   590
And, fashion'd all to harmony, alone
Know they to seize the captivated soul,
In rapture warbled from love-breathing lips ;
To teach the lute to languish : with smooth step,
Disclosing motion in its every charm,
To swim along, and swell the mazy dance ;
To train the foliage o'er the snowy lawn ;
To guide the pencil, turn the tuneful page ;
To lend new flavour to the fruitful year,
And heighten nature s dainties ; in their race   600
To rear their graces into second life ;
To give society its highest taste ;
Well-order'd home man's best delight to make ;
And, by submissive wisdom, modest skill,
With every gentle care-eluding art,
To raise the virtues, animate the bliss,
Even charm the pains to something more than joy,
And sweeten all the toils of human life.
This be the female dignity and praise.

A View of an Orchard.

Ye swains, now hasten to the hazel-bank,   610
Where, down yon vale, the wildly winding brook
Falls hoarse from steep to steep.   In close array
Fit for the thickets and the tangling shrub,
Ye virgins, come.   For you their latest song

The woodlands raise: the clustering nuts for you
The lover finds amid the secret shade;
And, where they burnish on the topmost bough,
With active vigour crushes down the tree,
Or shakes them ripe from the resigning husk,
A glossy shower, and of an ardent brown,   620
As are the ringlets of Melinda's hair;
Melinda, formed with every grace complete,
Yet these neglecting, above beauty wise,
And far transcending such a vulgar praise.

   Hence from the busy joy-resounding fields,
In cheerful error, let us tread the maze
Of Autumn, unconfin'd, and taste, reviv'd,
The breath of orchard big with bending fruit.
Obedient to the breeze and beating ray,
From the deep-loaded bough a mellow shower   630
Incessant melts away.   The juicy pear
Lies, in a soft profusion, scatter'd round.
A various sweetness swells the gentle race,
By nature's all-refining hand prepar'd;
Of temper'd sun, and water, earth, and air,
In ever-changing composition mix'd.
Such, falling frequent through the chiller night,
The fragrant stores, the wide-projected heaps
Of apples, which the lusty-handed year,
Innumerous, o'er the blushing orchard shakes.   640
A various spirit, fresh, delicious, keen,
Dwells in their gelid pores, and, active, points
The piercing cider for the thirsty tongue:
Thy native theme, and boon inspirer too,
Phillips, Pomona's bard, the second thou
Who nobly durst, in rhyme-unfetter'd verse,
With British freedom sing the British song:
How, from Silurian vats, high-sparkling wines

Foam in transparent floods; some strong, to cheer
The wintry revels of the labouring hind;   550
And tasteful some, to cool the summer hours.

Bub Dodington's Seat in Dorset.

In this glad season, while his sweetest beams
The sun sheds equal o'er the meeken'd day,
Oh lose me in the green delightful walks
Of, Dodington! thy seat, serene and plain,
Where simple nature reigns, and every view,
Diffusive spreads the pure Dorsetian downs,
In boundless prospect, yonder, shagg'd with wood,
Here rich with harvest, and there white with flocks.
Meantime, the grandeur of thy lofty dome,   660
Far-splendid, seizes on the ravished eye.
New beauties rise with each revolving day;
New columns swell; and still the fresh Spring finds
New plants to quicken, and new groves to green.
Full of thy genius all! the muses' seat,
Where, in the secret bower and winding walk,
For virtuous Young and thee they twine the bay.
Here, wandering oft, fir'd with the restless thirst
Of thy applause, I solitary court
Th' inspiring breeze, and meditate the book   670
Of nature ever open; aiming thence,
Warm from the heart, to learn the moral song.
Here, as I steal along the sunny wall,
Where Autumn basks, with fruit empurpled deep,
My pleasing theme continual prompts my thought;
Presents the downy peach, the shining plum,
With a fine bluish mist of animals
Clouded; the ruddy nectarine; and dark,
Beneath his ample leaf, the luscious fig.
The vine, too, here her curling tondrils shoots;   680

Hangs out her clusters, glowing, to the south;
And scarcely wishes for a warmer sky.

Picture of a Vineyard.

Turn we, a moment, fancy's rapid flight
To vigorous soils, and climes of fair extent,
Where, by the potent sun elated high,
The vineyard swells refulgent on the day,
Spreads o'er the vale, or up the mountain climbs,
Profuse, and drinks, amid the sunny rocks,
From cliff to cliff increas'd, the heighten'd blaze.
Low bend the weighty boughs.   The clusters clear,   690
Half through the foliage seen, or ardent flame,
Or shine transparent; while perfection breathes
White o'er the turgent film the living dew.
As thus they brighten with exalted juice,
Touch'd into flavour by the mingling ray,
The rural youth and virgins o'er the field,
Each fond for each to cull th' autumnal prime,
Exulting rove, and speak the vintage nigh.
Then comes the crushing swain: the country floats,
And foams unbounded with the mashy flood,   700
That, by degrees fermented and refin'd,
Round the rais'd nations pours the cup of joy:
The claret smooth, red as the lip we press
In sparkling fancy, while we drain the bowl;
The mellow-tasted burgundy; and, quick
As is the wit it gives, the gay champagne.

Autumn Fogs.

Now, by the cool, declining year condens'd,
Descend the copious exhalations, check'd
As up the middle sky unseen they stole,
And roll the doubling fogs around the hill.   710

No more the mountain, horrid, vast, sublime,
Who pours a sweep of rivers from his sides,
And high between contending kingdoms rears
The rocky long division, fills the view
With great variety ; but in a night
Of gathering vapour, from the baffled sense
Sinks dark and dreary.   Thence expanding far,
The huge dusk, gradual, swallows up the plain.
Vanish the woods.   The dim-seen river seems
Sullen, and slow, to roll the misty wave.   720
E'en in the height of noon oppress'd, the sun
Sheds weak and blunt his wide-refracted ray ;
Whence glaring oft, with many a broaden'd orb,
He frights the nations.   Indistinct on earth,
Seen through the turbid air, beyond the life
Objects appear ; and, wilder'd, o'er the waste
The shepherd stalks gigantic ; till at last
Wreath'd dun around, in deeper circles still
Successive closing, sits the general fog
Unbounded o'er the world ; and, mingling thick,   730
A formless grey confusion covers all ;
As when, of old (so sung the Hebrew bard)
Light, uncollected, through the chaos urg'd
Its infant way ; nor order yet had drawn
His lovely train from out the dubious gloom.

The Origin of Springs and Rivers.

These roving mists, that constant now begin
To smoke along the hilly country, these,
With weighty rains, and melted Alpine snows,
The mountain cisterns fill, those ample stores
Of water, scoop'd among the hollow rocks ;   740
Whence gush the streams, the ceaseless fountains play,
And their unfailing wealth the rivers draw.

Some sages say that, where the numerous wave
For ever lashes the resounding shore,
Drill'd through the sandy stratum, every way,
The waters with the sandy stratum rise;
Amid whose angles infinitely strain'd,
They joyful leave their jaggy salts behind,
And clear and sweeten, as they soak along.
Nor stops the restless fluid, mounting still,   750
Though oft amidst th' irriguous vale it springs;
But to the mountain courted by the sand,
That leads it darkling on in faithful maze,
Far from the parent main, it boils again
Fresh into day; and all the glittering hill
Is bright with spouting rills.   But hence this vain
Amusive dream! why should the waters love
To take so far a journey to the hills,
When the sweet valleys offer to their toil
Inviting quiet, and a nearer bed?   760
Or if, by blind ambition led astray,
They must aspire, why should they sudden stop
Among the broken mountain's rushy dells,
And, ere they gain its highest peak, desert
Th' attractive sand that charm'd their course so long?
Besides, the hard agglomerating salts,
The spoil of ages, would impervious choke
Their secret channels, or, by slow degrees,
High as the hills protrude the swelling vales.
Old Ocean too, suck'd through the porous globe,   770
Had long ere now forsook his horrid bed,
And brought Deucalion's watery times again.

    Say, then, where lurk the vast eternal springs,
That, like creating nature, lie conceal'd
From mortal eye, yet with their lavish stores
Refresh the globe, and all its joyous tribes?

O thou pervading genius, given to man,
To trace the secrets of the dark abyss,
Oh, lay the mountains bare ; and wide display
Their hidden structure to the astonish'd view !   780
Strip from the branching Alps their piny load ;
The huge incumbrance of horrific woods
From Asian Taurus, from Imaus stretch'd
Athwart the roving Tartar's sullen bounds.
Give opening Hæmus to my searching eye,
And high Olympus pouring many a stream.
Oh, from the sounding summits of the north,
The Dofrine hills, through Scandinavia roll'd
To farthest Lapland and the frozen main ;
From lofty Caucasus, far seen by those   790
Who in the Caspian and black Euxine toil ;
From cold Riphean rocks, which the wild Russ
Believes the stony girdle of the world ;
And all the dreadful mountains, wrapt in storm,
Whence wide Siberia draws her lonely floods—
Oh, sweep th' eternal snows !   Hung o'er the deep,
That ever works beneath his sounding base
Bid Atlas, propping heaven, as poets feign,
His subterranean wonders spread.   Unveil
The miny caverns, blazing on the day   800
Of Abyssinia's cloud compelling cliffs,
And of the bending Mountains of the Moon.
O'ertopping all these giant sons of earth,
Let the dire Andes, from the radiant Line
Stretch'd to the stormy seas that thunder round
The southern pole, their hideous deeps unfold !
Amazing scene !   Behold ! the glooms disclose :
I see the rivers in their infant beds ;
Deep, deep, I hear them labouring to get free.
I see the leaning strata, artful rang'd ;   810

The gaping fissures to receive the rains,
The melting snows, and ever-dripping fogs.
Strew'd bibulous above, I see the sands,
The pebbly gravel next, the layers then
Of mingled moulds, of more retentive earths,
The gutter'd rocks and mazy-running clefts,
That, while the stealing moisture they transmit,
Retard its motion, and forbid its waste.
Beneath the incessant weeping of these drains,
I see the rocky siphons stretch'd immense,   820
The mighty reservoirs of harden'd chalk,
Or stiff compacted clay, capacious form'd.
O'erflowing thence, the congregated stores,
The crystal treasures of the liquid world,
Through the stirr'd sands a bubbling passage burst,
And, welling out around the middle steep,
Or from the bottoms of the bosom'd hills,
In pure effusion flow.　United, thus,
The exhaling sun, the vapour-burthen'd air,
The gelid mountains, that, to rain condens'd,   830
These vapours in continual current draw,
And send them, o'er the fair-divided earth,
In bounteous rivers to the deep again,
A social commerce hold, and firm support
The full-adjusted harmony of things.

Migratory Birds and their Resorts.

When Autumn scatters his departing gleams,
Warn'd of approaching Winter, gather'd, play
The swallow-people; and, toss'd wide around,
O'er the calm sky, in convolution swift
The feather'd eddy floats, rejoicing once,   840
Ere to their wintry slumbers they retire;
In clusters clung, beneath the mouldering bank,
And where, unpierc'd by frost, the cavern sweats:

Or rather into warmer climes convey'd
With other kindred birds of season, there
They twitter cheerful, till the vernal months
Invite them welcome back ; for, thronging, now
Innumerous wings are in commotion all.
　　Where the Rhine loses his majestic force
In Belgian plains, won from the raging deep,　　850
By diligence amazing, and the strong
Unconquerable hand of liberty,
The stork assembly meets, for many a day,
Consulting deep, and various, ere they take
Their arduous voyage through the liquid sky.
And now, their route design'd, their leaders chose,
Their tribes adjusted, clean'd their vigorous wings,
And many a circle, many a short essay,
Wheel'd round and round—in congregation full
The figur'd flight ascends, and, riding high　　860
The aerial billows, mixes with the clouds.
　　Or where the Northern ocean, in vast whirls,
Boils round the naked melancholy isles
Of farthest Thule, and the Atlantic surge
Pours in among the stormy Hebrides,
Who can recount what transmigrations there
Are annual made? what nations come and go?
And how the living clouds on clouds arise,
Infinite wings, till all the plume-dark air
And rude-resounding shore are one wild cry?　　870
Here the plain harmless native his small flock,
And herd diminutive of many hues,
Tends on the little island's verdant swell,
The shepherd's sea-girt reign ; or, to the rocks
Dire clinging, gathers his ovarious food ;
Or sweeps the fishy shore ; or treasures up
The plumage, rising full, to form the bed
Of luxury.

Scotland and Her Patriotic Sons.

And here awhile the muse,
High hovering o'er the broad cerulean scene,
Sees Caledonia in romantic view ;   850
Her airy mountains, from the waving main,
Invested with a keen diffusive sky,
Breathing the soul acute ; her forests huge,
Incult, robust, and tall, by nature's hand
Planted of old ; her azure lakes between,
Poured out extensive, and of watery wealth
Full : winding deep, and green her fertile vales ;
With many a cool translucent brimming flood
Wash'd lovely, from the Tweed (pure parent stream
Whose pastoral banks first heard my Doric reed,   890
With sylvan Jed, thy tributary brook),
To where the north-inflated tempest foams
O'er Orca's or Berubium's highest peak :
Nurse of a people, in misfortune's school
Trained up to hardy deeds : soon visited
By learning, when before the Gothic rage
She took her western flight.   A manly race,
Of unsubmitting spirit, wise and brave,
Who still through bleeding ages struggled hard
(As well unhappy Wallace can attest,   900
Great patriot-hero ! ill-requited chief !)
To hold a generous undiminish'd state ;
Too much in vain !   Hence of unequal bounds
Impatient, and by tempted glory borne
O'er every land, for every land their life
Has flow'd profuse, their piercing genius plann'd,
And swell'd the pomp of peace their faithful toil;
As from their own clear north, in radiant streams,
Bright over Europe burst the Boreal morn.

Argyle and Forbes.

Oh ! is there not some patriot, in whose power   910
That best, that god-like luxury is plac'd,
Of blessing thousands, thousands yet unborn,
Through late posterity ? some, large of soul,
To cheer dejected industry, to give
A double harvest to the pining swain,
And teach the labouring hand the sweets of toil ;
How, by the finest art, the native robe
To weave ; how, white as hyperborean snow,
To form the lucid lawn ; with venturous oar
How to dash wide the billow, nor look on,   920
Shamefully passive, while Batavian fleets
Defraud us of the glittering finny swarms
That heave our friths, and crowd upon our shores
How all-enlivening trade to rouse, and wing
The prosperous sail from every growing port,
Uninjur'd, round the sea-encircled globe ;
And thus, in soul united as in name,
Bid Britain reign the mistress of the deep ?
    Yes, there are such. And full on thee, Argyle,
Her hope, her stay, her darling, and her boast,   930
From her first patriots and her heroes sprung,
Thy fond imploring country turns her eye ;
In thee, with all a mother's triumph, sees
Her every virtue, every grace combin'd,
Her genius, wisdom, her engaging turn,
Her pride of honour, and her courage tried,
Calm and intrepid, in the very throat
Of sulphurous war, on Taisniere's dreadful field.
Nor less the palm of peace inwreathes thy brow,
For, powerful as thy sword, from thy rich tongue   940
Persuasion flows, and wins the high debate ;

While, mix'd in thee, combine the charm of youth,
The force of manhood, and the depth of age.
Thee, Forbes, too, whom every worth attends,
As truth sincere, as weeping friendship kind,
Thee truly generous, and in silence great,
Thy country feels through her reviving arts,
Plann'd by thy wisdom, by thy soul inform'd;
And seldom has she known a friend like thee.

The Fading Woods and Verdure.

But see, the fading many-colour'd woods,   950
Shade deepening over shade, the country round
Imbrown; a crowded umbrage, dusk and dun,
Of every hue, from wan declining green
To sooty black. These now the lonesome muse,
Low-whispering, lead into their leaf-strown walks,
And give the season in its latest view.
Meantime, light-shadowing all, a sober calm
Fleeces unbounded ether: whose least wave
Stands tremulous, uncertain where to turn
The gentle current; while, illumin'd wide,   960
The dewy-skirted clouds imbibe the sun,
And, through their lucid veil, his soften'd force
Shed o'er the peaceful world. Then is the time,
For those whom wisdom and whom nature charm,
To steal themselves from the degenerate crowd,
And soar above this little scene of things;
To tread low-thoughted vice beneath their feet:
To soothe the throbbing passions into peace,
And woo lone quiet in her silent walks.
Thus solitary, and in pensive guise,   970
Oft let me wander o'er the russet mead,
And through the sadden'd grove, wherescarce is heard
One dying strain, to cheer the woodman's toil.

Haply some widow'd songster pours his plaint,
Far, in faint warblings, through the tawny copse;
While congregated thrushes, linnets, larks,
And each wild throat, whose artless strain so late
Swell'd all the music of the swarming shades,
Robb'd of their tuneful souls, now shivering sit
On the dead tree, a dull despondent flock, 980
With not a brightness waving o'er their plumes,
And nought save chattering discord in their note.
Oh, let not, aim'd from some inhuman eye,
The gun the music of the coming year
Destroy; and harmless, unsuspecting harm,
Lay the weak tribes, a miserable prey,
In mingled murder, fluttering on the ground.

The pale descending year, yet pleasing still,
A gentler mood inspires; for now the leaf
Incessant rustles from the mournful grove, 990
Oft startling such as, studious, walk below,
And slowly circles through the waving air.
But should a quicker breeze amid the boughs
Sob, o'er the sky the leafy deluge streams;
Till chok'd, and matted with the dreary shower,
The forest-walks, at every rising gale,
Roll wide the wither'd waste, and whistle bleak.
Fled is the blasted verdure of the field;
And, shrunk into their beds, the flowery race
Their sunny robes resign. Even what remain'd 1000
Of bolder fruits, falls from the naked tree;
And woods, fields, gardens, orchards, all around
The desolated prospect thrills the soul.

The Thoughts produced by Autumn.

He comes! he comes! in every breeze the power
Of philosophic melancholy comes.
His near approach the sudden-starting tear,

The glowing cheek, the mild dejected air,
The soften'd feature, and the beating heart,
Pierc'd deep with many a virtuous pang, declare.
O'er all the soul his sacred influence breathes,   1010
Inflames imagination, through the breast
Infuses every tenderness, and far
Beyond dim earth exalts the swelling thought.
Ten thousand thousand fleet ideas, such
As never mingled with the vulgar dream,
Crowd fast into the mind's creative eye.
As fast the correspondent passions rise,
As varied, and as high; devotion rais'd
To rapture and divine astonishment;
The love of nature unconfin'd, and, chief,   1020
Of human race; the large ambitious wish
To make them blest; the sigh for suffering worth
Lost in obscurity; the noble scorn
Of tyrant pride; the fearless great resolve;
The wonder which the dying patriot draws,
Inspiring glory through remotest time;
Th' awaken'd throb for virtue and for fame;
The sympathies of love and friendship dear;
With all the social offspring of the heart.
    Oh! bear me then to vast embowering shades,   1030
To twilight groves and visionary vales,
To weeping grottoes and prophetic glooms,
Where angel forms athwart the solemn dusk
Tremendous sweep, or seem to sweep along;
And voices more than human, through the void
Deep sounding, seize th' enthusiastic ear!

The Country-seat of Stowe.

    Or is this gloom too much? Then lead, ye powers
That o'er the garden and the rural seat
Preside, which shining through the cheerful land,

In countless numbers blest Britannia sees ;   1040
Oh, lead me to the wide-extended walks,
The fair majestic paradise, of Stowe !
Not Persian Cyrus on Ionia's shore
E'er saw such sylvan scenes, such varied art
By genius fired, such ardent genius tam'd
By cool judicious art, that in the strife,
All-beauteous nature fears to be outdone.
And there, O Pitt, thy country's early boast,
There let me sit beneath the shelter'd slopes,
Or in that temple where, in future times,   1050
Thou well shalt merit a distinguish'd name ;
And, with thy converse blest, catch the last smiles
Of Autumn beaming o'er the yellow woods.
While there with thee the enchanted round I walk,
The regulated wild, gay fancy then
Will tread in thought the groves of Attic land ;
Will from thy standard taste refine her own,
Correct her pencil to the purest truth
Of nature, or, the unimpassion'd shades
Forsaking, raise it to the human mind :   1060
Or if hereafter she, with juster hand,
Shall draw the tragic scene, instruct her thou
To mark the varied movements of the heart ;
What every decent character requires,
And every passion speaks.   Oh ! through her strain
Breathe thy pathetic eloquence, that moulds
Th' attentive senate, charms, persuades, exalts,
Of honest zeal th' indignant lightning throws,
And shakes corruption on her venal throne.
While thus we talk, and through Elysian vales   1070
Delighted rove, perhaps a sigh escapes.
What pity, Cobham, thou thy verdant files
Of order'd trees shouldst here inglorious range,

Instead of squadrons flaming o'er the field,
And long-embattled hosts; when the proud foe,
The faithless vain disturber of mankind,
Insulting Gaul, has rous'd the world to war;
When keen, once more, within their bounds to press
Those polish'd robbers, those ambitious slaves,
The British youth would hail thy wise command,   1080
Thy temper'd ardour, and thy veteran skill.

Moonlight in Autumn.

The western sun withdraws the shorten'd day;
And humid evening, gliding o'er the sky,
In her chill progress, to the ground condens'd
The vapours throws. Where creeping waters ooze,
Where marshes stagnate, and where rivers wind,
Cluster the rolling fogs, and swim along
The dusky-mantled lawn. Meanwhile the moon
Full-orb'd, and breaking through the scatter'd clouds,
Shows her broad visage in the crimson'd east.   1090
Turned to the sun direct, her spotted disk,
Where mountains rise, umbrageous dales descend,
And caverns deep, as optic tube descries,
A smaller earth, gives us his blaze again,
Void of its flame, and sheds a softer day.
Now through the passing cloud she seems to stoop,
Now up the pure cerulean rides sublime.
Wide the pale deluge floats, and streaming mild
O'er the skied mountain to the shadowy vale,
While rocks and floods reflect the quivering gleam,   1100
The whole air whitens with a boundless tide
Of silver radiance, trembling round the world.

Meteors and the Superstitious Fear of Them.

But when half-blotted from the sky her light,
Fainting, permits the starry fires to burn

With keener lustre through the depth of heaven;
Or near extinct her deaden'd orb appears,
And scarce appears, of sickly beamless white;
Oft in this season, silent from the north
A blaze of meteors shoots.   Ensweeping first
The lower skies, they all at once converge   1110
High to the crown of heaven, and all at once,
Relapsing quick, as quickly re-ascend,
And mix, and thwart, extinguish, and renew;
All ether coursing in a maze of light.
     From look to look, contagious through the crowd,
The panic runs, and into wondrous shapes
Th' appearance throws: armies in meet array,
Throng'd with aerial spears, and steeds of fire;
Till, the long lines of full-extended war
In bleeding fight commixt, the sanguine flood   1120
Rolls a broad slaughter o'er the plains of heaven.
As thus they scan the visionary scene,
On all sides swells the superstitious din,
Incontinent; and busy frenzy talks
Of blood and battle; cities overturn'd,
And late at night in swallowing earthquake sunk,
Or hideous wrapt in fierce-ascending flame;
Of sallow famine, inundation, storm;
Of pestilence, and every great distress;
Empires subvers'd, when ruling fate has struck   1130
The unalterable hour.   Even nature's self
Is deemed to totter on the brink of time.
Not so the man of philosophic eye,
And inspect sage.   The waving brightness he
Curious surveys, inquisitive to know
The causes and materials, yet unfix'd,
Of this appearance beautiful and new.

The Coming of Day.

Now, black and deep, the night begins to fall,
A shade immense.   Sunk in the quenching gloom,
Magnificent and vast, are heaven and earth.   1140
Order confounded lies; all beauty void;
Distinction lost; and gay variety
One universal blot; such the fair power
Of light, to kindle and create the whole.
Drear is the state of the benighted wretch,
Who then, bewilder'd, wanders through the dark,
Full of pale fancies and chimeras huge,
Nor visited by one directive ray,
From cottage streaming, or from airy hall.
Perhaps impatient as he stumbles on,   1150
Struck from the root of slimy rushes, blue,
The wild-fire scatters round, or gather'd trails
A length of flame deceitful o'er the moss;
Whither decoyed by the fantastic blaze,
Now lost and now renew'd, he sinks absorpt,
Rider and horse, amid the miry gulf;
While still, from day to day, his pining wife
And plaintive children his return await,
In wild conjecture lost.   At other times,
Sent by the better genius of the night,   1160
Innoxious, gleaming on the horse's mane,
The meteor sits, and shows the narrow path,
That winding leads through pits of death, or else
Instructs him how to take the dangerous ford.

   The lengthen'd night elaps'd, the morning shines
Serene, in all her dewy beauty bright
Unfolding fair the last autumnal day.
And now the mounting sun dispels the fog.
The rigid hoar-frost melts before his beam;
And, hung on every spray, on every blade   1170
Of grass, the myriad dew-drops twinkle round.

A Destroyed Beehive.

Ah, see where, robb'd and murder'd, in that pit
Lies the still-heaving hive! at evening snatch'd,
Beneath the cloud of guilt-concealing night,
And fixed o'er sulphur; while, not dreaming ill,
The happy people, in their waxen cells,
Sat tending public cares, and planning schemes
Of temperance for Winter poor; rejoic'd
To mark full flowing round, their copious stores.
Sudden the dark oppressive steam ascends;   1180
And, us'd to milder scents, the tender race,
By thousands, tumble from their honey'd domes,
Convolv'd, and agonizing in the dust.
And was it then for this you roam'd the Spring,
Intent from flower to flower? for this you toil'd
Ceaseless the burning Summer-heats away?
For this in Autumn search'd the blooming waste,
Nor lost one sunny gleam? for this sad fate?
O man! tyrannic lord! how long, how long,
Shall prostrate nature groan beneath your rage,   1190
Awaiting renovation? When oblig'd,
Must you destroy? Of their ambrosial food
Can you not borrow, and, in just return,
Afford them shelter from the wintry winds?
Or, as the sharp year pinches, with their own
Again regale them on some smiling day?
See where the stony bottom of their town
Looks desolate and wild, with here and there
A helpless number, who the ruin'd state
Survive, lamenting weak, cast out to death.   1200
Thus a proud city, populous and rich,
Full of the works of peace, and high in joy,
At theatre or feast, or sunk in sleep,
(As late, Palermo, was thy fate,) is seiz'd

By some dread earthquake, and convulsive hurl'd
Sheer from the black foundation, stench-involv'd,
Into a gulf of blue sulphureous flame.

Harvest Festivities.

Hence every harsher sight! for now the day,
O'er heaven and earth diffus'd, grows warm and high;
Infinite splendour, wide investing all.   1210
How still the breeze! save what the filmy threads
Of dew evaporate brushes from the plain.
How clear the cloudless sky! how deeply ting'd
With a peculiar blue! the ethereal arch
How swell'd immense! amid whose azure thron'd
The radiant sun how gay! how calm below,
The gilded earth! the harvest-treasures all
Now gathered in, beyond the rage of storms,
Sure to the swain; the circling fence shut up;
And instant Winter's utmost rage defied;   1220
While, loose to festive joy, the country round
Laughs with the loud sincerity of mirth;
Shook to the wind their cares.   The toil-strung youth,
By the quick sense of music taught alone,
Leaps wildly graceful in the lively dance.
Her every charm abroad, the village toast,
Young, buxom, warm, in native beauty rich,
Darts not unmeaning looks; and, where her eye
Points an approving smile, with double force
The cudgel rattles, and the wrestler twines.   1230
Age, too, shin s out, and garrulous, recounts
The feats of youth.   Thus they rejoice; nor think
That, with to-morrow's sun, their annual toil
Begins again the never-ceasing round.
Oh! knew he but his happiness, of men

The happiest he, who, far from public rage,
Deep in the vale, with a choice few retir'd,
Drinks the pure pleasures of the rural life.

The Joys and Blessings of a Country Life.

What though the dome be wanting, whose proud gate,
Each morning, vomits out the sneaking crowd   1240
Of flatterers false, and in their turn abus'd ?
Vile intercourse!   What though the glittering robe,
Of every hue reflective light can give,
Or floating loose, or stiff with mazy gold,
The pride and gaze of fools, oppress him not ?
What though, from utmost land or sea purvey'd,
For him each rarer tributary life
Bleeds not, and his insatiate table heaps
With luxury and death?   What though his bowl
Flames not with costly juice? nor sunk in beds,   1250
Oft of gay care, he tosses out the night,
Or melts the thoughtless hours in idle state?
What though he knows not those fantastic joys,
That still amuse the wanton, still deceive;
A face of pleasure, but a heart of pain;
Their hollow moments undelighted all?
Sure peace is his; a solid life estrang'd
To disappointment and fallacious hope;
Rich in content; in nature's bounty rich,
In herbs and fruits; whatever greens the Spring,   1260
When heaven descends in showers, or bends the bough
When Summer reddens, and when Autumn beams;
Or in the wintry glebe whatever lies
Conceal'd, and fattens with the richest sap—
These are not wanting; nor the milky drove,
Luxuriant, spread o'er all the lowing vale;

Nor bleating mountains, nor the chide of streams,
And hum of bees, inviting sleep sincere
Into the guiltless breast, beneath the shade,
Or thrown at large amid the fragrant hay;   1270
Nor aught beside of prospect, grove, or song,
Dim grottoes, gleaming lakes, and fountains clear.
Here too dwells simple truth; plain innocence;
Unsullied beauty; sound unbroken youth,
Patient of labour, with a little pleas'd;
Health, **ever** blooming; unambitious toil;
Calm contemplation, and poetic ease.
    Let others brave the flood in quest of gain
And beat for joyless months the gloomy wave.
Let such as deem it glory to destroy,   1280
Rush into blood, the sack of cities seek;
Unpierc'd, exulting in the widow's wail,
The virgin's shriek, and infant's trembling cry.
Let some, far distant from their native soil,
Urg'd or by want or harden'd avarice,
Find other lands beneath another sun.
Let this through cities work his eager way,
By legal outrage and establish'd guile,
The social sense extinct; and that ferment
Mad into tumult the seditious herd,   1290
Or melt them down to slavery.   Let these
Insnare the wretched in the toils of law,
Fomenting discord, and perplexing right;
An iron race! and those of fairer front
But equal inhumanity, in courts,
Delusive pomp and dark cabals, delight,
Wreathe the deep bow, diffuse the lying smile,
And tread the weary labyrinth of state.
While he from all the stormy passions free
That restless men involve, hears and but hears,   1300

At distance safe, the human tempest roar,
Wrapt close in conscious peace. The fall of kings
The rage of nations, and the crush of states,
Move not the man who, from the world escap'd,
In still retreats and flowery solitudes,
To nature's voice attends, from month to month,
And day to day, through the revolving year;
Admiring, sees her in every shape;
Feels all her sweet emotions at his heart;
Takes what she liberal gives, nor thinks of more.   1310
He when young Spring protrudes the bursting gems,
Marks the first bud, and sucks the healthful gale
Into his freshened soul. Her genial hours
He full enjoys; and not a beauty blows,
And not an opening blossom breathes, in vain.
In summer, he, beneath the living shade,
Such as o'er frigid Tempe wont to wave,
Or Hæmus cool, reads what the muse, of these
Perhaps, has in immortal numbers sung,
Or what she dictates writes; and oft, an eye   1320
Shot round, rejoices in the vigorous year.
When Autumn's yellow lustre gilds the world,
And tempts the sickled swain into the field,
Seiz'd by the general joy, his heart distends
With gentle throes; and through the tepid gleams
Deep musing, then he best exerts his song.
Even Winter wild to him is full of bliss.
The mighty tempest, and the hoar waste,
Abrupt and deep, stretch'd o'er the buried earth,
Awake to solemn thought. At night, the skies,   1330
Disclos'd and kindled by refining frost,
Pour every lustre on the exalted eye.
A friend, a book, the stealing hours secure,
And mark them down for wisdom. With swift wing,

O'er land and sea imagination roams;
Or truth, divinely breaking on his mind,
Elates his being and unfolds his powers;
Or in his breast heroic virtue burns.
The touch of kindred, too, and love he feels;
The modest eye, whose beams on his alone   1340
Ecstatic shine; the little strong embrace
Of prattling children, twin'd around his neck,
And emulous to please him, calling forth
The fond parental soul.   Nor purpose gay,
Amusement, dance, or song, he sternly scorns;
For happiness and true philosophy
Are of the social, still, and smiling kind.
This is the life which those who fret in guilt,
And guilty cities, never knew; the life
Led by primeval ages, uncorrupt,   1350
When angels dwelt, and God himself, with man.

The Poet's Devotion to Nature.

O Nature! all-sufficient! over all!
Enrich me with the knowledge of thy works;
Snatch me to heaven; thy rolling wonders there,
World beyond world, in infinite extent,
Profusely scatter'd o'er the blue immense,
Show me; their motions, periods, and their laws,
Give me to scan; through the disclosing deep
Light my blind way; the mineral strata there;
Thrust, blooming, thence the vegetable world;   1360
O'er that the rising system, more complex,
Of animals; and higher still, the mind,
The varied scene of quick-compounded thought,
And where the mixing passions endless shift;
These ever open to my ravish'd eye;
A search the flight of time can ne'er exhaust!

But if to that unequal, if the blood,
In sluggish streams about my heart, forbid
That best ambition, under closing shades,
Inglorious, lay me by the lowly brook,   1370
And whisper to my dreams. From thee begin,
Dwell all on thee, with thee conclude, my song;
And let me never, never stray from thee!

END OF AUTUMN.

WINTER.

SEE, Winter comes, to rule the varied year,
Sullen and sad, with all his rising train,
Vapours, and clouds, and storms. Be these my theme,
These, that exalt the soul to solemn thought
And heavenly musing. Welcome, kindred glooms!
Congenial horrors, hail! With frequent foot,
Pleas'd have I, in my cheerful morn of life,
When nurs'd by careless solitude I liv'd,
And sung of nature with unceasing joy,
Pleas'd have I wander'd through your rough domain;   10
Trod the pure virgin snows, myself as pure;
Heard the winds roar, and the big torrents burst;
Or seen the deep fermenting tempest, brew'd,
In the grim evening sky. Thus pass'd the time,
Till, through the lucid chambers of the south
Look'd out the joyous Spring—look'd out, and smil'd.

Dedication

To thee, the patron of her first essay,
The muse, O Wilmington! renews her song.
Since has she rounded the revolving year;
Skimm'd the gay Spring; on eagle pinions borne,   20
Attempted through the Summer-blaze to rise;
Then swept o'er Autumn with the shadowy gale;
And now among the Wintry clouds again,
Roll'd in the doubling storm, she tries to soar;
To swell her note with all the rushing winds;
To suit her sounding cadence to the floods;
As is her theme, her numbers wildly great:
Thrice happy! could she fill thy judging ear
With bold description and with manly thought.
Nor art thou skill'd in awful schemes alone,   30

And how to make a mighty people thrive;
But equal goodness, sound integrity,
A firm, unshaken, uncorrupted soul,
Amid a sliding age, and burning strong,
Not vainly blazing, for thy country's weal—
A steady spirit, regularly free.
These, each exalting each, the statesman light
Into the patriot; these the public hope
And eye to thee converting, bid the muse
Record what envy dares not flattery call.

Approach of Winter.

Now, when the cheerless empire of the sky
To Capricorn and Centaur Archer yields,
And fierce Aquarius stains th' inverted year,
Hung o'er the farthest verge of heaven, the sun
Scarce spreads through ether the dejected day.
Faint are his gleams; and ineffectual shoot
His struggling rays, in horizontal lines,
Through the thick air, as, cloth'd in cloudy storm,
Weak, wan, and broad, he skirts the southern sky,
And, soon descending, to the long dark night,
Wide-shading all, the prostrate world resigns.
Nor is the night unwish'd, while vital heat,
Light, life, and joy, the dubious day forsake.
Meantime, in sable cincture, shadows vast,
Deep-ting'd and damp, and congregated clouds,
And all the vapoury turbulence of heaven,
Involve the face of things. Thus Winter falls
A heavy gloom oppressive o'er the world,
Through nature shedding influence malign,
And rouses up the seeds of dark disease.
The soul of man dies in him, loathing life,
And black with more than melancholy views.

The cattle droop ; and o'er the furrow'd land,
Fresh from the plough, the dun-discolour'd flocks,
Untended spreading, crop the wholesome root.
Along the woods, along the moorish fens,
Sighs the sad genius of the coming storm ;
And up among the loose disjointed cliffs,
And fractur'd mountains wild, the brawling brook,
And cave, presageful, send a hollow moan,   70
Resounding long in listening fancy's ear.

A Rain-storm.

Then comes the father of the tempest forth,
Wrapt in black glooms.   First, joyless rains obscure
Drive through the mingling skies with vapour foul ;
Dash on the mountain's brow, and shake the woods,
That grumbling wave below.   Th' unsightly plain
Lies, a brown deluge ; as the low-bent clouds
Pour flood on flood, yet unexhausted still
Combine, and, deepening into night, shut up
The day's fair face.   The wanderers of heaven,   80
Each to his home, retire, save those that love
To take their pastime in the troubled air,
Or skimming flutter round the dimply pool.
The cattle from the untasted fields return,
And ask, with meaning low, their wonted stalls,
Or ruminate in the contiguous shade.
Thither the household feathery people crowd ;
The crested cock, with all his female train,
Pensive and dripping ; while the cottage hind
Hangs o'er the enlivening blaze, and taleful there   90
Recounts his simple frolic : much he talks,
And much he laughs, nor recks the storm that blows
Without, and rattles on his humble roof.
Wide o'er the brim, with many a torrent swell'd,

And the mix'd ruin of its banks o'erspread,
At last the rous'd-up river pours along.
Resistless, roaring, dreadful, down it comes,
From the rude mountain and the mossy wild,
Tumbling through rocks abrupt, and sounding far;
Then o'er the sanded valley floating spreads,   100
Calm, sluggish, silent; till again, constrain'd
Between two meeting hills, it bursts away,
Where rocks and woods o'erhang the turbid stream.
There, gathering triple force, rapid and deep,
It boils, and wheels, and foams, and thunders through.

A Wind-storm and Its Effects.

Nature! great parent! whose unceasing hand
Rolls round the seasons of the changeful year,
How mighty, how majestic, are thy works!
With what a pleasing dread they swell the soul,
That sees astonish'd, and astonish'd sings!   110
Ye, too, ye winds! that now begin to blow
With boisterous sweep, I raise my voice to you.
Where are your stores, ye powerful beings! say,
Where your aerial magazines reserv'd
To swell the brooding terrors of the storm?
In what far distant region of the sky,
Hush'd in deep silence, sleep ye when 'tis calm?

When from the pallid sky the sun descends,
With many a spot, that o'er his glaring orb
Uncertain wanders, stain'd, red fiery streaks   120
Begin to flush around. The reeling clouds
Stagger with dizzy poise, as doubting yet
Which master to obey; while, rising slow,
Blank, in the leaden-colour'd east, the moon
Wears a wan circle round her blunted horns.
Seen through the turbid fluctuating air,

The stars obtuse emit a shiver'd ray,
Or frequent seem to shoot athwart the gloom,
And long behind them trail the whitening blaze.
Snatch'd in short eddies plays the wither'd leaf ;   130
And on the flood the dancing feather floats.
With broaden'd nostrils to the sky up-turn'd.
The conscious heifer snuffs the stormy gale.
Even as the matron, at her nightly task,
With pensive labour draws the flaxen thread,
The wasted taper and the crackling flame
Foretell the blast.   But chief the plumy race,
The tenants of the sky, its changes speak.
Retiring from the downs, where all day long
They pick'd their scanty fare, a blackening train   140
Of clamorous rooks thick urge their weary flight,
And seek the closing shelter of the grove.
Assiduous, in his bower, the wailing owl
Plies his sad song.   The cormorant on high
Wheels from the deep, and screams along the land.
Loud shrieks the soaring hern ; and with wild wing
The circling sea-fowl cleave the flaky clouds.
Ocean, unequal press'd, with broken tide
And blind commotion heaves ; while, from the shore,
Eat into caverns by the restless wave,   150
And forest-rustling mountains, comes a voice,
That, solemn sounding, bids the world prepare.
Then issues forth the storm, with sudden burst,
And hurls the whole precipitated air
Down in a torrent.   On the passive main
Descends the ethereal force, and with strong gust
Turns from its bottom the discolour'd deep.
Through the black night that sits immense around,
Lash'd into foam, the fierce conflicting brine
Seems o'er a thousand raging waves to burn.   160

Meantime the mountain-billows, to the clouds
In dreadful tumult swell'd, surge above surge,
Burst into chaos with tremendous roar,
And anchor'd navies from their stations drive,
Wild as the winds, across the howling waste
Of mighty waters: now the inflated wave
Straining they scale, and now impetuous shoot
Into the secret chambers of the deep,
The wintry Baltic thundering o'er their head.
Emerging thence again, before the breath   170
Of full-exerted heaven they wing their course,
And dart on distant coasts; if some sharp rock,
Or shoal insidious, break not their career,
And in loose fragments fling them floating round.
   Nor less at land the loosen'd tempest reigns.
The mountain thunders; and its sturdy sons
Stoop to the bottom of the rocks they shade.
Lone on the midnight steep, and all aghast,
The dark wayfaring stranger breathless toils,
And, often falling, climbs against the blast.   180
Low waves the rooted forest, vex'd, and sheds
What of its tarnish'd honours yet remain;
Dash'd down, and scatter'd by the tearing wind's
Assiduous fury, its gigantic limbs.
Thus, struggling through the dissipated grove,
The whirling tempest raves along the plain,
And on the cottage thatch'd, or lordly roof,
Keen-fastening, shakes them to the solid base.
Sleep frighted flies; and round the rocking dome,
For entrance eager, howls the savage blast.   190
Then too, they say, through all the burthen'd air,
Long groans are heard, shrill sounds, and distant sighs,
That, utter'd by the demon of the night,
Warn the devoted wretch of woe and death

Huge uproar lords it wide.   The clouds commix'd
With stars, swift gliding, sweep along the sky.
All nature reels; till nature's King, who oft
Amid tempestuous darkness dwells alone,
And on the wings of the careering wind
Walks dreadfully serene, commands a calm.   200
Then, straight, air, sea, and earth, are hush'd at once.

Reflections During the Night.

As yet 'tis midnight deep.   The weary clouds,
Slow meeting, mingle into solid gloom.
Now, while the drowsy world lies lost in sleep,
Let me associate with the serious night,
And contemplation, her sedate compeer ;
Let me shake off the intrusive cares of day,
And lay the meddling senses all aside.
    Where now, ye lying vanities of life !
Ye ever-tempting, ever-cheating train !   210
Where are you now, and what is your amount ?
Vexation, disappointment, and remorse.
Sad, sickening thought !   And yet deluded man,
A scene of crude disjointed visions past,
And broken slumbers, rises, still resolv'd,
With new-flush'd hopes, to run the giddy round.
    Father of light and life ! thou Good Supreme !
Oh ! teach me what is good ! teach me Thyself !
Save me from folly, vanity, and vice,
From every low pursuit, and feed my soul   220
With knowledge, conscious peace, and virtue pure,
Sacred, substantial, never-fading bliss !

A Snow-storm; its Effects on the Animal Creation.

The keener tempests rise ; and, fuming dun
From all the livid east or piercing north,
Thick clouds ascend, in whose capacious womb

A vapoury deluge lies, to snow congeal'd.
Heavy they roll their fleecy world along;
And the sky saddens with the gather'd storm.
Through the hush'd air the whitening shower descends,
At first thin-wavering, till at last the flakes   230
Fall broad, and wide, and fast; dimming the day,
With a continual flow.   The cherish'd fields
Put on their winter robes of purest white.
'Tis brightness all; save where the new snow melts
Along the mazy current.   Low, the woods
Bow their hoar head; and ere the languid sun
Faint from the west emits his evening ray,
Earth's universal face, deep hid, and chill,
Is one wild dazzling waste, that buries wide
The works of man.   Drooping, the labourer-ox   240
Stands cover'd o'er with snow, and then demands
The fruit of all his toil.   The fowls of heaven,
Tam'd by the cruel season, crowd around
The winnowing store, and claim the little boon
Which Providence assigns them.   One alone,
The red-breast, sacred to the household gods,
Wisely regardful of the embroiling sky,
In joyless fields and thorny thickets leaves
His shivering mates, and pays to trusted man
His annual visit.   Half-afraid, he first   250
Against the window beats; then, brisk, alights
On the warm hearth; then, hopping o'er the floor,
Eyes all the smiling family askance,
And pecks, and starts, and wonders where he is;
Till, more familiar grown, the table-crumbs
Attract his slender feet.   The foodless wilds
Pour forth their brown inhabitants.   The hare,
Though timorous of heart, and hard beset
By death in various forms, dark snares, and dogs,

And more unpitying men, the garden seeks,   260
Urg'd on by fearless want.   The bleating kind
Eye the bleak heaven, and next the glistening earth,
With looks of dumb despair; then, sad dispers'd,
Dig for the wither'd herb through heaps of snow.

    Now, shepherds, to your helpless charge be kind,
Baffle the raging year, and fill their pens
With food at will : lodge them below the storm,
And watch them strict; for, from the bellowing east,
In this dire season, oft the whirlwind's wing
Sweeps up the burden of whole wintry plains   270
In one wide waft, and o'er the hapless flocks,
Hid in the hollow of two neighbouring hills,
The billowy tempest whelms; till, upward urg'd,
Th · valley to a shining mountain swells,
Tipp'd with a wreath high curling in the sky.

The Man Perishing in the Snow.

    As thus the snows arise, and, foul and fierce,
All winter drives along the darken'd air,
In his own loose-revolving fields, the swain
Disaster'd stands ; sees other hills ascend,
Of unknown joyless brow, and other scenes,   280
Of horrid prospect, shag the trackless plain ;
Nor finds the river, nor the forest, hid
Beneath the formless wild, but wanders on
From hill to dale, still more and more astray ;
Impatient flouncing through the drifted heaps,
Stung with the thoughts of home : the thoughts of home
Rush on his nerves, and call their vigour forth
In many a vain attempt.   How sinks his soul !
What black despair, what horror, fills his heart !
When, for the dusky spot, which fancy feign'd   290
His tufted cottage rising through the snow,

He meets the roughness of the middle waste,
Far from the track and blest abode of man ;
While round him night resistless closes fast,
And every tempest howling o'er his head,
Renders the savage wilderness more wild.
Then throng the busy shapes into his mind,
Of cover'd pits, unfathomably deep,
A dire descent ! beyond the power of frost ;
Of faithless bogs ; of precipices huge,   300
Smooth'd up with snow ; and, what is land, unknown,
What water ; of the still unfrozen spring,
In the loose marsh or solitary lake,
Where the fresh fountain from the bottom boils.
These check his fearful steps ; and down he sinks
Beneath the shelter of the shapeless drift,
Thinking o'er all the bitterness of death.
Mix'd with the tender anguish nature shoots
Through the wrung bosom of the dying man,
His wife, his children, and his friends, unseen.   310
In vain for him the officious wife prepares
The fire fair-blazing and the vestment warm.
In vain his little children, peeping out
Into the mingling storm, demand their sire,
With tears of artless innocence.   Alas !
Nor wife, nor children, more shall he behold ;
Nor friends, nor sacred home.   On every nerve
The deadly Winter seizes, shuts up sense,
And, o'er his inmost vitals creeping cold,
Lays him along the snows, a stiffen'd corse,   320
Stretch'd out and bleaching in the northern blast.

The Prevalence of Human Pain and Misery.

Ah ! little think the gay licentious proud,
Whom pleasure, power, and affluence, surround ;
They who their thoughtless hours in giddy mirth,

And wanton, often cruel, riot waste ;
Ah ! little think they, while they dance along,
How many feel, this very moment, death
And all the sad variety of pain ;—
How many sink in the devouring flood,
Or more devouring flame ;—how many bleed,   330
By shameful variance betwixt man and man ;—
How many pine in want and dungeon glooms,
Shut from the common air, and common use
Of their own limbs ;—how many drink the cup
Of baleful grief, or eat the bitter bread
Of misery ;—sore pierc'd by wintry winds,
How many shrink into the sordid hut
Of cheerless poverty ;—how many shake
With all the fiercer tortures of the mind,
Unbounded passion, madness, guilt, remorse ;   840
Whence tumbled headlong from the heart of life,
They furnish matter for the tragic muse ;—
Even in the vale where wisdom loves to dwell,
With friendship, peace and contemplation join'd,
How many, rack'd with honest passions, droop
In deep retir'd distress ;—how many stand
Around the deathbed of their dearest friends,
And point the parting anguish.   Thought fond man
Of these, and all the thousand nameless ills
That one incessant struggle render life,   350
One scene of toil, of suffering, and of fate,
Vice in his high career would stand appall'd,
And heedless rambling impulse learn to think.
The conscious heart of charity would warm,
And her wide wish benevolence dilate.
The social tear would rise, the social sigh,
And into clear perfection, gradual bliss,
Refining still, the social passions work.

The Prisons and Their Wretched Inmates.

And here, can I forget the generous band,
Who, touch'd with human woe, redressive search'd   360
Into the horrors of the gloomy jail ;
Unpitied, and unheard, where misery moans ;
Where sickness pines ; where thirst and hunger burn ,
And poor misfortune feels the lash of vice .
While in the land of liberty, the land
Whose every street and public meeting glow
With open freedom, little tyrants rag'd ;
Snatch'd the lean morsel from the starving mouth ;
Tore from cold wintry limbs the tatter'd weed ;
Even robb d them of the last of comforts, sleep ;   370
The free-born Briton to the dungeon chain'd,
Or, as the lust of cruelty prevail'd,
At pleasure mark'd him with inglorious stripes,
And crush'd out lives, by secret barbarous ways,
That for their country would have toil'd, or bled ?
Oh great design ! if executed well,
With patient care, and wisdom-temper'd zeal.
Ye sons of mercy ! yet resume the search.
Drag forth the legal monsters into light.
Wrench from their hands oppression's iron rod ;   380
And bid the cruel feel the pains they give.
Much still untouch'd remains : in this rank age,
Much is the patriot's weeding hand requir'd.
The toils of law (what dark insidious men
Have cumbrous added to perplex the truth,
And lengthen simple justice into trade),
How glorious were the day that saw these broke,
And every man within the reach of right !

Descent of the Wolves.

By wintry famine rous'd, from all the tract
Of horrid mountains which the shining Alps,   390

And wavy Apennines, and Pyrenees,
Branch out stupendous into distant lands,
Cruel as death, and hungry as the grave,
Burning for blood, bony, and gaunt, and grim,
Assembling wolves in raging troops descend,
And, pouring o'er the country, bear along,
Keen as the north wind sweeps the glossy snow.
All is their prize.   They fasten on the steed,
Press him to earth, and pierce his mighty heart.
Nor can the bull his awful front defend,   400
Or shake the murdering savages away.
Rapacious, at the mother's throat they fly,
And tear the screaming infant from her breast.
The godlike face of man avails him nought.
Even beauty, force divine! at whose bright glance
The generous lion stands in soften'd gaze,
Here bleeds, a hapless undistinguish'd prey.
But if, appriz'd of the severe attack,
The country be shut up, lur'd by the scent,
On church-yards drear (inhuman to relate!)   410
The disappointed prowlers fall, and dig
The shrouded body from the grave, o'er which,
Mix'd with foul shades and frighted ghosts, they howl.

An Avalanche.

Among those hilly regions, where, embrac'd
In peaceful vales, the happy Grisons dwell,
Oft, rushing sudden from the loaded cliffs,
Mountains of snow their gathering terrors roll.
From steep to steep, loud thundering, down they come,
A wintry waste in dire commotion all ;
And herds, and flocks, and travellers, and swains,   420
And sometimes whole brigades of marching troops,
Or hamlets sleeping in the dead of night,
Are deep beneath the smothering ruin whelm'd

Literary Converse for a Winter Evening.

Now, all amid the rigours of the year,
In the wild depth of winter, while, without,
The ceaseless winds blow ice, be my retreat,
Between the groaning forest and the shore
Beat by the boundless multitude of waves,
A rural, shelter'd, solitary scene.
Where ruddy fire and beaming tapers join,   430
To cheer the gloom. There studious let me sit,
And hold high converse with the mighty dead,
Sages of ancient time, as gods rever'd,
As gods beneficent, who bless'd mankind
With arts, with arms, and humaniz'd a world.
Rous'd at the inspiring thought, I throw aside
The long-liv'd volume, and, deep-musing, hail
The sacred shades that slowly-rising pass
Before my wondering eyes.

Illustrious Grecians.

First, Socrates,
Who, firmly good in a corrupted state,   440
Against the rage of tyrants single stood,
Invincible; calm reason's holy law,
That voice of God within the attentive mind,
Obeying, fearless, or in life or death;
Great moral teacher, wisest of mankind!
Solon, the next, who built his commonweal
On equity's wide base; by tender laws
A lively people curbing, yet undamp'd
Preserving still that quick peculiar fire,
Whence in the laurel'd field of finer arts,   450
And of bold freedom, they unequall'd shone,
The pride of smiling Greece and human kind.
Lycurgus, then, who bow'd beneath the force

Of strictest discipline, severely wise,
All human passions.   Following him, I see,
As at Thermopylæ he glorious fell,
The firm devoted chief, who prov'd by deeds
The hardest lesson which the other taught.
Then Aristides lifts his honest front ;
Spotless of heart, to whom the unflattering·voice   460
Of freedom gave the noblest name of Just ;
In pure majestic poverty rever'd ;
Who, even his glory to his country's weal
Submitting, swell'd a haughty rival's fame.
Rear'd by his care, of softer ray appears,
Cimon, sweet-soul'd, whose genius, rising strong,
Shook off the load of young debauch ; abroad,
The scourge of Persian pride ; at home, the friend
Of every worth and every splendid art ;
Modest, and simple, in the pomp of wealth.   470
Then the last worthies of declining Greece,
Late call'd to glory, in unequal times,
Pensive, appear.   The fair Corinthian boast,
Timoleon, temper'd happy, mild, and firm,
Who wept the brother, while the tyrant bled.
And, equal to the best, the Theban pair
Whose virtues, in heroic concord join'd,
Their country rais'd to freedom, empire, fame.
He, too, with whom Athenian honour sunk,
And left a mass of sordid lees behind,   480
Phocion, the good ; in public life severe,
To virtue still inexorably firm ;
But when, beneath his low illustrious roof,
Sweet peace and happy wisdom smooth'd his brow,
Not friendship softer was, nor love more kind.
And he, the last of old Lycurgus' sons,
The generous victim to that vain attempt

To save a rotten state ; Agis, who saw
Even Sparta's self to servile avarice sunk.
The two Achæan heroes close the train : 490
Aratus, who awhile relum'd the soul
Of fondly-lingering liberty in Greece ;
And he, her darling, as her latest hope,
The gallant Philopœmen, who to arms
Turned the luxurious pomp he could not cure ;
Or toiling in his farm, a simple swain ;
Or, bold and skilful, thundering in the field.

Illustrious Romans.

Of rougher front, a mighty people come !
A race of heroes ! in those virtuous times,
Which knew no stain, save that, with partial flame, 500
Their dearest country they too fondly lov'd.
Her better founder first, the light of Rome,
Numa, who soften'd her rapacious sons ;—
Servius, the king, who laid the solid base
On which, o'er earth the vast republic spread.
Then the great consuls venerable rise :
The public father who the private quelled,
As on the dread tribunal sternly sad ;—
He whom his thankless country could not lose,
Camillus, only vengeful to her foes ;— 510
Fabricius, scorner of all-conquering gold ;—
And Cincinnatus, awful from the plough ;—
Thy willing victim, Carthage, bursting loose
From all that pleading nature could oppose,
From a whole city's tears, by rigid faith
Imperious called, and honour's dire command ;—
Scipio, the gentle chief, humanely brave,
Who soon the race of spotless glory ran,
And, warm in youth, to the poetic shade

With friendship and philosophy retir'd ;—   520
Tully, whose powerful eloquence awhile
Restrain'd the rapid fate of rushing Rome ;—
Unconquered Cato, virtuous in extreme ;
And thou, unhappy Brutus, kind of heart,
Whose steady arm, by awful virtue urg'd,
Lifted the Roman steel against thy friend.
Thousands besides, the tribute of a verse
Demand ; but who can count the stars of heaven ?
Who sing their influence on this lower world ?
     Behold, who yonder comes, in sober state,   530
Fair, mild and strong, as in a vernal sun ?
'Tis Phœbus' self, or else the Mantuan swain !
Great Homer, too, appears, of daring wing,
Parent of song ! and, equal by his side,
The British muse : join'd hand in hand they walk,
Darkling, full up the middle steep to fame.
Nor absent are those shades whose skilful touch
Pathetic drew the impassion'd heart, and charm'd
Transported Athens with the moral scene ;
Nor those who, tuneful, wak'd the enchanting lyre.   540
     First of your kind ! society divine !
Still visit thus my nights, for you reserv'd,
And mount my soaring soul to thoughts like yours.
Silence, thou lonely power ! the door be thine.
See on the hallow'd hour that none intrude,
Save a few chosen friends, who sometimes deign
To bless my humble roof, with sense refin'd,
Learning digested well, exalted faith,
Unstudied wit, and humour ever gay.
Or, from the Muses' hill will Pope descend,   550
To raise the sacred hour, to bid it smile,
And with the social spirit warm the heart ?
For though not sweeter his own Homer sings,

Yet is his life the more endearing song.
   Where art thou, Hammond? thou the darling pride,
The friend and lover of the tuneful throng!
Ah, why, dear youth, in all the blooming prime
Of vernal genius, where disclosing fast
Each active worth, each manly virtue lay,
Why wert thou ravish'd from our hopes so soon?   560
What now avails that noble thirst of fame,
Which stung thy fervent breast; that treasur'd store
Of knowledge, early gained; that eager zeal
To serve thy country, glowing in the band
Of youthful patriots who sustain her name?
What now, alas! that life-diffusing charm
Of sprightly wit; that rapture for the muse,
That heart of friendship and that soul of joy,
Which bade, with softest light, thy virtues smile?
Ah! only show'd, to check our fond pursuits,   570
And teach our humbled hopes that life is vain!

Subjects Proposed.

   Thus, in some deep retirement would I pass
The winter glooms, with friends of pliant soul,
Or blithe or solemn, as the theme inspir'd;
With them would search, if nature's boundless frame
Was call'd late rising, from the void of night,
Or sprung eternal from the Eternal Mind;
Its life, its laws, its progress, and its end.
Hence larger prospects of the beauteous whole
Would, gradual open on our opening minds;   580
And each diffusive harmony unite
In full perfection, to the astonish'd eye.
Then would we try to scan the moral world,
Which, though to us it seems embroil'd, moves on
In higher order; fitted and impell'd

By Wisdom's finest hand, and issuing all
In general good.   The sage historic muse
Should next conduct us through the deeps of time ;
Show us how empire grew, declin'd and fell,
In scattered states ; what makes the nations smile,   590
Improves their soil, and gives them double suns ;
And why they pine beneath the brightest skies,
In nature's richest lap.   As thus we talk'd,
Our hearts would burn within us, would inhale
That portion of divinity, that ray
Of purest heaven, which lights the public soul
Of patriots and of heroes.   But if doom'd,
In powerless, humble fortune to repress
These ardent risings of a kindling soul ;
Then, even superior to ambition, we   600
Would learn the private virtues ; how to glide
Through shades and plains, along the smoothest stream
Of rural life ; or snatch'd away by hope,
Through the dim spaces of futurity,
With earnest eye anticipate those scenes
Of happiness and wonder, where the mind,
In endless growth and infinite ascent,
Rises from state to state, and world to world.
But when with these the serious thought is foil'd,
We, shifting for relief, would ply the shapes   610
Of frolic fancy ; and incessant form
Those rapid pictures, that assembled train
Of fleet ideas, never join'd before,
Whence lively wit excites to gay surprise ;
Or folly-painting-humour, grave himself,
Calls laughter forth, deep-shaking every nerve.

Winter Evening in the Country.

Meantime the village rouses up the fire ;
While, well attested, and as well believ'd,

Heard solemn, goes the goblin story round,

Till superstitious horror creeps o'er all ; 620

Or, frequent in the sounding hall, they wake

The rural gambol. Rustic mirth goes round ;

The simple joke that takes the shepherd's heart,

Easily pleas'd ; the long loud laugh sincere ;

The kiss, snatch'd hastily from the sidelong maid,

On purpose guardless, or pretending sleep ;

The leap, the slap, the haul ; and, shook to notes

Of native music, the respondent dance.

Thus jocund fleets with them the winter-night.

Winter Evening in the City.

The city swarms intense. The public haunt, 630

Full of each theme, and warm with mix'd discourse,

Hums indistinct. The sons of riot flow

Down the loose stream of false enchanted joy

To swift destruction. On the rankled soul

The gaming fury falls ; and in one gulf

Of total ruin, honour, virtue, peace,

Friends, families, and fortune, headlong sink.

Up springs the dance along the lighted dome,

Mix'd and evolv'd, a thousand sprightly ways.

The glittering court effuses every pomp. 640

The circle deepens : beamed from gaudy robes,

Tapers, and sparkling gems, and radiant eyes,

A soft effulgence o'er the palace waves ;

While, a gay insect in his summer-shine,

The fop, light-fluttering, spreads his mealy wings.

Dread o'er the scene, the ghost of Hamlet stalks ;

Othello rages ; poor Monimia mourns ;

And Belvidera pours her soul in love.

Terror alarms the breast ; the comely tear

Steals o'er the cheek ; or else the comic muse 650

Holds to the world a picture of itself,
And raises sly the fair impartial laugh.
Sometimes she lifts her strain, and paints the scenes
Of beauteous life; whate'er can deck mankind,
Or charm the heart, in generous Bevil show'd.

Panegyric on Lord Chesterfield.

O thou, whose wisdom, solid, yet refin'd,
Whose patriot-virtues, and consummate skill
To touch the finer springs that move the world,
Join'd to whate'er the graces can bestow,
And all Apollo's animating fire,   660
Give thee, with pleasing dignity, to shine
At once, the guardian, ornament, and joy,
Of polish'd life—permit the rural muse,
O Chesterfield, to grace with thee her song!
Ere to the shades again she humbly flies,
Indulge her fond ambition in thy train,
(For every muse has in thy train a place,)
To mark thy various full-accomplish'd mind;
To mark that spirit which, with British scorn,
Rejects the allurements of corrupted power;   670
That elegant politeness, which excels,
Even in the judgment of presumptuous France,
The boasted manners of her shining court;
That wit, the vivid energy of sense,
The truth of nature, which, with Attic point,
And kind, well-temper'd satire, smoothly keen,
Steals through the soul, and without pain, corrects.
Or, rising thence, with yet a brighter flame,
Oh, let me hail thee on some glorious day,
When to the listening senate, ardent, crowd   680
Britannia's sons to hear her pleaded cause.
Then, dress'd by thee, more amiably fair,

Truth the soft robe of mild persuasion wears.
Thou to assenting reason giv'st again
Her own enlighten'd thoughts : call'd from the heart
The obedient passions on thy voice attend ;
And even reluctant party feels awhile
Thy gracious power ; as through the varied maze
Of eloquence, now smooth, now quick, now strong,
Profound and clear, you roll the copious flood   690

Frost and its Effects.

To thy lov'd haunt return, my happy muse ;
For now, behold, the joyous winter days,
Frosty, succeed ; and through the blue serene,
For sight too fine, the ethereal nitre flies,
Killing infectious damps, and the spent air
Storing afresh with elemental life.
Close crowds the shining atmosphere, and binds
Our strengthened bodies in its cold embrace,
Constringent ; feeds and animates our blood ;
Refines our spirits, through the new-strung nerves,   700
In swifter sallies darting to the brain,
Where sits the soul, intense, collected, cool,
Bright as the skies, and as the season keen.
All nature feels the renovating force
Of Winter, only to the thoughtless eye
In ruin seen.   The frost-concocted globe
Draws in abundant vegetable soul,
And gathers vigour for the coming year.
A stronger glow sits on the lively cheek
Of ruddy fire ; and luculent along   710
The purer rivers flow ; their sullen deeps,
Transparent, open to the shepherd's gaze,
And murmur hoarser, at the fixing frost.
    What art thou, frost ? and whence are thy keen stores

Deriv'd, thou secret, all-invading power,
Whom even the illusive fluid cannot fly?
Is not thy potent energy, unseen,
Myriads of little salts, or hook'd, or shap'd
Like double wedges, and diffus'd immense
Through water, earth, and ether?   Hence at eve,   720
Steam'd eager from the red horizon round,
With the fierce rage of Winter deep suffus'd,
An icy gale, oft shifting, o'er the pool
Breathes a blue film, and in its mid career
Arrests the bickering stream.   The loosen'd ice,
Let down the flood, and half-dissolv'd by day,
Rustles no more; but to the sedgy bank
Fast grows, or gathers round the pointed stone,
A crystal pavement, by the breath of heaven
Cemented firm; till, seized from shore to shore,   730
The whole imprison'd river growls below.
Loud rings the frozen earth, and hard reflects
A double noise; while, at his evening watch,
The village dog deters the nightly thief.
The heifer lows: the distant water-fall
Swells in the breeze; and with the hasty tread
Of traveller, the hollow-sounding plain
Shakes from afar.   The full ethereal round,
Infinite worlds disclosing to the view,
Shines out intensely keen; and all one cope   740
Of starry glitter glows from pole to pole.
From pole to pole the rigid influence falls,
Through the still night, incessant, heavy, strong,
And seizes nature fast.   It freezes on,
Till morn, late rising o'er the drooping world,
Lifts her pale eye unjoyous.   Then appears
The various labour of the silent night:
Prone from the dripping cave, and dumb cascade,

Whose idle torrents only seem to roar,
The pendent icicle; the frost-work fair,   750
Where transient hues and fancied figures rise;
Wide-spouted o'er the hill, the frozen brook,
A livid tract, cold gleaming on the morn;
The forest bent beneath the plumy wave;
And by the frost refin'd, the whiter snow
Incrusted hard, and sounding to the tread
Of early shepherd, as he pensive seeks
His pining flock, or from the mountain top,
Pleas'd with the slippery surface, swift descends.

Various Winter Amusements.

On blithesome frolics bent, the youthful swains,   760
While every work of man is laid at rest,
Fond o'er the river crowd, in various sport
And revelry dissolv'd; where mixing glad,
Happiest of all the train! the raptur'd boy
Lashes the whirling top. Or, where the Rhine
Branched out in many a long canal extends,
From every province swarming, void of care,
Batavia rushes forth; and as they sweep,
On souding skates, a thousand different ways,
In circling-poise, swift as the winds, along,   77
The then gay land is madden'd all to joy.
Nor less the northern courts, wide o'er the snow,
Pour a new pomp. Eager, on rapid sleds,
Their vigorous youth in bold contention wheel
Their long-resounding course. Meantime, to raise
The manly strife, with highly-blooming charms,
Flush'd by the season, Scandinavia's dames,
Or Russia's buxom daughters, glow around.
    Pure, quick, and sportful, is the wholesome day;
But soon elaps'd. The horizontal sun,   780

Broad o'er the south, hangs at his utmost noon,
And, ineffectual, strikes the gelid cliff.
His azure gloss the mountain still maintains,
Nor feels the feeble touch.   Perhaps the vale
Relents awhile to the reflected ray.
Or from the forest falls the cluster'd snow,
Myriads of gems, that in the waving gleam
Gay-twinkle as they scatter.   Thick around
Thunders the sport of those who, with the gun
And dog impatient bounding at the shot,   790
Worse than the season, desolate the fields ;
And, adding to the ruins of the year,
Distress the footed or the feather'd game.

Winter in Extreme Northern Regions.

But what is this? our infant Winter sinks,
Divested of his grandeur, should our eye
Astonish'd shoot into the frigid zone ;
Where, for relentless months, continual night
Holds o'er the glittering waste her starry reign.
There, through the prison of unbounded wilds,
Barr'd by the hand of nature from escape,   800
Wide roams the Russian exile.   Nought around
Strikes his sad eye, but deserts lost in snow ;
And heavy-loaded groves ; and solid floods,
That stretch, athwart the solitary vast,
Their icy horrors to the frozen main ;
And cheerless towns, far-distant, never bless'd,
Save when its annual course the caravan
Bends to the golden coast of rich Cathay,
With news of human kind.   Yet there life glows ;
Yet, cherished there, beneath the shining waste,   810
The furry nations harbour ; tipp'd with jet,
Fair ermines, spotless as the snows they press ;

Sables, of glossy black ; and dark embrown'd,
Or beauteous freak'd with many a mingled hue,
Thousands besides, the costly pride of courts.
There, warm together press'd, the trooping deer
Sleep on the new-fall'n snows ; and, scarce his head
Rais'd o'er the heapy wreath, the branching elk
Lies slumbering sullen in the white abyss.
The ruthless hunter wants not dogs nor toils,   820
Nor with the dread of sounding bows he drives
The fearful, flying race : with ponderous clubs,
As weak against the mountain heaps they push
Their beating breast in vain, and piteous bray,
He lays them quivering on the ensanguin'd snows,
And with loud shouts rejoicing bears them home.
There through the piny forest half absorpt,
Rough tenant of these shades, the shapeless bear,
With dangling ice all horrid, stalks forlorn.
Slow-pac'd, and sourer as the storms increase,   830
He makes his bed beneath the inclement drift,
And, with stern patience, scorning weak complaint,
Hardens his heart against assailing want
    Wide o'er the spacious regions of the north,
That see Bootes urge his tardy wain,
A boisterous race, by frosty Caurus pierc'd,
Who little pleasure know, and fear no pain,
Prolific swarm.   They once relum'd the flame
Of lost mankind in polish'd slavery sunk,
Drove martial horde on horde, with dreadful sweep   840
Resistless rushing o'er the enfeebled south,
And gave the vanquish'd world another form.
Not such the sons of Lapland : wisely they
Despise the insensate barbarous trade of war.
They ask no more than simple nature gives ;
They love their mountains and enjoy their storms.

No false desires, no pride-created wants,
Disturb the peaceful current of their time,
And through the restless, ever-tortured maze
Of pleasure or ambition, bid it rage.   850
Their rein-deer form their riches. These their tents,
Their robes, their beds, and all their homely wealth,
Supply, their wholesome fare, and cheerful cups.
Obsequious at their call, the docile tribe
Yield to the sled their necks, and whirl them swift
O'er hill and dale, heap'd into one expanse
Of marbled snow, as far as eye can sweep,
With a blue crust of ice, unbounded, glaz'd.
By dancing meteors then, that ceaseless shake
A waving blaze refracted o'er the heavens,   860
And vivid moons, and stars that keener play
With double lustre from the glossy waste,
Even in the depth of polar night, they find
A wondrous day; enough to light the chase,
Or guide their daring steps to Finland fairs.
Wish'd spring returns; and from the hazy south,
While dim Aurora slowly moves before,
The welcome sun, just verging up at first,
By small degrees extends the swelling curve;
Till seen at last for gay rejoicing months,   870
Still round and round his spiral course he winds;
And, as he nearly dips his flaming orb,
Wheels up again, and re-ascends the sky.
In that glad season, from the lakes and floods,
Where pure Niemi's fairy mountains rise,
And fring'd with roses, Tenglio rolls his stream,
They draw the copious fry. With these at eve,
They cheerful—loaded to their tents repair;
Where, all day long in useful cares employ'd,
Their kind, unblemished wives the fire prepare.   880

Thrice happy race! by poverty secur'd
From regal plunder and rapacious power:
In whom fell interest never yet has sown
The seeds of vice: whose spotless swains ne'er knew
Injurious deed, nor, blasted by the breath
Of faithless love, their blooming daughters woe.

Still pressing on beyond Tornea's lake,
And Hecla flaming through a waste of snow,
And farthest Greenland, to the pole itself,
Where, failing gradual, life at length goes out,   890
The muse expands her solitary flight;
And. hovering, o'er the wild stupendous scene,
Beholds new seas beneath another sky.
Thron'd in his palace of cerulean ice,
Here winter holds his unrejoicing court;
And, through his airy hall, the loud misrule
Of driving tempest is for ever heard;
Here the grim tyrant meditates his wrath;
Here arms his winds with all-subduing frost;
Moulds his fierce hail, and treasures up his snows,   900
With which he now oppresses half the globe.

Thence, winding eastward, to the Tartar's coast,
She sweeps the howling margin of the main;
Where, undissolving, from the first of time,
Snows swell on snows amazing to the sky;
And icy mountains high on mountains pil'd,
Seem to the shivering sailor from afar,
Shapeless and white, an atmosphere of clouds.
Projected huge, and horrid, o'er the surge,
Alps frown on Alps; or, rushing hideous down,   910
As if old chaos was again return'd,
Wide rend the deep, and shake the solid pole.
Ocean itself no longer can resist
The binding fury; but in all its rage

Of tempest, taken by the boundless frost,
Is many a fathom to the bottom chain'd,
And bid to roar no more : a bleak expanse,
Shagg'd o'er with wavy rocks, cheerless and void
Of every life, that from the dreary months
Fli s conscious southward.   Miserable they !   920
Who, here entangled in the gathering ice,
Take their last look of the descending sun ;
While, full of death, and fierce with tenfold frost,
The long, long night, incumbent o'er their heads,
Falls horrible.   Such was the Briton's fate,
As with first prow (what have not Britons dar'd ?)
He for the passage sought, attempted since
So much in vain, and seeming to be shut
By jealous Nature with eternal bars.
In these fell regions, in Arzina caught,   930
And to the stony deep his idle ship
Immediate seal'd, he with his hapless crew,
Each full exerted at his several task,
Froze into statues ; to the cordage glued
The sailor and the pilot to the helm.

    Hard by these shores, where scarce his freezing stream
Rolls the wild Oby, live the last of men ;
And, half-enliven'd by the distant sun,
That rears and ripens man as well as plants,
Here human nature wears its rudest form.   940
Deep from the piercing season, sunk in caves,
Here, by dull fires, and with unjoyous cheer,
They waste the tedious gloom.   Immers'd in furs,
Doze the gross race.   Nor sprightly jest, nor song,
Nor tenderness, they know ; nor aught of life,
Beyond the kindred bears that stalk without ;
Till morn at length, her roses drooping all,
Sheds a long twilight, brightening o'er their fields,
And calls the quiver'd savage to the chase.

Panegyric on Peter the Great.

What cannot active government perform ;   950
New-moulding man ? Wide stretching from these shores,
A people savage from remotest time,
A huge neglected empire, one vast mind,
By Heaven inspir'd, from Gothic darkness call'd.
Immortal Peter ! first of monarchs ! He
His stubborn country tam'd, her rocks, her fens,
Her floods, her seas, her ill-submitting sons ;
And, while the fierce barbarian he subdued,
To more exalted soul he rais'd the man.
Ye shades of ancient heroes, ye who toil'd   960
Through long successive ages to build up
A labouring plan of state, behold at once
The wonder done ! Behold the matchless prince
Who left his native throne, where reign'd till then
A mighty shadow of unreal power ;
Who greatly spurn'd the slothful pomp of courts ;
And roaming every land—in every port,
His sceptre laid aside, with glorious hand
Unwearied plying the mechanic tool—
Gather'd the seeds of trade, of useful arts,   970
Of civil wisdom, and of martial skill.
Charg'd with the stores of Europe, home he goes ;
Then cities rise amid the illumin'd waste ;
O'er joyless deserts smiles the rural reign ;
Far-distant flood to flood is social join'd.
The astonish'd Euxine hears the Baltic roar ;
Proud navies ride on seas that never foam'd
With daring keel before ; and armies stretch
Each way their dazzling files, repressing here
The frantic Alexander of the north,   980
And awing there stern Othman's shrinking sons.
Sloth flies the land, and ignorance, and vice,

Of old dishonour proud ; it glows around,
Taught by the royal hand that rous'd the whole,
One scene of arts, of arms, of rising trade :
For what his wisdom plann'd, and power enforc'd,
More potent still, his great example show'd.

A Thaw Producing Floods and Icebergs.

Muttering, the winds at eve, with blunted point,
Blow hollow-blustering from the south.   Subdued,
The frost resolves into a trickling thaw.   900
Spotted the mountains shine : loose sleet descends,
And floods the country round.   The rivers swell,
Of bonds impatient.   Sudden from the hills,
O'er rocks and woods, in broad brown cataracts,
A thousand snow-fed torrents shoot at once ;
And, where they rush, the wide-resounding plain
Is left one slimy waste.   Those sullen seas,
That wash'd the ungenial pole, will rest no more
Beneath the shackles of the mighty north ;
But, rousing all their waves, resistless heave.   1000
And, hark ! the lengthening roar continuous runs
Athwart the rifted deep : at once it bursts,
And piles a thousand mountains to the clouds.
Ill fares the bark, with trembling wretches charg'd,
That, toss'd amid the floating fragments, moors
Beneath the shelter of an icy isle,
While night o'erwhelms the sea, and horror looks
More horrible.   Can human force endure
The assembled mischiefs that besiege them round?
Heart-gnawing hunger, fainting weariness,   1010
The roar of winds and waves, the crush of ice,
Now ceasing, now renew'd with louder rage,
And in dire echoes bellowing round the main.
More to embroil the deep, Leviathan

And his unwieldy train, in **dreadful** sport,
Tempest the loosen'd brine, while, through the gloom,
Far from the bleak inhospitable shore,
Loading the winds, is heard the hungry howl
Of famish'd monsters there awaiting wrecks.
Yet Providence, that ever-waking eye,   1020
Looks down with pity on the feeble toil
Of mortals lost to hope, and lights them safe,
Through all this dreary labyrinth of fate.

Human Life Compared to the Changing Seasons.

'Tis done! dread Winter spreads his latest glooms,
And reigns tremendous o'er the conquer'd year.
How dead the vegetable kingdom lies!
How dumb the tuneful! Horror wide extends
His desolate domain. Behold, fond man !
See here thy pictur'd life ! Pass some few years,
Thy flowering Spring, thy Summer's ardent strength,   1030
Thy sober Autumn fading into age,
And pale concluding Winter comes at last,
And shuts the scene. Ah! whither now are fled
Those dreams of greatness? those unsolid hopes
Of happiness? those longings after fame?
Those restless cares? those busy bustling days?
Those gay-spent festive nights? those veering thoughts,
Lost between good and ill, that shar'd thy life?
All now are vanish'd! Virtue sole survives,
Immortal, never-failing friend of man,   1040
His guide to happiness on high. And see !
'Tis come, the glorious morn ! the second birth
Of heaven and earth ! Awakening nature hears
The new-creating word, and starts to life,
In every heighten'd form, from pain and death
For ever **free**. The great eternal scheme,

Involving all, and in a perfect whole
Uniting, as the prospect wider spreads,
To reason's eye refin'd clears up apace.
Ye vainly wise! ye blind presumptuous! now,   1050
Confounded in the dust, adore that Power.
And Wisdom oft arraign'd : see now the cause,
Why unassuming worth in secret liv'd,
And died neglected ; why the good man's share
In life was gall and bitterness of soul ;
Why the lone widow and her orphans pin'd
In starving solitude—while luxury,
In palaces, lay straining her low thought,
To form unreal wants : why heaven-born truth,
And moderation fair, wore the red marks   1060
Of superstition's scourge ; why licens'd pain,
That cruel spoiler, that embosom'd foe,
Embittered all our bliss.   Ye good distres'd !
Ye noble few ! who here unbending stand
Beneath life's pressure, yet bear up awhile ;
And what your bounded view, which only saw
A little part, deem'd evil, is no more.
The storms of wintry time will quickly pass,
And one unbounded Spring encircle all.

END OF WINTER.

NOTES.

AUTUMN.

1. Crown'd limits **Autumn**.

sickle.—Contrast with modern implements.

Wheaten.—Of wheat. Seldom used now.

3. jovial.—Like Jove (Jupiter), merry and sociable. If the planet Jupiter were in the ascendant at one's birth, it was prognostic of a happy and successful life. Compare *mercurial* and *saturnine*.

Doric reed, *i.e.*, pastoral poetry, which among the Greeks was confined to the Doric dialect, and was written by Theocritus, Bion and Moschus. Reeds were the origin of musical pipes of all kinds. What are the chief characteristics of pastoral poetry? Name any English writers of this variety of poetry.

5. Nitrous is an adv. The meaning of the word here is hard to see, unless allusion is made to the great fertilizing power of nitre and other salts. The construction is, "Whatever has been prepared by Winter, promised by Spring, and ripened by Summer, now rushes perfected to view." —*Morris.* But see notes to *Winter,* l. 694.

6-7. promise.—Blossom.

concocted.—Ripened. Lat. meaning. Parse *rush* and *swell*.

9. Onslow.—Speaker of the House of Commons from 1728 to 1761. His duty would be to *listen* to the public voice (11), to keep order, and not to make speeches (15).

13-14. A strange succession of images ; the virtues **distend** his mind, are **spread** on his brow, and *burn* in his bosom. Compare Burke, "thousands hung with rapture on his accents." *Panegyric on Sheridan.*

15-18. Senate would better apply to the House of Lords, but is here used poetically for any deliberative assembly.

devolving.—Employed in an unusual sense. Derive, and exemplify its ordinary meaning.

periods.—In oratory and poetry the usual word for sentence. Strictly speaking, a *period*, as compared with a *loose* sentence, is one in which the meaning remains in suspense till the sentence is finished.

she too.—The muse, referring to the poets and other literary men opposed to Walpole and calling themselves patriots. Walpole was essentially a peace minister.

pants for.—Eagerly desires.

[77]

19. Notice the **of** after weak, yet **in** after strong.

23-4. Virgo, the Virgin.—The 6th division or sign of the Zodiac, beginning on the 21st August. Libra, the balance, is the next, beginning 21st September, when the days and nights are equal. Libra would be just halfway in the old Roman year, which began in March.

25. The effulgence (nom. abs.) of parting Summer being *shaken* from heaven's *canopy*.

26-7. **enlivened.**—Notice the antithesis to the idea in *serene*. We apply the term *relieved* to occasional and pleasing changes from a dull monotony of colour.

  attempered.—Softened.

29. **lucid.**—Clear, from the light of the sun. *Pellucid* is common in this sense.

30-2. Notice the alliteration, and the beauty of the picture.

33. Many poets have this thought, but few have so happily expressed it as Thomson in this line; so in lines 37-9.

34. **ruffled.**—Disturbed; we speak of ruffled temper, and ruffled water, but never of ruffled air.

  poise.—Equilibrium.

35-6. **gives,** *i.e.*, causes the breezes to blow. A similar use of *gives* occurs in Coleridge's lines to Genevieve,

> "Yet not your heavenly beauty *gives*
> This heart with passion soft *to glow.*"

37. **different.**—In different direction; the root meaning (derive), but seems very harsh here. Note the frequency and freedom with which T. uses adjectives with an adverbial force.

38. Give different meanings of the word **fit.**

40-2. **a view unbounded tossing.**—Nom. absol.

41. **shoot.**—See W., lines 795-6.

43. Why is Industry called a rough power?
  These.—What?

45. **source.**—In apposition with Industry.

46. **civility.**—Refinement, opposite of wild, savage. Latin use. Compare *urbanity.*

47. Notice T. says cast out by **Nature,** not by God. Explain the allusion.

50. *et seq.* Compare a passage at the close of Browning's Paracelsus, commencing, "Wherefore take accounts of feverish starts."—*Morris.*

52. (with) materials poured around.

53. **unconscious,** *i.e.*, of these seeds and **materials.**

54. **corruption.**—Produce of nature allowed to rot and spoil.

56. **savage,** *i.e.*, the year of the savage—transferred epithet.

57-9. **sad.**—Gloomy, sullen, like Lat. *tristis.*
   tusky.—Commonly *tusked.*

60-62. What figure here?
   let fly seems a low expression for this place.

63-4. he sordid pined away the season.
   sordid.—Dirty and uncared for.
   season.—What case?

65. **resort of** is usually followed an object denoting a person; "frequented by " is an equivalent phrase.

70. Is **even** correctly placed?

74. Is **unfolded** trans. or intrans. ?

75-6. **lavish.**—Synonyme?
   to raise.—Increase.

77. **mechanic.**—What is the usual word?

78. **vaulted.**—What is meant?

79. Extracting metals from their ores.

80. Does this line refer in a general way to the employment of water and wind in the mechanical arts, or has it special reference to their use in connection with mineral products?

82. **chip.**—Chop.

84. **blood polluted,** *i.e.*, untanned.

86. **bright.**—Adv.
   lawn.—A fine kind of linen used for bishops' sleeves, and in consequence the words *lawn-sleeves* are often used to designate a bishop. Compare *ermine;* see note on *Winter,* l. 812.

88. **generous glass inspired.**—T. probably had in his mind the words of Jotham, Judges 9-18, " Wine which cheereth God and man." But in the next line, if he had put *indecent* instead of *decent,* many will think he would have been nearer the mark.

90. **barren** and **bare** are here properly enough used together, for although they are probably from the same root (A. S. *bar,* naked), they have diverged in their later applications. This process of divergence and discrimination goes on in every language, but the English being very composite in its character, and having borrowed so largely, has had very many such points of departure, and hence the language is very rich in synonymes.

96. There are two theories as to the origin of society ; one that it was made ; the other that it grew. The first is called the doctrine of the original contract, and is fully expounded by Hume in his essays. According to it, men feeling the isolation of living separately, met together in a large plain, and agreed to form a society and give that society a government.

It is almost needless to add, that this theory is opposed to historical evidence; there is no record or trace of the meeting. The other theory is that society began with the family, grew larger, and so became the state. On this theory, with its proofs, vide *Maine's Ancient Law*, chap. v., Thomson evidently favours the first view, which is now antiquated but was then generally accepted. It is rather a stretch, even of this theory, to make parliamentary institutions after the English model, the earliest form of government.—*Morris*. T., always an admirer of the British Constitution, seems quite unconscious of its defects; for instance, line 100 is quite misleading, and an advanced English Radical or Irish Home Ruler would see considerable satire in ll. 105-8.

96. Scan this line and point out others with similar irregularities.

104. If his reference is to England, as is probably the case, the Hanoverians were certainly the nominees of the Parliament. The first two Georges, being foreigners and incapable of wielding personal political influence, left the helm of state to their ministries, which was no doubt best for the country. The third George wished to be King again in the old pre-revolution way, and our American colonies were lost to us.

108. ... This line means those who are not patriots, but merely eager for their own advancement.

111. **wrought.**—Intrans. This form instead of *worked* is used chiefly by the northern folk in England. *Wrought* might be taken as a participle, and *sprang* or some such verb supplied with *form*.

112. **high.**—In aim.

115-17. Construe, "Drew her sons from twining woody haunts or from strong-straining the tough yew to bows." From earliest times the yew was preferred for bows. . . . With what else is the *yew* associated in English literature? See *e.g.*, *sepulchral yew*, *Lady of the Lake*, iii., 8, 9.

120. **crane.**—The most common form consists of an upright, revolving shaft with a projecting arm at the top. At the end of the arm is a fixed pulley, by which the weight is raised, and by the revolution of the shaft it can be deposited anywhere within the length of the arm.

122. **large.**—Capacious. The Thames (literally broad-water) is navigable for barges 200 miles up; vessels of 1,400 tons can come within five miles of London Bridge. At the Nore it is six miles wide, and eight miles below eighteen miles wide.

king.—On account of its shipping.

124. **groves.**—Applicable enough on account of the various docks in which the different classes of vessels are laid up.

126. **sooty.**—Black, perhaps referring to the colliers.

127. **barge.**—The barges used on ceremonial occasions by the City of London and the Admiralty are splendid affairs and supplied with many rowers. A man of war's barge is not usually showy, and is light enough to

be easily hoisted in or out.   On our lakes, rivers and canals, barges are clumsy vessels of burden or draught, and are divided into coal-barges, sand-barges, etc.

128. **rowed.**—Being rowed, or better, intransit. past tense.

133. What is the British thunder? Why is the epithet *black* used?
main.—Ocean.

134. **magnific.**—Not used now ; magnificent.
heaved.—Raised would seem to be a better word here.

136. Why is the word **glittering** used?

137. **embodied.**—The paintings being so life-like, stand out *(protuber-ant)* from the canvas as if they were the real objects instead of their repre-sentations. What three arts are referred to in ll. 134-40? Notice the antithesis in smooth and protuberant.

138. **breathe.**—Compare Macaulay, *Prophecy of Capys*, 28,
"The stone that breathes and struggles,
The brass that seems to speak."

140. **imagination-flushed** is an unusual compound, but a very expressive one.

143. **him.**—Notice the gender? Why masc.? What principles influence us in personification?

145. **idly.**—In gusts, or doing no damage.

146. The luxuriant wealth of Spring reduced to order and symmetry ; notions which underlie our ideas of beauty.

148. Nor could Summer transmit, etc.
waving stores is an awkward expression.

154. The peasant women of England often assist in the harvest field. The scene described belongs to the old sickle or reaping-hook days.

154. Note the derivation of *lass* from *lad*.

156. **offices.**—Dutiful services, its former meaning.

157. **lusty.**—Vigorous, bulky (here). The noun means desire, and that in a bad sense.

160. Thomson's apology for the "rural scandal."
to.—So as to.

162. The picture of the master behind, **shocking** or stooking the sheaves, is not an unfamiliar one, even in Canada.

163. **conscious.**—Feeling and showing satisfaction.

165. Leaving a small portion on the ground for the poor is a very old cus-tom. The Jews were commanded to do so. Read Boaz's instructions to the reapers, Ruth i., 16.

166. **spike.**—Used here for an ear of corn or wheat. In botany an in-florescence, consisting of several flowers sessile on an axis or single stem, as in the mullein.

167. **narrow,** *i.e.,* stingy. Why does he add in the next line "with stealth"?

172. **partners of your kind.**—Fellow members of your race.

173. **hover.**—To hang fluttering over or about, and thus gives the idea of anxiety and expectancy.

174. **dole.**—Same root as deal, that which is distributed grudgingly and in small portions.

175. Supply *think* or *reflect* before *that.* Paraphrase the sentence, 174-6.

179. What word in 178 does the clause beginning with **for** explain?

180. **stay.**—Support. Explain why **innocence** is a stay.

183-4. Compare line 115, and notice the alliteration.

188-9. **giddy.**—Give the various meanings.
 Almost . . . . . fed.—Explain what is meant.

190. **gay.**—In plumage or in song? Which meaning agrees best with the rest of the line?

193. Notice the awkward accumulation of s-sounds in "wets its leaves."

196. **dejected.**—Cast down through modesty, not through sadness.

197. Why *humid?*

198. Explain why **the** is better than *a* would be in this line.

200. Construe, "(she being) thrilled in her thought, they (the eyes) shone."

 dewy star of evening.—Not necessarily Venus, but any star.

205-6. . . . Much quoted lines; the idea is not original with Thomson, but his expression of it is a masterpiece.

207-17. T. sent an interleaved copy of the 1736 edition of the *Seasons* of Pope. This passage then stood:

> "Thoughtless of beauty she was Beauty's self
> Recluse among the woods; if city dames
> Will deign their faith; and thus she went, compelled
> By strong necessity, with as serene
> And pleased a look as Patience e'er put on,
> To glean Palemon's fields."

Pope drew his pen through these lines and wrote those in the text. Their beauty makes us regret Pope's writing in rhyme instead of blank verse. Thomson was too shrewd and too pleased not to adopt all of Pope's corrections, of which there are several. The friendship and intimacy of the two poets is honourable to both.

208. **recluse.**—Distinguish recluse and hermit.

211. The myrtle among the ancients was sacred to Venus as the symbol of youth and beauty, and is much referred to in poetry. Give the points of resemblance between the myrtle and Lavinia.

215. *et seq.* The story of Boaz and Ruth has evidently been in the poet's mind.

220. Arcadia, the centre division of the Peloponnesus, inhabited by a pastoral people passionately fond of music and dancing. The elegance, however, was rudeness to. the rest of Greece, and the term "Arcadian youth" was only another name for a dunce. Compare the phrases "Arcades ambo," and "Arcadian simplicity."—Virg. *Ecl.* vii. 5, x. 32.

222. T. means the tyranny of fashion or social usage, but customs have been the foundation of the Common Law as well.

223. Construe, "To follow nature freely was the mode," or "The mode was free to follow nature."

229-30. Much quoted lines, expressive through their suggestiveness. "He saw her charming." Supply "to be." The verbs *see* and *know* are used in this way, with the omission of the "to be," which omission is the regular construction with the verb "find."

232-5. The connection and coherence of these lines are somewhat obscure. The sequence of tenses is not good. **For** introduces the reason of the previous statement implied in the word **unknown.** Construe "Unknown to himself, for still the world and its dread laugh (would have) prevailed if his heart should have owned (for its mistress) a gleaner, etc." The sentiment seems contradictory to ll. 222-3, and represents the rustic as fully alive to social distinctions.

236. Notice the alliterative beauty and the imagery of this line recalling the notion of the attendant and guiding dæmon of the ancients. See note on *Winter*, ll. 439-435.

237. **What pity** !—Compare the common phrase, "what a pity."
　　　delicate.—Pleasing to the eye or taste. Explain how this word has acquired the meaning of "*feeble*," the opposite of "robust."

238. Explain the meaning of **kindled** and **enlivening sense.**

239. **vulgar goodness.**—Common goodness ; or perhaps the meaning is those virtues that belong only to the vulgar (common people).

241. **indecent.**—Ugly, awkward.
　　　looks.—Appears to be. Parse **methinks.**

245. **gone down.**—Limits **patron.** Notice the peculiar use of **dissolved.**

248. "Urged (to retire) by sad remembrance and becoming pride."

252. Parse **would** and **were.**

256. **surprised.**—Took unawares. Comp. ll. 231-2.

258. **smothered.**—By what?

259-60. Two very expressive lines.

261. **confused, frightened,** may be taken with **beauties,** (she), or with **her,** if *her* be parsed as a pers. pron.

262. **To flush a bloom** is a rather strange phrase. **Bloom** may perhaps be taken in apposition with **beauties.**

263. **passionate.**—Full of strong emotion – the root meaning. Compare the phrases, "Passion Week," "The Passionate Pilgrim," etc.

264. **rapture.**—A state of mind in which the attention is carried away (*rapere*) from the ordinary things of life and completely engrossed by the ruling passion or feeling. Compare Byron,

> "There is a pleasure in the pathless woods,
> There is a *rapture* on the lonely shore."

265. Lavinia is called his **remains,** *i.e.,* what is left or representative of him. His widow would be called his *relict,* which has the same root meaning.

266-7. "Art thou she whom, etc." "Thou art the very same, etc."

269. Construe "being alive," or "is here alive."

272. **ah.**—Weak, seems like padding.

273. **sequestered.**—"Secluded. In Lat. *sequester (secus)* is a trustee in whose hands contested property is placed *pendente lite.* To sequester is (1) so to place property, (2) to put aside, to withdraw."—*Morris.* In the first sense *sequestrate* is more commonly used. In Scotch law, sequestration corresponds to bankruptcy.

274-5. May be paraphrased freely, "Thy smiling and beauteous form, expanding and blossoming into the perfection of womanhood."

276-7. So Gray says, "chill penury."

keen applies to the wind. **heavy** to the rain. A rather awkward construction.

282. Notice the effective repetition, and the change from the second person to the third.

283. **his.**—In apposition with **Acasto's,** antecedent of **whose.** The construction is not uncommon in Latin. Or supply **daughter** after **his,** and parse *his* as poss. adj.

285. Notice the limping construction, **father** in apposition with **Acasto's,** a poss. case.

288. **shameful pittance.**—Why shameful, and to whom?

289. **But ill-applied.**--Ill fitted for.

293. **power of blessing thee.**—Providing for her various needs and for her comfort.

294. Compare *Kg. Lear* iv. 5, 25.

297. **vulgar joy.**—What is Thomson's meaning?

299. **all.**—Quite.

302. **pierced.**—Engrossed in thought for Lavinia's fate. Compare *Winter*, 286.

304. (She) amazed and scarce believing, etc., joy seized her withered veins.

307. (She being) not less enraptured.

311. **defeating.**—Undoing.

314. **murmur** is not a good word—rustle would be more imitative of the sound made.

315. **soft-inclining.**—Pliant, and consequently bending before the breeze.

316. **fuller.**—Adj. for adv.

322. **high-beat.**—Beaten in their higher parts.
　　eddy.—Cause to move as an eddy, *i.e.*, collect.

325. **Exposed, naked.**—Limit *plain*.

327. Nor can it being whirled in air or shaken wastefully into worthless chaff, evade, etc.

332. **continuous** cannot refer to time ; there is only a burst of rain, for a time descending in one broad, continuous, connected sheet. Compare *Georgic* i., 318.

335. **flatted.**—The water filling up the hollows and thus levelling the whole.
　　sordid.—Full, and therefore unsightly with floating matter.

337. **red.**—From the soil washed away.

343-4.—**painful.**—Laborious.
　　fled.—Having fled. Æneid ii., 305-8.

347. **descending.**—On the flood.

349-50. **unprovided** for.
　　clamant.—Crying out, clamouring for food.

353. **russet.**—Reddish brown cloth worn by country people and labourers on account of its serviceable colour. So, too, from their colour there are apples called russets.

354. Whose toil is warmth and ornament to your limbs.

355. **sparing board.**—What is meant ? What figure ?

357. **sparkle.**—With what ?
　　sense.—Meaning of this word ?

358-9. Although these lines are not inconsistent with the payment of a money-rent, yet perhaps T. had in mind the *metayer* system of letting land, which gives the landlord a part of the produce as rent. In Canada it is not uncommon, and is called letting on shares. The moral effect of the system is maintained by some to be beneficial, but the political economist views it as unworthy of general adoption, as it is inconsistent with the cultivation of large areas or the employment of large capital. See Sismondi, and Rogers' Pol. Econ.

361. Distinguish wīnded, wĭnded, and wound.

362-4. **game.**—Sport.

tainted.—With the scent of the game. The pure-bred Pointer or Setter does not advance upon the game.

365-6. **draws full on.**—Approaches.

sensible.—Perceptive.

latent.—Hiding, the root meaning. What is the derived meaning?

367-8. **covey.**—A small flock of birds. (Fr. *couver*, to hatch), most commonly said of partridges.

every way.—In every direction.

373-7. **glanced.**—Aimed.

gun o'ertakes.—What figure?

again.—This word seems to relate to the phrase "to the ground."

towering wing.—Soaring flight.

378. **various.**—Notice how very freely T. uses adjectives with an adverbial force.

381. Then she is most delighted. Does **social** limit **she** or **creation**?

384. **game of death,** *i.e.*, the chase, in apposition with it in 383. All the Germanic nations have been fond of it. A humorous story is told of a French traveller, who observed that whenever one Englishman said to another, "it is a fine day," the answer generally was, "yes, let us go and kill something."—*Morris*.

385-8. **rage of pleasure.**—Would rage *for* pleasure have exactly the same force?

youth.—Obj. after "awakes."

ranged.—Prov. 28, 15. Give the other meanings of range.

389. **conscious.**—Transferred epithet.

390. **steady.**—Constant of purpose, never ceasing.

395. **gentle days.**—Explain the force of the epithet.

396. **ravening.**—Voracious. See Genesis 49, 27.

wanton.—Given to excess. The root meaning is "unrestrained;" see Skeat.

398-400. Relation of **fed** and **rolled**? Account for the singular **is.**

horrid.—T. uses this word in two senses, "bristling," the root meaning, and "terrible," the common meaning. For the first, see A. 400, 772, 782, W. 390, 829. Of course there are many places where either meaning will do.

401. Compare Cowper's opinion of the sport, *Task* iii., 326-331.

timid hare.—See n. on *W.*, 258. Hares *(Leporidæ)* are found in both American continents, but in far greater numbers in the temperate parts of N. A. The chief species are the northern hare and the wood hare or grey rabbit. They change colour more or less in winter.

402. **Scare** is a good word here, as the meaning is suddenly frighted. In Canada "scared" is often improperly used for "afraid."

seat or **form** is the technical word for the place in which the hare takes refuge.

404. **chapped.**—In gaps or cracks; often applied to the hands.

405. **lawn.**—Here simply a green field.

broom.—The broom and furze (called also whin and gorse) are varieties of the same order, Papilionaceæ. The broom grows farther to the north than the furze; they are both shrub-like in form, and both inhabit sandy upland tracts, and are covered with numerous solitary yellow flowers. Broom has been used to some extent in the arts, as tanning, dyeing, and its fibres have been even made into a coarse cloth. Furze in some countries, as Normandy, is cultivated as fodder, but only of course upon otherwise unproductive soils.

406. **fern.**—The two preceding plants are not indigenous to Ontario, but the ferns are numerous and found on every woody upland and river bottom.

407. **fallow.**—Ploughed, but lying idle for the season; often incorrectly pronounced "follow" in Canada.

408. **concoctive.**—Ripening. See *W.*, 706 n.

nodding.—Overhanging, sheltering.

412. The wide range of the eye being a provision for its safety.

413. To escape observation and the better to hear.

415-16. **labyrinth.**—Involved course.

openings.—Barking of the dogs on first catching sight of the game.

417. **coming storm.**—What is meant?

418. **nearer, more frequent.**—Attributive to **it**; an unusual inversion.

loads.—See *W.*, 1018.

amazed.—Struck with sudden fear. Usually derived from *a* (intensive, Skeat) and *maze*: but, according to Stormonth, from the same source as *dismayed* (O. F. s'esmaier, to be sad), a derivation which suits the use of the word in the text.

421. **full-opening.**—See n. on 416.

various.—In different tones; see n. on 378.

424. **all.**—Sums up the nom. abs., pack, horn, steed, shout.

426. Is **where** correctly used?

427. **ranged.**—See n. on 388.

monarch.—Case?

428. **tempest.**—Compare 317.

 drives.—Intr.

429. **sprightly,** *i.e.,* sprite-like or spirit-like Has the notion of cheerfulness added to that of "aerial soul" (430).

431-2. Are these lines true to nature? Parse **way** and **more.**

435-6.—These lines have been much admired. Give reasons why. How would the employment of singular nouns affect the lines?

437-40. The inhuman rout adhesive—come sure, if slow, etc.

 ... **rout.**—Clamorous crowd.

  shift.—Expedient. Give the other meanings of these two words.

441. **sobbing.**—Compare Scott's "While every gasp with sobs he drew." *L. of L.* 1, vii.

444. **wont.**—Was wont. The word as a verb is now out of use; but as a noun and an adj., in the senses of "custom" and "accustomed," is quite common.

446. Tries to lose the scent and tries to lave; *laves* would seem to be better. Notice the causative force of *lose.*

449. **vivid** seems to have same meaning as "so full of buoyant spirit." Compare above (429-30) "sprightly" and "aerial soul."

452. **sick** refers to "toil," but the whole expression is awkward. "Sick at heart" is the common phrase used of mental states. Great anxiety of mind affects powerfully the stomach and the heart; this is no doubt true of the lower animals also. See Darwin on the "Expression of Emotions in Men and Animals."

 at bay, *i.e.,* in a bay formed by the dogs surrounding. Another and better derivation makes *bay* signify the baying (Fr. aboiement) of the dogs from the O. F. aboi, the barking of a dog.

454.—**big tears.**—See As You Like It, ii. 1-38. Horses and seals are said to weep.

456. **Blood-happy.**—Happy at the taste of blood. This would seem a rather startling compound with any other poet.

457. **chequered.**—Streaked and spotted with blood.

459. Notice the similar root meanings of "fervent" and "boil."

460. **despising flight.**—Not strictly true; all wild animals seem by instinct to recognize man's superiority, and very soon learn to fear and avoid him. See W., 406 n.

461. **roused up.**—*Gen.* 49, 9, "Who will rouse him up."

462. **protended.**—Stretched forward, the root meaning.

463. **coward-band.**—Must refer to times or places in which the rifle was unknown.

464. **slunk.**—Having slunk, or by poetic license for slinking, creeping.
troubled.—By what?

465-6. **shaggy foe.**—The wolf-dog.
ruffian.—Seldom used of beasts.

467. **brindled.**—Coloured in stripes : also "brinded," a form Shaks. used, as in Macbeth ; the first witch says, "Thrice the brinded cat hath mew'd."—Act iv.

growling horrid.—Attributive to **boar.** See n. on 418.

468. **grins.**—Refers to the tusks (the canine teeth) which protrude, and are formidable weapons of defence.

469. **lighten.**—Light or alight would now be used ; *in* or *on* would be a more suitable preposition than *to.*

nervous.—Has the same meaning as in the phrase, "a nervous style," *i.e.,* full of strength and vigour. Note the very opposite meaning, weak and spiritless.

470. **These Britain knows not.**—Yet T. recommends the youth to hunt them. The lion in historic times never inhabited Britain, but wild boars and wolves were numerous and had rewards offered for their heads. Wolves were not entirely extinct at the middle of the last century.

470-2. **loose.**—Adj. to **fury** or adv. to **pour.** With the phrase "give your fury to pour," compare "give thee to shine." W. 661 and note.

nightly.—What two meanings? Which preferable here?

473. Driven from his burrow.

475. Bound high o'er.

throw.—What is the usual word?

477. **shaking wilderness.**—Explain the force of these words.

478-9. **nice.**—This is a word much used (and abused) in America. The original meanings, "foolish, particular," may be traced through the Fr. *nice,* foolish, simple to the Latin *nescius.* This is supported by Pope's rhyme,

"Thus critics, of less judgment than caprice,
    Curious, not knowing, not exact but nice."

Bear.—Advance.

481. **sonorous, running, tossed.**—Limits **triumph.**

485. So Shaks. *Henry IV.,* i. 1, "He seemed in running to devour the way."

488. **guile.**—A doublet of *wile.* Which is the more common word in this sense? Compare the similar doublets, guard and ward, guarantee and warrant.

489. **Disclosed.**—Parse.

494. ... **ghostly** seems unexpected and out of place, as introducing an idea quite irrelevant to this description.

495-7. fox's fur depending.—In a fox hunt, to be first in at the death, and to secure the brush mark the hero of the day.

    depending.—Hanging down.

497. antic.—Antique, ancient. So Milton, *Il. Pens.*,

        "And love the high embowed roof
        With *antic* pillars massy proof."

499. Some paraphrase thus: "They stagger under the excessive drinking which even the Centaurs couldn't equal, although they were noted drinkers." See Hor. *Odes* i., 18-8, and *W.* n., l. 42. Or it may mean, "When the night, exhausted by the recounting of feats unequalled by the Centaurs, is retreating before the coming day."

501. their.—What is the antecedent? See ll. 493-4.

    wonders.—What figure?

502-5. foam. With ale.

    sirloin.—The loin is said to have been sportively knighted by Charles II., or, according to others, James I., but unfortunately for this derivation the word is found to have been in existence before the time of James I. Probably the same as Fr. *sur-longe.*

    desperate.—Although it seems an overstrong word, it gives us a lively idea of their appetites made keen by exercise, and their consequent rude way of eating.

508. hence, *i.e.*, from the "Roast Beef of Old England," which is the theme and title of Fielding's song. Beef-eating is popularly supposed to b the real cause of England's superiority in arms and industry, if not in literature ; but the lowest classes eat very little meat of any kind on account of its dearness ; to which fact some sarcastically say their content and humility is due. (See Mr. Bumble's observations in *Oliver Twist.*)

508. amain.—From A. S. mægen, strength, with energy. Compare the phrase "with might and main."

513. bowl.—The punch bowl. Punch was named, it is said, from being composed of five ingredients (Hindoo "panch" five). As now made, the basis is some form of spirit, *e.g.*, whiskey, brandy or rum, with lemon, nutmeg, sugar, hot water, milk, etc. Fifty or sixty years ago it was a common drink, but it is now rarely seen, being perhaps a little too potent for the moderation and decorum of these latter days.

516. Maia.—Daughter of Atlas and mother of Mercury by Jove, was the eldest of the Pleiades. As there is no aptness in her being named, Maia is here probably put for the month of May.—*Morris.*

517.—diffused.—Reclining—probably in imitation of Virgil's "fusi per herbam."

519. brown October.—October refers to the month of brewing. Ale is doubtless meant, although the term *brown* better applies to porter, invented by Harwood in 1722. As Autumn was published in 1730, and T.

mentions thirty years as the age of the liquor, he must refer to ale. The brown colour of porter is due to the employment of malt roasted till it becomes brown.

520. **mature.**—Mellows and strengthens by keeping.

521. **honest front.**—Why is this expression used of the ale as against the wine?

522. **produce.**—Note the accent.

525. **grave sound**—Grave (dull in some editions) may refer to the fact that whist (from *whist !* be silent), more than most games at cards, requires close attention and thought; perhaps because it is chiefly played by elderly people.

527. **thunder.**—An absurd hyperbole.

528. **gammon.**—The backgammon board. Distinguish gammon in its different meanings and derivations.

531. **puling.**—Whimpering, but here "feeble," "inane."
frequent.—Crowded. Compare Lat. *frequens senatus.*

531. **Divan** is a Persian word with various meanings :
　　(i.) A register of payments or accounts.
　　(ii) A collection of poems by an author.
　　(iii.) An executive board, as the Privy Council of the Sultan.
　　(iv.) A reception room in palaces.
　　(v.) A low sofa or cushioned seat.
　　(vi.) (Eng.) A coffee-house where smoking is the chief pastime.

534. **sober-shift,** *i.e.*, expedient to keep sober.

536-7. Swimming, as we say, before their eyes.
fuddled.—Stupefied or unsteady with drink.

538. **mutual.**—Common.
swill.—Drinking greedily. *Comus,* 178.

544. **catch.**—A short vocal composition, sung by two or more voices which come in after one other, one *catching* up the melody as another drops it. Frequently, too, the different parts have different words.

546. **full-mouthed cry.**—A hunting term applied to the opening cry of the pack ; in full cry.

547. **jocund curse.**—An unusual coupling.

548. **shook.**—Give the proper form, and the meaning.

550. Supply the clause with **as** in this line, and in 559.

553. **cumbrous.**—Show the force of the epithet.

554. **dissolved.**—Paralyzed.
maudlin.—Swollen and bleared with the tears that flow in this stage of intoxication. Derived from Mary Magdalen, whom the old painters represented with suffused, inflamed eyes.

555-6. double tapers.--The same cause for this as for the floating table and faithless pavement ; indistinct vision.

558. gazetteers.—Newspapers or journals. Derivation said to be from gazetta, a Venetian coin less than a farthing, paid for hearing read the first newspapers ever issued, in the war between the Venetians and the Turks, 1563.

561. Slaughter among so-called good fellows.

562. lubber power.—Besotting drunkenness. Lubber from the Gaelic (leobhar) means a clumsy fellow.

inclining.—Swaying. The passage suggests the picture of drunken old Silenus (in the Greek mythology) supported on an ass.

564. steeped.—Soaks, saturates. Distinguish drench and drink.

565. Doctor.—From the word *flock* and the word *black*, referring to his clerical garb, this must be a doctor of divinity. Parsons rode to hounds and took their part in the evening wassail equally with their parishioners. They may have risen somewhat from the low social position they held, as described by Macaulay (c. ii.), but their illiteracy and religious apathy were still extreme. (See Stevens' Hist. of Methodism, chap. i.).

566-7. awful and deep.--Sarcastic.
     outlives.—Outdrinks.

571. hurried wild.—Made wild. Note the opposing ideas in **horrid joy,** *i.e.*, horrid to others.

576. cap.—Fitting closely to the head for riding. It was not at all uncommon for the daughters of the nobility and gentry to follow the hounds. The number of such is now small, and we may agree with T. that they could easily find something better to do.

578. softness.—Compare Milton, speaking of Adam and Eve, *P. L.* iv., 297-8,

> "For contemplation he, and valour formed :
> For softness she, and sweet attractive grace."

Also see *A.,* ll. 268-270.

579. dissolve.—What is meant ?

580-1. wave, kindling.—Explain the figures.

583. unequal.—Predicative after **shrink** to (them).

584-5. "And engaging man more to their protection by, etc." Parse engaging.

the silent adulation. What is referred to and why is it so called ? What kind of flattery is adulation generally applied to ?

588. Through.—By means of.
     fled.—Being avoided ; a use not allowable in prose,

589. ambiguous.—Sometimes the pursuer, sometimes the pursued. Some have deplored those rules of decorum which forbid the woman to show her preferences too plainly. However scornfully some may deny the imputation conveyed in ll. 587-8, yet no doubt this unwritten but not the less imperative law of modesty and fashion has consigned many a one to the supposed unloved shades of ancient spinsterhood.

590. Read again the description of Lavinia, 201-205. This indicates T.'s opposition to the tremendous hoop-petticoat, which was a revival of the Elizabethan fardingale, but differed from that monstrosity of fashion by being elastic and gathered at the waist. These hoops were wonderful structures of canvas and whalebone, and many of them would cover a space in which six men could stand comfortably. Sir Roger de Coverley says: " My grandmother appeared as if she stood in a large drum (fardingale), whereas the ladies now walk as if they were in a go-cart."

592. May they know (how) to seize, etc.

594. lute.—To languish, *i.e.*, to utter tender, plaintive sounds. The lute is now obsolete, having been superseded by the harp and the guitar. The strings were of cat-gut, in number from five to twenty-four, and were stretched on a fingerboard with frets or stops, at intervals, on which to form with the left hand the various notes, which were struck or thrummed with the right. It lacked in resonance and carrying power, but was exceedingly sweet, and the beauty of the hand and arm was well set off by playing on it.

595. Notice the inversion and its effect; the meaning is, disclosing charms in every motion.

596-600. Morris discovers an anticlimax in these lines, preserving or the making of jams coming after the higher employments of botany, drawing, and music. But l. 597 merely refers to ornamental gardening, and perhaps T. means that to make the perfect woman (as a help-meet for man), to those accomplishments (ll. 590-8) which render her an attractive and social creature, must be added those solider and more useful qualities (ll. 599-607) which every wife and mother should possess, and which are the real foundation of domestic happiness.

600-1. race.—Offspring.

second life.—Explain the thought clearly.

602. To give to society the highest models of taste and refinement, which are to be found in the well-ordered home of the cultured and virtuous woman.

603-7. Compare Rogers' beautiful lines :

" His house she enters,—there to be a light
Shining within when all without is night ;
A guardian angel o'er his life presiding,
· Doubling his pleasures, and his cares dividing,

Winning him back when mingling in the throng,
Back from a world we love, alas ! too long,
To fireside happiness, to hours of ease,
Blest with that charm, the certainty to please.

611. The idea of a dale hardly accords with that of a brook falling from steep to steep. The word *ravine* would seem better.

609. Hazels are common enough in England and in America, especially the beaked variety in the north. ... There are large importations from the south of Europe both into Britain and America. The oil is a good dryer and consequently used by painters, and by perfumers as a base for fragrant oils. Filberts are a variety of hazelnuts.

609. this, *i.e.*, ll. 594-608. How does the length of the enumeration affect the force and the beauty of the picture ?

611. close array.—In close-fitting garb. Why ?

616. burnish.—Intrans.=shine. Cognate with *brown*.

619. resigning.—Show the force of the epithet.

621-4. Melinda.—A name taken for one of these rustic virgins at random. T. overshoots the mark here ; women, however wise and good, are not generally ignorant or neglectful of those charms (621-3) with which nature has endowed them. The vulgar praise meant is that which dwells exclusively upon the beauties of feature and form, ignoring the higher and better attributes of the mind.

626-7. error.—In its classical meaning of "wandering." Give the force of "maze" in this connection.

revived.—Attributive to (us).

629. beating ray of the sun ripens the fruit so that it is much more easily blown down.

633-6. A sweetness prepared and mixed swells (fills) the gentle race (of fruits).

635. of=from.—T. has the four elements, fire, air, earth, and water, which were by the earlier Greek philosophers assumed to make up in various proportions the constitution of material things. It corresponds somewhat to our division into imponderable, gaseous, solid and liquid. Thales, as his first principle, took water, Anaximenes air, Heraclitus fire, etc.

637-40. Such (are) lusty-handed.—With vigorous hand.
innumerous.—Now obsolete, innumerable.

641-2. spirit.—Juice.
gelid.—Cool.
points.—Gives sharpness to.

644. boon.—A favour granted, comes from A. S., *ben*, a petition ; *boon*, as in boon companion, comes from Lat. *bonus* (Fr. *bon*) gay, merry. The latter is the meaning in this passage.

645. John Philips (not Namby-Pamby Philips) was a clergyman's son, born in 1676, in Oxfordshire, a county noted for cider. He published in 1706 a poem called *Cider*, in blank verse. It was an imitation of the *Georgics*, hence P. is called here Pomona's bard, Pomona being the goddess of orchards and fruits.—*Morris.*

646. **rhyme-unfettered.**—The first example of blank verse in England was by the Earl of Surrey, executed by Henry VIII. in 1547, being a translation of Virgil's *Æneid*, books ii. and iii. The fitness of blank verse for the drama was immediately recognized, and its employment in that species of poetry was general. But in other kinds of poetry, Milton's Paradise Lost was the first great work in blank verse. Between Milton and Philips the rhyming metres were the fashion.

648. **Silurian.**—The Silures, a tribe of ancient Britons living west of the Severn and in the south of Wales. The story of Caractacus, and how his noble bearing won a pardon from Claudius, is familiar to all.

648. **wines.**—Must be used here for cider of different qualities.

vats.—Sometimes in older English written *fats, e.g., Mark* xii. 1.

650. **revels.**—Noisy jollity.

hind.—See *W.* 89 n.

653-4. **Meekened.**—Softened by the absence of the fierce rays of the sun.

lose.—It's a pleasure to be lost.

655. Doddington, commonly called Bub Doddington, was a prominent political member of the House of Commons, a man of distinguished ability, and to some extent a patron of letters. He left a diary, published after his death, which made a great noise in the political world.

Summer was intended to be dedicated to Lord Binning, but on his advice it was addressed to D. instead. Macaulay says that D. stood "so low in public estimation that the only service he could have rendered to any government would have been to oppose it." However, this refers to a time considerably later than that of T.'s writing. His seat in Dorsetshire was not in very good taste, certainly not plain.

661. **Far-splendid.**—One of T.'s characteristic compounds, due to his classical reading ; shining from afar.

662-4. Morris thinks l. 662 refers to the house being built at that time, and l. 664 to the plantings each year.

667. **Virtuous Young.**—1684-1756, author of the celebrated *Night Thoughts.* He was, at this time (1770), well known as an author by his satires. The *Night Thoughts* display in passages a fine but somewhat gloomy imagination, and the most exemplary piety, which last, however, did not seriously interfere with Y.'s advancement in life ; for he was a most persevering and unblushing toady, ever keeping a sharp eye to his interests where money was concerned.

667. Twine the bay.—Victor's laurel, or sweet bay, was sacred to Apollo, and twigs of it with berries adhering were wound about the forehead of victorious heroes and poets. Compare the phrases, "wear the laurel," "laurel crown," said metaphorically of poets and artists, etc.

669. of.—What is the usual preposition after *thirst?*

670-5. Meditate.—Trans. or supply *on*, which is the proper preposition. What is the book of nature; why ever open; what is to be learned from it?

The ideas in these lines are not original with T. Nature has formed the material of poetic inspiration in all countries. And even that poetry in which the poet is most subjective—almost wholly occupied with self, his thoughts and feelings—must be relieved here and there by touches of description and narration.

672. warm.—Modifying *song*.

677. Some editions leave out this line, and with reason, and read in 678 "The ruddy fragrant nectarine," etc.

Animals.—Compare *living dew* in l. 693.

678. nectarine.—Differs from the peach only in not being covered with down, but smooth.

679. The fig, peach and grape do not succeed well in Britain—the summer not being sufficiently warm. They require a southern exposure (673), and even then are uncertain. In America peaches and grapes are not very successful north of New York State, nor figs north of Maryland.

685. elated.—Now used only of persons and mental states; here in its Lat. meaning "exalted," *i.e.*, it grows and climbs towards the sun.

692-3. While o'er the swelling skin, perfection (over-ripeness) breathes a white living dew.

The **living** refers to the supposed minute insects, as in the case of the plum (677). Fortunately it is only a supposition.

694-8. exalted.—To perfection.

mingling ray.—Either simply mingled rays, or, perhaps, mingling the different elements that make the flavour. See 633-6.

fond.—Desirous.

prime.—That which is first in quality.

speak.—The *fact* of their being in the vineyard bespeaks, etc.

699-702. crushing swain.—Who presses out the juice.

mashy.—The *mash* is the name given by brewers to the mixture of malt and water; here the crushed mass.

floats.—Decidedly hyperbolic.

pours round.—Distributes to.

raised.—Explain the force; compare the vulgar "elevated."

703-6. claret.—The English name (unknown in France) for wines from the Garonne district, which being usually shipped at Bordeaux go by that name.

red as the lip.—Of some fair lady. Love and wine are often associated in poetry.

burgundy.—The produce of the hilly district between Dijons and Chalons. In richness of flavour and the more delicate qualities it surpasses most wines. There are two varieties, the red and the white. *Champagnes*, from the province of that name, are also white and red. Sparkling *(gay)* champagnes are produced by a special treatment. The wine is bottled before fermentation is complete, and a large amount of carbonic acid gas is dissolved in it. Not one-third of these three wines as commonly sold is genuine.

707-17. Discuss the faithfulness of the account here given (707-10).

checked.—By what? Is roll trans. or intrans. ?

division.—The use of this word for *boundary* probably led to the employment of *contending*, or *vice versa*.

baffled sense.—Explain.

up the middle sky.—Lat. *per medium cœlum.* See 826 and *W*. 536 n.

718-27. On 721-4, see *W*. 45-29 n. If **whence** is an adv. of place, it refers back to **vapor**, l. 716, or **dusk**, l. 718 ; but it may be " on which account."

beyond the life.—Beyond the natural size.

wildered.—What is the usual form ?

The apparent increase in the size of objects during fogs is well known. Why is the gloom called *dubious?*

732-5. Bard.—The passage seems to refer to the creation, Gen. i., in which case *bard* would mean Moses ; but he may refer to David. See Ps. 74, 16.

uncollected.—As though light were a material substance, and dispersed throughout the universe.

738. Alpine.—Only where there is perpetual snow would any be remaining in autumn.

741-2. Supply the ellipsis.

744. " But when loud surges lash the sounding shore,
The hoarse rough verse should like the torrent roar."

—*Essay on Criticism*, 368

745-55. Drill.—To drop in rows, as in a seed drill, is, according to Skeat, only another form of *trickle*. *Drill, thrill*, to pierce, is a different word. The ideas of *dropping* and rising (by capillary attraction, we suppose) clash awkwardly.

Jaggy.—Literally having notches or teeth, refers to the irregular crystals of the salts, which are strained out as the waters rise. The whole theory of the mountain cisterns, and the way they are filled, is rather trying to one's gravity.

Irriguous.—Well-watered
courted.—Attracted.
darkling.—See *W*. 536 n.
main.—Open sea.
boils.—See *W*. l. 306.

757-72. Distinguish *amusive* and amusing. T.'s deductions from the above theory are a little startling. The salts strained through the sands would gradually fill the valleys as high as the hills, consequently there would be no hills! And if there were no hills, to what top could Deucalion (the Noah of the Greek mythology) retire, and how could the cisterns inundate the earth?

forsook.—Give the correct form.

777-90. What faculty of man does T. here personify?

Taurus.—In the south of Asia Minor.
Imaus.—The ancient name for the Himalayas.
Haemus.—The Balkans.
Olympus.—Where? The fabled residence of the gods.
Dofrine.—The Dovre-fjelds are hills (2,500-4,000 ft.) by contrast with the preceding.
Euxine.—The Black Sea.
Riphean rocks.—The Ural Mts., the residence, according to Aeschylus, of the three Gorgons.

793. **girdle.**—What is the construction?

797. Bid Atlas, propping heaven, being, etc., spread. Atlas, one of the Titans who fought against Jove, and condemned by him to support the world, is said to have been turned into a mountain of the same name by Perseus showing to him the head of Medusa, one of the Gorgons mentioned above. The fables in regard to him are rather mixed.

800. **miny.**—Not full of mines, but underground.
blazing.—From the precious metals or stones in them.
cloud-compelling.—Explain.

802. The word *bending* is well applied to the Mts. of the Moon, if reference is had to their location by geographers. They were put as running from e. to w., and varying in latitude from 10 s. to 10 n. Beke's theory was that they ran from n. to s. parallel to the Zanzibar coast, but Speke, in 1858, thought the mountains which he discovered lying in a *crescent* shape around the n. of L. Tanganyika were Ptolemy's Mts. of the Moon; but they are not sufficiently high to be snow-clad in that latitude.

804. **dire.**—Perhaps from the many volcanic peaks and the frequency of earthquakes.

Line.—The sailor's word for the equator.

deeps.—Valleys.

807-12. **disclose.**—Intrans.

bibulous.—Adj., parse and explain the force.

815. Give the various meanings of the word *mould*. *More retentive*—Than what? What transmits the moisture, and why does it retard it?

820. **siphons.**—Here merely pipes; what is the technical meaning?

827. **bosomed,** *i.e.*, with bosoms.

828-35. **effusion.**—One of T.'s padded phrases. Flowing and effusion are too nearly alike in meaning. Profusion would be better.

What three things hold social commerce? Write in logical order ll. 828-35, and justify the various epithets.

837-40. **swallow-people.**—So *W.* 811, furry-nations.

feathered eddy.—What is meant, and why so called?

841-3. The fact that some of the species (as the sand martin) burrow deeply in cliff sides, river banks, etc., to make their nests, led many to think they remained torpid during winter, but they all migrate.

sweats.—Explain.

849. It divides into several streams.

850. **Belgian plains.**—Holland, as Belgium was not then a separate kingdom. It was united to Holland by the Congress of Vienna, 1815, but owing to religious and political differences, which arose from the Belgians not being sufficiently represented in the government, they separated from Holland, 1830. The ancient Belgæ had their home in this region.

851. **won from the raging sea.**—Explain what is meant. Compare Goldsmith's description. *Traveller*, 281-96.

852. The heroic struggles of the Netherlands against Spain and France are too well known to need mention here.

853. **Stork-assembly**—See 838. Storks are common in Holland, loving marshy and low ground. They are protected by law in some countries because they act the part of scavengers, eating reptiles, offal and garbage. Before migrating to their summer haunts, they meet together, making a great clatter with their large mandibles (consultation). Their nesting on the top of one's house was considered a good omen. They go to the n. of Africa, and there seems considerable regularity and design in their arrangements for the journey. Notice the change of number from *meets* to *they take*, and defend it if you can.

855. **liquid.**—Clear, in its Latin sense, *e.g.*, "liquidus æther."

860. **figured,** *i.e.,* in the form of certain figures.

864. With the ancients the Island of Thule was the most northern part of the world (*ultima Thule*). Some say they meant Iceland, others Norway, others, again, one of the Faroes.

866-7. **transmigrations, nations.**—Of what?

874. **reign.**—Realm, in apposition with swell.

875. **dire-clinging.**—In a manner dreadful to witness.
   ovarious.—Of eggs—a word rarely used.
   sweeps.—With nets.
   rising full.—Heaped up.

880-5. **in romantic view.**—In fancy's view, or, presenting a romantic prospect.
   airy.—From the breezes off the sea.
   diffusive sky.—Widely spread atmosphere.
   breathing the soul acute.—Inspiring a keen, vigorous intellect.
   incult.—Uncultivated or in a state of nature; an obsolete word.

890-1. **Doric reed.**—See 3 n.
   Jed.—A tributary of the Teviot, which is itself a tributary of the Tweed. See Life.

893. **Orca's.**—The ancient name for the Orkneys.
   Berubium's.—Duncansby Head, or St. Andrew's Cape.

895.—**soon** (*i.e.* early) **visited by learning.**—Probably referring to the landing of St. Columba and his twelve disciples in Iona in 563 A.D., and the founding of a monastery.
   before the Gothic rage, *i.e.* fleeing from it. See note on W., 836 *et seq.*

901. **too much in vain.**—This awkward phrase means, perhaps, "too vainly." If a comma were put after *too,* and the dash erased after 902, the next sentence would follow more logically.

903-7. **unequal bounds** may refer to the religious persecutions. Many Scotchmen took service with France during Scotland's long connexion with that kingdom, and Scotch mercenaries assisted the Netherlanders against Spain. See Schiller's *Siege of Antwerp.*

The enterprise and capacity for leadership which the Scotch have shown in a superior degree to the English or Irish is attributed by Macaulay to the establishment of parish schools in 1696. See *Mac. Hist.,* chap. xxii.

909-15. **Boreal Morn.**—See W. 1. 859 n.
   double harvests.—Bountiful or increased.

918. **hyperborean.**—Extreme north. The Hyperboreans were a people who lived beyond the wind *Boreas,* which term was applied by the Greeks to that which blew from the N.N.E. Both words are synonyms for north.

919.—lucid lawn.—See l. 86 n. White and very thin.

921-3.- Batavian.—See W . 768 n. The coast fisherics (Br.) were largely in the hands of the Dutch at this time.

Heave.—Fill or swell.

frith, or firth.—(See fjord) is properly the mouth of a river opening into the sea. A Scottish word.

928. The disputes with Spain were principally in relation to the commerce with the New World. British merchantmen were harassed by Spanish privateers and pirates, and a generally hostile policy, which was returned in kind. Much to the delight of the patriot party (to which T. belonged), and to the chagrin of Walpole, war was declared in 1739.

929. Argyle.—Second Duke and eleventh Earl, born 1678, distinguished himself under Marlborough at Ramilies, Oudenarde, Lille, Ghent and Malplaquet, to which last the text refers, Taisnière being the name of a forest near that little village, where Marshal Villars was so signally defeated by Marlborough and Eugene. On Marlborough's disgrace, Argyle became as keen a Tory as he had been a Whig. Not being sufficiently rewarded for his *ratting*, he became a Whig again, and in the troubles of 1715 his services were such as to secure him an English peerage. He seems to have been a firm believer in the principle of expediency rather than the expediency of principle, but lax and selfish as he was in public life, in private life he was kind and courteous. His politic course during the Porteous Riots made him immensely popular, and this, added to his benevolence among the common people, procured for him the title of "The Good Duke."

937. very throat of war.—So the common quotations from Sh. :

    " Seeking the bubble reputation
      Even in the cannon's mouth,"

and Tennyson,

    "Into the jaws of death,
      Into the mouth of hell
        Rode the six hundred."

939. It was a Roman custom to give to a victorious gladiator a branch of a palm-tree.

944. Duncan Forbes, 1685-1747, of Culloden. He was a connection of the first Duke of Argyle, by whose influence he became sheriff of Midlothian. In '15 he was active on the side of the Government. His moderation and leniency to the Jacobites roused some suspicion of his loyalty, but he was too important a man to be ignored, and he was made Lord Advocate in 1725 and Lord President in 1737. He was an intimate friend of Thomson in his early days, a convivial soul and cultivated acquaintance with the chief literary men of his day.

746. in silence great may refer to the fact that he was no speaker.

948. The word **informed**, endowed with life, is very aptly used here.

950. Compare Bryant's description in *Autumn Woods*.

952. **imbrown.**—Verb, having shade for its subj.; also written *embrown*. Notice the inharmonious succession of the same sound in *round* and *imbrown*.

      umbrage.—Properly means the shade cast by the leafage, but is put here for the leafage itself. In what sense is the word commonly used now?

954. **sooty dark.**—This phrase is so uncommon as to surprise us.
      These, *i.e.*, the leaves, subj. of *lead*.

955-6. **low-whispering.**—Notice the transferred epithet. In what lies its appropriateness here?
      view.—Phase.

957-63. **fleeces.**—Covers with fleecy clouds.
      ether.—In Lat. and Gr. the pure upper air.
      dewy-skirted.—Compare Shelley with the above passage:

> "I bear light shade for the leaves when laid
>> In their noon-day dreams, . . .
> From my *wings* are shaken the dews that 'waken
>> The sweet birds everyone."

      softened force.—Compare 1095.
      lucid.—Full of light.

965-7. **Degenerate.**—Gr. *Elegy* 73; scene of *little* things.
      low-thoughted, *i.e.*, which has low thoughts.

970. **pensive.**—Meditative. "The mind must not be impelled to solitude by melancholy and discontent, but by a real distaste to the idle pleasures of the world, a rational contempt for the deceitful joys of life, and a just apprehension of being corrupted by its insinuating and destructive gaieties."—*Zimmerman on Solitude*.

971-5. **Russet.**—353 n.
      dying strain.—On the point of ceasing, or feeble.
      widowed.—Without a mate.

976. **thrushes, linnets, larks.**—Perhaps the song thrush, throstle or mavis is meant, which sings finely from early spring to autumn. It frequents copses, is a snail and worm eater, and its flesh is very good. There are many varieties in America, but they are found principally in the Southern and Middle States.

The linnets belong to the finch family, and have many representatives in Northern Europe and America. Their song is mellow and varied and they make good cage birds.

The sky-lark or meadow-lark, so celebrated in British poetry and song is not found in America, the sky-lark or shore-lark with us being of a different genus. Its song is even sweeter than that of the Old Country lark, but not nearly so varied or continuous.

978-80. Note the alliteration.

981-2. As their sweetest notes are for the spring and the mating season, so is their most brilliant plumage.

983-6. Let not the gun aimed destroy the music, and lay the harmless unsuspecting tribes a prey, fluttering, etc.

   aimed from.—What is the usual preposition?

986. **tribes.**—Not a good word as applied to the birds.
   mingled.—Indiscriminate.

988. **pale descending.**—Pale refers to the blanching, and **descending** to the fall of the leaves.

992. **sob** seems a very strong word here. What is the usual one?

997. In connection with this and the preceding lines read first two stanzas of Bryant's *Death of the Flowers*.

1003. **prospect.**—In apposition with woods, etc.

1004. There are different kinds of melancholy, caused by grief, indigestion, etc., but this is simply the result of the surroundings. Notice the gradation of feelings, and how one merges into another. Discuss the appropriateness of the sequence which the poet has here given to them, *e.g.*, devotion, rapture, astonishment, ambition (for good), sympathy, scorn, resolution.

1010. **his sacred influence.**—T. makes melancholy masc.; Milton, fem. Which do you think is better? Justify Thomson's use. See *Il Penseroso*, 11, 12:

   "But hail thou *goddess*, sage and holy,
    Hail divinest Melancholy!"

1014-5. **ten thousand thousand.**—A very effective way of saying innumerable.

   vulgar.—Common or humdrum.
There is a slight incongruity in saying that *ideas* crowd into the *eye*.

1017. **As fast,** etc., *i.e.*, equally fast, etc.

1020-2. **unconfined,** *i.e.*, in its whole extent, of which that (love) of the human race is *chief.*

1030-1. Compare Cowper (Timepiece):

   "Oh for a lodge in some vast wilderness
    Some boundless contiguity of shade."

   visionary prophetic. Which forecast the future.
Give the full force of the words weeping, enthusiastic; paraphrase 1030-6.

1042. **Stowe.** -Near Buckingham, then the property of Viscount Cobham. Cotton says of it:

> "It puzzles much the sage's brains
> Where Eden stood of yore,
> Some place it in Arabia's plains,
> Some say it is no more ;
> But Cobham can these tales confute,
> As all the curious know,
> For he has proved beyond dispute
> That Paradise is Stowe,"

and Pope, *Moral Essay*, iv., 70, says (quoted by Morris):

> "Nature shall join you ; Time shall make it grow
> A work to wonder at--perhaps a Stowe."

1043. **Ionia.**—A beautiful and fertile district on the west coast of Asia Minor. It was settled by Greeks, but fell under the dominion of Persia about 500 years later. (Cyrus the Great.)

1046. **Pitt.**—This was Pitt the elder, commonly known as Lord Chatham, to distinguish him from his son, William Pitt. This passage appeared first in the 1744 edition of the *Seasons*. Two years later Pitt was in the Ministry.

1050. There was a temple of British worthies in Stowe Park which contained busts of eminent British statesmen, heroes, and authors.—*Morris*.

1056-7. **Attic land.**—See W., l. 446, *et seq.*
       standard.—The best of its kind.

1058. What objection to the phrase "purest truth?"

1062. T. had already published *Sophonisba*. See **Life.**

1069. It will be a good exercise here to contrast the private and public characters of Pitt and Walpole.

1070. **Elysium.**—That part of Hades, according to the later classical mythology, to which the souls of the departed good were consigned. *Æneid*, vi., 342 and 637-43. The word now conveys the idea of extreme happiness.

1072. **Cobham.**—Sir Richard Temple, the proprietor of Stowe, served in the wars under Marlborough, became a lieutenant-general, and was, in 1714, created a peer under the title of Lord Cobham. His opposition to the prime minister, Walpole, caused him to be deprived of his military rank, to which circumstance the poet here alludes. Lord C. was, however, afterwards restored to his offices. He died in 1749.
       squadrons, host.—What different meanings have these words ? Give the derivation.

1077. France (anciently Gallia or Gaul) had gained, during the reign of Louis XIV., the most prominent position in arms, in letters, and in that polished courtliness which was thought essential to successful diplomacy. The wars with France for the balance of power were still fresh in the minds of all, and just now hostilities were again impending. By the lower classes in England the French were despised as slaves, as frog-eaters, and as wearers of wooden shoes. There are still some lingering remnants of this contempt.

1083. **humid evening.**—Virgil's *humida nox., Æn.*, ii., 8. The old mythology represented the sun and night as traversing the firmament in chariots.

1087. The fogs **cluster and glide** *(swim)*. Notice in connection with fogs and rain the difference between England and Canada.

1092. **where.**—In the disc.

umbrageous.—Not from being wooded, but from being deep.

1093. **optic tube.**—What is meant?

1094-5. Reflects the light void of heat.

earth.—In apposition with *disc.*

1096. **stoop.**—Milton, *Il Pens.*, 72. :

> "And oft, as if her head she bowed,
> Stooping through a fleecy cloud."

1097. **cerulean.**—Usually an adjective.

sublime.—In its original sense of aloft, on high.

1098. **deluge.**—An uncommon use of the word, though we often speak of a flood of light.

1099. **skied.**—Surrounded by or enveloped in the sky. Sky originally meant a cloud. Compare Gr. *skia*, a shadow.

1102. What is the real meaning of **half-blotted**?

1107. This line seems hardly necessary after 1106.

appears.—Is visible.

1109. **a blaze of meteors.**—The term "meteors" is especially applied to fire-balls, and the masses of stone or other substances which sometimes fall from them to the earth, and to shooting stars. Showers of the latter occur periodically in the months of August and November. Meteors, however, in the wider sense of the term, include any phenomena in the atmosphere, and are sometimes classed as aerial, aqueous, luminous, and igneous, the last named including auroras and lightning. The description in ll. 1109-1114 and 1117-21 makes it evident that the poet is speaking of an auroral display.

1112. **thwart, extinguish.**—Both intrans.

1115. **From face to face.**—Why is the poet's phrase more expressive?

1117. **meet.**—Full.

1119-20. **lines.**—Nom. abs.

sanguine flood.—Explain.

1124. incontinent.—Irrepressible; according to Morris "imme-diately."

1122-30. "Under the influence of fear men conjure up resemblances be-tween the meteors and various terrible or ominous objects. Such appear-ances in the heavens have, in all ages, greatly disturbed men. Compare 2 *Maccabees*, v., 1, and also Tacitus *Hist.*, ii., xiii., of the portents before the siege of Jerusalem."—*Morris.*

1125. Compare 1201-7.

1128. sallow.—Explain the force of the epithet.

1130. subversed.—Subverted is the usual form.

1134. inspect.—Power of inspection, rarely, if ever, now used as a noun.

1141. Insert *is* or *being* after "beauty," "distinction," "variety."

1147. Chimeras.—The chimera was a monster, described by Homer as having the head of a lion, the body of a goat and the tail of a serpent, and vomiting fire. Hence the word came to mean, as here, a wild baseless fancy, also a visionary hare-brained project.

1148. directive.—Distinguish in force from *directing.*

1152. wild fire.—*Ignis fatuus.* Will o' the wisp, etc., has never been produced artificially, occurs in low marshy places and churchyards, is sup-posed to be due to the gas generated from decaying animal and vegetable matter, perhaps phosphuretted ($P.H._3$), or carburetted hydrogen ($Cr. H._2$); is generally seen about two feet above the ground. It is said that a match has been lighted at its flame!

1155. absorpt.—See W., 827.

1157-8. Compare W., 311-13-14. Why is the latter picture so much more effective?

T. is no doubt true to nature in ll. 1147-59, but he oversteps it in the remaining lines 1160-4.

1162. meteor.—See n. on 1109.

1170. spray.—Another form of *sprig.* Compare "Gentle music melts on every spray."—*Traveller*, 322.

1172. murdered.—Here and in 987 applied to lower animals.

1173. still-heaving.—With life. See 1198-1200.

1175. fixed o'er sulphur.—This unfortunate phrase spoils what is otherwise a fair poetical account of the old method of extracting the honey by means of the fumes of sulphur. In the modern beehives this is un-necessary.

1178. temperance.—Regulated distribution.

1183-4. **convolved.**—Rolled or twisted together. Compare
"Then Satan first knew pain,
And writhed him to and fro convolved."
—*Milton.*

agonizing.—Writhing with pain—the original sense.

spring.—The fields in spring; or adv. of time.

toil away.—Trans.

1191-2. **obliged.**—Laid under an obligation.

ambrosia was the food of the gods, as nectar was their drink.

1295-6. Explain the force of **pinches, with their own.** The force of **smiling** is not clear. Morris suggests "propitious or festive." It may refer to the rule given that "bees should be fed only when the weather is fine and warm, to prevent the temperature of the hive from being injured.

1197. **stony.**—From the appearance of the hardened wax on the floor of the hive.

1204. **Palermo.**—The capital of Sicily, the scene of many contests in the Punic wars. In modern times perhaps its most notable event is the Sicilian Vespers, 1283. Though earthquakes have been common enough there, yet none is recorded to have occurred about T.'s time.

1206. **sheer.**—Completely, so as to leave no part; of different origin from *sheer*, the nautical term.

the day.—The sun. What figure?

1211-12. Save what brushes the filmy threads of evaporated dew from the plain. These lines probably refer to gossamer, a light filament, often found in late autumn spread over the ground, or stretching from leaf to leaf, the meshes laden with entangled dewdrops, which glisten and sparkle in the sunshine. It is also found floating in the air, but this, perhaps, is not produced by the same variety of spiders. A viscid fluid is shot from their spinnerets with great force, and this soon hardens into threads. These are caught by the slightest breeze, and carry the spider with them; the spider likely exercising some volition in the aerial flight.

The derivation commonly given is God-summer (in German Marienfäden), from the legend that gossamer is formed from the Virgin Mary's winding sheet, which fell away in fragments when she was taken up to heaven. See, however, Skeat, who derives it from goose-summer.

1214-15. **peculiar.**—Different from that of spring or summer.

swelled.—Explain why it appears thus.

1220-3. **instant.**—Threatening, the classical sense of the word.

Parse **shook,** and point out anything peculiar in the syntax of 1221-3.

toil-strung.—Made strong by toil.

1226-9. **abroad.**—Not closed in, or unfolded.

the village-toast.—Bring out the meaning by a paraphrase.

points.—directs.

1230. **cudgel.**—Referring to the old and rough game of *singlestick*, in which he who first drew blood from his adversary's head was the victor.

1232. **The harvest home.**—Common after harvest in most European countries.

"The Roman *Saturnalia*, which were held in December, at the end of the agricultural labours of the year, were probably of this nature."—*Morris.*

1236. T. again eulogizes the life rural and retired in an almost literal translation of Virgil, *Georgic II.*, 458, *et seq.*

1239-41. The word **vomits**, if taken in the ordinary sense, gives an idea of nastiness, in strict accordance with the character of place hunters and sycophants. The words **sneaking** and **abused in turn** refer to their generally disappointed and injured appearance.

1244. **mazy.**—With the intricately embroidered patterns. Some editions have *massy.*

oppress.—Explain the force.

1246. **purveyed.**—Conveyed or brought. The proper meaning of purvey is "to buy in provisions," "to provide."

1247. **tributary life.**—The lower animals which, for clothing or food, contribute to the sybarite's pleasures. Supply *not* after *heaps.*

1249. Note the fine contrast in "heaps with luxury and death."

sure.—Probably in the original sense of secure (of which it is a doublet (free from care).

1251. **gay care.**—T. is fond of phrases like this (known as the figure *oxymoron*), the words of which have opposing meanings; compare *still breeze*, 1211 ; care which is the result of dissipation.

tosses out the night.—Explain the meaning of this, and of the following line by a paraphrase.

1257. **estranged to.**—A very awkward phrase meaning free from. Estranged takes *from* not *to* after it.

1267. The word **chide** has been applied in a *good* sense to the constant and pleasant sound of water in summer time. Contrast Shakespeare's use of it in, "As doth a rock against the chiding flood." Compare *brawling.* Notice the transferred epithets in 1266-7.

1268. **sincere.**—Pure, dreamless.

1270. **at large.**—Compare 517, "on violets *diffused.*"

1274. **sound unbroken.**—*Unbroken* is used in the sense of "continued."

1277. **poetic ease.**—This seems a harsh antithesis to "unambitious toil." In what way can these two epithets be justified as said of qualities resident in the same person ?

1282. **unpierced.**—Unmoved.

1284-5. Emigration has been caused (from the British Islands at least) as much by poverty and oppressive laws as by love of gain, and this among a people confessedly the most enterprising in Europe.

1287-94. Notice the use of the demonstratives, let this, let that, let these, let those. Compare W., ll. 375-85.

1289. **the social sense extinct,** *i.e.,* the feeling that he owes certain duties to society being extinguished in his breast.

1290. Into mad tumult.

1291. **melt.**—Is this an appropriate metaphor ?

1292. **toils.**—Snares. A word of different origin from *toils,* labours.

1294. **those,** *i.e.,* And let those delight in, etc.

1296. **cabals.**—Taken immediately from the Fr. *cabale,* a club, remotely from Hebr. *gabbalah,* a mysterious doctrine. The word is found earlier, but first came into common use in 1671, when by a mere coincidence it was found that it could be formed from the initials of the names of Chas. the Second's cabinet. "These ministers soon made that appellation so infamous that it has never since their time been used, except as a term of reproach."—*Macaulay.*

1297. **To wreathe a bow** is T.'s hyperbolic way of expressing the crafty and calculating politeness of the politicians of his day. One edition has " brow" instead of " bow."

1300. Notice the *nice* use of "but." Morris prints the passage thus, " hears (and but hears at distance safe) the human tempest roar."

1301. Compare Gray's " Far from the madding crowd's ignoble strife."

1311. **gems.**—(Latin gemma) and *buds* are precisely the same; the word *gem* or *gemma* is used only in botanical language.

1314-15. For him the flowers unfold their beauties, for him the opening blossoms breathe out their fragrance.

1317-18. The vale of Tempe, in Thessaly, about five miles long, lies between Mt. Olympus on the n. and Mt. Ossa on the s., the Peneus flowing through it. It has been much celebrated by the poets for its beauty, and in the matter of valleys is a principal article of their stock in trade, and the word Tempe has almost become a common noun.

Hæmus (l. 785) was covered with forests.

1320-1. **an eye shot round.**—An awkward absolute phrase, " glancing quickly round."

1325. **tepid.**—Lukewarm ; scarcely ever said of anything but liquids.

1331. **frost.**—During which the skies are free from clouds, and the stars look brightly down upon the eye that is raised to contemplate the beauty of the heavens.

1333-4. secure, mark.—Should properly be singular, as the subject is a friend (or) a book. Would *secures* sound equally well?

1337-9. elates.—Exalts.

touch.—Claims.

1341-2. See the *Elegy*, 13. *Georgic II.*, 523.

1347. Are still (nevertheless) of the social, etc.

1348. fret. Are the prey of remorse.

1350. uncorrupt or incorrupt : also un- or in-corrupted.

1356. blue.—Morris reads *void*. What difference will it make in the parsing of *immense* ?

1358-64. disclosing.—Which is disclosed. The construction is loose. "Strata" and "world" seem to depend on "through."

thrust thence, *i.e.*, the vegetable world pushed up from the strata. After "o'er that" supply "is placed"; *where*=the place in which.

1365. ravished.—Delighted even to rapture.

open.—Intrans.

search.—It is a search which, etc.

1367. But if I am unequal to that task.

1371-3. Compare Dryden's translation of the same lines of Virgil (*Ecl.*, viii., 11) :

" Amidst thy laurels let this ivy twine ;
Thine was my earliest Muse ; my latest shall be thine."

WINTER.

1. **Varied,** *i.e.,* by the seasons.

2. **sad.**—A Vergilian epithet=*tristis hiems.*
   rising.—Coming up from the horizon.
   kindred.—Congenial. These two words, nearly synonymous, illustrate the two main sources of our vocabulary.

6. Par. Lost, I. 250.
   frequent.—Similarly Chaucer's "hote foote."

7-16. Refers to his life at the Southdean Manse.

8. **careless.**—Free from care.

10. **Pleased have I.**—Why the repetition?

12. **big.**—Pregnant, teeming.

13. Note Thomson's fondness for such compounds as *deep-fermenting, virgin-snows.*

15. **lucid.**—Bright. See Job ix., 9. Note the beauty of the image.

17. **first,** *i.e.,* of the *Seasons,* published (1726), and then scarcely half its present length, and without this fulsome dedication.

18. **Wilmington.**—Sir Spencer Compton, Speaker of the H. of C. (1714-17), was made a peer (1727), and finally became Premier; was of very moderate ability and quite undeserving of such praise as this of Thomson's.
   renews.—*Winter* being republished with the other *Seasons,* 1730.

19. **since.**—Adv. here.

20-26. What figures? Discuss their appropriateness.

22. **shadowy.**—That makes shadows.

24. **doubling.**—Increasing, or turning back on itself.

27. **numbers.**—Notes; what case?

32. **sound integrity.**—A good example of one of Thomson's faults.

34. **sliding.**—Corrupt. The evil effects of the Restoration on literature, politics and the church still continued. In this connection note the names and influence of Pitt, Cowper, Wesley.
   burning.—John v. 35, attributive to *spirit.*

36. **free,** but obedient to law, *i.e.,* British freedom.

37. **these** (qualities) **light.**—Lead the way for.

39. **converting** (turning), attributive to *these.*

41. **Capricorn.**—The sun passes from Sagittarius, the 9th sign of the Zodiac, here called the Centaur-Archer, to Capricorn, the 10th sign about 21st Dec., and of course a month after enters Aquarius. The Centaurs of

[111]

the old Greek mythology were monsters, half man and half horse, armed with bow and arrow. When the Spanish cavalry invaded Mexico the Mexicans thought the man and the horse were one creature.

43. inverted.—The three preceding seasons give the idea of advancement or progress; here, however, there is retrogression. Thomson copies the idea from Horace, and Cowper (Task iv., 120) from Thomson.

stains.—Discolors with excessive rain.

45. ether, or **æther,** means here the air or the firmament, and not that medium which, for the production of the phenomena of heat, light, etc., theory supposes to fill all space.

49. broad.—Caused by refraction.—The preceding picture seems very accurate.

54. cincture.—Robe, dress.

59. gloom.—In apposition with *winter*.

61-2. loathing life.—Statistics show that suicides are not more common at this season than at any other; but melancholia is more prevalent in the north of Europe than in the South, due partly to climate and partly to race.

65. This line seems to disagree with ll. 63 and 84.

moorish.—Marshy.

67-71. What three personifications here; which is the weakest?

presageful.—Foreboding.

73-4. obscure.—Dark.

skies.—Used here in its original meaning of *clouds*.

77-9. brown.—From the soil washed down.

combine.—Close in as night comes on.

83. This line seems out of harmony with the rest of the description.

85. low.—Subst. The sound made by cattle.

86. ruminate.—Chew the cud, as the cow, sheep, camel. This class of animals has the power of returning the food from the stomach to the mouth for more thorough mastication. The stomach is divided into four distinct cavities, into each of which the food may be sent directly from the œsophagus.

89-90. L. Allegro, 49.

hind.—A peasant or servant, but used in some parts as a name for a farm foreman.

92. recks.—Trans., but often followed by *of, e.g.*, "recks not of a wound."

94-105. This description of the effects of the storm has been much admired for its faithfulness and correspondence of sound to sense.

109-10. **pleasing dread.**—What figure? 114 makes us think of Æolus and his bag.

120. **streaks.**—Sun's rays struggling through the clouds.

122. **poise.**—Balancing.

124-5. **blank.**—Pale, white.

    circle, or halo about the sun or moon portends a storm.

126-141. Almost transl. from the 1st Georgic 365-390.

    obtuse.—Dulled.

128. Falling stars are more common in Autumn, especially in November.

130-1. See note to 83.

    eddies.—In nautical language "cat's paws."

135. In the Latin, "carding their tasks" (pensa), hence, remotely, pensive.

139. **downs.**—Any sandy uplands covered with grass, originally sand-hills by the sea.

141. **thick-urge.**—Not a good compound, as *thick* refers to the numbers.

143. **waiting.**—Compare Gray's "moping," Elegy, 10. Shakespeare is more faithful when he speaks of it as "clamoring," Macb. II. 3.63.

146. The hern (more commonly heron) and cormorant (lit. sea crow, L. corvus marinus) generally keep close to land.

148. **unequal.**—Adv.

150. **eat.**—For eaten.

151. **forest-rustling.**—Is this compound properly formed for the meaning intended?

157. Hyperbole; in the greatest storms the sea is tranquil at 200 or 300 feet deep, and the highest waves, from trough to crest probably never exceed 40 feet.

167-8. A vivid picture; see Ps. 104, 3.

169. **Baltic.**—Storms are frequent and navigation dangerous from its shallowness (15 to 20 fathoms), narrowness and irregular coastline.

176. Mountains attract the clouds, consequently thunder is more frequent.

    sons.—Trees.

178-80. These lines relieve the monotony of the natural descriptions.

182. **tarnished-honours.**—Withered foliage. A Latinism.

184. **limbs.**—Nom. absol. Compare

        As falls on Mount Alvernus
        A thunder-smitten oak.
        Far o'er the crashing forest
        Its giant limbs lie spread.—Macaulay, *Horatius.*

185. Is **dissipated** a good word here, and why?

188. **them.**—What is the antecedent?

191. **burthened.**—Better than *burdened* for a grave subject.

193. **demon.**—See l. 67.   Among the ancients the extraordinary conditions or actions of men not capable of being referred to the natural or apparent laws of the mind or body were attributed to the influence of one or more attendant spirits (genii or daemons).   Plato gives one to each mortal, accompanying him through life and finally bearing his soul to Hades ; others give two.   The Jews during the Captivity copied some of the Persian demonology.   At the advent of Christ, the popular meaning of demon with them was evil spirit, and the early Christian writers intensified it.

194. **devoted.**—Doomed.

199-201. Ps. 104, 3.   **at once.**—Is the redundancy a weakness ?

206. **compeer.**—Companion.

207-8. **intrusive, meddling.**—In the Lockian philosophy all ideas are due to Sensation or Reflection.   The first is the perception of the external objects through the five senses which act independently of the will. The mind is more free to reflect during the night, not being so subject to the annoyance of the external world through these avenues of approach.

217-222. A beautiful prayer, few more so in the language.   Compare P. L. I., 17-26.

223-4. **dun.**—Adv.

livid, piercing.—Are these epithets well used ? Why ?

227. **heavy** and **fleecy** are somewhat incongruous terms.

229-231. Cowper, Task IV. 326.   Cowper is generally more minute in descriptions.

232. **cherished.**—Tended.

236. **hoar.**—As an aged man.

240. **labourer-ox.**—Is this better than labouring-ox, or (as Milton) laboured-ox ?

241. **demands.**—Wilson says, "this notion is a fantastic one.   Call it doubtful, for Jemmy was never wholly in the wrong."

244. **winnowing.**—Being winnowed.   This use of the pres. part., although still good English, is dying out.

246. The name robin is applied in America to a kind of thrush (turdus migratorius), a larger bird than the European robin, but resembling it in its colour, general appearance, and familiar habits.   In Germany the robin is called Thomas, in Norway, Peter.   The line simply means "sacred to the family," as the term "household gods" is a classical allusion to certain minor tutelary duties of the Romans, whose statues were placed about the house and worshipped regularly every day, at meal time, on rising, retiring, etc.

253. **askance.**—Sideways, obliquely from the corner of the eye ; akin to *aslant.*

257. **brown.**—Wilson says, "a touch like one of Cowper's. That one word proves the poet."

258. **timorous.**—The hare matched with its own kind or even another of equal size shows considerable courage.

263. **dumb despair.**—The poet seems a little illogical ; the next line says they dig. Besides, do the lower animals ever give way to despair ?

267. **at will.**—Does this limit *fill* or *food ?*

271. **o'er..whelms.**—Is this a case of *tmesis ?*

277. **drives.**—Intr.

278. **loose revolving.**—Explain what is meant.

279. **disaster'd.**—Seldom used as a verb ; here either attributive in its old astrological sense "illstarred," or better, predicative in the sense of "overwhelmed with calamity."

279-80. **other hills of unknown brow.**—Explain.

280. **shag.**—Roughen, deform.
   trackless.—Prolepsis.

285. **flouncing.**—This word, which generally has far different associations, seems very expressive here. What is the usual word ?

286. What figure ? Is **stung** an appropriate word ?

292. **middle waste.**—A Latinism for "midst of the waste."

300. **faithless.**—Explain 301-2. "What is land, what is water, being unknown ?"

305. **fearful.**—Distinguish the two meanings of this word.

307. 1 Sam. 15, 32.

310. Nom. Abs.

311. **officious.**—Duteous. What is the ordinary meaning ?

316-17. What is the effect of the repetition of the conj. ? Give other examples.

320. Distinguish **corse**, corpse, carcass.

329. Is **in** correct ?

333. Notice the two meanings of **common.**

335. **baleful.**—In a passive sense, "caused by calamity."

337. **sordid.**—Has its root meaning "filthy." What is the ordinary meaning ?

340. **whence.** By which.
   tumbled.—A factitive verb, passive.

343-5. Thomson's **vale**, where most happiness is found, is evidently the middle condition of life; *see* 333-8. What passions are honest? How does the idea of *racking* agree with *peace* and *contemplation?*

348. **point.**—Give point to. So Johnson of Ch. XII. *Van. of Hum. Wishes.*

> "He left the name at which the world grew pale,
> To point a moral, or adorn a tale."

fond.—Foolish, its root meaning.

thought.—Supply "if."

349. So Hamlet. "The heart-ache and the thousand natural shocks
That flesh is heir to."

350-1. "That render life one struggle, one scene."

351. **one scene of fate.**—Fate or destiny was the only monotheistic conception of the Greeks and Romans. In some writers it takes the form of fatalism, in others of the superintendence of a guiding will, in others of chance (Epicureans). In Mohammedanism it presents itself as an inexorable and arbitrary law, allowing little scope for the development of human nature. In Christianity it appears under the forms of Predestination and of the Law of Necessity. The first gives a dominating influence to the Divine Will and approaches Fatalism, its opponents say, by leaving no power of free action to the individual. The latter regards everything in nature as subject to law, and approaches Fatalism by supposing this law immutable and self-existent. Thomson's training as a Calvinist perhaps led him to take a pessimistic view of fate, as in this line.

353. **Impulse.**—Towards *good* or *evil*, or both.

355. **wide.**—Prolepsis.

356-8. **social.**—Of sympathy with one's fellow-creatures. If *work* be taken as transitive, then *bliss* is its subject; if not, *bliss* is object of *into.*

359. **generous band.**—The jail committee of 1729, appointed to enquire into the condition of prisons, especially of the Fleet. The revelations made were something awful and furnished material for some of Hogarth's best pictures. Dirt, vice of the most revolting kind, starvation and torture were common. Such was their state from a sanitary point of view that the foulest diseases were bred in them. Twenty years later the lord mayor, two aldermen, two judges, most of the jury and many spectators caught the jail fever at an assize of the Old Bailey and most of them died. The jails, too, were crowded on account of imprisonment for debt, which now may hardly be said to exist. The terrible abuses of the prison discipline of those times, truly needed the exertions of men like Oglethorpe (the founder of Georgia) and Howard, the philanthropist.

360. **redressive.**—Relief-giving.

364. **lash of vice.**—*i.e.*, which vice should feel.

367. **tyrants.**—The jailers.

369. **weed.**—Weeds usually.   Not used now for clothing in general but as mourning clothes for a widow.

372. **lust.**—Desire.

The whole picture (360-75) is certainly not overdrawn.

383. What image ?

384. **toils.**—Snares.

385. **cumbrous.**—These lines are a fit enough conclusion to the preceding pictures, and no doubt correctly represent the popular idea.   The codification and simplification of law have no doubt made justice cheaper, but the percentage of litigation has not diminished.   Some aver the contrary, and that the intervention of lawyers is as necessary as ever.

390. **horrid.**—In its root meaning of " rough," " bristling."

   shining.—With snow.

   Alps.—From *albus* white.

391. **wavy.**—Refers either to their varying heights or to their curving course through Italy.

392. **branch.**—Transitive.

394. **burning.**—Thirsting.

   gaunt.—How pronounced ?

396. **bear** (intr.) **along keenly.**

406. The nobility and generosity have no foundation in reality.   In fact Cumming's account of him gives him no superiority, except in strength, over the other Felidae.

407. **hapless.**—Unfortunate.

   undistinguished.—Not favoured at all on account of the beauty.

408. The following is the substance of Wilson's criticism on this passage, 389-413 : " The first fifteen lines are equal to anything in the whole range of descriptive poetry, but the last ten are positively bad.   Wild beasts do not like the look of the human eye—they think us ugly customers. But that the godlike face of man should terrify an army of wolves is ludicrous, and still more so the trash about beauty force divine !   'Tis all stuff, too, about the generous lion.   True he has been known to walk past a pretty Caffre girl without eating her, but the secret lay in his stomach ; he had dined an hour or two before on a Hottentot Venus.   Again famished wolves howking up a dead body is a dreadful image ; but the expression *inhuman to relate* is not heavily laden with meaning.   In the last line why are the shades foul and only the ghosts frightened ?   Wherein lies the specific difference between a shade and a ghost ?   If the ghosts were frightened why were they not off ?"

415. Grisons.—The largest but most thinly peopled of the Swiss Cantons, being an assemblage of mountains intersected by narrow valleys. Its area is 2,770 square miles, and population about 100,000. The Rhine and Inn rise here and it also feeds the Ticino and Addua to some extent. Both the French and German names, Grisons and Granbunden, have their origin in the Grey League formed against the nobility in 1424. In 1472 they allied with the Swiss Cantons, and in 1803 were formally admitted into the Swiss Confederation. On account of its mountainous character and the different exposures resulting, the climate and products are exceedingly varied, including not only northern products like barley, rye and wheat, but also Indian corn, the vine, fig, and almond. Cattle, lumber and cheese are exported. Mining is done in the mountains, and the rivers are stocked with salmon and trout. The district is rather subject to avalanches.

417. Avalanches are of various kinds, as the drift, sliding and rolling, and are generally of snow, hence often called snow-slips. But glaciers in their advance down the sides of the steep Alps sometimes break away. Avalanches occur most frequently in the months of July, August and September.

420-1. Discuss the effectiveness of the enumeration.

424. The digression seems abrupt.

all amid.—In the very midst of.

426. blow ice. –What is meant?

430. tapers.—Candles. Would "candles" do equally well here?

435. humanized.—Civilized.

437. long-lived.—Ancient.

438. shades.--Shadows (imaginary) of the dead.

439. Socrates, 469-399 B.C., son of an Athenian sculptor, and followed his father's trade till about middle age, when he took up the role of philosopher. He had served in the Peloponnesian war as a hoplite, was of excelling physical strength, fortified by an abstemious diet and a regular life. He belonged to the walking school and had among his intimate friends and disciples Plato and Xenophon, to whom we are chiefly indebted for information about him. As to the subject of his teaching, he was the first to proclaim that the proper study of man is man, his nature, duties and happiness. Other speculations might be useful practically to certain special classes, but morality, justice and happiness were necessary for all. As to method, he insisted on an accuracy in definition and classification seldom thought of before. To ascertain the exact *connotation* of each term, he would pretend ignorance (the Socratic irony) and ask for a definition from his opponent. Then by a series of questions (a manner peculiarly his own), he would involve his opponent in self-contradiction. Socrates' boast was that he at least knew his ignorance, and a great part of the dialogues in

Plato and Xenophon close with this merely negative result. The object of Socrates was by means of induction from particular conceptions to form a general notion and hence formulate a logical definition. The only positive tenet of Socrates that has come down to us is that virtue consists in knowledge and intellectual discernment, and proceeds from a clear cognition of the notion of what any particular action contemplates, of its ends, means, and conditions. Vice can result only from ignorance; no person is willingly wicked or knowingly does wrong. The proper corrective of vice is the teaching of the consequences of actions, hence virtue as knowledge is teachable and is promoted by exercise. But the practice of Socrates was wider than his theories; his advice and exhortations were addressed to men's feelings as well as to their intellects. In his own person, too, he shewed an exaltation over sensuous cravings, a calmness of mind amid enmity and misfortune, and a consciousness of his own strength and integrity which served to exemplify his notions of united virtue and felicity. In after times his life and character became the archetype and inspiration of other philosophers, who, though they could not rival him in personal excellence, yet left more enduring results in the way of regularly formulated and developed philosophical systems.

440-4. Who—obeying–law.

443. This line and a few others just here are due to Pope's emendation. are *Essay on Man*, Ep. II. 204.

445. **wisest.**–So *Par. Reg.* IV. 275.

446. **Solon.**—An Athenian lawgiver, one of the seven wise men, b. 638 B.C. He introduced the plutocratic principle and divided the citizens into four classes according to amount of income, with corresponding privileges and burdens. Legislation originated in an upper house of 400, left as strictly aristocratic by Solon as he found it, but he required ratification by a lower house or assembly, composed of all the classes. His constitution and his laws with some alterations remained in force for 400 or 500 years.

   common-weal, commonwealth. Distinguish the ordinary meanings.

   next.—Not in time, but in order of presentation to the poet's mind.

447-8. **tender.**—So different from the stern laws of Draco, which preceded.

   lively.—A very expressive epithet as regards the Athenians, who were as full of vivacity as of intelligence.

450. *Par. Reg.* IV. 240. Give lists of Athenians distinguished in sculpture, painting, poetry, the drama and eloquence.

452. **Smiling.**—A common epithet for Greece with the poets. See Byron in several passages·

   Lycurgus.—The great Spartan lawgiver (about 881 B.C.), made Sparta a close aristocracy based on caste, the majority of the people having no political rights. L. is a semi-mythical personage and probably did little more than collect and arrange previously existing laws. These developed a nation of brave and hardy soldiers, but repressed intellectual, commercial, or even moral progress. The example of Sparta proved that the sources of a nation's strength are not in the perfectness of any military system. Her insolent tyranny after the Peloponnesian War brought her into collision with Thebes, by which she was reduced to her ancient boundaries, and later on she was quite unable to make head against Macedon or Rome.

bowed.—Trans.

455. **following.**—Parse.

457-8. **chief.**—Leonidas, King of Sparta, killed at Thermopylae in opposing Xerxes, 480 B.C.

the other.—Lycurgus.
hardest lesson.—To lay down his life for Sparta.

459. **Aristides.**—An Athenian of such probity that his fellow citizens called him the Just. He fought at Marathon under Miltiades (490), and was chief Archon next year. Themistocles, called by the poet, his *haughty rival*, procured his ostracism. A. returned, however, to assist Themistocles against the invading Persians, fought at Salamis, and led the Athenians at Plataea. In 477 he introduced a constitutional change admitting all classes of citizens to political offices. He died in 468, respected by all, being so poor that his funeral and his family had to be provided for at the public expense.

465. **his.**—Aristides.

ray.—*i.e.*, disposition. An allusion to the belief in the influence of the planets and their relative positions on the character of the child. In the east, especially among the Mohammedans, astrology is still believed in.

466. Cimon, son of Miltiades, by Aristides' advice shook off his bad habits and distinguished himself against the Persians. Having acquired great wealth he employed it freely in embellishing his native city, Athens, and assisting the deserving poor. He became the leader of the aristocratic party and the rival of Pericles, who procured his ostracism for five years.

471. **declining.**—After the Peloponnesian War.

472. **unequal.**—*i.e.*, to the former.

474. **Timoleon.**—b. 394. Consented to the death of his brother, Timophanes, who had made himself tyrant of Corinth, his native city. It being doubtful whether he was a murderer or a patriot, he was sent to help the people of Syracuse, a colony of Corinth, against their tyrant Dionysius and the Carthaginians. Here he was successful, defeating even Hasdrubal and Hamilcar with one-seventh the number of their men. He expelled the tyrants from the Greek cities of Sicily and defined the boundaries of the Carthaginian colony. He organized the laws of Syracuse on a democratic basis and died there an honoured private citizen in 335.

476. **pair.**—Epaminondas and Pelopidas. Their friendship is one of the most beautiful things recorded in Greek history. P. expelled the Spartans and organized and trained the celebrated "sacred band" of Thebes, which contributed so much to the victories of E. over the Spartans at Leuctra, 371, and Mantinea, 362. Under E., Thebes, which had never had much influence, rose to be the head of Greece.

481. **Phocion,** b. 402 B.C.—An Athenian general and statesman. Although he defeated Philip of Macedon in several engagements, yet he recognized the real strength of Macedon as opposed to Greece and proposed an alliance. He was in consequence an opponent of Demosthenes and the war party and fell into disrepute. He strongly opposed the proposed rejoicings at Philip's assassination (336), and after the defeat of the Athenians by Antipater, procured a considerable mitigation of their punishment. Forced to flee the city he took refuge among the Phocians, who basely delivered him up, and he was compelled like Socrates, by the ungrateful Athenians, to drink the hemlock, 317. In private life, a model of courtesy and in public life of integrity, he may be considered as the compeer of Timoleon.

486-8. **sons.**—Descendants. *Agis III.*, one of the two Kings of Sparta 244 B.C., thought to restore the old Spartan spirit and to stay the *decadence* of the state by restoring in their strictness the institutions and laws of Lycurgus. He carried the abolition of debts, and in the new partition of the lands awakened so much opposition that he was put to death along with all his family by his colleague Leonidas.

491. After the death of Epaminondas the superiority of Thebes rapidly declined, and the Achaeans for sometime held it by means of their famous League, which they wished to extend to the whole of Greece. *Aratus* was General of the League in 245 B.C., and held the office many times. He recovered Corinth from Macedon, but Sparta's jealousy forced him to become her ally. Philopœmen, General of the League in 208, revived the martial spirit (l. 495), and forced the Spartans and Aetolians to join the League, which was allowed by the Romans to exist as an aid against Macedon, till 146 B.C., when it was dissolved. P. has been called the last of the Greeks.

491. **relumed.**—Lighted again. Give other words from the same root (*lumen*).

493. **hope.**—Case?

496. **toiling swain.**—Relation?

498. **people.**—The Romans.
too fondly.—See l. 503.
virtuous times of the republic.

502. better founder.—Because *Numa* founded the religious institutions of Rome. By some regarded as mythical.

504. Servius Tullius, the 6th King, founded the Roman Constitution. In a general way, Solon's principle may be said to be the basis, that greater possessions should have a greater influence in the councils of the nation.

505. The Kings were expelled shortly after, and Rome became a republic. L. J. Brutus, consul of the new republic, ordered his sons to be put to death for attempting to restore the expelled King (Tarquin).

507. who the private quelled. Subordinated his feelings as a parent to his conviction of duty to the state.

508. as. Supply *he sat* an unusual ellipsis with *as*, though similar ones are quite common with *while*.

510. Camillus.—Consul 403 B.C., was victorious against the Volscians and Veii, Falerii. The democratic party accused him of inordinate greed after the spoils, and also of peculation. In consequence he retired to Ardea, but was recalled in 390 to expel the Gauls under Brennus. Camillus in this, as in all other things, was wonderfully successful; in fact his recorded feats rather strain one's powers of belief.

only.—Is this word in its proper place?

511. Fabricius.—Consul 282 B.C., sent to treat with Pyrrhus, King of Epirus, who had invaded Italy, refused all his offers of money, and on the other hand spurned the proposal of Pyrrhus's doctor to dispose of the King by poison.

Cincinnatus.—Consul 460 B.C., was found at his plough by the Senate's messengers in 458, when they implored his acceptance of the dictatorship to save the state from the Æqui and Volsci. In three weeks he had done his work, resigned his office and retired to his farm. He was dictator a second time, but resigned after nearly as short a period.

513. willing victim.—Regulus, a consul in the first Punic war. He invaded Africa, but falling into the hands of the Carthaginians was sent to Rome, under parole, to propose an exchange of prisoners. He advised the Senate to continue the war, and in spite of the entreaties of his family and friends returned to Carthage, although certain of a cruel death. See Horace, bk. iii., ode 5. Niebuhr casts doubt on the story of his barbarous death. History and poetry have lent their embellishments to many names of the monarchy and early republic.

517. Scipio, called *Africanus* (minor), from destroying Carthage 146 B.C., and *Numantinus*, from his capture of Numantia in Spain, B.C. 133. Unpopular on account of his aristocratic feelings and his opposition to the reforms of his brother-in-law, Tiberius Gracchus; murdered, probably by some of the supporters of the Sempronian law. A man of culture, well versed in Greek literature ; a close friend of the consul Laelius, (their friendship was celebrated throughout Rome and led Cicero to make Laelius the chief speaker in his *De Amicitia),* the historian Polybius, and the poet Terence, whom he and Laelius are said to have assisted in his plays.

521. **Tully.**—*Marcus Tullius Cicero,* 106-43 B.C., Rome's great orator and man of letters, was at 27 the first man at the Roman bar, quæstor in Sicily 76, ædile 69, prætor 66, consul 63, and in this last office earned the title of Father of his Country by crushing the conspiracy of that political desperado, Catiline. In the struggle between Cæsar and Pompey, was a lukewarm friend of Pompey's, but after Pharsalia went over to Cæsar and was graciously received. Till Cæsar's death was in retirement and engaged on his chief works in philosophy and rhetoric. In the proscription that followed the formation of the 2nd triumvirate, Cicero was on Antony's list and was overtaken and slain by his soldiers while attempting to leave Italy. Cicero was devoid of heroism of character, and although he had legislative ability due to his acute mind and wide information, he was too deficient in courage and political sagacity to become a leader of men in those troublous and corrupt times. But he was the greatest master of rhetoric that ever lived, and at that time eloquence was relatively of more importance than now. His love of applause, his unwearied diligence, his great natural faculties quickened and strengthened by study, his unlimited power of expression, language, and the luminous treatment of his subject, have all combined to make his orations our most splendid examples of forensic eloquence. Even now, when the subject matter has lost all living interest and classical study is on the wane, they are still read with pleasure and furnish models for imitation to aspirants in our own tongue.

523. **Cato,** 234-149 B.C., commonly called the Censor. In his youth distinguished himself at the bar, became consul and exhibited considerable military talent in quelling disturbances in Spain (206). When 50 years old was appointed Censor at Rome, and the duties of this office gave him fine opportunities for exhibiting that strictness in morals and that unflinching honesty which had now become but too rare. He did great service in paving and draining the city and in checking the rapacity of contractors for public works. But his interference in matters relating to wages, dress, furniture, etc., failed, as sumptuary laws always do. His severity and sternness gained for him by way of prominence the title of Censor.

As Cato Major (above) is not in proper chronological order with the rest, perhaps Thomson referred to Cato Minor, 95-46, who served in the army against Spartacus with credit, and afterwards became quæstor and tribune. He was an adherent of Pompey, and after Pharsalia (48 B.C.) fled to Africa, and on hearing of the defeat by Cæsar of Pompey's party at Thapsus, stabbed himself. He belonged to the Stoics and possessed great decision and energy of character.

524. Brutus, 85-42, after Pharsalia, received a province from Cæsar. On returning to Rome, Cassius prevailed on him to join the conspiracy against Cæsar. The eloquence of Antony over Cæsar's dead body so incensed the populace that he fled from Rome and from Italy. In Asia Minor he kept up a sort of guerilla warfare against Octavianus and Antony, but being defeated by them at Phillippi, 42 B.C., he fell upon his sword. Shakespeare (*Julius Cæsar*) is perhaps responsible for the popular idea of Brutus's character, a character not too heroic.

526. Roman stool.—Cæsar being stabbed at the foot of Pompey's pillar, and seeing Brutus among the number, is reported to have said reproachfully, "Et tu Brute!" The epithet *Roman* may be applied because the deed was one of vengeance against him who had destroyed the liberties of Rome and had become its tyrant, or may refer to the stern and determined character of these republican conspirators, who unfortunately could find no cure for the ills of the state but in assassination.

527. verse.—Give the meaning and derivation.

528. demand.—In what sense used here.

count.—A doublet of *compute.* Give similar pairs of doublets, and account for their existence.

532. Phœbus.—Apollo, God of light, therefore of poetry and the fine arts ; the type of beauty for painting and sculpture.

Mantuan swain.—Virgil, 70-19 B.C., born near Mantua, here called *swain* either because his father was a farmer, or because his early works, the *Eclogues,* were pastoral in their character, and the *Georgics* related to husbandry. His most finished production was the *Georgics,* but his greatest work was the *Æneid,* next to the *Iliad* and *Odyssey* of Homer, the greatest epic poem among the ancients. Its subject, the origin of the Roman people, was suggested by Augustus. In many instances he copies from earlier poets, Homer, Theocritus, Ennius, but generally with added grace of diction, if not with added strength or vividness of imagination. No other Latin poets but Horace can dispute the palm with him, and his amiable and retiring disposition endeared him to all.

533. Homer.—Author of the *Iliad* and *Odyssey,* the greatest epics of Greece, and perhaps of the world. There is nothing known with certainty of his life, and his very existence has been denied. See Grote I., c. 21.

534. parent.—About 900 B.C. Very few earlier poems of any merit exist.

535. British muse.—Milton. Dryden's lines, adjudging Milton as even superior to the other two, though often quoted are worth quoting again :

> "Three poets, in three distant ages born,
> Greece, Italy, and England did adorn.
> The first in loftiness of thought surpassed,
> The next in majesty, in both the last.
> The force of nature could no further go,
> To make a third she joined the other two."

Schiller has the same idea:

> "da sie (the British Muse)
> Einst mit der Maeonid, und jener,
> Am Kapitol den heiszen Sand trat."

536. darkling.—Being in the dark, both Homer and Milton being blind,—an adverb formed from *dark* by the adverbial suffix *ling*. Compare *hedling* O.E. form of *headlong*; *full up*, right up. Note the common phrase "to climb Parnassus."

537-9. those shades.—The Attic tragedians, Æschylus, Sophocles, and Euripides, in whose hands the drama, which had originated in the choral services accompanying the worship of Dionysus, was not a mere amusement, but a means employed for religious and moral teaching. Æschylus introduced action and dramatic dialogue, in place of the perpetual chorus; also scenery, masks, dresses, etc. Sophocles improved on A. and gained the prize over him (464 B.C.), Cimon being judge. In the tragedies of these two there is a constant subjection of the action of the play to the disposing of destiny. S. is accounted the most perfect of the three, his verse being soft and harmonious, and a faithful reflex of the human passions. Euripides was rather unequal, although on some occasions he was preferred to his elder rival, Sophocles. It may be added that the Athenians were very fond of dramatic entertainments, and that under Pericles the poorer classes were provided out of the public funds with the means of attending the theatre.

540. lyre.—The chief lyric poets of Greece were Alcaeus, Sappho, Anacreon, Simonides and Pindar. Anacreon has been imitated and some say improved on by our own poet Moore. Give a list of English lyric poets.

543. mount, trans. causative; *soaring,* so the phrase "flight of imagination."

544. door be thine.—Be my doorkeeper.

546-7. friends . . . roof.—See life.

547. sense.—Literary taste.

548. digested, *i.e.* so as to affect the judgment and taste, not like cram, the memory alone, and even that not lastingly.

549. Distinguish *wit and humour.*

550. Muses' hill.—Parnassus.

551. sacred to contemplation.

553. sweeter is a better epithet for Pope's translation of Homer than for the original. Bentley, the great classical scholar, in acknowledging a copy, said, "It is a very pretty poem, Mr. Pope, but it is not Homer."

554. This statement may seem open to doubt, yet in spite of his peevishness, his jealousy, his vanity, and his stinging satire, the "wicked wasp of Twickenham" was not devoid of generosity or a manly spirit.

556. Hammond. Member for Truro, and a friend of Thomson, wrote elegiacs of no merit, and was often among the tuneful throng of poets visiting Thomson's cottage. He died at 32.

558-64. Discuss the appropriateness of the words *vernal, ravished, stung, glowing.*

565-6. patriots.—Those opposed to Walpole. *What* avails now.

570. They were only shewed (shewn) ; *fond*, foolish.

575. If—whether ; *sprung* for sprang, supply *if it.*

578. Supply *would search.*

580. gradual—Adv.

581. diffusive.—Diffused.

583. embroiled. Confused.

586. historic muse.—Clio. Name some of the others.

591 2. double suns.—As the sun is the source of all animal and vegetable life, this means double prosperity ; *brightest skies*, tropics.

594-5. Luke xxiv. 32.—*Portion of divinity*, a doctrine of Socrates.

597-9. doomed.—Sentenced ; *repress*, Gr. Elegy 51-59.
        ardent, kindling.—Compare the meanings.

609-10. foiled, shifting.—The metaphor is probably taken from fencing.
        play.—Display.
        is foiled, would play.—Is this a proper correspondence of tenses ?

612. assembled train. The ideas are somewhat incongruous ; probably *assembled* is loosely used for "connected." Derive the words, accounting for the *b* in *assembled*, and showing how the different meanings of *train* are connected.

614. A fair poetical definition of wit ; see l. 549.

616. Milton is much more expressive : "And laughter, holding both his sides." *L'Allegro*, l. 32.

625. Compare Goldsmith : "The bashful virgin's side-long look of love." D.V. 29. Is putting the serious before the gay in this picture, 617-628, a natural order ?

626-8. on purpose guardless.—Explain what figure ?
        haul.—Is this an effective word ?
        shook for shaken.
        respondent.—Responsive.

631. mixed.—In old editions spelled *mixt*. It is a great pity that these past tenses and participles in *t* have gone out of use. In many cases of rhyme the eye as well as the ear would be satisfied by their use.

632. sons of riot. Compare Milton's "sons of Belial flown with insolence and crime." P.L. 1. 502.

633-4. loose.—Lawless.

rankled.—Festered. Festering is the common term.

638-9. The ideas in *along* and *dome* seem to clash a little. *Ways,* parse ; *evolved,* involved.

640-41. Effuses.—Pours forth. Effulgence *beam'd.*

644-5. As an insect's wings are covered with powder, so the fop's arms (wings) were covered with the powder which fell from his hair. The use of powder was then general among the fashionable. By act of parliament it was to be pure starch, and at one time the tax on it yielded a revenue of £20,000. As a bit of sarcastic wit, these lines are among Thomson's happiest examples.

646-55. Hamlet and **Othello** are well known Shakespearian characters.

Monimia and **Belvidera** are characters, the first in Otway's *Orphan,* the second in his *Venice Preserved.*

Bevil.—A character in Steele's *Conscious Lovers.*

fair impartial.—Are the two epithets needed ?

With this passage compare *Il Pens.* 97, and *L'Allegro* 132.

656. Lord Chesterfield, 1694-1773, well-known as the model of a polite (671) and dignified (661) gentleman. He was an opponent of Walpole (669-70), held, however, several important posts, and was Viceroy of Ireland. His eloquence was marked by delicacy and irony (658 and 675). He is best known by his famous " Letters to his Son, ' the general purport of which is that success in life is due as much to good manners as to ability and probity. Several of Thomson's lines are tinged with exaggeration.

659. Graces.—According to the Greek mythology, three beautiful goddesses that lend their grace and beauty to everything that delights and elevates gods and men.

660. Apollo.—See note on 532.

661. give.—Permit or enable.

662. guardian.—In what case ?

663. rural.—Why this epithet ?

665. shades of retirement.

672. Even.—Parse.

presumptuous, in setting the fashions, etc.

675. Attic point and Attic salt are phrases expressive of the pungency and sparkle of Athenian wit.

678-9. or let me hail thee rising thence, *i.e.,* from these qualities.

680. Senate.—House of Lords.

684-5. Other men's thoughts are made clearer by his reasoning.

687. **reluctant party.** Wm. III., by the Earl of Sunderland's advice in 1693, selected the chief officers of state from that party which had the majority in the House of Commons, giving origin to what is known party government. There are evils seemingly inseparable from the system ; one is hinted at here, the tendency to sink one's private judgment before the demands of the party. Others might be mentioned, as, "To the victors belong the spoils," "The minority has no rights to be respected.' But it is easier to point evils than to suggest a remedy.

690. **you roll.**—Is this correct after using *thou* and *thy* above

691-3. **haunt.**—The country.

serene.—Sky.

694. "**Nitre** is a salt of potassium, commonly called Saltpetre. Here used for any salt capable of subtle intermixture with the air. Nitre cools gas under heat with great rapidity. The poet's notion seems to have been that frost was not only an effect of a certain condition of the atmosphere, but an actually existing thing, which he here likens to a finely divided salt. Compare l. 718. But it may mean only oxygen, which Priestly calls *nitre*. See *Task*, iii., 32, and *Autumn*, l. 5."—Bright. The last explanation seems an odd one, seeing that Priestly was born some years after Thomson's lines were written.

695-6. Frost exercises a drying influence on damp soils and arrests the progress of contagious disease, or the effects of malaria, being destructive to the morbific germs which thrive by heat and moisture.

698. **constringent,** *i.e.*, binding binds, etc., in T.'s pleonastic manner. The greater vigour of northern nations is no doubt due to climatic influence and to the greater and enforced care taken of youth.

699-703. **feeds** is nonsense ; cold animates because it necessitates motion to quicken the circulation. The vigorous body makes the vigorous mind. "Mens sana in sano corpore."

intense.—Alert and powerful.

706. **concocted** seems to mean *ripened*. *Georgic*, l. 65-6 ; so Bacon. The effect of snow and frost on soils is well known to be beneficial, rendering them friable, and so more absorptive of those constituents (carbonic acid, water and ammonia) necessary to plant life.

707. **soul.**—Life.

709-10. Give the cause of this.

luculent.—Beauteous or shining. Notice the fine effect of the contrast in (the once) *sullen* deeps (now) *transparent*, and the imitative harmony of *murmur hoarser*.

716-21. **illusive.**—Water eluding the grasp. *Elusive* would be more appropriate. Distinguish elude, illude, evade.

> **salts.**—See note to 694.
>
> **ether.**—Air.

721. **Steamed.**—"An icy gale steamed eager—breathes." The idea ems to be that the frost rising like a vapour from these particles fills the gale and makes it *icy*.

> **red horizon** in the west at sunset, a sign of frost.—*Georgic iii. 358.*

723-4. Wilson finds great beauty in the words "breathes a blue film." The words "oft shifting" don't seem natural here.

> **Bicker.**—Formed from *pick*, to *peck* with the *beak* (Skeat).
>
> **bickering.**—Originally then, fighting—here quickly moving, quivering. Compare "that, as they bickered through the sunny shade, a lulling murmur made."—*Castle of Indolence*, Canto 1, st. 3.

725. **Let.**—Permitted to go.

> **sedgy.**—Covered with river-flags (water-iris).

731. Cowper says,

> " While silently beneath,
> And unperceived, the current steals away."

Which is truer to nature ?

732-4. **reflects.**—Gives back.
> **double.**—Very loud.
> **deters.**—Frightens away.
> **nightly.**—By night.

736. **swells.**—What is meant?

738. **Ethereal round.**—Explain.

740-6. **cope.**—Canopy.
> **rigid influence.**—Frost, which makes rigid.
> **unjoyous.**—Not in use now.

748-9. **Prone** means with face downwards ; can only mean pendent here. The next line is very expressive.

751. **fancied.**—Fanciful, fantastic.
> **transient.**—Distinguish from *transitory*.

754. **plumy.**—The branches covered with feathery snow, nodding like the plumes of a hearse.

755-9. **refined and incrusted hard** seem rather contradictory. Why would putting the word *shepherd* and the attendant words in the plural spoil the effect of the picture?

763. **dissolv'd**—Separated.

764. **raptured.**—Enraptured.

767.—**void of care.** This rather misrepresents the industrious Dutchman, to whom skating is not always a pleasure, but sometimes a matter of business, going to market, etc.

768. **Batavia.**—The old classical name of Holland, from Batavi, a German nation (Catti according to Tacitus) who immigrated there before Cæsar's time. Notice the change of number in *rushes* and *they*. How may it be defended?

771. **then gay.**—The Dutch being proverbially phlegmatic.

772. **courts,** *i.e.,* royalty and nobility of Norway, Sweden, etc.

773. Distinguish sled, sledge, and sleigh.

775. **manly strife.** – See *L'Allegro*, 121.

777. Why are the Norwegian and Swedish ladies flushed by the season?
   buxom.—Lively and handsome.

780-82. **elapses,** *i.e.,* slips by. See note 47-49.
   gelid. – Cold as ice.
   ineffectual.—Explain why.

783-5. **azure.**—From the ice.
   relents.—Thaws.

793. **game.**—Here, any object of the chase. In England certain animals are protected at certain seasons by *game laws*. A revenue is also derived from licenses given for shooting. Are there any game laws in Canada?

794. **our infant winter.**—Explain the force of the epithet.

796-7. **shoot.**—Swiftly glance.

   relentless months.—At the poles there are six months of day and then six months of night—shortening, of course, as you proceed towards the equator.

799. **there.**—Siberia, the ordinary place of banishment for Russian subjects who have fallen under the czar's displeasure. Thomson has rather exaggerated the horrors of a Siberian winter.

805. **main.**—Arctic Ocean.

808. **Cathay.**—China. The transit trade by caravan is chiefly done at Kiahta, a town of about 5,000, 150 m. south of Lake Baikal, on the Chinese frontier – tea and furs being of course the principal articles of exchange.

809. **with.**—What is the relation?

811. **furry nations.**—For similar epithets see 87, 137.

814. **freaked.**—Mottled, or rather with irregular and broken lines What are the chief fur-bearing animals and their habitats?

818. **heapy.**—In heaps, formed, it is said, by the animal itself, with its antlers.

elk.—It is getting very scarce in Siberia now, and is not common in North America. The antlers sometimes weigh 120 lbs., and the whole animal from 800 to 1200 lbs.

822. With the exception of the substitution of **clubs** for knives (*ferro*) the passage 816-826 is a close imitation of Virgil's account of the Scythians. —*Geo. iii.* 369-375.

824. **bray** is not expressive of the elk's cry ; there seems to be no word especial to this animal. *Bell* is used by Scott for the noise the deer makes.

811. **jet.**—A variety of lignite, very black and capable of high polish, found in many parts of the world, and used for crosses, mourning ornaments. Here of course a jet colour is meant.

812-13. **ermine, sable,** are both animals of the weasel kind. Ermines in winter become perfectly white, except the tip of the tail, which always remains black. The fur forms a distinctive border for the robes of judges ; the word ermine being in consequence often used as a synonyme for the office of judge. The sable is perfectly black, found chiefly in Siberia, and its fur, like that of the ermine, is extremely valuable.

827. **piny.**—In cold regions pines are among the trees that last survive.

absorpt.—Half sunk in snow ; for *absorbed* and more euphonic. See note on *mixed*, l. 413.

828. **shapeless.**—From its long shaggy hair.

horrid.—Bristling.

833. May refer to its hibernation, or being torpid during winter.

835. **Boötes.**—The two stars in the handle of the plough point to the constellation of Boötes, the ploughman, of which Arcturus is the chief star.

wain.—An older and chiefly poetical spelling of wagon. The constellation of the Great Bear (*Ursà Major*), is also known as the Plough, the Dipper, and Charles's Wain (coorl's or peasant's wagon) ; called here **tardy,** because revolving slowly about the North pole.

836. **boisterous.**—Turbulent.

Caurus. The North-West wind.—*Geo. iii.* 356.

838. **swarm.**—Four great tides of immigration from Asia into Europe may be marked : first that into Greece and Italy ; then the Celtic and Cimbrian, who occupied Britain, France and Spain ; then the Germanic, into the north and centre ; then the Slavonic, peopling the North-East, pressed upon by Huns beyond the Ural Mountains, and the Tartars beyond the Caspian. Perhaps Thomson had specially in mind the Goths. Their earliest home was Scandinavia, but about 200 A.D., they began to move southward in three great divisions, one of which under Alaric, sacked the city of Rome (410) ; another founded a kingdom in Spain.

relumed.—See 491 note.

flame of liberty.—Being a migratory nation they were necessarily warriors and free. Later on, becoming more settled, the feudal system (l. 842) was introduced, which in time developed for the great mass of the people into a new kind of slavery, as burdensome, if not as completely destitute of civil rights, as that of Rome under the Empire. In England the people were a little more fortunate.

840. **drove,** *intrans.* Note Milton's greater force and vividness in referring to the same subject.—*P. L. l.* 301.

> A multitude, like which the populous North
> Poured never from her frozen loins, to pass
> Rhene or the Danaw, where her barbarous sons
> Came like a deluge on the South, and spread
> Beneath Gibraltar to the Libyan sands.

844. **insensate.**—The usual meaning is stupid, *i.e.*, without sense (perceptive); here perhaps means "mad" or "without reason."

846. Compare what Goldsmith says of the Swiss.—*Traveller,* 199-208.

847. No desires bid it (the current) rage thro', etc.

853. **cheerful cups.**—What is meant?

855. Sledge is more common.

them.—The Lapps.

854. **obsequious.**—Has this word its ordinary meaning here?

857. **marbled.**—Meaning here? Give the other.

859. The Aurora Borealis, or Northern Lights, gives some relief to the Arctic inhabitants during their dreary nights of months in duration.

They are probably of electrical origin, and in some way connected with disturbances in the magnetic currents of the earth. Their frequency and brilliancy seem greatest in the latitude of Spitzbergen. It is doubtful whether any noise occurs with them, as has been alleged.

by.—They find by meteors.

862. **doubled lustre.**—Reflection.

867. **Aurora.** - Goddess of the morning.

875. Maupertius in his book on the Figure of the Earth, after describing the beautiful lake and mountain of Niemi, in Lapland, says: "We had been frighted with stories of bears that haunted this place, but saw none. It seemed rather a resort for fairies and genii than bears. . . . . I was surprised to see on the banks of this river (the Tenglio) roses of as lively a red as any that are in our garden."

877. **fry**—Young fish just produced from the spawn.

tents.—Covered with reindeer hide, or conical mud huts raised on stakes.

884-6. Is **whose swains—nor—their daughters**—a correct construction? **spotless** and **blooming** must be understood in a Pickwickian sense.

883. **interest.**—Love of power and riches.
   Why fell?

887-8. **Tornea.**—Where?
   Hecla flaming—Explain.

893. **new seas.**—In the other hemisphere.
   cerulean.—Sky-colored. Compare *azure*, 783. Winter's Court is decorated. Show the points of resemblance in the comparison.

895-901.—This image has been much admired.

903. **she**—The Muse.
   main.—Arctic Ocean.

909. **projected.**—Projecting.

910. **Alps.**—Here for any mountain; properly, pastures on the mountain sides. See n. 445-8.

911. **chaos.**—With some of the ancients, one of the oldest gods.
   was.—Is this grammatically correct?

912. Notice the effective use of the words *shake* and *solid*.

914. **binding.**—Explained by what follows. Compare 730-1.

915. **taken.**—As a captive.
   boundless.—Of limitless power.

920. **conscious** of coming evil to itself.

922. **descending.**—To an absence of months.

924. **incumbent.**—Brooding.

925. **Briton's fate.**—An expedition sent by a company of adventurers in 1553, to discover a north-east passage to India, under Sir Hugh Willoughby, Richard Chancellor and Stephen Burroughs. After experiencing much stormy weather two of the ships entered the river Arzina, which is east of the North Cape. There both commanders and crews perished, their bodies, together with the journal of the voyage, having been discovered by some Russian sailors. The other ship, Chancellor's, escaping, was wrecked on its way home off the coast of Scotland.—*Morris.*

928. **in vain,** *i.e.,* in search of a north-west passage. Give an account of the various expeditions. One may be excused for wondering what prospect of commercial advantage there can be to justify such an expenditure of money and energy and life.

930-35. One of the most expressive, although gruesome pictures in all Thomson's poetry, or indeed in anybody's poetry.
   froze (intrans), *i.e.,* while in motion. So "arrests the bicker. stream" (725).

glued.—being glued.

935. Bell says: "This account is imaginary (930-5); the poet describes the process of petrifaction, not of freezing."

937. Ostiacs and Samoyedes, chiefly between the Obi and Yenesei, little influenced as yet by Russian civilization or Christianity.

enlivened.—Has this its usual meaning here ?

distant.—Is this a correct word ?

942-3. unjoyous cheer.—What figure ?

waste.—Spend uselessly.

944-5. gross.—Refers to their filthy habits and dull intellects, no doubt due in a measure to the severity of the cold, which scarcely permits cleanliness, and which necessitates the almost exclusive use of fatty animal food.

946. kindred.—From their appearance or sluggishness.

quivered.—With quiver.

950-4. active government.—Paternal government may be suited to society in its early stages, but as people become civilized and educated, the most successful results come from giving, consistent with peace and order, the widest scope to individual freedom of action. When Thomson wrote, the Russians were hardly accounted as belonging to the family of European nations.

gothic.—Here a common adjective. So the word vandalism. See n. l. 836 et seq.

955. Peter, Czar of Russia, 1672-1725, a man of brutal and passionate disposition, but of indomitable energy. What he did for Russia is pretty accurately recounted in the text, making allowance for the exaggeration natural in poetry. Despite his almost superhuman exertions, the Russians are still behind the rest of Europe, and retain traces of their Tartar origin (l. 952). It was a saying of Bonaparte's, "Scratch a Russian and you'll find a Tartar."

960-2. Ye shades.—See l. 437 et seq.

labouring.—In distress, as a ship labours.

964. left.—In 1697, visiting Prussia, Hanover, Holland, England, etc.

966. greatly.—Grandly.

967-9. At Saardam, in Holland, he worked for some time as a common shipwright. "That large mind, equal to the highest duties of the general and the statesman, contracted itself to the most minute details of naval architecture and naval discipline." He spent three months in England, living at Deptford, in John Evelyn's house, and left it in such a dirty state that the Government quieted his (E.'s) grumblings with a sum of money. On Peter and his visit, read Macaulay, chap. xxiii., vol. 5.

970-3. Scarcely anything escaped Peter's reforming zeal.   He took away with him from England, engineers, artificers, surgeons, artisans, artillery-men, etc., to the number of 500.   The organization and discipline of an army, the building of a navy, trade with foreign countries, improvements in dress, manners and etiquette, the education of the nobility, the introduction of indirect taxation, the keeping of accounts in the modern way instead of by the old Tartar method of balls strung on a wire, the encouragement of architecture, painting and sculpture, are among the many benefits conferred on Russia by this large-minded tyrant.

He laid the foundation of St. Petersburgh, the new capital, in May, 1703, and it speedily became the commercial depot of the Baltic.

975. Alluding to Peter's projects of joining the Don and Volga by a canal; also the Black Sea (Euxine) and Baltic.

977. Would *to* be more effective than **with**?

980. Charles XII, King of Sweden, Peter's chief rival.   Peter coveted the provinces on the Baltic which then belonged to Sweden, and taking advantage of Charles' youth, allied himself with Poland and Denmark against Sweden.   In the battle of Narva, and several succeeding battles, the Swedes were victorious, but at Poltawa, in 1709, Charles was totally routed and became a fugitive among the Turks.   Peter was at war with the Turks also, as he desired possession of the Black Sea coast as well as the Baltic. Charles has been called here the Alexander of the North on account of his passion for war, although he possessed great abilities in other directions. See note, l. 318.   He got back to Sweden, and was making head against his numerous enemies when he was killed before Frederickshald, Nov. 1718. After his death Sweden sank from the preeminence it had acquired under him.

981. Othman was third caliph of the Moslems after Mahomet, and the Turks perhaps got their name of Ottomans from him.   The word *shrinking* is contrary to the truth, as in the war referred to (see n. 980) Peter was surrounded and in danger of captivity; Catherine, his mistress--his wife a few years later—procured his escape by bribing the Turkish officials with her jewels and articles of her wardrobe.

983. Proud of deeds now reckoned dishonorable.
    it.—The land.

988. **blunted.**—Is not keen.
    resolves.—Loosens.

991. **spotted.**—Explain how this agrees with the idea of shining.

993. What are the **bonds**?

995. **brown.**—From alluvial matter.

997-9. **sullen, shackles.**—Because bound by the ice.

1002. **rifted.**—Riven, split.
    it bursts.—What?

1004. **charged.**—Loaded.
    wretches.—In what sense used?

1005. **moors.**—From what language have we borrowed most of our nautical words? Compare *Par. Lost*, i., 206-8.

1007. Explain, if possible, the meaning of the words:
        "And horror looks more horrible."

1008. **force.**—"Strength" would seem more appropriate with "endure."

1013. **bellowing.**—Compare Dryden's
    " And rocks the bellowing voice of boiling seas rebound."

1014. **more to embroil.**—To disturb still more.

    Leviathan.—Compare Job xli. 31, and *Par. Lost*, i. 200-8, and vii. 410-6. The whale needs no description; it is sufficient to say that, like the dolphin, porpoise, and some others, it is not a fish, as it brings forth its young alive and suckles them like an ordinary mammal; breathes with lungs, and can, like some land animals, be drowned by being kept too long under water. The tail (**train** in the text) moves like a sculler's oar, or like the screw of a steamer, with a combined downward and lateral motion; but when urged to speed, directly up and down.

1015-26. **tempest.**—Verb.
    loading.—The ordinary phrase is "borne by the winds."
    monsters.—White bears, etc.

    Milton makes great use of the suggestive in his poetry, Thompson very little. The phrase, "there awaiting wrecks," fitly concludes these two powerful lines, and gives a vividness to the picture which, perhaps, no direct statement could give.

1027. **the tuneful,** *i.e.*, the birds.

1029-32. A theatrical image. Compare Shakespeare's celebrated passage. "All the world's a stage, etc." Man's life has been compared to changing seasons by numberless poets.
    shuts the scene, *i.e.*, the curtain of death falls.

1037. **veering.**—Like a weather-cock with the wind.

1038. The meaning is a little obscure, but the poet probably refers to the thousand schemes and plans for action that remain unaccomplished.

1039. " Virtue alone is happiness below."—*Pope.*

1042-5. See Rev. xxi. 1-4.

1052. **now.**—After viewing the works of God, as shown in the seasons.

1055. Acts viii. 23.

1058. **low thoughts.**—Luxury lolling in ease and plenty, still craving for more and keener physical (low) enjoyment.

1061. **licensed pain.**—Licensed callings – like liquor-selling and slave-holding, which have great evils connected with them. Thomson had no such special reference here.

1067. What seemed evil to the earthly eye, unknowing of the Great Architect's plan, is now seen to be no evil, but only a hitherto misunder-stood part of one harmonious whole.

SOUTHEY'S LIFE OF NELSON,

CHAPTERS VII., VIII. & IX.

WITH

LIFE OF SOUTHEY, SOUTHEY'S LITERATURE

AN

ARTICLE ON PROSE COMPOSITION, NOTES, &c.

BY
T. C. L. ARMSTRONG, B. A.

.

FOR THE USE OF CANDIDATES PREPARING FOR
UNIVERSITY MATRICULATION AND
TEACHERS' CERTIFICATES.

TORONTO:

The Copp, Clark Company (Limited), Publishers, Front Street West.

1886.

LIFE OF SOUTHEY.

ROBERT SOUTHEY was born at Bristol, on the 19th of August, 1774. His father was a small linen draper of that town, and managed from his business to make a living for his family but nothing more. Young Robert's prospects, however, were thought to have a brighter outlook when he, as a mere child, was adopted by his aunt, Miss Tyler, a maiden lady of some means. This lady was somewhat imperious in manner, but was kind and devoted in her own way to literature.

At her home, in Bath, the boy lived a rather solitary life, devoted to quietness, neatness and decorum. This was not a very attractive life for a young boy, but Miss Tyler had one amusement which young Robert greatly enjoyed: she was passionately fond of the theatre. Naturally he, too, became fascinated with it, and soon caught all his aunt's admiration for theatrical plays, play actors and play writers. The strong bias his young mind thus received, led him irresistibly towards literature. His aunt's library, which consisted chiefly of the early dramatists, fed this taste, and even at this early age he had a young ambition to become a writer of dramas, and spent much of his leisure time in composing juvenile plays.

In 1788, he went to Westminster School, the expense being borne by his uncle, the Reverend Herbert Hill, English Chaplain at Lisbon. Here he devoted more of his time to old books of romance and legends than to the ordinary routine of studies. Spenser and Tasso captivated his imagination, and Gibbon's Decline and Fall of the Roman Empire had a great influence on his mind. His head was too full of his own literary schemes to allow him to become a devoted or an accurate scholar; but he was laying the foundation for his future life work, and actually conceived the plan, at this early age, of most of his future works. It was while at Westminster that he conceived the idea of *Madoc; Thalaba* and the *Curse of Kehama* were also the after elaboration of a youthful idea he had there conceived of writing a poem on each of the great mythological religions in the world.

In his fourth year at Westminster he was expelled from the school on account of an article against flogging, written for a school journal which had been established by himself and some of his schoolmates. This was in the year 1792, a glorious age for poetic youth to live in. It was the age of Washington; of the fall of the Bastile, and of the rise of the revolutionary spirit. All the world was worshipping young liberty rising from the grave of centuries and bursting her iron fetters. Liberty is of slow growth however ; she comes timidly and reluctantly to dwell with men, but people, especially the young, did not then recognize this fact. Their hearts were full of enthusiasm for the impulse that would "Ring out the old, ring in the new," and all looked for the speedy advent of a millennial age of higher and purer existence. Years after, when Southey's heart had became somewhat sobered by age, he wrote : "I left Westminster in a perilous state—a heart full of piety and feeling—a head full of Rosseau and Werther, and my religious principles shaken by Gibbon. Many circumstances tended to give me a wrong bias, none to lead me right, except adversity, the wholesomest of all discipline."

At the time of Southey's expulsion from Westminster School, his father had failed in business, and the young man had to look forward to the prospect of abandoning his studies to aid in the support of the family, but by his uncle Hill's generosity he was enabled to go to Oxford, and in the autumn of the same year he matriculated into Balliol College.

He never liked Oxford, and learned but little during his course there. One book, however, made a deep impression on him—this was Epictetus, the stoic, of which he afterwards wrote : "Twelve years ago I carried Epictetus in my pocket till my very heart was ingrained with it, and the longer I live and the more I learn the more I am convinced that stoicism, properly understood, is the best and noblest of systems."

The impression then made never wore off—a philosophic stoicism, mellowed in later life by Christian faith, characterized him till the last. We have but few records of his college life ; his autobiography stops with his school-days, and his letters cover only his later years. It was, however, a repetition of his school-days ; the literary aspirations were intensified and modified by the stirring events of the French Revolution. His *Joan of Arc*, finished in 1793, reveals his ardent sympathy with Republicanism and hatred of tyranny. But in that very year the terrible excesses in Paris threw him into despair. The removal of hereditary rulers had not converted the ignorance and vice of the masses into wisdom and virtue. The age of prejudice, abuse and tyranny was not to be suddenly replaced by an age of culture, reason and liberty. Southey therefore began to despair of a purer age ever being established in Europe, and in this frame of mind he naturally thought of America. His mother's and his uncle's wish was that he should enter the church, but this his way of thinking did not allow him to do, much as he regretted it. He thought at one time of studying medicine, but his mind was too strongly biassed toward literature and was full of Utopian dreams.

America was, he thought, the only place in which he could live his Arcadian life of cultured innocence ; and meeting, about this time, another Utopian dreamer in Coleridge, he began to consider the matter seriously. A scheme was soon mutually concocted of settling on the Susquehanna, in America, where they could found a small colony of their own—a pantisocracy, each sharing in the government. Lovell, a friend, was to join them.

and as each member was to be married, the two sisters of Mrs. Lovell, Edith and Martha Fricker, were to be invited to share the fortunes of the young pantisocrats. The marriages were afterwards, indeed, consummated, but the scheme fell through. Money was the root from which all this good was to spring, and money was just what each lacked most; and moreover, Miss Tyler came to hear of Miss Fricker and the rest of the scheme, and Southey was ordered to leave her house. This was a crisis in his life. The publication of *Joan of Arc*, and a series of lectures by Southey and Coleridge still failing to raise money, Southey accepted his uncle's invitation to spend six months in Lisbon, a step which highly offended Coleridge. Before going he secretly married his Edith; but pantisocracy was dead; the Susquehanna was allowed to roll its sleepy waters through vales of unenlightened darkness. The revolutionary ardour of the young author of *Joan of Arc* and *Wat Tyler* was from this day merged in the embryo Toryism of the future poet laureate.

On his return from Lisbon he took up the study of law, but devoted his time to his poem *Madoc*, which he had now begun. He also wrote regularly for several magazines. In 1800, he again went to Portugal, where he utilized his visit by collecting materials for a *History of Portugal*, which, however, was never finished, and a *History of Brazil*, which he afterwards published. He also while there prepared *Thalaba* for the press.

On returning to Britain he became Secretary to Mr. Corry, Chancellor of the Exchequer for Ireland, but soon resigned the post and, in 1803, took up his residence with Coleridge, at Exeter Hall, near Keswick, in the lake district.

Keswick, from this time forward, became his home; with him lived Coleridge, and near him lived Wordsworth; hence the three were called by Jeffrey the Lake School, but there was little in common among them to constitute a school of poets.

The chief revenue for Exeter Hall came from Southey's busy pen, assisted by an annuity of £160, which had been given him by his college friend Wynn. He now devoted himself almost entirely to his literary work, and was in the habit of carrying on several works at the same time; when tired of one, he would rest himself by working at another. He was fond of books, and in time had a collection of 14,000, "the pride of his eye and the joy of his heart."

In 1805, he visited Scotland and spent three days with Scott, where he met Lord Jeffrey, the critic of the *Edinburg Review*. This magazine was becoming too liberal for Scott and Southey, and a new one, the *Quarterly*, was started in 1809, to which Southey became a regular contributor. His *Life of Nelson* was originally an article in the fifth number of the new quarterly.

He had by this time become quite conservative in his views and orthodox in his belief, and although he could discuss in theory political and social reform as desirable when the people were prepared for them, he opposed the

Reform Bill, Free Trade and Catholic Emancipation as going too far and too fast. He was appointed Poet Laureate in 1813, on the death of Pye. The position added £90 a year to his income, with which he insured his life. Other honours came to him now. He was given the degree of LL.D. by Oxford in 1820; elected to Parliament in 1826, but he never sat; he was offered and declined Knighthood in 1835, and had instead an annual pension of £300 conferred upon him by Sir Robert Peel. But, while these public honours were being heaped upon him, domestic affliction was darkening his life. In this same year, 1835, his wife died. His favourite son Herbert, and a daughter had previously died, and the loss of his wife gave his faculties a blow from which they never fully recovered; a gloom seemed to settle on him and his mind became gradually weaker. Two years later he married Caroline Bowles, an old lady friend, fifty-two years of age, a step he took merely for the sake of companionship in the weakness of his old age, now rapidly approaching; and the end was not long in coming. In 1840 he had to give up writing and abandon his beloved books. Wordsworth, on one of his visits, found him in that year in a state of mental stupor, and left him " patting with both hands his books affectionately like a child." In this state he continued, with occasional gleams of intelligence, but he gradually sank till his death occurred in 1843.

Southey as a man had many noble qualities; his purity, kind-hearted sympathy, and self-sacrificing devotion present a picture of a good and true man. He himself lived, as far as man could, the pure ideal he taught in his books. Busy as his life was, he found time to devote to others whose lot was worse than his own. At one time we find him editing Chatterton's poems, after the death of that strange genius, by which he netted £300 to assist his sisters, at another time, through sympathetic kindness, editing Kirk White's Remains. In manner, he was constitutionally bashful and reserved, qualities that were intensified by his long devotion to retirement and study. He had a large heart, but he cloaked his feelings under a studied stoicism; thus he writes to Coleridge: "Your feelings go naked; I cover mine with a bearskin. I will not say you harden yours by your mode, but I am sure that mine are the warmer for their clothing." He had not the imagination of Coleridge, that could call forth real beings out of the ideal world, nor that of his neighbour, Wordsworth, that could converse with a Divine Presence in external nature. He wrote and spoke little of nature, but he enjoyed her charms and the rugged beauty of his mountain home, where he spent the best part of his life devoted to his pleasant task.

SOUTHEY'S LITERATURE.

Southey's whole life was devoted to letters, yet his influence on the course of English Literature has been comparatively small. His poetry is chiefly of the narrative form, which had been made popular by Scott, but with Southey it labours under the disadvantage of being foreign in subject and cold in treatment. The pleasure derived is intellectual rather than emotional, and his heroes are too often like abstract types of right fighting against tyranny and fraud. Southey is the pure-toned moralist, approving and admiring great qualities and heroic deeds, rather than the divine-taught poet speaking to the hearts of his fellowmen. If he had followed his early impulses he might have given the world burning words on the wonderful events going on around him ; but his sudden conversion to the side of order closed his mouth or drove him to moralize coldly on the evils with which foreign lands were grappling.

His style is not characterized by artifice or peculiarities, it is simple and straightforward ; he believed in the use of plain words and avoided everything that approached the ornate.

From narrative poetry he glided naturally into prose, where he attained a somewhat higher position. His works in this department consist of histories, biographies and magazine articles. With him, history is a plain, simple narrative of events judged from a pure moral standard ; the style is easy, natural and unassuming.

In biography his relative position is higher. In this minor department of literature he stands among the first. His three leading biographies, the Lives of Nelson, Cowper and Wesley, are couched in graceful prose, and catch much of the spirit of the respective subjects. His *Life of Nelson*, written in 1817, when his powers were at their best, was originally an article in the *Quarterly Magazine*, afterwards expanded. It is in his best style. The devotion, the loyalty, and the heroic fortitude in Nelson's character appealed to similar qualities in Southey himself, the cause was a great national cause, and the feeling was intensified by centuries of tradition, while the incidents were wonderful in themselves. All these appealed strongly to Southey's nature, yet he tells the stirring tale in easy, graceful prose, his feelings, indeed, at glowing heat throughout, but the style maintained in an equable stoic calmness till the impassioned close when, for a moment, it bursts forth into flame in a tribute of praise and gratitude to the departed hero. The heroic spirit and devoted loyalty of Nelson are kept prominent throughout the narrative of his wonderful achievements in fighting for the safety and honour of his country :—

> " That white-faced shore
> Whose foot spurns back the ocean's roaring tides,—
> Even that England, hedged in with the main,
> That water-walled bulwark, still secure
> And confident from foreign purposes."

PROSE COMPOSITION.

FAMILIARITY with the best models and practice in composition are essential requisites in producing a good prose style. These are sufficient if the student is fortunate enough to possess an artistic literary sensibility that will lead him to appreciate and imitate the great masters, but in the case of each, it is neverthless true that

> "True ease in writing comes by art, not chance,
> As those move easiest who have learned to dance."

This art must be acquired by individual effort guided by a knowledge of the principles of rhetoric. A few of those principles, as far as they relate to prose composition, are given below. They are founded on Professor Bain's Composition and Rhetoric, to which the student is directed for a fuller treatment of the subject.

VOCABULARY.

The student should cultivate the habit of carefully selecting the proper words and phrases to express his thoughts. Our language is rich in synonymous terms, owing largely to the fact that our stock of words has come to us from various other languages. This peculiarity necessitates a thorough knowledge of the meaning and use of each word, and often requires nice taste in selecting the most suitable word. It affords us also a means of varying our diction to suit the language to the subject or to the nature of the thoughts. Our diction and phraseology thus differ in conversation and oratory, in common prose and in impassioned prose, while poetry differs from all prose in much of its diction and phraseology. A correct taste in the use of words, phrases and idioms should, therefore, be cultivated, and the student cannot begin too early in acquiring the habit of neatness and accuracy of expression. The habit once formed will "grow by what it feeds on," and may help to develop in the student the keen sensibility that marks the cultured mind.

THE SENTENCE.

As the sentence is the foundation of composition, great care should be taken in its formation. Skill in sentence building requires a knowledge of the principles of rhetoric as far as they relate to the order and the number of words used, the melody and rhythm of their sounds, and the various kinds of sentences the loose, the periodic, the balanced and the condensed—all of which are very important, but beyond the scope of these notes ; a few general principles in sentence structure, however, are the following :—

1. A series of long or of short sentences is tiresome.

2. Words, phrases and clauses should be so placed that their grammatical relation may be readily seen.

3. The beginning and the end are the emphatic places in a sentence, and it is a common rhetorical expedient to emphasize important words or phrases by transferring them from their natural place to the beginning or the end of the sentence.

4. A sentence should have unity ; one main thought should be prominent throughout. This unity may be preserved by the following means :

(1) Do not shift the scene in the course of a sentence.

(2) Do not crowd into one sentence heterogeneous ideas.

(3) Avoid excess of parentheses.

(4) Add nothing after a full and perfect close.

THE PARAGRAPH.

The present tendency of English prose writers is to make subjects prominent and distinct by exactness in paragraphing. Our prose has reduced sentence structure to a science, but the paragraph has been comparatively neglected up to the present. Like the sentence, it was formerly long and disjointed, and like the sentence, it is now made shorter, more compact and distinct. Professor Bain's rules for the paragraph are the following :—

1. It should have unity of subject matter, and should be free from digressions or irrelevant sentences.

2. The opening sentence, unless obviously preparatory, should indicate with prominence the subject of the paragraph.

3. The bearing of each sentence upon what precedes should be explicit and unmistakable. This is most important. The relation of one sentence or of one paragraph to another, should be clearly shown by the careful use of the proper conjunctions or phrases.

4. A paragraph should be consecutive. The thread of thought ought to run through it without interruption or dislocation.

5. When several consecutive sentences iterate or illustrate the same idea, they should, as far as possible, be formed alike. This may be called the rule of parallel construction. The principal subject and predicate should retain their places throughout.

6. There should be a due proportion between principal and subordinate statements. Everything should have bulk and prominence according to its importance.

Of ordinary composition, the most usual varieties are description and narration.

In description, the object is to present a definite picture to the mind by means of words. The art here is to follow some general plan, so as to avoid confusing the mind with a multiplicity of details. A general outline is sometimes taken, and the details are methodically filled in afterwards, or a description may follow a succession of aspects disclosed to a spectator surveying the whole. The imagination is assisted in following the description by allusions to individual objects and their associated circumstances, or by combining both methods of description, e. g., the plan and enumeration may be followed by the travellers point of view.

NARRATION.

Narrative composition is generally a series of descriptive pictures. It therefore requires careful attention to all the requirements of the art of description, but a few additional cautions are necessary :—

1. The scene should not be shifted oftener or to a greater extent than is absolutely necessary, and when shifted, clear intimation should be given of the change.

2. The first principle of narrative is to follow the order of events.

3. In narrating two or more streams of events, the forms of language announcing the transition from one to the other should be explicit. Separating them into distinct paragraphs, or chapters, contributes to this end.

In resuming an interrupted thread of narrative, a backward view is sometimes taken by means of a summary.

In history there are many concurrent streams of events to be conducted. These must be carefully distinguished ; the transitions from one to the other must be clearly indicated, and the memory should be occasionally refreshed by introductory summaries. History recounting the grand stream of human or national life admits of a certain elevation of style, and of many of the arts of poetry. But Southey's easy narrative has little embellishment. He followed his own directions as to historical style given to his brother : "A Welsh triad might comprehend all the rules of style. Say what you have to say as perspicuously as possible, as briefly as possible, and as rememberably as possible, and take no other thought about it. Omit none of those little circumstances which give life to narration, and bring old manners, old feeling and old times before your eyes."

Biography gives the experience of a life as illustrative of important truths respecting man's physical and mental nature. But the lives of distinguished men are always interesting, and a biography has often no further aim than to gratify that interest. The leading characteristics and guiding principle of the life should be clearly indicated, and the details illustrating these should be as full as possible. It admits more fully than history of poetic embellishment.

SOUTHEY'S LIFE OF NELSON.

1. NELSON was welcomed in England with every mark of popular honour. At Yarmouth, where he landed, every ship in the harbour hoisted her colours. The mayor and corporation waited upon him with the freedom of the town, and accompanied him in procession to church, with all the naval officers on shore and the principal inhabitants. Bonfires and illuminations concluded the day; and on the morrow the volunteer cavalry drew up and saluted him as he departed, and followed the carriage to the borders of the county. At Ipswich the people came out to meet him, drew him a mile into the town and three miles out. (*a*) When he was in the *Agamemnon* he wished to represent this place in Parliament, and some of his friends had consulted the leading men of the corporation; the result was not successful, and Nelson, observing that he would endeavour to find out a preferable path into Parliament, said there might come a time when the people of Ipswich would think it an honour to have had him for their representative. In London he was feasted by the City, drawn by the populace from Ludgate Hill to Guildhall, and received the thanks of the Common Council for his great victory, (*b*) and a golden-hilted sword studded with diamonds. Nelson had every earthly blessing except domestic happiness: he had forfeited (*c*) that for ever. Before he had been three months in England he separated from Lady Nelson. Some of his last words to her were: "I call God to witness there is nothing in you or your conduct that I wish otherwise." (*d*) This was the consequence of his infatuated attachment to Lady Hamilton. (*e*) It had before caused a quarrel with his son-in-law, and (*f*)

occasioned remonstrances from his truest friends, which produced no other effect than that of making him displeased with them and more dissatisfied with himself.

2. The (*a*) Addington administration was just at this time formed, and Nelson, who had solicited employment, and been made vice-admiral of the (*b*) blue, was sent to the Baltic, as second in command under Sir Hyde Parker, by (*c*) Earl St. Vincent, the new First Lord of the Admiralty. The three northern Courts had formed a confederacy for making England resign her (*d*) naval rights. Of these Courts, Russia was guided by the passions of its emperor, Paul, a man not without fits of generosity and some natural goodness, but subject to the wildest humours of caprice, and (*e*) crazed by the possession of greater power than can ever be safely or perhaps innocently possessed by weak (*f*) humanity. Denmark was (*g*) French at heart; ready to co-operate in all the views of France, to recognize all her usurpations, and obey all her injunctions. Sweden, under a king whose principles were right and whose feelings were generous, but who had a taint of hereditary insanity, acted in acquiescence with the dictates of two powers whom it feared to offend. The Danish navy at this time consisted of twenty-three ships of the line, with about thirty-one frigates and smaller vessels, exclusive of guardships. The Swedes had eighteen ships of the line, fourteen frigates and sloops, seventy-four galleys and smaller vessels, besides gunboats; and this force was in a far better state of equipment than the Danish. The Russians had eighty-two sail of the line and forty frigates. Of these, there were forty seven sail of the line at Cronstadt, Revel, Petersburg, and Archangel; but the Russian fleet was ill-manned, ill-officered, and ill-equipped. Such a combination under the influence of France would soon have become formidable; and never did the British Cabinet display more decision than in instantly preparing to crush it. They erred, however, in permitting any petty consideration to prevent them from

appointing Nelson to the command. The public properly
murmured at seeing it entrusted to another; and he himself
said to Earl St. Vincent, that, circumstanced as he was, this
expedition would probably be the last service that he should
ever perform. The Earl, in reply, besought him, for God's
sake, not to suffer himself to be carried away by any sudden
impulse.

3. The season happened to unusually favourable; so mild a
winter had not been known in the Baltic for many years.
When Nelson joined the fleet at Yarmouth he found the admiral "a little nervous about dark nights and fields of ice."
" But we must brace up," (a) said he; "these are not times for
nervous systems. I hope we shall give our northern enemies
that hailstorm of bullets which gives our dear country the
dominion of the sea. We have it, and all the devils in the
north cannot take it from us, if our wooden walls have fair
play." Before the fleet left Yarmouth it was sufficiently known
that its destination was against Denmark. Some Danes, who
belonged to the *Amazon* frigate, went to Captain Riou, and
telling him what they had heard, begged that he would get
them exchanged into a ship bound on some other destination.
"They had no wish," they said, "to quit the British service;
but they entreated that they might not be forced to fight
against their own country." There was not in our whole navy
a man who had a higher and more chivalrous sense of duty
than Riou. Tears came into his eyes while the men were
speaking; without making any reply, he instantly ordered his
boat, and did not return to the *Amazon* until he could tell them
that their wish was effected.

4. The fleet sailed on the 12th of March. Mr. Vansittart
sailed in it, the British Cabinet still hoping to obtain its end
by negotiation. It was well for England that Sir Hyde Parker
placed a fuller confidence in Nelson than the Government seems
to have done at this most important crisis. Her enemies

might well have been astonished at learning that any other
man should for a moment have been thought of for the
command. But so little deference was paid, even at this time,
to his intuitive and all-commanding genius, that when the fleet
had reached its first rendezvous, at the entrance of the Cattegat,
he had received no official communication whatever of the
intended operations. His own mind had been made up upon
them with its accustomed decision. "All I have gathered of
our first plans," said he, "I disapprove most exceedingly.
Honour may arise from them; good cannot. I hear we are
likely to anchor outside of Cronenburg Castle, instead of
Copenhagen, which would would give weight to our negotiation.
A Danish minister would think twice before he would put his
name to war with England, when the next moment he would
probably see his master's fleet in flames and his capital in ruins.
The Dane should see our flag every moment he lifted up his
head."

5. Mr. Vansittart left the fleet at the Scaw, and preceded
it in a frigate with a flag of truce. Precious time was lost by
this delay, which was to be purchased by the dearest blood of
Britain and Denmark: according to the Danes themselves, the
intelligence that a British fleet was seen off the Sound produced
a much more general alarm in Copenhagen than its actual
arrival in the roads; for their means of defence were at that
time in such a state that they could hardly hope to resist, still
less to repel, an enemy. On the 21st Nelson had a long conference with Sir Hyde; and the next day addressed a letter
to him worthy of himself and of the occasion. Mr. Vansittart's
report had then been received. It represented the Danish
Government as in the highest degree hostile, and their state of
preparation as exceeding what our Cabinet had supposed
possible; for Denmark had profited, with all activity, of the
leisure (a) which had so impolitically been given her. "The
more I have reflected," said Nelson to his commander, "the

more I am confirmed in opinion that not a moment should be
lost in attacking the enemy. They will every day and every
hour be stronger: we shall never be so good a match for them
as at this moment. The only consideration is, how to get at
them with the least risk to our ships. Here you are, with
almost the safety—certainly with the honour—of England
more entrusted to you than ever (*b*) yet fell to the lot of any
British officer. On your decision depends whether our country
shall be degraded in the eyes of Europe, or whether she shall
rear her head higher than ever. Again I do repeat, never did
our country depend so much upon the success of any fleet as
on this. How best to honour her and abate the pride of her
enemies must be the subject of your deepest consideration."

6. (*a*) Supposing him to force the passage of the Sound,
Nelson thought some damage might be done among the masts
and yards, though perhaps not one one of them but would be
serviceable again. "If the wind be fair," said he, "and you
determine to attack the ships and Crown Islands, you must
expect the natural issue of such a battle—ships crippled, and
perhaps one or two lost, for the wind which carries you in
will most probably not bring out a crippled ship. This method
I call taking the bull by the horns. It, however, will not prevent
the Revel ships or the Swedes from joining the Danes; and to
prevent this is, in my humble opinion, a measure absolutely
necessary, and still to attack Copenhagen." For this he proposed two modes. One was to pass Cronenburg, taking the
risk of danger, take the deepest and straightest channel along
the Middle Grounds, and then coming down the Garbar, or
King's Channel, attack the Danish line of floating batteries
and ships as might be found convenient. This would prevent
a junction, and might give an opportunity of bombarding
Copenhagen. Or to take the passage of the Belt, which might
be accomplished in four or five days, and then the attack by
Draco might be made and the junction of the Russians prevented.

Supposing them through the Belt, he proposed that a detach
ment of the fleet should be sent to destroy the Russian squadron
at Revel, and that the business at Copenhagen should be attempted with the remainder. "The measure," he said, "might
be thought bold: but the boldest measures are the safest."

7. The pilots, as men who had nothing but safety to think
of, were terrified by the formidable report of the batteries of
Elsinore, and the (a) tremendous preparations which our
negotiators, who were now returned from their fruitless mission,
had witnessed. They therefore persuaded Sir Hyde to prefer
the passage of the Belt. "Let it be by the Sound, by the
Belt, or anyhow," cried Nelson; "only lose not an hour!" On
the 26th they sailed for the Belt: such was the habitual reserve
of Sir Hyde that his own captain, the (b) captain of the fleet,
did not know which course he had resolved to take till the fleet
were getting under (c) weigh. When Captain Domett was
thus apprised of it, he felt it his duty to represent to the admiral
his belief that, if that course were persevered in, the ultimate
object would be totally defeated. It was liable to long delays
and to (d) accidents of ships grounding. In the whole fleet
there were only one captain and one pilot who knew anything
of this formidable passage (as it was then deemed), and their
knowledge was very slight. Their instructions did not authorize
them to attempt it. Supposing them safe through the Belts,
the heavy ships could not come over the Grounds to attack
Copenhagen, and light vessels would have no effect on such a
line of defence as had been prepared against them. Domett
urged these reasons so forcibly that Sir Hyde's opinion was
shaken, and he consented to bring the fleet to, and send for
Nelson on board. There can be little doubt (e) but that the
expedition would have failed if Captain Domett had not thus
timely and earnestly given his advice. Nelson entirely agreed
with him, and it was finally determined to take the passage of
the Sound, and the fleet returned to its former anchorage.

8. The next day was more idly expended in despatching a flag of truce to the governor of Cronenburg Castle, to ask whether he had received orders to fire at the British fleet, as the admiral must consider the first gun to be a declaration of war on the part of Denmark. A soldier-like and becoming answer was returned to this formality. The governor said that the British Minister had not been sent away from Copenhagen, but had obtained a passport at his own demand. He himself, as a soldier, could not meddle with politics, but he was not at liberty to suffer a fleet, of which the intention was not yet known, to approach the guns of the castle which he had the honour to command, and he requested, if the British admiral should think proper to make any proposals to the King of Denmark, that he might be apprised of it before the fleet approached nearer. During this intercourse a Dane, who came on board the commander's ship, having occasion to express his business in writing, found the pen blunt, and holding it up, sarcastically said, "If your guns are not better pointed than your pens, you will make little impression on Copenhagen!"

9. On that day intelligence reach the admiral of the loss of one of his fleet, the *Incincible*, seventy-four, wrecked on a sandbank as she was coming out of Yarmouth: 400 of her men perished in her. Nelson, who was now appointed to lead the van, shifted his flag to the *Elephant*, Captain Foley—a lighter ship than the *St. George*, and therefore fitter for the expected operations. The two following days were calm. Orders had been given to pass the Sound as soon as the wind would permit, and on the afternoon of the 29th the ships were cleared for action with an alacrity characteristic of British seamen. At daybreak on the 30th it blew a topsail breeze from N.W. The signal was given and the fleet moved on in order of battle; Nelson's division in the van, Sir Hyde's in the centre, and Admiral Graves' in the rear.

10. Great actions, whether military or naval, have generally given celebrity to the scenes from whence they are denominated, and thus petty villages, and capes, and bays, known only to the coasting trader, become associated with mighty deeds, and their names are made conspicuous in the history of the world. Here, however, the scene was every way worthy of the drama. The political importance of the Sound is such that grand objects are not needed there to impress the imagination, yet is the channel full of grand and interesting objects, both of art and nature. This passage, which Denmark had so long considered as the key of the Baltic, is in its narrowest part about three miles wide, and here the city of Elsinore is situated, except Copenhagen the most flourishing of the Danish towns. Every vessel which passes lowers her top-gallant-sails and pays toll at Elsinore, a toll which is believed to have had its origin in the consent of the traders to that sea, Denmark taking upon itself the charge of constructing lighthouses and erecting signals to mark the shoals and rocks from the Cattegat to the Baltic; and they on their part agreeing that all ships should pass this way in order that all might pay their shares; none from that time using the passage of the Belt, because it was not fitting that they who enjoyed the benefit of the beacons in dark and stormy weather should evade contributing to them in fair seasons and summer nights. Of late years about ten thousand vessels had annually paid this contribution in time of peace. Adjoining Elsinore, and at the edge of the peninsular promontory, upon the (a) nearest point of land to the Swedish coast, stands Cronenburg Castle, built after (b) Tycho Brahe's design, a magnificent pile—at once a palace and fortress and state prison, with its spires and towers, and battlements and batteries. On the left of the strait is the old Swedish city of Helsinburg, at the foot and on the side of a hill. To the north of Helsinburg the shores are steep and rocky ; they lower to the south, and the distant spires of Landscrona, Lund, and Malmoe are seen

in the flat country. The Danish shores consist (c) partly of
ridges of sand, but more frequently their slopes are covered
with rich wood, and villages and villas, denoting the vicinity
of a great capital. The islands of Huen, Satholm, and Amak
appear in the widening channel; and at the distance of twenty
miles from Elsinore stands Copenhagen, in full view—the best
city of the North, and one of the finest capitals of Europe,
visible, with its stately spires, far off. Amid these magnificent
objects there are some which possess a peculiar interest for the
recollections which they call forth. The isle of Huen, a lovely
domain, about six miles in circumference, had been the munifi-
cent gift of Frederic the Second to Tycho Brahe. Here most
of his discoveries were made, and here the ruins are to be seen
of his observatory, and of the mansion where he was visited by
princes, and where, with a princely spirit, he received and
entertained all comers from all parts, and promoted science by
his liberality as well as by his labours. (d) Elsinore is a name
familiar to English ears, being inseparably associated with
Hamlet, and one of the noblest works of human genius.
Cronenburg had been the scene of deeper tragedy: here (e)
Queen Matilda was confined, the victim of a foul and murderous
Court intrigue. Here, amid heart-breaking griefs, she found
consolation in nursing her infant. Here she took her everlasting
leave of that infant, when, by the interference of England, her
own deliverance was obtained, and as the ship bore her away
from a country where the venal indiscretions of youth and
unsuspicious gaiety had been so cruelly punished, upon these
towers she fixed her eyes, and stood upon the deck, obstinately
gazing towards them till the last speck had disappeared.

11. The Sound being the only frequented entrance to the
Baltic, the great Mediterranean of the North, few parts of the sea
display so frequent a navigation. In the height of the season
not fewer than a hundred vessels pass every four-and-twenty
hours for many weeks in succession; but never (a) had so busy

or so splendid a scene been exhibited there as on this day, when
the British fleet prepared to force that passage where till now
all ships had vailed their top-sails to the flag of Denmark.
The whole force consisted of fifty-one sail of various descriptions,
of which sixteen were of the line. The greater part of the
boom and gun vessels took their stations off Cronenburg Castle,
to cover the fleet ; while others, on the larboard, were ready to
engage the Swedish shore. The Danes having improved every
moment which ill-timed negotiation and battling weather gave
them, had lined their shore with batteries ; and as soon as the
Monarch, which was the leading ship, came abreast of them,
a fire was opened from about a hundred pieces of cannon and
mortars : our light vessels immediately, in return, opened their
fire upon the castle. Here were all the (*b*) pompous circumstance and exciting reality of war without its effects ; for this
ostentatious display was but a bloodless prelude to the wide
and sweeping destruction which was soon to follow. The
enemy's shot (*c*) fell near enough to splash the water on board
our ships : not relying upon any forbearance of the Swedes, (*d*)
they meant to have kept the mid-channel ; but when they perceived that not a shot was fired from Helsinburg, and that
no batteries were to be seen on the Swedish shore, they inclined
to that side, so as (*e*) completely to get out of reach of the
Danish guns. The uninterrupted blaze which was kept up
from them till the fleet had passed served only to exhilarate
our sailors, and afford them matter for jest, as the shot fell in
showers a full cable's length short of its destined aim. A few
rounds were returned from some of our leading ships till they
perceived its inutility : this, however, occasioned the only
bloodshed of the day, some of our men being killed and
wounded by the bursting of a gun. As soon as the main body
had passed, the gun-vessels followed, desisting from their bombardment, which had been as (*f*) innocent as that of the enemy ;
and about midday the whole fleet anchored between the island

of Huen and Copenhagen. Sir Hyde, with Nelson, Admiral Graves, some of the senior captains, and the commanding officers of the artillery and the troops, then proceeded in a lugger to reconnoitre the enemy's means of defence—a formidable line of ships, radeaus, pontoons, galleys, fire-ships and gunboats, flanked and supported by extensive batteries, and occupying, from one extreme point to the other, an extent of nearly four miles.

12. A council of war was held in the afternoon. It was apparent that the Danes could not be attacked without great difficulty and risk ; and some of the members of the council spoke of the number of the Swedes and the Russians whom they should afterwards have to engage as a consideration which ought to be borne in mind. Nelson, who kept pacing the cabin, impatient as he ever was of anything which savoured of irresolution, repeatedly said, "The more numerous the better: I wish they were twice as many—the easier the victory, depend on it." The plan upon which he had determined, if ever it should be his fortune to bring a Baltic fleet to action, was to attack the head of their line, and confuse their movements. "Close with a Frenchman," he used to say, "but out-manoeuvre a Russian." He offered his services for the attack, requiring ten sail of the line and the whole of the smaller craft. Sir Hyde gave him two more line-of-battle ships than he asked, and left everything to his judgment.

13. The enemy's force was not the only nor the greatest obstacle with which the British fleet had to contend ; there was another to overcome before they could come in contact with it. The channel was little known and extremely intricate ; all the buoys had been removed, and the Danes considered (a) this difficulty as almost insuperable, thinking the channel impracticable for so large a fleet. Nelson himself saw the soundings made and the buoys laid down, boating it on this exhaustive service, (b) day and night, till it was effected. When this was

done he thanked God for having enabled him to get through this difficult part of his duty. "It had worn him down," he said, "and was infinitely more grievous to him than any resistance which he could experience from the enemy."

14. At the first council of war opinions inclined to an attack from the eastward : but the next day, the wind being southerly, after a second examination of the Danish position, it was determined to attack from the south, approaching in the manner which Nelson had suggested in his first thoughts. On the morning of the 1st of April the whole fleet removed to an anchorage within two leagues of the town, and off the N.W. end of the Middle Ground; a shoal lying exactly before the town, at about three-quarters of a mile (*a*) distance, and extending along its whole sea front. The King's Channel, where there is deep water, is between this shoal and the town, and here the Danes had arranged their line of defence as near the shore as possible : nineteen ships and floating batteries, flanked, at the end nearest the town, by the Crown Batteries, which were two artificial islands at the mouth of the harbour—most formidable works; the larger one having, by the Danish account, sixty-six guns, but, as Nelson believed, eighty-eight. The fleet having anchored, Nelson, with Riou in the *Amazon*, made his last examination of the ground, and about one o'clock, returning to his own ship, threw out the signal to weigh. It was received with a shout throughout the whole division ; they weighed with a light and favourable wind : the narrow channel between the island of Saltholm and the Middle Ground had been accurately buoyed ; the small craft pointed out the course distinctly ; Riou led the way : the whole division coasted along the outer edge of the shoal, doubled its further extremity, and anchored there off Draco Point, just as the darkness closed—the headmost of the enemy's line not being more than two miles distant. The signal to prepare for action had been made early in the evening, and, as his own anchor dropped, Nelson called out : "I will

fight them the moment I have a fair wind." It had been arranged that Sir Hyde, with the remaining ships, should weigh
on the following morning at the same time as Nelson, to menace
the Crown Batteries on his side, and the four ships of the line
which lay at the entrance of the arsenal, and to cover our own
disabled ships as they came out of action.

15. The Danes, meantime, had not been idle : no sooner did
the guns of Cronenburg make it known to the (a) whole city
that all negotiation was at end, that the British fleet was passing the Sound, and that the dispute between the two crowns
must now be decided by arms, than a spirit displayed itself,
most honourable to the Danish character. All ranks offered
themselves to the service of their country ; the university furnished a corps of twelve hundred youths, the flower of Denmark : it was one of those emergencies in which little drilling
or discipline is necessary to render courage available ; they had
nothing to learn but how to manage the guns, and were employed day and night in practising them. When the movements of Nelson's squadron were perceived, it was known when
and where the attack was to be expected, and the line of defence
was manned indiscriminately by soldiers, sailors and citizens.
Had not the whole attention of the Danes been directed to
strengthen their (b) own means of defence, they might most
materially have annoyed the invading squadron, and perhaps
frustrated the impending attack, for the British ships were
crowded in an anchoring ground of little extent ; it was calm,
so that mortar boats might have acted against them to the utmost advantage, and they were within range of shells from Amak
Island. A few fell among them, but the enemy soon ceased to
fire. It was learnt afterwards that, fortunately for the fleet, the
bed of the mortar had given way, and the Danes either could
not get it replaced, or in the darkness lost the direction.

16. This was an awful night for Copenhagen— far more so
than for the British fleet, where the men were accustomed to

battle and victory, and had none of those objects before their
eyes which render death terrible. Nelson sat down to table
with a large party of his officers ; he was, as he was ever wont
to be when on the eve of action, in high spirits, and drank to a
leading wind and to the success of the morrow. After supper
(a) they returned to their respective ships, except Riou, who
remained to arrange the order of battle with Nelson and Foley,
and to draw up instructions ; Hardy, meantime, went in a
small boat to examine the channel between (b) them and the
enemy, approaching so near that he sounded round their leading ship with a pole, lest the noise of throwing the lead should
discover him. The incessant fatigue of body as well as (c) mind
which Nelson had undergone during the last three days had so
exhausted him that he was earnestly urged to go to his cot,
and his old servant, Allen, using that kind of authority which
long and affectionate services entitled and enabled him to
assume on such occasions, insisted upon his complying. The
cot was placed on the floor, and he continued to dictate from
it. About eleven, Hardy returned, and reported the practic-
ability of the channel, and the depth of water up to the enemy's
line. About one the orders were completed, and half-a-dozen
clerks in the foremost cabin proceeded to transcribe them,
Nelson frequently calling out to them from his cot to hasten
their work, for the wind was becoming fair. Instead of attempting to get a few hours of sleep, he was constantly receiving reports on this important point. At daybreak it was
announced as becoming perfectly fair. The clerks finished
their work about six. Nelson, who was already up, breakfasted
and made signal for all captains. The land forces and five
hundred seamen, under Captain Freemantle and the Honourable Colonel Stewart, were to storm the Crown Battery as soon
as its fire should be silenced ; and Riou--whom Nelson had
never seen till this expedition, but whose worth he had instantly perceived, and appreciated as it deserved--had the

Blanche and *Alcmene* frigates, the *Dart* and *Arrow* sloops, and the *Zephyr* and *Otter* fire-ships, given him, with a special command to act as circumstances might require : every other ship had its station appointed.

17. Between eight and nine the pilots and masters were ordered on board the admiral's ship. The pilots were mostly men who had been mates in Baltic traders, and their hesitation about the bearing of the east end of the shoal and the exact line of deep water gave ominous warning of how little their knowledge was to be trusted. The signal for action had been made, the wind was fair—not a moment to be lost. Nelson urged them to be steady, to be resolute, and to decide : but they wanted the only ground for steadiness and decision in such cases, and Nelson had reason to regret that he had not trusted to Hardy's single report. This was one of the most painful moments of his life, and he always spoke of it with bitterness. " I experienced in the Sound," said he, "the misery of having the honour of our country intrusted to a set of pilots who have no other thought than to keep the ships clear of danger, and their own silly heads clear of shot. Everybody knows what I must have suffered, and if any merit attaches itself to me, it was for combating the dangers of the shallows in defiance of them." At length Mr. Bryerly, the master of the *Bellona*, declared that he was prepared to lead the fleet : his judgment was acceded to by the rest ; they returned to their ships, and at half-past nine the signal was made to weigh in succession.

18. Captain Murray, in the *Edgar*, led the way, the *Agamemnon* was next in order, but on the first attempt to leave her anchorage she could not weather the edge of the shoal, and Nelson had the grief to see his old ship, in which he had performed so many years' gallant services, immovably aground at a moment when her help was so greatly required. Signal was then made for the *Polyphemus*, and this change in the order of

sailing was executed with the utmost promptitude, yet so much
delay had thus been unavoidably occasioned that the *Edgar*
was for some time unsupported, and the *Polyphemus*, whose
place should be at the end of the enemy's line, where their
strength was the greatest, could get no farther than the beginning, owing to the difficulty of the channel ; there she occupied
indeed an efficient station, but one where her presence was
less required.   The *Isis* followed, with better fortune, and took
her own berth.   The *Bellona*, Sir Thomas Boulden Thompson,
kept too close on the starboard shoal, and grounded abreast of
the outer ship of the enemy ; this was the more vexatious, in-
asmuch as the wind was fair, the room ample, and three ships
had led the way.   The *Russell*, following the *Bellona*, grounded
in like manner ; both were within reach of shot, but their
absence from their intended stations was severely felt.   Each
ship had been ordered to pass her leader on the starboard side,
because the water was supposed to shoal on the larboard shore.
Nelson, who came next after these two ships, thought they had
kept too far on the starboard direction, and made signal for
them to close with the enemy, not knowing that they were
aground, but when he perceived that they did not obey the
signal, he ordered the *Elephant's* helm to starboard, and went
within these ships ; thus quitting the appointed order of sailing, and guiding those which were to follow.   The greater part
of the fleet were probably, by this act of promptitude on his
part, saved from going on shore.   Each ship, as she arrived
nearly opposite to her appointed station, let her anchor go by
the stern, and presented her broadside to the Danes.   The distance between each was about half a cable.   The action was
fought nearly at the distance of a cable's length from the
enemy.   This, which rendered its continuance so long, was
owing to the ignorance and consequent indecision of the pilots.
In pursuance of the same error which had led the *Bellona* and
the *Russell* aground, they, when the lead was at a quarter less

five, refused to approach nearer, in dread of shoaling their water on the larboard shore, a fear altogether erroneous, for the water deepened up to the very side of the enemy's line.

19. At five minutes after ten the action began. The first half of our fleet was engaged in about half an hour, and by half past eleven the battle became general. The plan of the attack had been complete; but seldom has any plan been more disconcerted by untoward accidents. Of twelve ships of the line, one was entirely useless, and two others in a situation where they could not render half the service which was required of them. Of the squadron of gun-brigs only one could get into action : the rest were prevented by baffling currents from weathering the eastern end of the shoal; and only two of the bomb-vessels could reach their station on the Middle Ground, and open their mortars on the Arsenal, firing over both fleets. Riou took the vacant station against the Crown Battery with his frigates, attempting with that unequal force a service in which three sail of the line had been directed to assist.

20. Nelson's agitation had been extreme when he saw himself, before the action began, deprived of a fourth part of his ships of the line; but no sooner was he in battle, where his squadron was received with the fire of more than a thousand guns, than, as if that artillery, like music, had driven away all care and painful thoughts, his countenance brightened, and, as a bystander describes him, his conversation became joyous, animated, elevated, and delightful. The commander-in-chief, meantime, near enough to the scene of action to know the unfavourable accidents which had so materially weakened Nelson, and yet too distant to know the real state of the contending parties, suffered the most dreadful anxiety. To get to his assistance was impossible; both wind and current were against him. Fear for the event in such circumstances would naturally preponderate in the bravest mind; and at one o'clock, perceiving that after three hours' endurance, the enemy's fire

was unslackened, he began to despair of success. "I will make the signal of recall," said he to his captain, (*a*) "for Nelson's sake. If he is in a condition to continue the action successfully, he will disregard it; if he is not, it will be an excuse for his retreat, and no blame can be imputed to him." Captain Domett urged him (*b*) at least to delay the signal till he could communicate with Nelson, but, in Sir Hyde's opinion, the danger was too pressing for delay. "The fire," he said, "was too hot for Nelson to oppose; a retreat, he thought, must be made. He was aware of the consequences to his own personal reputation, but it would be cowardly in him to leave Nelson to bear the whole shame of the failure, if shame it should be deemed." Under a mistaken judgment,* therefore, but with this disinterested and generous feeling, he made the signal for retreat.

21. Nelson was at this time, in all the excitement of action, pacing the quarter-deck. A shot through the mainmast knocked the splinters about, and he observed to one of his officers with a smile, "It is warm work; and this day may be the last to any of us at a moment;" and then, stopping short at the gangway, added, with emotion—"but mark you, I would not be elsewhere for thousands." About this time the signal lieutenant called out that No. 39 (the signal for discontinuing the action) was thrown out by the commander-in-chief. He continued to walk the deck, and appeared to take no notice of it. The signal officer met him at the next turn, and asked him if he should repeat it. "No," he replied, "acknowledge it." Presently he called after him to know if the signal for close action was still hoisted, and being answered in the affirmative said, "Mind you keep it so." He now paced the deck, moving the stump of his lost arm in a manner which always indicated great emotion. "Do you know," said he to Mr. Ferguson, "what is shown on board the commander-in-chief? No. 39." Mr. Fergu-

---

* I have great pleasure in rendering this justice to Sir Hyde Parker's reasoning. The fact is here stated upon the highest and most unquestionable authority

son asked what that meant. "Why, to leave off action!" Then, shrugging up his shoulders, he repeated the words—"Leave off action? Now, damn me if I do! You know, Foley," turning to the captain, "I have only one eye; I have a right to be blind sometimes." And then, putting the glass to his blind eye, in that mood of mind which sports with bitterness, he exclaimed, "I really do not see the signal!" Presently he exclaimed, "Damn the signal! Keep mine for closer battle flying! That's the way I answer such signals! Nail mine to the mast!" Admiral Graves, who was so situated that he could not discern what was done on board the *Elephant*, disobeyed Sir Hyde's signal in like manner; whether by fortunate mistake or by a like brave intention has not been made known. The other ships of the line, looking only to Nelson, continued the action. The signal, however, saved Riou's little squadron, but did not save its heroic leader. This squadron, which was nearest the commander-in-chief, obeyed and hauled off. It had suffered severely in its most unequal contest. For a long time the *Amazon* had been firing, enveloped in smoke, when Riou desired his men to stand fast and let the smoke clear off, that they might see what they were about. A fatal order, for the Danes then got clear sight of her from the batteries, and pointed their guns with such tremendous effect that nothing but the signal for retreat saved this frigate from destruction. "What will Nelson think of us?" was Riou's mournful exclamation when he unwillingly drew off. He had been wounded in the head by a splinter, and was sitting on a gun, encouraging his men, when, just as the *Amazon* showed her stern to the Trekroner Battery, his clerk was killed by his side, and another shot swept away several marines who were hauling in the main-brace. "Come, then, my boys," cried Riou, "let us die all together!" The words had scarcely been uttered before a raking shot cut him in two. Except had it been Nelson himself, the British navy could not have suffered a severer loss.

22. The action continued along the line with unabated vigour on our side, and with the most determined resolution on the part of the Danes. They fought to great advantage, because most of the vessels in their line of defence were without masts; the few which had any standing had their top-masts struck, and the hulls could only be seen at intervals. The *Isis* must have been destroyed by the superior weight of her enemy's fire, if Captain Inman, in the *Desirée* frigate, had not judiciously taken a situation which enabled him to rake the Dane, and if the *Polyphemus* had not also relieved her. (*a*) Both in the *Bellona* and the *Isis* many men were lost by the bursting of their guns. The former ship was about forty years old, and these guns were believed to be the same which she had first taken to sea; they where probably originally faulty, for the fragments were full of little air-holes. The *Bellona* lost seventy five men; the *Isis*, 110; the *Monarch*, 210. She was, more than any other line-of-battle ship, exposed to the great battery; and supporting at the same time the united fire of the *Holstein* and the *Zealand*, her loss this day exceeded that of any (*b*) single ship during the whole war. Amid the (*c*) tremendous carnage in this vessel some of the men displayed a singular instance of coolness; the pork and peas happened to be in the kettle; a shot knocked its contents about; they picked up the pieces, and ate and fought at the same time.

23. The Prince Royal had taken his station upon one of the batteries, from whence he beheld the action and issued his orders. Denmark had never been engaged in so arduous a contest, and never did the Danes more nobly display their national courage—a courage not more unhappily than impoliticly exerted in subserviency to the interest of France. Captain Thura, of the *Indfoedsretten*, fell early in the action, and all his officers, except one lieutenant and one marine officer, were either killed or wounded. In the confusion the colours were either struck or shot away; but she was moored athwart one of

the batteries in such a situation that the British made no attempt to board her, and a boat was despatched to the prince to inform him of her situation. He turned to those about him, and said, "Gentlemen, Thura is killed; which of you will take the command?" Schroedersee, a captain who had lately resigned on account of extreme ill health, answered in a feeble voice, "I will!" and hastened on board. The crew, perceiving a new commander coming alongside, hoisted their colours again, and fired a broadside. Schroedersee, when he came on deck, found himself surrounded by the dead and wounded, and called to those in the boat to get quickly on board; a ball struck him at that moment. A lieutenant who had accompanied him then took the command, and continued to fight the ship. A youth of seventeen, by name Villemoes, particularly distinguished himself on this memorable day. He had volunteered to take the command of a floating battery, which was a raft, consisting merely of a number of beams nailed together with a flooring to support the guns; it was square, with a breastwork full of port-holes, and without masts—carrying twenty-four guns and 120 men. With this he got under the stern of the *Elephant*, below the reach of the stern-chasers, and under a heavy fire of small arms from the marines, fought his raft, till the truce was announced, with such skill as well as courage as to excite Nelson's warmest admiration.

24. Between one and two the fire of the Danes slackened; about two it ceased from the greater part of their line, and some of their lighter ships were adrift. It was, however, difficult to take possession of those which struck, because the batteries on Amak Island protected them, and because an irregular fire was kept up from the ships themselves as the boats approached. This arose from the nature of the action. The crews were continually reinforced from the shore, and fresh men coming on board did not inquire whether the flag had been struck, or perhaps did not heed it; many or most of them never

having been engaged in war before, knowing nothing therefore
of its laws, and thinking only of defending their country to
the last extremity. The *Danbrog* fired upon the *Elephant's*
boats in this manner, though her commodore had removed her
pendant and deserted her, though she had struck, and though
she was in flames. After she had been abandoned by the
commodore, Braun fought her till he lost his right hand,
and then Captain Lemming took the command. This unexpected renewal of her fire made the *Elephant* and *Glatton*
renew theirs, till she was not only silenced, but nearly every
man in the praams ahead and astern of her was killed. When
the smoke of their guns died away she was seen drifting in
flames before the wind, those of her crew who remained alive
and able to exert themselves throwing themselves out at her
port-holes.

25. Captain Rothe commanded the *Nyeborg* praam, and perceiving that she could not much longer be kept afloat, made for
the inner road. As he passed the line he found the *Aygershuus*
praam in a more miserable condition than his own; her masts
had all gone by the board, and she was on the point of sinking.
Rothe made fast a cable to her stern and towed her off, but he
could get her no farther than a shoal called Stubben, when she
sunk, and soon after he had worked the *Nyeborg* up to the
landing-place that vessel also sunk to her gunwale. Never did
any vessel come out of action in a more dreadful plight. The
stump of her foremast was the only stick standing; her cabin
had been stove in; every gun, except a single one, was dis-
mounted; and her deck was covered with shattered limbs and
dead bodies.

26. By half-past two the action had ceased along that part
of the line which was astern of the *Elephant*, but not with the
ships ahead and the Crown Batteries. Nelson, seeing the manner in which his boats were fired upon when they went to take
possession of the prizes, became angry, and said he must either

send on shore to have this irregular proceeding stopped, or send a fire-ship and burn them. Half the shot from the Trekroner and from the batteries at Amak at this time struck the surrendered ships, four of which had got close together, and the fire of the English in return was equally or even more destructive to these poor devoted Danes. Nelson, who was as humane as he was brave, was shocked at this massacre—for such he called it—and, with a presence of mind peculiar to himself, and never more signally displayed than now, he retired into the stern galley, and wrote thus to the Crown Prince :—" Vice-Admiral Lord Nelson has been commanded to spare Denmark when she no longer resists. The line of defence which covered her shores has struck to the British flag; but if the firing is continued on the part of Denmark, he must set on fire all the prizes that he has taken, without having the power of saving the men who have so nobly defended them. The brave Danes are the brothers and should never be the enemies of the English." A wafer was given him, but he ordered a candle to be brought from the cockpit, and sealed the letter with wax, affixing a larger seal than he ordinarily used. " This," said he, " is no time to appear hurried and informal." Captain Sir Frederick Thesiger, who acted as his aide-de-camp, carried this letter with a flag of truce. Meantime the fire of the ships ahead, and the approach of the *Ramilies* and *Defence* from Sir Hyde's division, which had now worked near enough to alarm the enemy, though not to injure them, silenced the remainder of the Danish line to the eastward of the Trekroner. That battery, however, continued its fire. This formidable work, owing to the want of the ships which had been destined to attack it, and the inadequate force of Riou's little squadron, was comparatively uninjured. Towards the close of the action it had been manned with nearly fifteen hundred men, and the intention of storming it, for which every preparation had been made, was abandoned as impracticable.

27. During Thesiger's absence Nelson sent for Freemantle from the *Ganges*, and consulted with him and Foley, whether it was advisable to advance with those ships which had sustained least damage against the yet uninjured part of the Danish line. They were decidedly of opinion that the best thing which could be done was, while the wind continued fair, to remove the fleet out of the intricate channel from which it had to retreat. In somewhat more than half-an-hour after Thesiger had been despatched the Danish adjutant-general, Lindholm, came bearing a flag of truce; upon which the Trekroner ceased to fire, and the action closed, after four hours continuance. He brought an inquiry from the prince; What was the object of Nelson's note? The British Admiral wrote in reply: "Lord Nelson's object in sending the flag of truce was humanity; he therefore consents that hostilities shall cease, and that the wounded Danes may be taken on shore. And Lord Nelson will take his prisoners out of the vessels, and burn or carry off his prizes as he shall think fit. Lord Nelson, with humble duty to his Royal Highness the Prince, will consider this the greatest victory he has ever gained if it may be the cause of a happy reconciliation and union between his own most gracious sovereign and his Majesty the King of Denmark." Sir Frederick Thesiger was despatched a second time with the reply; and the Danish adjutant-general was referred to the commander-in-chief for a conference upon this overture. Lindholm assenting to this, proceeded to the *London*, which was riding at anchor full four miles off; and Nelson losing not one of the critical moments which he had thus gained, made signal for his leading ships to weigh in succession—they had the shoal to clear, they were much crippled, and their course was immediately under the guns of the Trekroner.

28. The *Monarch* led the way. This ship had received six-and-twenty shot between wind and water. She had not a shroud standing; there was a double-headed shot in the heart

of her foremast; and the slightest wind would have sent every
mast over her side.* The imminent danger from which Nelson
had extricated himself soon became apparent; the *Monarch*
touched immediately upon a shoal, over which she was pushed
by the *Ganges* taking her amidships; the *Glatton* went clear;
but the other two, the *Defiance* and the *Elephant*, grounded
about a mile from the Trekroner, and there remained fixed for
many hours, in spite of all the exertions of their wearied crews.
The *Desirée* frigate also, at the other end of the line, having
gone toward the close of the action to assist the *Bellona*,
became fast on the same shoal. Nelson left the *Elephant*, soon
after she took the ground, to follow Lindholm. The heat of
action was over, and that kind of feeling which the surrounding
scene of havoc was so well fitted to produce pressed heavily
upon his exhausted spirits. The sky had suddenly become
overcast; white flags were waving from the mastheads of so
many shattered ships; the slaughter had ceased; but the grief
was to come, for the account of the dead was not yet made up,
and no man could tell for what friends he would have to mourn.
The very silence which follows the cessation of such a battle
becomes a weight upon the heart at first, rather than a relief:
and though the work of mutual destruction was at an end, the
Danbrog was at this time drifting about in flames; presently
she blew up, while our boats, which had put off in all directions to assist her, were endeavouring to pick up her devoted
crew, few of whom could be saved. The fate of these men,
after the gallantry which they had displayed, particularly
affected Nelson; for there was nothing in this action of that
indignation against the enemy, and that impression of retribu-
tive justice, which at the Nile had given a sterner temper to

---

* It would have been well if the fleet, before they went under the batteries,
had left their spare spars moored out of reach of shot. Many would have
been saved which were destroyed lying on the booms, and the hurt done by
their splinters would have been saved also. Small craft could have towed
them up when they were required, and after such an action so many must
necessarily be wanted, that if those which were not in use were wounded, it
might thus have been rendered impossible to refit the ships.

his mind, and a sense of austere delight in beholding the vengeance of which he was the appointed minister. The Danes were an honourable foe; they were of English mould as well as English blood; and now that the battle had ceased, he regarded them rather as brethren than as enemies. There was another reflection also, which mingled with these melancholy thoughts, and predisposed him to receive them. He was not here master of his own movements, as at Egypt; he had won the day by disobeying his orders; and in so far as he had been successful, had convicted the commander-in-chief of an error in judgment. "Well," said he as he left the *Elephant*, "I have fought contrary to orders, and I shall perhaps be hanged! Never mind, let them!"

29. This was the language of a man who, while he is giving utterance to an uneasy thought, clothes it half in jest because he half repents that it has been disclosed. His services had been too eminent on that day, his judgment too conspicuous, his success too signal, for any commander, however jealous of his own authority, or envious of another's merits, to express anything but satisfaction and gratitude, which Sir Hyde heartily felt and sincerely expressed. It was speedily agreed that their should be a suspension of hostilities for four-and-twenty hours; that all the prizes should be surrendered and the wounded Danes carried on shore. There was a pressing necessity for this, for the Danes, either from too much confidence in the strength of their position and the difficulty of the channel; or (*a*) supposing that the wounded might be carried on shore during the action, which was found totally impracticable; or perhaps from the confusion which the attack excited, had provided no surgeons; so that when our men boarded the captured ships they found many of the mangled and mutilated Danes bleeding to death for want of proper assistance—a scene of all (*b*) others the most shocking to a brave man's feelings.

30. The boats of Sir Hyde's division were actively employed all night in bringing out the prizes, and in getting afloat the ships which were on shore. At daybreak, Nelson, who had slept in his own ship, the *St. George*, rowed to the *Elephant*, and his delight at finding her afloat seemed to give him new life. There he took a hasty breakfast, praising the men for their exertions, and then pushed off to the prizes, which had not yet been removed. The *Zealand*, seventy-four, the last which struck, had drifted on the shoal under the Trekroner, and relying, as it seems, upon the protection which that battery might have afforded, refused to acknowledge herself captured, saying that, though it was true her flag was not to be seen, her pendant was still flying, Nelson ordered one of our brigs and three long-boats to approach her, and rowed up himself to one of the enemy's ships to communicate with the commodore. This officer proved to be an old acquaintance whom he had known in the West Indies; so he invited himself on board, and with that urbanity as well as decision which always characterised him, urged his claim to the *Zealand* so well that it was admitted. The men from the boats lashed a cable round her bowsprit, and the gun-vessel towed her away. It is affirmed, and probably with truth, that the Danes felt more pain at beholding this than at all their misfortunes on the preceding day ; and one of the officers, Commodore Steen Bille, went to the Trekroner Battery, and asked the commander why he had not sunk the *Zealand* rather than suffer her thus to be carried off by the enemy.

31. This was indeed a mournful day for Copenhagen ! It was Good Friday ; but the general agitation and the mourning which was in every house made all distinction of days be forgotten. There were at that hour thousands in that city who felt, and more perhaps who needed, the consolations of Christianity, but few or none who could be calm enough to think of its observances. The English were actively employed in

refitting their own ships, securing the prizes, and distributing the prisoners; the Danes, in carrying on shore and disposing of the wounded and the dead. It had been a murderous action. Our loss in killed and wounded was nine hundred and fifty-three. Part of this slaughter might have been spared. The commanding officer of the troops on board one of our ships asked where his men should be stationed? He was told that they could be of no use; that they were not near enough for musketry, and were not wanted at the guns; they had therefore better go below. This, he said, was impossible—it would be a disgrace that could never be wiped away. They were therefore drawn up upon the gangway, to satisfy this cruel point of honour; and there, without the possibility of annoying the enemy, they were mowed down! The loss of the Danes, including prisoners, amounted to about six thousand. The negotiations meantime went on, and it was agreed that Nelson should have an interview with the prince the following day. Hardy and Freemantle landed with him. This was a thing as unexampled as the other circumstances of the battle. A strong guard was appointed to escort him to the palace, as much for the purpose of security as of honour. The populace according to the British account, showed a mixture of admiration, curiosity, and displeasure at beholding that man in the midst of them who had inflicted such wounds upon Denmark. But there were neither acclamations nor murmurs. "The people," says a Dane, "did not degrade themselves with the former, nor disgrace themselves with the latter: the Admiral was received as one brave enemy ever ought to receive another. He was received with respect." The preliminaries of the negotiation were adjusted at this interview. During the repast which followed Nelson, with all the sincerity of his character, bore willing testimony to the valour of his foes. He told the prince that he had been in a hundred and five engagements, but that this was the most tremendous of all.

"The French," he said, "fought bravely; but they could not have stood for one hour the fight which the Danes had supported for four." He requested that Villemoes might be introduced to him; and shaking hands with the youth, told the prince that he ought to be made an admiral. The prince replied: "If, my lord, I am to make all my brave officers admirals, I should have no captains or lieutenants in my service."

32. The sympathy of the Danes for their countrymen who had bled in their defence was not weakened by distance of time or place in this instance. Things needful for the service or the comfort of the wounded were sent in profusion to the hospitals, till the superintendents gave public notice that they could receive no more. On the third day after the action the dead were buried in the naval churchyard; the ceremony was made as public and as solemn as the occasion required—such a procession had never before been seen in that or perhaps in any other city. A public monument was erected upon the spot where the slain were gathered together. A subscription was opened on the day of the funeral for the relief of the sufferers, and collections in aid of it throughout all the churches in the kingdom. This appeal to the feelings of the people was made with circumstances which gave it full effect. A monument was raised in the midst of the church, surmounted by the Danish colours; young maidens, dressed in white, stood round it, with either one who had been wounded in the battle, or the widow and orphans of some one who had fallen; a suitable oration was delivered from the pulpit, and patriotic hymns and songs were afterwards performed. Medals were distributed to all the officers, and to the men who had distinguished themselves. Poets and painters vied with each other in celebrating a battle which, disastrous as it was, had yet been honourable to their country; some, with pardonable sophistry, represented the advantage of the day as on their

own side. One writer discovered a more curious but less dis-
putable ground of satisfaction in the reflection that Nelson, as
may be inferred from his name, was of Danish descent, and
his actions therefore, the Dane argued, were attributable to
Danish valour.

33. The negotiation was continued during the five following days, and in that interval the prizes were disposed of in
a manner which was little approved by Nelson. Six line-of-
battle ships and eight praams had been taken. Of these, the
Holstein, sixty-four, was the only one which was sent home.

The *Zealand* was a finer ship, but the *Zealand* and all the
others were burned, and their brass battering cannon sunk
with the hulls in such shoal water that when the fleet returned
from Revel they found the Danes with craft over the wrecks
employed in getting the guns up again. Nelson, though he
forbore from any public expression of displeasure at seeing the
proofs and trophies of his victory destroyed, did not forget to
represent to the Admiralty the case of those who were thus
deprived of their prize-money. "Whether," said he to Earl
St. Vincent, "Sir Hyde Parker may mention the subject to
you, I know not, for he is rich and does not want it; nor is it,
you will believe me, any desire to get a few hundred pounds
that actuates me to address this letter to you; but justice to
the brave officers and men who fought on that day. It is true
our opponents were in hulks and floats, only adapted for the
position they were in; but that made our battle so much the
harder, and victory so much the more difficult to obtain. Believe me, I have weighed all the circumstances, and in my
conscience I think that the King should send a gracious
message to the House of Commons for a gift to this fleet; for
what must be the natural feelings of the officers and men
belonging to it, to see their rich commander-in-chief burn all
the fruits of their victory, which, if fitted up and sent to England (as many of them might have been by dismantling part of
our fleet), would have sold for a good round sum."

34. On the 9th Nelson landed again, to conclude the terms of the armistice. During its continuance the armed ships and vessels of Denmark were to remain in their then actual situation as to armament, equipment, and hostile position; and the treaty of armed neutrality, as far as related to the co-operation of Denmark, was suspended. The prisoners were to be sent on shore; an acknowledgment being given for them, and for the wounded also, that they might be carried to Great Britain's credit in the account of war, in case hostilities should be renewed. The British fleet was allowed to provide itself with all things requisite for the health and comfort of its men. A difficulty arose respecting the duration of the armistice. The Danish commissioners fairly stated their fears of Russia; and Nelson, with that frankness which sound policy and the sense of power seem often to require as well as justify in diplomacy, told them his reason for demanding a long term was, that he might have time to act against the Russian fleet, and then return to Copenhagen. Neither party would yield upon this point; and one of the Danes hinted at the renewal of hostilities. " Renew hostilities!" cried Nelson to one of his friends—for he understood French enough to comprehend what was said, though not to answer it in the same language. " Tell him we are ready at a moment!—ready to bombard this very night!" The conference, however, proceeded amicably on both sides; and as the (a) commissioners could not agree upon this head, they broke up, leaving Nelson to settle it with the prince. A (b) levee was held forthwith in one of the state-rooms; a scene well suited for such a consultation, for all these rooms had been stripped of their furniture, in fear of a bombardment. To a bombardment also Nelson was looking at this time; fatigue and anxiety, and vexation at the dilatory measures of the commander-in-chief, combined to make him irritable; and as he was on the way to the prince's dining-room he whispered to the officer on whose

arm he was leaning, "Though I have only one eye, I can see that all this will burn well." After dinner he was closeted with the prince, and they agreed that the armistice should continue fourteen weeks, and that at its termination fourteen days' notice should be given before the recommencement of hostilities.

35. An official account of the battle was published by Olfert Fischer, the Danish commander-in-chief, in which it was asserted that our force was greatly superior; nevertheless, that two of our ships of the line had struck, that the others were so weakened, and especially Lord Nelson's own ship, as to fire only single shots for an hour before the end of the action; and that this hero himself, in the middle and very heat of the conflict, sent a flag of truce on shore to propose a cessation of hostilities. For the truth of this account the Dane appealed to the prince, and all those who, like him, had been eye-witnesses of the scene. Nelson was exceedingly indignant at such a statement, and addressed a letter, in confutation of it, to the adjutant-general, Lindholm; thinking this incumbent upon him for the information of the prince, since his Royal Highness had been appealed to as a witness: "Otherwise," said he, "had Commodore Fischer confined himself to his own veracity, I should have treated his official letter with the contempt it deserved, and allowed the world to appreciate the merits of the two contending officers." After (a) pointing out and detecting some of the misstatements in the account, he proceeds: "As to his nonsense about victory, his Royal Highness will not much credit him. I sunk, burned, captured, or drove into the harbour the whole line of defence to the southward of the Crown Islands. He says he is told that two British ships struck. Why did he not take possession of them? I took possession of his as fast as they struck. The reason is clear, that he did not believe it; he must have known the falsity

of the report. He states that the ship in which I had the
honour to hoist my flag fired latterly only single guns. It is
true; for steady and cool were my brave fellows, and did
not wish to throw away a single shot. He seems to exult
that I sent on shore a flag of truce. You know, and his
Royal Highness knows, that the guns fired from the shore
could only fire through the Danish ships which had surrendered, and that if I fired at the shore, it could only be
in the same manner. God forbid that I should destroy an
unresisting Dane ! When they became my prisoners I became
their protector."

36. This letter was written in terms of great asperity against
the Danish commander. Lindholm replied in a manner every
way honourable to himself. He vindicated the commodore in
some points and excused him in others, reminding Nelson that
every commander-in-chief was liable to receive incorrect reports.
With a natural desire to represent the action in a most favourable light to Denmark, he took into the comparative strength
of the two parties the ships which were aground, and which could
not get into action; and omitted the Trekroner and the batteries upon Amak Island. He disclaimed all idea of claiming
as a victory " what to every intent and purpose," said he,
" was a defeat, but not an inglorious one. As to your lordship's motive for sending a flag of truce, it never can be mis-
construed; and your subsequent conduct has sufficiently
shown that humanity is always the companion of true valour.
You have done more; you have shown yourself a friend to
the re-establishment of peace and good harmony between this
country and great Britain. It is therefore with the sincerest
esteem I shall always feel myself attached to your lordship."
Thus handsomely winding up his reply, he soothed and con-
tented Nelson, who, drawing up a memorandum of the comparative force of the two parties for his own satisfaction,
assured Lindholm that if the commodore's statement had been

4

in the same manly and honourable strain, he would have been the last man to have noticed any little inaccuracies which might get into a commander-in-chief's public letter.

For the battle of Copenhagen Nelson was raised to the rank of Viscount, an inadequate mark of reward for services so splendid and of such paramount importance to the dearest interests of England. There was, however, some prudence in dealing out honours to him step by step; had he lived long enough he would have fought his way up to a dukedom.

_____

CHAPTER VIII.

1. WHEN Nelson informed Earl St. Vincent that the armistice had been concluded, he told him also without reserve his own discontent at the dilatoriness and indecision which he witnessed and could not remedy. "No man," said he, "but those who are on the spot can tell what I have gone through and do suffer. I make no scruple in saying that I would have been at Revel fourteen days ago; that without this armistice the fleet would never have gone but by order of the Admiralty, and with it I dare say we shall not go this week. I wanted Sir Hyde to let me at least go and cruise off Carlscrona, to prevent the Revel ships from getting in. I said I would not go to Revel to take any of those laurels which I was sure he would reap there. Think for me, my dear lord, and if I have deserved well let me return; if ill, for Heaven's sake supersede me, for I cannot exist in this state."

2. Fatigue, incessant anxiety, and a climate little suited to one of a tender constitution, which had now for many years been accustomed to more genial latitudes, made him at this time seriously determine upon returning home. "If the northern business were not settled," he said, "they must send more admirals, for the keen air of the North had cut him to

the heart." He felt the want of activity and decision in the commander-in-chief more keenly, and this affected his spirits, and consequently his health, more than the inclemency of the Baltic. Soon after the armistice was signed Sir Hyde proceeded to the eastward with such ships as were fit for service, leaving Nelson to follow with the rest as soon as those which had received slight damages should be repaired and the rest sent to England. In passing between the isles of Amak and Saltholm most of the ships touched the ground, and some of them stuck fast for a while; no serious injury, however, was sustained. It was intended to act against the Russians first before the breaking up of the frost should enable them to leave Revel; but learning on the way that the Swedes had put to sea to effect a junction with them, Sir Hyde altered his course in hopes of intercepting this part of the enemy's force. Nelson had at this time provided for the more pressing emergencies of the service, and prepared on the 18th to follow the fleet. The *St. George* drew too much water to pass the channel between the isles without being lightened; the guns were therefore taken out and put on board an American vessel. A contrary wind, however, prevented Nelson from moving, and on that same evening, while he was thus delayed, information reached him of the relative situation of the Swedish and British fleets, and the probability of an action. The fleet was nearly ten leagues distant, and both wind and current contrary, but it was not possible that Nelson could wait for a favourable season under such an expectation. He ordered his boat immediately, and stepped into it. Night was setting in—one of the cold spring nights of the North—and it was discovered, soon after they had left the ship, that in their haste they had forgotten to provide him with a boat-cloak. He, however, forbade them to return for one, and when one of his companions offered him his greatcoat, and urged him to make use of it, he replied: "I thank you very much; but, to tell you the truth, my anxiety keeps me sufficiently warm at present."

3. "Do you think," said he presently, "that our fleet has quitted Bornholm? If it has, we must follow it to Carlscrona." About midnight he reached it, and once more got on board the *Elephant.* On the following morning the Swedes were discovered; as soon, however, as they perceived the English approaching they retired, and took shelter in Carlscrona, behind the batteries on the island at the entrance of that port. Sir Hyde sent in a flag of truce, stating that Denmark had concluded an armistice, and requiring an explicit declaration from the Court of Sweden, whether it would adhere to or abandon the hostile measures which it had taken against the rights and interests of Great Britain? The commander, Vice-Admiral Cronstadt, replied that " he could not answer a question which did not come within the particular circle of his duty, but that the king was then at Maloe, and would soon be at Carlscrona." Gustavus shortly afterwards arrived, and an answer was then returned to this effect: " That his Swedish Majesty would not for a moment fail to fulfil, with fidelity and sincerity, the engagements he had entered into with his allies, but he would not refuse to listen to equitable proposals made by deputies furnished with proper authority by the King of Great Britain to the united northern powers." Satisfied with this answer, and with the known disposition of the Swedish Court, Sir Hyde sailed for the Gulf of Finland, but he had not proceeded far before a dispatch boat from the Russian ambassador at Copenhagen arrived, bringing intelligence of the death of the (a) Emperor Paul, and that his successor, Alexander, had accepted the offer made by England to his father—of terminating the dispute by a convention. The British admiral was therefore required to desist from all further hostilities.

4. It was Nelson's maxim, that, to negotiate with effect, force should be at hand, and in a situation to act. The fleet having been reinforced from England, amounted to eighteen sail of the line, and the wind was fair for Revel. There he would have sailed immediately, to place himself between that

division of the Russian fleet and the squadron at Cronstadt, in
case this offer should prove insincere. Sir Hyde, on the other
hand, believed that the death of Paul had effected all that was
necessary. The manner of that death, indeed, rendered it
apparent that a change of policy would take place in the
Cabinet of Petersburg; but Nelson never trusted anything to
the uncertain events of time which could possibly be secured
by promptitude or resolution. It was not therefore without
severe mortification that he saw the commander-in-chief return
to the coast of Zealand, and anchor in Kioge Bay, there to wait
patiently for what might happen.

5. There the fleet remained till despatches arrived from
home, on the 5th of May, recalling Sir Hyde and appointing
Nelson commander-in-chief.

6. Nelson wrote to Earl St. Vincent that he was unable to
hold this honourable station. Admiral 'Graves also was so ill
as to be confined to his bed, and he entreated that some person
might come out and take the command. "I will endeavour,"
said he, "to do my best while I remain, but, my dear lord, I
shall either soon go to heaven, I hope, or must rest quiet for a
time. If Sir Hyde were gone, I would now be under sail." On
the day when this was written he received news of his appointment. Not a moment was now lost. His first signal as commander-in-chief was to hoist in all launches and prepare to
weigh, and on the 7th he sailed from Kioge. Part of his
fleet was left at Bornholm to watch the Swedes, from whom he
required and obtained an assurance that the British trade in
the Cattegat and in the Baltic should not be molested; and
saying how unpleasant it would be to him if anything should
happen which might for a moment disturb the returning harmony between Sweden and Great Britain; he apprised them
that he was not directed to abstain from hostilities should he
meet with the Swedish fleet at sea. Meantime, he himself,
with ten sail of the line, two frigates, a brig, and a schooner,

made for the Gulf of Finland. Paul, in one of the freaks of his tyranny, had seized upon all the British effects in Russia, and even considered British subjects as his prisoners. "I will have all the English shipping and property restored," said Nelson, "but I will do nothing violently ; neither commit the affairs of my country, nor suffer Russia to mix the affairs of Denmark or Sweden with the detention of our ships." The wind was fair, and carried him in four days to Revel roads. But the bay had been clear of firm ice on the 29th of April, while the English were lying idly at Kioge. The Russians had cut through the ice in the mole, six feet thick, and their whole squadron had sailed for Cronstadt on the third. Before that time it had lain at the mercy of the English. "Nothing," Nelson said, " if it had been right to make the attack, could have saved one ship of them in two hours after our entering the bay."

7. It so happened that there was no cause to regret the opportunity which had been lost, and Nelson immediately put the intentions of Russia to the proof. He sent on shore to say that he came with friendly views, and was ready to return a salute. On their part the salute was delayed till a message was sent to them to inquire for (a) what reason ; and the officer whose neglect had occasioned the delay was put under arrest. Nelson wrote to the Emperor, proposing to wait on him personally, and congratulate him on his accession, and urged the immediate release of British subjects and restoration of British property.

8. The answer arrived on the 16th ; Nelson meantime had exchanged visits with the governor, and the most friendly intercourse had subsisted between the ships and the shore. Alexander's ministers in their (a) reply expressed their surprise at the arrival of a British fleet in a Russian port, and their wish that it should (b) return ; they professed, on the part of Russia, the most friendly disposition towards Great Britain,

but declined the personal visit of Lord Nelson unless he came in a single ship. There was a suspicion implied in this which stung Nelson, and he said the Russian ministers would never have written thus if their fleet had been at Revel. He wrote an immediate reply expressing what he felt ; he told the Court of Petersburg that "the word of a British admiral, when given in explanation of any part of his conduct, was as sacred as that of any sovereign in Europe." And he (c) repeated, that "under other circumstances it would have been his anxious wish to (d) have paid his personal respects to the emperor, and signed with his own hand the act of amity between the two countries." Having despatched this, he stood out to sea immediately, leaving a brig to bring off the provisions which had been contracted for, and to settle the accounts. "I hope all is right," said he, writing to our ambassador at Berlin ; "but seamen are but bad negotiators, for we put to issue in five minutes what diplomatic forms would be five months doing."

9. On his way down the Baltic, however, he met the Russian admiral, Tchitchagof, whom the Emperor, in reply to Sir Hyde's overtures, had sent to communicate personally with the British commander-in-chief. The reply was such as had been wished and expected, and these negotiators, going, seamanlike, straight to their object, satisfied each other of the friendly intentions of their respective governments. Nelson then anchored off Rostock, and there he received an answer to his last despatch from Revel, in which the Russian Court expressed their regret that there should have been any misconception between them, informed him that the British vessels which Paul had detained were ordered to be liberated, and invited him to Petersburg in whatever mode might be most agreeable to himself. Other honours awaited him : the Duke of Mecklenburg Strelitz, the queen's brother, came to visit him on board his ship ; and towns of the inland parts of Mecklen-

burg sent deputations, with their publi· books of record, that they might have the name of Nelson in them, written by his own hand.

10. From Rostock the fleet returned to Kioge Bay. Nelson saw that the temper of the Danes towards England was such as naturally arose from the chastisement which they had so recently received. "In this nation," said he, "we shall not be forgiven for having the upper hand of them; I only thank God we have, or they would try to humble us to the dust." He saw also that the Danish Cabinet was completely subservient to France; a French officer was at this time the companion and counsellor of the Crown Prince, and things were done in such open violation of the armistice that Nelson thought a (*a*) second infliction of vengeance would soon be necessary. He wrote to the Admiralty, requesting a clear and explicit reply to his inquiry, whether the commander-in-chief was at liberty to hold the language becoming a British admiral?—"which very probably," said he, "if I am here, will break the armistice and set Copenhagen in a blaze. I see everything which is dirty and mean going on, and the Prince Royal at the head of it. Ships have been masted, guns taken on board, floating batteries prepared, and, except hauling out and completing their rigging, everything is done in defiance of the treaty. My heart burns at seeing the word of a prince, nearly allied to our good King, so falsified; but his conduct is such that he will lose his kingdom if he goes on, for (*b*) Jacobins rule in Denmark. I have made no representations yet, as it would be useless to do so until I have the power of correction. All I beg, in the name of the future commander-in-chief, is that the orders may be clear, for enough is done to break twenty treaties if it should be wished, or to make the Prince Royal humble himself before British (*c*) generosity."

11. Nelson was not deceived in his judgment of the Danish Cabinet, but the battle of Copenhagen had crippled its power.

The death of the Czar Paul had broken the confederacy, and that Cabinet therefore was compelled to defer till a more convenient season the indulgence of its enmity towards Great Britain. Soon afterwards, Admiral Sir Charles Maurice Pole arrived to take the command. The business, military and political, had by that time been so far completed that the presence of the British fleet soon became no longer necessary. Sir Charles, however, made the short time of his command memorable by passing the Great Belt for the first time with line-of-battle ships; working through the channel against adverse winds. When Nelson left the fleet, this speedy termination of the expedition, though confidently expected, was not certain; and he, in his willingness to weaken the British force, thought at one time of traversing J land in his boat by the canal to Tonningen, on the Eydei, and finding his way home from thence. This intention was not executed, but he returned in a brig, declining to accept a frigate, which few admirals would have done; especially if, like him, they suffered from sea-sickness in a small vessel. On his arrival at Yarmouth the first thing he did was to visit the hospital and see the men who had been wounded in the late battle; that victory which had added new glory to the name of Nelson, and which was of more importance (*a*) even than the battle of the Nile to the honour, the strength, and security of England.

12. He had not been many weeks on shore before he was called upon to undertake a service for which no Nelson was required. Bonaparte, who was now First Consul and in reality sole ruler of France, was making preparations upon a great scale for invading England, but his schemes in the Baltic had been baffled; fleets could not be created as they were wanted; and his armies therefore were to come over in gun-boats, and such small craft as could be rapidly built or collected for the occasion. From the former governments of France such threats have only been matter of insult or policy; in Bonaparte they

were sincere, for this adventurer, intoxicated with success, already began to imagine that all things were to be submitted to his fortune. We had not at that time proved the superiority of our soldiers over the French, and the unreflecting multitude were not to be persuaded that an invasion could only be effected by numerous and powerful fleets. A general alarm was excited, and in condescension to this unworthy feeling Nelson was appointed to a command extending from Orfordness to Beachy Head, on both shores; a sort of service, he said, for which he felt no other ability than what might be found in his zeal.

13. To this service, however, such as it was, he applied with his wonted alacrity; and having hoisted his flag in the *Medusa* frigate, he went to reconnoitre Boulogne, the point from which it was supposed the great attempt would be made, and which the French, in fear of an attack themselves, were fortifying with all care. He approached near enough to sink two of their floating batteries and destroy a few gun-boats which were without the pier; what damage was done within could not be ascertained. " Boulogne," he said, " was certainly not a very pleasant place that morning; but," he added, " it is not my wish to injure the poor inhabitants, and the town is spared as much as the nature of the service will admit." Enough was done to show the enemy that they could not with impunity come outside their own ports. Nelson was satisfied by what he saw that they meant to make an attempt from this place, but that it was impracticable, for the least wind at W. N.W. (a) and they were lost. The ports of Flushing and Flanders were better points; there we could not tell by our eyes what means of transport were provided. From thence, therefore, if it came forth at all, the expedition would come. "And what a forlorn undertaking!" said he; "consider cross-tides, etc. As for rowing, that is impossible. It is perfectly right to be prepared for a mad government, but with the active force which has been given me I may pronounce it almost impracticable."

14. The force had been got together with an alacrity which has seldom been equalled. On the 28th of July we were, in Nelson's own words, literally at the foundation of our fabric of defence ; and twelve days afterwards we were so prepared on the enemy's coast that he did not believe they could get three miles from their ports. The *Medusa*, returning to our own shores, anchored in the rolling ground off Harwich; and when Nelson wished to get to the Nore in her, the wind rendered it impossible to proceed there by the usual channel. In haste to be at the Nore, remembering that he had been a tolerable pilot for the mouth of the Thames in his younger days, and thinking it necessary that he should know all that could be known of the navigation, he requested the maritime surveyor of the coast, Mr. Spence, to get him into the Swin by any channel, for neither the pilots whom he had on board, nor the Harwich ones, would take charge of the ship. No vessel drawing more than fourteen feet had ever before ventured over the Naze. Mr. Spence, however, who had surveyed the channel, carried her safely through. The channel has since been called Nelson's, though he himself wished it to be named after the *Medusa :* his name needed no new memorial.

15. Nelson's eye was upon Flushing. "To take possession of that place," he said, "would be a week's expedition for four or five thousand troops." This, however, required a consultation with the Admiralty ; and that something might be done meantime, he resolved upon attacking the flotilla in the mouth of Boulogne harbour. This resolution was made in deference to the opinion of others, and to the public feeling which was so preposterously excited. He himself scrupled not to assert that the French army would never embark at Boulogne for the invasion of England ; and he owned that this boat warfare was not congenial to his feelings. Into Helvoet or Flushing he should be happy to lead, if Government turned their thoughts that way. "While I serve," said he, "I will do it actively,

and to the very best of my abilities.   I require nursing like a
child," he added ; "my mind carries me beyond my strength,
and will do me up.   But such is my nature."

16. The attack was made by the boats of the squadron in
five divisions, under Captains Somerville, Parker, Cotgrave,
Jones, and Conn.   The previous essay had taught the French
the weak parts of their position, and they omitted no means of
strengthening it, and of guarding against the expected attempt.
The boats put off about half-an-hour before midnight ; but
owing to the darkness and tide and half-tide, which must
always make night attacks so uncertain on the coasts of the
channel, the divisions separated.   One could not arrive at all ;
another not till near daybreak.   The others made their attack
gallantly ; but the enemy were fully prepared ; every vessel
was defended by long poles, headed with iron spikes, projecting
from their sides ; strong nettings were braced up to their lower
yards ; they were moored by the bottom to the shore ; they
were strongly manned with soldiers and protected by land
batteries, and the shore was lined with troops.   Many were
taken possession of ; and though they could not have been
brought out, would have been burned, had not the French
resorted to a mode of offence which they have often used, but
which no other people have ever been wicked enough to employ.
The moment the firing ceased on board one of their own vessels,
they fired upon it from the shore, perfectly regardless of their
own men.

17. The commander of one of the French divisions acted
like a generous enemy.   He hailed the boats as they approached and cried ou' in English, " Let me advise you, my
brave Englishmen, to keep your distance—you can do nothing
here ; and it is only uselessly shedding the blood of brave men to
make the attempt."   The French official account boasted of the
victory.   "The combat," it said, "took place in sight of both
countries ; it was the first of the kind, and the historian would

have cause to make this remark." They guessed our loss at four or five hundred; it amounted to one hundred and seventy-two. In his private letters to the Admiralty, Nelson affirmed that had our force arrived as he intended, it was not all the chains in France which could have prevented our men from bringing off the whole of the vessels. There had been no error committed, and never did Englishmen display more courage. Upon this point Nelson was fully satisfied; but he said he should never bring himself again to allow any attack wherein he was not personally concerned, and that his mind suffered more than if he had had a leg shot off in the affair. He grieved particularly for Captain Parker, an excellent officer, to whom he was greatly attached, and who had an aged father looking to him for assistance. His thigh was shattered in the action, and the wound proved mortal after some weeks of suffering and manly resignation. During this interval Nelson's anxiety was very great. "Dear Parker is my child," said he, "for I found him in distress." And when he received the tidings of his death, he replied: "You will judge of my feelings: God's will be done. I beg that his hair may be cut off and given me; it shall be buried in my grave. Poor Mr. Parker! what a son has he lost! If I were to say I was content, I should lie; but I shall endeavour to submit with all the fortitude in my power. His loss has made a wound in my heart which time will hardly heal."

18. He now wished to be relieved from his service. The country, he said, had attached a confidence to his name which he had submitted to, and therefore had cheerfully repaired to the station; but this boat business, though it might be part of a great plan of invasion, could never be the only one, and he did not think it was a command for a vice-admiral. It was not that he wanted a more lucrative situation, for, seriously indisposed as he was, and low-spirited from private considerations, he did not know, if the Mediterranean were vacant, that

he should be equal to undertake it. Just at this time the peace
of Amiens was signed. Nelson rejoiced that the experiment
was made, but was well aware that it was an experiment : he
saw what he called the misery of peace, unless the utmost
vigilance and prudence were exerted ; and he expressed in
bitter terms his proper indignation at the manner in which the
mob of London (a) welcomed the French general who brought
the ratification ; saying that "they made him ashamed of his
country."

19. He had purchased a house and estate at Merton, in
Surrey, meaning to pass his days there in the society of Sir
William and Lady Hamilton. This place he had never seen
till he was now welcomed there by the friends to whom he
had so passionately devoted himself, and who were not less
sincerely attached to him. The place, and everything which
Lady Hamilton had done to it, delighted him ; and he declared
that the longest liver should possess it all. His pensions for
his victories and for the loss of his eye and arm amounted,
with his half-pay, to about £3,400 a-year. From this he gave
£1,800 to Lady Nelson, £200 to a brother's widow and £150
for the education of his children, and he paid £500 interest
for borrowed money ; so that Nelson was comparatively a poor
man, and though much of the pecuniary embarrassment which
he endured was occasioned by the separation from his wife,
even if that cause had not existed, his income would not have
been sufficient for the rank which he held, and the claims
which would necessarily be made upon his bounty. The depres-
sion of spirits under which he had long laboured arose partly
from this state of his circumstances and partly from the other
disquietudes in which his connection with Lady Hamilton had
involved him—a connection which it was not possible his
father could behold without sorrow and displeasure. Mr.
Nelson, however, was soon persuaded that the attachment,
which Lady Nelson regarded with natural jealousy and resent-

ment, did not in reality pass the bounds of ardent and romantic admiration : a passion which the manners and accomplishments of (*a*) Lady Hamilton, fascinating as they were, would not have been able to excite if they had not been accompanied by more uncommon intellectual endowments, and by a character which, both in its strength and in its weakness, resembled his own. It did not therefore require much explanation to reconcile him to his son; an event the more essential to Nelson's happiness because a few months afterwards the good old man died, at the age of seventy-nine.

20. Soon after the conclusion of peace tidings arrived of our final and decisive successes in Egypt; in consequence of which the Common Council voted their thanks to the army and navy for bringing the campaign to so glorious a conclusion. When Nelson, after the action of Cape St. Vincent, had been entertained at a City feast, he had observed to the Lord Mayor, that "if the city continued its generosity, the navy would ruin them in gifts." To which the Lord Mayor (*a*) replied, putting his hand upon the admiral's shoulder, "Do you find victories, and we will find rewards." Nelson, (*b*) as he said, had kept his word—had doubly fulfilled his part of the contract; but no thanks had been voted for the battle of Copenhagen, and feeling that he and his companions in that day's glory had a fair and honourable claim to this reward, he took the present opportunity of addressing a letter to the Lord Mayor, complaining of the omission and the injustice. "The smallest services," said he, "rendered by the army or navy to the country have always been noticed by the great city of London, with one exception—the glorious 2nd of April—a day when the greatest dangers of navigation were overcome, and the Danish force, which they thought impregnable, totally taken or destroyed by the consummate skill of our commanders and and by the undaunted bravery of as gallant a band as ever defended the rights of this country. For myself, if I were

only personally concerned, I should bear the stigma attempted
to be now first placed upon my brow with humility.   But, my
lord, I am the natural guardian of the fame of all the officers
of the navy, army, and marines, who fought, and so profusely
bled, under my command on that day.   Again I disclaim for
myself more merit than naturally falls to a successful commander; but when I am called upon to speak of the merits of
the captains of his Majesty's ships, and of the officers and men,
whether seamen, marines, or soldiers, whom I that day had the
happiness to command, I then say that never was the glory of
this country upheld with more determined bravery than on
that occasion ; and if I may be allowed to give an opinion as a
Briton, then I say that more important service was never rendered to our King and country.   It is my duty, my lord, to
prove to the brave fellows, my companions in danger, that I
have not failed, at every proper place, to represent, as well as
I am able, their bravery and meritorious conduct."

21. Another honour, of greater import, was withheld from
the conquerors.   The King had given medals to those captains
who were engaged in the (a) battles of the 1st of June, of Cape
St. Vincent, of Camperdown, and of the Nile.   Then came the
victory at Copenhagen, which Nelson truly called the most
difficult achievement, the hardest-fought battle, the most glorious result, that ever graced the annals of our country.   He of
course expected the medal, and in writing to Earl St. Vincent
said he "longed to have it, and would not give it up to be
made an English duke."   The medal, however, was not given
—"For what reason," said Nelson, "Lord St. Vincent best
knows."   Words plainly implying a suspicion that it was withheld by some feeling of jealousy ; and that suspicion estranged
him, during the remaining part of his life, from one who had
been at one time essentially, as well as sincerely, his friend,
and of whose professional abilities he ever entertained the
highest opinion.

22. The happiness which Nelson enjoyed in the society of his chosen friends was of no long continuance. Sir William Hamilton, who was far advanced in years, died early in 1803. He expired in his wife's arms, holding Nelson by the hand, and almost in his last words left her to his protection; requesting him that he would see justice done her by the Government, as he knew what she had done for her country. He left him her portrait in enamel, calling him his dearest friend—the most virtuous, loyal, and truly brave character he had ever known. The codicil containing this bequest concluded with these words: " God bless him, and shame fall on those who do not say Amen." Sir William's pension of £1,200 a year ceased with his death. Nelson applied to Mr. Addington in Lady Hamilton's behalf, stating the important service which she had rendered to the fleet at Syracuse; and Mr. Addington, it is said, acknowledged that she had a just claim upon the gratitude of the country. This barren acknowledgment was all that was obtained; but a sum equal to the pension which her husband had enjoyed was settled on her by Nelson, and paid in monthly payments during his life. A few weeks after this event the war was renewed, and the day after his Majesty's message to Parliament Nelson departed to take the command of the Mediterranean fleet.

23. He took his station immediately off Toulon, and there, with incessant vigilance, waited for the coming out of the enemy. When he had been fourteen months thus employed he received a vote of thanks from the city of London for his skill and perseverance in blockading that port, so as to prevent the French from putting to sea. Nelson had not forgotten the wrong which the city had done to the Baltic fleet by their omission, and did not lose the opportunity which this vote afforded of recurring to that point. " I do assure your lordship," said he, in his answer to the Lord Mayor, " that there is not that man breathing who sets a higher value upon the

b

thanks of his fellow-citizens of London than myself; but I should feel as much ashamed to receive them for a particular service, marked in the resolution, if I felt that I did not come within that line of service, as I should feel hurt at having a great victory passed over without notice. I beg to inform your lordship that the port of Toulon has never been blockaded by me—quite the reverse. Every opportunity has been offered the enemy to put to sea, for it is there we hope to realize the hopes and expectations of our country." Nelson then remarked that the junior flag officers of his fleet had been omitted in this vote of thanks, and his surprise at the omission was expressed with more asperity, perhaps, than an offence, so entirely and manifestly unintentional, deserved; but it arose from that generous regard for the feelings as well as interests of all who were under his command, which made him as much beloved in the fleets of Britain as he was dreaded in those of the enemy.

24. Never was any commander more beloved. He governed men by their reason and their affections; they knew that he was incapable of caprice or tyranny, and they obeyed him with alacrity and joy, because he possessed their confidence as well as their love. "Our Nel," they used to say, "is as brave as a lion and as gentle as a lamb." Severe discipline he detested, though he had been bred in a severe school; he never inflicted corporal punishment if it were possible to avoid it, and when compelled to enforce it he who was familiar with wounds and death suffered like a woman. In his whole life Nelson was never known to act unkindly towards an officer. If he was asked to prosecute one for ill-behaviour, he used to answer that "there was no occasion for him to ruin a poor devil who was sufficiently his own enemy to ruin himself." But in Nelson there was more than the easiness and humanity of a happy nature; he did not merely abstain from injury; his was an active and watchful benevolence, ever desirous not only to

render justice, but to do good. During the peace he had spoken in (a) Parliament upon the abuses respecting prize-money, and had submitted plans to Government for more easily manning the navy, and preventing desertion from it, by bettering the condition of the seamen. He proposed that their certificates should be registered, and that every man who had served with a good character five years in war should receive a bounty of two guineas annually after that time, and of four guineas after eight years. "This," he said, "might at first sight appear an enormous sum for the State to pay, but the average life of a seaman is, from hard service, finished at forty-five: he cannot therefore enjoy the annuity many years, and the interest of the money saved by their not deserting would go far to pay the whole expense."

25. To his midshipmen he ever showed the most winning kindness, encouraging the diffident, tempering the hasty, counselling and befriending both. "Recollect," he used to say, "that you must be a seaman to be an officer, and also that you cannot be a good officer without being a gentleman." A lieutenant wrote to him to say that he was dissatisfied with his captain. Nelson's answer was in that spirit of perfect wisdom and perfect goodness which regulated his whole conduct toward those who were under his command. "I have just received your letter, and I am truly sorry that any difference should arise between your captain, who has the reputation of being one of the bright officers of the service, and yourself, a very young man and a very young officer, who must naturally have much to learn; therefore the chance is that you are perfectly wrong in the disagreement. However, as your present situation must be very disagreeable, I will certainly take an early opportunity of removing you, provided your conduct to your present captain be such that another may not refuse to receive you." The gentleness and benignity of his disposition never made him forget what was due to discipline. Being on one

occasion applied to to save a young officer from a court-martial
which he had provoked by his misconduct, his reply was, that
"he would do everything in his power to oblige so gallant and
good an officer as Sir John Warren," in whose name the inter-
cession had been made; "but what," he added, "would he do
if he were here? Exactly what I have done and am still willing to do. The young man must write such a letter of contri-
tion as would be an acknowledgment of his great fault, and
with a sincere promise, if his captain will intercede to prevent
the impending court-martial, never to so misbehave again. On
his captain enclosing me such a letter, with a request to cancel
the order for the trial, I might be induced to do it; but the
letters and reprimand will be given in the public order-book of
the fleet, and read to all the officers. The young man has
pushed himself forward to notice, and he must take the consequence. It was upon the quarter-deck, in the face of the ship's
company, that he treated his captain with contempt; and I
am in duty bound to support the authority and consequence of
every officer under my command. A poor ignorant seaman is
for ever punished for contempt to *his* superiors."

26. A dispute occurred in the fleet while it was off Toulon,
which called forth Nelson's zeal for the rights and interests of
the navy. Some young artillery officers, serving on board the
bomb-vessels, refused to let their men perform any other duty
but what related to the mortars. They wished to have it
established that their corps was not subject to the captain's
authority. The same pretensions were made in the Channel
Fleet about the same time, and the artillery rested their claims
to separate and independent authority on board upon a clause
in the Act which they interpreted in their favour. Nelson
took up the subject with all the earnestness which its importance deserved. "There is no real happiness in this world,"
said he, writing to Earl St. Vincent as First Lord. "With
all content and smiles around me, up start these artillery boys

(I understand they are not beyond that age) and set us at defiance; speaking in the most disrespectful manner of the navy
and its commanders. I know you, my dear lord, so well, that
with your quickness the matter would have been settled, and
perhaps some of them been broke. I am perhaps more
patient, but, I do assure you, not less resolved, if my plan of
conciliation is not attended to. You and I are on the eve of
quitting the theatre of our exploits; but we hold it due to our
successors never, whilst we have a tongue to speak or a hand
to write, to allow the navy to be in the smallest degree injured
in its discipline by our conduct." To Trowbridge he wrote in
the same spirit: "It is the old history, trying to do away the
Act of Parliament; but I trust they will never succeed, for
when they do, farewell to our naval superiority. We should
be prettily commanded! Let them once gain the step of being
independent of the navy on board a ship, and they will soon
have the other, and command us. But, thank God, my dear
Trowbridge, the King himself cannot do away the Act of
Parliament. Although my career is nearly run, yet it would
embitter my future days and expiring moments to hear of our
navy being sacrificed to the army." As the surest way of
preventing such disputes, he suggested that the navy should
have its own corps of artillery, and a corps of marine artillery
was accordingly established.

27. Instead of lessening the power of the commander,
Nelson would have wished to see it increased. It was absolutely necessary, he thought, that merit should be rewarded at
the moment, and that the officers of the fleet should look up
to the commander-in-chief for their reward. He himself was
never more happy than when he could promote those who were
deserving of promotion. Many were the services which he
thus rendered unsolicited, and frequently the officer in whose
behalf he had interested himself with the Admiralty did not
know to whose friendly interference he was indebted for his

good fortune. He used to say, "I wish it to appear as a God-send." The love which he bore the navy made him promote the interests and honour the memory of all who had added to its glories. "The near relations of brother officers," he said, "he considered as legacies to the service." Upon mention being made to him of a son of Rodney by the Duke of Clarence, his reply was: "I agree with your Royal Highness most entirely, that the son of a Rodney ought to be the *protege* of every person in the kingdom, and particularly of the sea officers. Had I known that there had been this claimant, some of my own lieutenants must have given way to such a name, and he should have been placed in the *Victory;* she is full, and I have twenty on my list, but whatever numbers I have, the name of Rodney must cut many of them out." Such was the proper sense which Nelson felt of what was due to splendid services and illustrious names. His feelings toward the brave men who had served with him are shown by a note in his diary, which was probably not intended for any other eye than his own:—"Nov. 7. I had the comfort of making an old '*Agamemnon*,' George Jones, a gunner into the *Chameleon* brig."

28. When Nelson took the command it was expected that the Mediterranean would be an active scene. Nelson well understood the character of the (*a*) perfidious Corsican who was now sole tyrant of France, and knowing that he was as ready to attack his friends as his enemies, knew therefore that nothing could be more uncertain than the direction of the fleet from Toulon, whenever it should put to sea. "It had as many destinations," he said, "as there were countries." The momentous revolutions of the last ten years had given him ample matter for reflection as well as opportunities for observation. The (*b*) film was cleared from his eyes, and now, when the French no longer went abroad with the cry of liberty and equality, he saw that the oppression and misrule of the

powers which had been opposed to them had been the main causes of their success, and that those causes would still pre- pare the way before them.   Even in Sicily, where, if it had been possible longer to blind himself, Nelson would willingly have seen no evil, he perceived that the people wished for a change, and acknowledged that they had reason to wish for it. In Sardinia the same burden of misgovernment was felt, and the people, like the Sicilians, were impoverished by a govern- ment so utterly incompetent to perform its first and most essential duties, that it did not protect its own coasts from the Barbary pirates.   He would fain have had us purchase this island (the finest in the Mediterranean) from its sovereign, who did not receive £5,000 a year from it after its wretched establishment was paid.   There was reason to think that France was preparing to possess herself of this important point, which afforded our fleet facilities for watching Toulon not to be obtained elsewhere.   An expedition was preparing at Corsica for the purpose, and all the Sardes who had taken part with revolutionary France were ordered to assemble there.   It was certain that if the attack were made it would succeed.   Nelson thought that the only means to prevent Sardinia from becoming French was to make it English, and that half a million would give the king a rich price and England a cheap purchase.   A better and therefore a wiser policy would have been to exert our influence in re- moving the abuses of the government, for foreign dominion is always in some degree an evil, and allegiance neither can nor ought to be made a thing of bargain and sale.   Sardinia, like Sicily and Corsica, is large enough to form a separate state.   Let us hope that these islands may ere long be made free and independent.   Freedom and independence will bring with them industry and prosperity ; and wherever these are found, arts and letters will flourish and the improvement of the human race proceed.

29. The proposed attack was postponed. Views of wider
ambition were opening upon Bonaparte, who now almost undis-
guisedly aspired to make himself master of the continent of Europe,
and Austria was preparing for another struggle, to be conducted
as weakly and terminated as miserably as the former. Spain,
too, was once more to be involved in war by the policy of France ;
that perfidious government having in view the double object of
employing the Spanish resources against England, and exhaust-
ing them in order to render Spain herself finally its prey. Nelson, who knew that England and the Peninsula ought to be in
alliance, for the common interest of both, frequently expressed
his hopes that Spain might resume her national rank among
the nations. "We ought," he said, "by mutual consent, to be
the very best friends, and both to be ever hostile to France."
But he saw that Bonaparte was meditating the destruction of
Spain, and that, while the wretched Court of Madrid professed
to remain neutral, the appearances of neutrality were scarcely
preserved. An order of the year 1771, excluding British ships
of war from the Spanish ports, was revived and put in force,
while French privateers from these very ports annoyed the British
trade, carried their prizes in, and sold them even at Barcelona.
Nelson complained of this to the captain-general of Catalonia,
informing him that he claimed for every British ship or squadron the right of lying as long as it pleased in the ports of
Spain while that right was allowed to other powers. To the
British ambassador he said, "I am ready to make large allow-
ances for the miserable situation Spain has placed herself in,
but there is a certain line beyond which I cannot submit to
be treated with disrespect. We have given up French vessels
taken within gunshot of the Spanish shore, and yet French
vessels are permitted to attack our ships from the Spanish
shore. Your excellency may assure the Spanish Government
that in whatever place the Spaniards allow the French to attack us, in that place I shall order the French to be attacked."

30. During this state of things, to which the weakness of
Spain, and not her will, consented, the enemy's fleet did not
venture to put to sea.   Nelson watched it with unremitting
and almost unexampled perseverence. The station off Toulon he
called his home. "We are in the right fighting trim," said he :
"let them come as soon as they please. I never saw a fleet
altogether so well officered and manned : would to God the
ships were half so good ! The finest ones in the service would
soon be destroyed by such terrible weather. I know well
enough that if I were to go into Malta I should save the ships
during this bad season ; but if I am to watch the French I
must be at sea, and if at sea, must have bad weather ; and if
the ships are not fit to stand bad weather they are useless."
Then only he was satisfied and at ease when he had the enemy
in view. Mr. Elliot, our Minister at Naples, seems at this
time to have proposed to send a confidential Frenchman to
him with information. "I should be very happy," he replied,
"to receive authentic intelligence of the destination of the
French squadron, their route, and time of sailing. Anything
short of this is useless, and I assure your excellency that I
would not upon any consideration have a Frenchman in the
fleet except as a prisoner. I put no confidence in them. You
think yours good ; the queen thinks the same ; I believe they
are all alike. Whatever information you can get me I shall
be very thankful for ; but not a Frenchman comes here. For-
give me, but my mother hated the French !"

31. M. Latouche Treville, who had commanded at Boulogne,
commanded now at Toulon. "He was sent for on purpose,"
said Nelson, "as he *beat me* at Boulogne, to beat me again ;
but he seems very loath to try." One day, while the main
body of our fleet was out of sight of land, Rear-Admiral Campbell, reconnoitring with the *Canopus, Donegal,* and *Amazon,*
stood in close to the port, and M. Latouche, taking advantage
of a breeze which sprung up, pushed out with four ships of the

line and three heavy frigates, and chased him about four
leagues. The Frenchman, delighted at having found himself
in so novel a situation, published a boastful account, affirming
that he had given chase to the whole British fleet, and that
Nelson had fled before him. Nelson thought it due to the
Admiralty to send home a copy of the *Victory's* log upon this
occasion. "As for himself," he said, "if his character was not
established by that time for not being apt to run away, it was
not worth his while to put the world right." "If this fleet
gets fairly up with M. Latouche," said he, to one of his corres-
pondents, "his letter, with all his ingenuity, must be different
from his last. We had fancied that we chased him into
Toulon, for, blind as I am, I could see his water-line when he
clued his topsails up, shutting in Sepet. But from the time of
his meeting Captain Hawker in the *Isis* I never heard of his
acting otherwise than as a poltroon and a liar. Contempt is
the best mode of treating such a miscreant." In spite, however, of contempt, the impudence of this Frenchman half
angered him. He said to his brother, "You will have seen
Latouche's letter; how he chased me, and how I ran. I keep
it, and if I take him, by God he shall eat it!"

32. Nelson, who used to say that in sea affairs nothing is
impossible and nothing improbable, feared the more that this
Frenchman might get out and elude his vigilance because he
was so especially desirous of catching him, and administering
to him his own lying letter in a sandwich. M. Latouche, however, escaped him in another way. He died, according to the
French papers, in consequence of walking so often up to the
signal-post upon Sepet to watch the British fleet. "I always
pronounced that would be his death," said Nelson. "If he
had come out and fought me, it would at least have added ten
years to my life." The patience with which he had watched
Toulon he spoke of truly as a perseverance at sea which had
never been surpassed. From May, 1803, to August, 1805, he

himself went out of his ship but three times; each of those times was upon the King's service, and neither time of absence exceeded an hour. The weather had been so unusually severe that he said the Mediterranean seemed altered. It was his rule never to contend with the gales, but either run to the south-ward to escape their violence, or furl all the sails and make the ships as easy as possible. The men, though he said flesh and blood could hardly stand it, continued in excellent health, which he ascribed in great measure to a plentiful supply of lemons and onions. For himself he thought he could only last till the battle was over. One battle more it was his hope that he might fight. "However," said he, "whatever happens I have run a glorious race." He was afraid of blindness, and this was the only evil which he could not contemplate without unhappiness. More alarming symptoms he regarded with less apprehension, describing his own "shattered carcase" as in the worst plight of any in the fleet, and he says : "I have felt the blood gushing up the left side of my head, and the moment it covers the brain I am fast asleep." The fleet was in worse trim than the men, but when he compared it with the enemy's, it was with a right English feeling. "The French fleet yester-day," said he in one of his letters, " was to appearance in high feather, and as fine as paint could make them ; but when they may sail, or where they may go, I am very sorry to say is a secret I am not acquainted with. Our weather-beaten ships, I have no fear, will make their sides like a plum-pudding."

33. Hostilities at length commenced between Great Britain and Spain. That country, whose miserable government made her subservient to France, was once more destined to lavish her resources and her blood in furtherance of the designs of a perfidious ally. The immediate occasion of the war was the seizure of four treasure-ships by the English. The act was (a) perfectly justifiable, for those treasures were intended to fur-nish means for France ; but the circumstances which attended

it were as unhappy as they were unforeseen. Four frigates had been despatched to intercept them. They met with an equal force. Resistance therefore became a point of honour on the part of the Spaniards, and one of their ships soon blew up with all on board. Had a stronger squadron been sent this deplorable catastrophe might have been spared—a catastrophe which excited not more indignation in Spain than it did grief in those who were its unwilling instruments, in the English Government and in the English people. On the 5th of October this unhappy affair occurred, and Nelson was not apprised of it till the 12th of the ensuing month. He had indeed sufficient mortification at the breaking out of the Spanish war, an event which it might reasonably have been supposed would amply enrich the officers of the Mediterranean fleet, and repay them for the severe and unremitting duty on which they had been so long employed. But of this harvest they were deprived, for Sir John Orde was sent with a small squadron and a separate command to Cadiz. Nelson's feelings were (b) never wounded so deeply as now. "I had thought," said he, writing in the first flow of freshness of indignation : " I fancied—but nay, it must have been a dream, an idle dream—yet, I confess it, I *did* fancy that I had done my country service, and thus they use me! And under what circumstances and with what pointed aggravation! Yet if I know my own thoughts, it is not for myself, or on my own account chiefly, that I feel the sting and the disappointment. No! it is for my brave officers, for my noble-minded friends and comrades. Such a gallant set of fellows! Such a band of brothers! My heart swells at the thought of them!"

34. War between Spain and England was now declared, and on the 18th of January the Toulon fleet, having the Spaniards to co-operate with them, put to sea. Nelson was at anchor off the coast of Sardinia, where the Madelena Islands form one of the finest harbours in the world, when at three in

the afternoon of the 19th the *Active* and *Seahorse* frigates brought this long-hoped-for intelligence. They had been close to the enemy at ten on the preceding night, but lost sight of them in about four hours. The fleet immediately unmoored and weighed, and at six in the evening ran through the straits between Biche and Sardinia, a passage so narrow that the ships could only pass one at a time, each following the stern lights of its leader. From the position of the enemy when they were last seen it was inferred that they must be bound round the southern end of Sardinia. Signal was made the next morning to prepare for battle. Bad weather came on, baffling the one fleet in its object and the other in its pursuit. Nelson beat about the Sicilian seas for ten days without obtaining any other information of the enemy than that one of their ships had put into Ajaccio dismasted, and having seen that Sardinia, Naples, and Sicily were safe, believing Egypt to be their destination, for Egypt he ran. The disappointment and distress which he had experienced in his former pursuits of the French through the same seas were now renewed, but Nelson, while he endured these anxious and unhappy feelings, was still consoled by the same confidence as on the former occasion, that though his judgment might be erroneous, under all circumstances he was right in having formed it. "I have consulted no man," said he to the Admiralty, "therefore the whole blame of ignorance in forming my judgment must rest with me. I would allow no man to take from me an atom of my glory had I fallen in with the French fleet, nor do I desire any man to partake any of the responsibility. All is mine, right or wrong." Then stating the grounds upon which he had proceeded, he added : "At this moment of sorrow I still feel that I have acted right." In the same spirit he said to Sir Alexander Ball : "When I call to remembrance all the circumstances, I approve, if nobody else does, of my own conduct."

35. Baffled thus, he bore up for Malta, and met intelligence from Naples that the French, having been dispersed in a gale, had put back to Toulon. From the same quarter he learned that a great number of saddles and muskets had been embarked; and this confirmed him in his opinion that Egypt was their destination. That they should have put back in consequence of storms which he had weathered, gave him a consoling sense of British superiority. "These gentlemen," said he, "are not accustomed to a Gulf of Lyons gale; we have buffeted them for one-and-twenty months, and not carried away a spar." He, however, who had so often braved these gales was now, though not mastered by them, vexatiously thwarted and impeded; and on February 27 he was compelled to anchor in Pulla Bay, in the Gulf of Cagliari. From the 21st of January the fleet had remained ready for battle, without a bulkhead up night or day. He anchored here that he might not be driven to leeward. As soon as the weather moderated he put to sea again; and after again beating about against contrary winds, another gale drove him to anchor in the Gulf of Palma on the 8th of March. This he made his rendezvous; he knew that the french troops still remained embarked, and wishing to lead them into a belief that he was stationed upon the Spanish coast, he made his appearance off Barcelona with that intent. About the end of the month he began to fear that the plan of the expedition was abandoned, and sailing once more towards his old station off Toulon, on the 4th of April he met the *Phœbe*, with news that Villeneuve had put to sea on the last of March with eleven ships of the line, seven frigates, and two brigs. When last seen they were steering toward the coast of Africa. Nelson first covered the channel between Sardinia and Barbary, so as to satisfy himself that Villeneuve was not taking the same route for Egypt which Gantheaume had taken before him, when he attempted to carry reinforcements there. Certain of this, he

bore up on the 7th for Palermo, lest the French should pass to the north of Corsica, and he despatched cruisers in all directions. On the 11th he felt assured that they were not gone down the Mediterranean, and sending off frigates to Gibraltar, to Lisbon, and to Admiral Cornwallis, who commanded the squadron off Brest, he endeavoured to get to the westward, beating against westerly winds. After five days a neutral gave intelligence that the French had been seen off Cape de Gatte on the 7th. It was soon afterwards ascertained that they had passed the Straits of Gibraltar on the day following; and Nelson, knowing that they might already be half-way to Ireland or to Jamaica, exclaimed that he was miserable. One gleam of comfort only came across him in the reflection that his vigilance had rendered it impossible for them to undertake any expedition in the Mediterranean.

36. Eight days after this certain intelligence had been obtained he described his state of mind thus forcibly in writing to the governor of Malta: "My good fortune, my dear Ball, seems flown away. I cannot get a fair wind, or even a side wind. Dead foul! Dead foul! But my mind is fully made up what to do when I leave the Straits, supposing there is no certain account of the enemy's destination. I believe this ill-luck will go near to kill me; but as these are times for exertion, I must not be cast down, whatever I may feel." In spite of every exertion which could be made by all the zeal and all the skill of British seamen, he did not get in sight of Gibraltar till the 30th April, and the wind was then so adverse that it was impossible to pass the Gut. He anchored in Mazari Bay, on the Barbary shore; obtained supplies from Tetuan; and when on the 5th a breeze from the eastward sprang up at last, sailed once more, hoping to hear of the enemy from Sir John Orde, who commanded off Cadiz, or from Lisbon. "If nothing is heard of them," said he to the Admiralty, "I shall probably think the rumours which have been spread are true, that their

object is the West Indies, and in that case I think it my duty to follow them ; or to the Antipodes, should I believe that to be their destination." At the time when this resolution was taken the physician of the fleet had ordered him to return to England before the hot months.

37. Nelson had formed his judgment of their destination, and made up his mind accordingly, when Donald Campbell, at that time an admiral in the Portuguese service, the same person who had given important tidings to Earl St. Vincent of the movements of that fleet from which he won his title, a second time gave timely and momentous intelligence to the flag of his country. He went on board the *Victory*, and communicated to Nelson his certain knowledge that the combined Spanish and French fleets were bound for the West Indies. Hitherto all things had favoured the enemy. While the British commander was beating up against strong southerly and westerly gales, they had wind to their wish from the N.E., and had done in nine days what he was a whole month in accomplishing. Villeneuve, finding the Spaniards at Carthagena were not in a state of equipment to join him, dared not wait, but hastened on to Cadiz. Sir John Orde necessarily retired at his approach. Admiral Gravina, with six Spanish ships of the line and two French, came out to him, and they sailed without a moment's loss of time. They had about three thousand French troops on board and fifteen hundred Spanish ; six hundred were under orders expecting them at Martinique, and one thousand at Guadaloupe. General Lauriston commanded the troops. The combined fleet now consisted of eighteen sail of the line, six forty-four gun frigates, one of twenty-six guns, three corvettes, and a brig. They were joined afterwards by two new French line-of-battle ships and one forty-four. Nelson pursued them with ten sail of the line and three frigates. "Take you a Frenchman apiece," said he to his captains, "and leave me the Spaniards ; when I haul down my colours I expect you to do the same, and not till then."

38. The enemy had five-and-thirty days' start, but he calcu-
lated that he should gain eight or ten days upon them by his
exertions. May 15th he made Madeira, and on June 4th
reached Barbadoes, whither he had sent despatches before him.
and where he found Admiral Cochrane, with two ships, part of
our squadron in those seas being at Jamaica. He found here
also accounts that the combined fleets had been seen from St.
Lucia on the 28th, standing to the southward, and that Tobago
and Trinidad were there objects. This Nelson doubted, but he
was alone in his opinion, and yielded with these foreboding
words—"If your intelligence proves false, you lose me the
French fleet." Sir William Myers offered to embark here with
two thousand troops ; they were taken on board, and the next
morning he sailed for Tobago. Here accident confirmed the
false intelligence which had, whether from intention or error,
misled him. A merchant at Tobago, in the general alarm, not
knowing whether this fleet was friend or foe, sent out a schooner
to reconnoitre, and acquaint him by signal. The signal which
he had chosen happened to be the very one which had been
appointed by Colonel Shipley, of the Engineers, to signify that
the enemy were at Trinidad ; and as this was at the close of
the day there was no opportunity of discovering the mistake.
An American brig was met with about the same time, the
master of which, with that propensity to deceive the English
and assist the French in any manner which has been but too
common among his countrymen, affirmed that he had been
boarded off Granada a few days before by the French, who
were standing towards the Bocas of Trinidad. This fresh intelligence removed all doubts. The ships were cleared for
action before daylight, and Nelson entered the Bay of Paria
on the 7th, hoping and expecting to make the mouths of the
Orinoco as famous in the annals of the British navy as those
of the Nile. Not an enemy was there ; and it was discovered
that accident and artifice had combined to lead him so far to

leeward 'hat there could have been little hope of fetching to windward of Granada for any other fleet. Nelson, however, with skill and exertions never exceeded and almost unexampled, bore for that island.

39. Advices met him on the way, that the combined fleets, having captured the Diamond Rock, were then at Martinique, on the 4th, and were expected to sail that night for the attack of Granada. On the 9th Nelson arrived off that island, and there learned that they had passed to leeward of Antigua the preceding day, and taken a homewardbound convoy. Had it not been for false information, upon which Nelson had acted reluctantly and in opposition to his own judgment, he would have been off Port Royal just as they were leaving it, and the battle would have been fought on the spot where Rodney defeated De Grasse. This he remembered in his vexation; but he had saved the colonies and above two hundred ships laden for Europe, which would else have fallen into the enemy's hands, and he had the satisfaction of knowing that the mere terror of his name had effected this, and had put to flight the allied enemies, whose force nearled doubled that before which they fled. That they were flying back to Europe he believed, and for Europe he steered in pursuit on the 13th, having disembarked the troops at Antigua, and taking with him the *Spartiate*, 74, the only addition to the squadron with which he was pursuing so superior a force. Five days afterwards, the *Amazon* brought intelligence that she had spoke a schooner who had seen them, on the evening of the 15th, steering to the north, and by computation eighty-seven leagues off. Nelson's diary at this time denotes his great anxiety and his perpetual and all-observing vigilance :—"June 21, midnight.—Nearly calm ; saw three planks, which I think came from the French fleet. Very miserable, which is very foolish." On the 17th of July he came in sight of Cape St. Vincent, and steered for Gibraltar. "June 18th," his diary says, "Cape Spartel in sight, but

no French fleet, nor any information about them. How sorrowful this makes me, but I cannot help myself." The next day he anchored at Gibraltar, and on the 20th, says he, "I went on shore for the first time since June 16th, 1803; and from having my foot out of the *Victory*, two years, wanting ten days."

40. Here he communicated with his old friend Collingwood, who, having been detached with a squadron when the disappearance of the combined fleets and of Nelson in their pursuit was known in England, had taken his station off Cadiz. He thought that Ireland was the enemy's ultimate object; that they would now liberate the Ferrol squadron, which was blocked up by Sir Robert Calder, call for the Rochefort ships, and then appear off Ushant with three or four and thirty sail, there to be joined by the Brest fleet. With this great force he supposed they would make for Ireland, the real mark and bent of all their operations; and their flight to the West Indies, he thought, had been merely undertaken to take off Nelson's force, which was the great impediment to their undertaking.

41. Collingwood was gifted with great political penetration. As yet, however, all was conjecture concerning the enemy, and Nelson having victualled and watered at Tetuan, stood for Ceuta on the 24th, still without information of their course. Next day intelligence arrived that the *Curieux* brig had seen them on the 19th standing to the northward. He proceeded off Cape St. Vincent, rather cruising for intelligence than knowing whither to betake himself, and here a case occurred that, more than any other event in real history, resembles those whimsical proofs of sagacity which Voltaire, in his "Zadig," has borrowed from the Orientals. One of our frigates spoke an American, who, a little to the westward of the Azores, had fallen in with an armed vessel, appearing to be a dismasted privateer, deserted by her crew, which had been run on board by another ship, and had been set fire to, but the

fire had gone out. A log-book and a few seamen's jackets were found in the cabin, and these were brought to Nelson. The log-book closed with these words: "Two large vessels in the W.N.W.;" and this led him to conclude that the vessel han been an English privateer cruising off the Western Islands. But there was in this book a scrap of dirty paper filled with figures. Nelson, immediately upon seeing it, observed that the figures were written by a Frenchman, and after studying this for a while, said: "I can explain the whole. The jackets are of French manufacture, and prove that the privateer was in possession of the enemy. She had been chased and taken by the two ships that were seen in the W.N.W. The prize-master, going on board in a hurry, forgot to take with him his reckoning; there is none in the log-book, and the dirty paper contains her work for the number of days since the privateer last left Corvo, with an unaccounted-for run, which I take to have been the chase, in his endeavour to find out her situation by back-reckonings. By some mismanagement, I conclude, she was run on board of by one of the enemy's ships, and dismasted. Not liking delay (for I am satisfied that those two ships were the advanced ones of the French squadron), and fancying we were close at their heels, they set fire to the vessel, and abandoned her in a hurry. If this explanation be correct, I infer from it that they have gone more to the northward, and more to the northward I will look for them." This course accordingly he held, but still without success. Still persevering and still disappointed, he returned near enough to Cadiz to ascertain that they were not there, traversed the Bay of Biscay, and then, as a last hope, stood over for the north-west coast of Ireland, against adverse winds, till on the evening of the 12th of August he learned that they had not been heard of there. Frustrated thus in all his hopes, after a pursuit to which, for its extent, rapidity, and perseverance, no parallel can be produced, he judged it best to reinforce the Channel Fleet with his squadron, lest the enemy, as Collingwood apprehended, should bear down upon Brest with their whole collected force. On the 15th he joined Admiral Cornwallis off Ushant. No news had yet been obtained of the enemy, and on the same evening he received orders to proceed with the *Victory* and *Superb* to Portsmouth.

CHAPTER IX.

1. At Portsmouth Nelson at (*a*) length found news of the combined fleets. Sir Robert Calder, who had been sent out to intercept their return, had fallen in with them on the 22nd of July, sixty leagues west of Cape Finisterre. Their force consisted of twenty sail of the line, three fifty-gun ships, five frigates, and two brigs; his, of fifteen line-of-battle ships, two frigates, a cutter, and a lugger. After an action of four hours he had captured an eighty-four and a seventy-four, and then thought it necessary to bring-to the squadron for the purpose of securing their prizes. The hostile fleets remained in sight of each other till the 26th, when the enemy bore away. The capture of two ships from so superior a force would have been considered as no inconsiderable victory a few years earlier, but Nelson had introduced a new era in our naval history, and the nation felt respecting this action as he had felt on a (*b*) somewhat similar occasion. They regretted that Nelson, with his eleven ships, had not been in Sir Robert Calder's place, and their disappointment was generally and loudly expressed.

2. Frustrated as his own hopes had been, Nelson had yet the high satisfaction of knowing that his judgment had never been more conspicuously approved, and that he had rendered essential service to his country by (*a*) driving the enemy from those islands where they expected there could be no force capable of opposing them. The West India merchants in London, as men

whose interests were more immediately benefited, appointed a deputation to express their thanks for his great and judicious exertions. It was now his intention to rest awhile from his labours, and recruit himself, after all his fatigues and cares, in the society of those whom he loved. All his stores were brought up from the *Victory*, and he found in his house at Merton the enjoyment which he had (*b*) anticipated. (*c*) Many days had not elapsed before Captain Blackwood, on his way to London with despatches, called on him at five in the morning. Nelson, who was already dressed, exclaimed, the moment he saw him : "I am sure you bring me news of the French and Spanish fleets! I think I shall yet have to beat them ! " They had refitted at Vigo, after the indecisive action with Sir Robert Calder ; then proceeded to Ferrol, brought out the squadron from thence, and with it, (*d*) entered Cadiz in safety. " Depend on it, Blackford," he repeatedly said, " I shall yet give M. Villeneuve a drubbing." But when Blackford had left him he wanted resolution to declare his wishes to Lady Hamilton and his sisters, and endeavored to drive away the thought. He had done enough ; he said, " Let the man trudge it who has lost his budget ! " His countenance belied his lips ; and as he was pacing one of the walks in the garden, which he used to call the quarter deck, Lady Hamilton came up to him and told him she saw he was uneasy. He smiled, and said : " No, he was as happy as possible ; he was surrounded by his family, his health was better since he had been on shore, and he would not give sixpence to call the king his uncle." She replied that she did not believe him, that she knew he was longing to get at the combined fleets, that he considered them as his own property, that he would be miserable if any man but himself did the business, and that he ought to have them as the price and reward of his two years' long watching and his hard chase. "Nelson," said she, however we may lament your absence, offer your services; they will be accepted, and you will gain a quiet heart by it : you will have a glorious victory, and then you may return here, and be happy. He looked at her with tears in his eyes : " Brave Emma ! Good Emma ! If there were more Emmas, there would be more Nelsons."

3. His services were as willingly accepted as they were offered, and Lord Barham, giving him the list of the navy, desired him to choose his own officers. " Choose yourself, my lord," was his reply ; " the same spirit actuates the whole profession ; you cannot choose wrong." Lord Barham then desired him to say what ships and how many he would wish, in addition to the fleet which he was going to command, and said they should follow him as soon as each was ready. No appointment was ever more in unison with the feelings and judgment of the whole nation. They, like Lady Hamilton, thought that the destruction of the combined fleets ought properly to be Nelson's work : that he who had been

> Half around the sea-girt ball,
> The hunter of the recreant Gaul,*

ought to reap the spoils of the chase, which he had watched so long and so perseveringly pursued.

4. Unremitting exertions were made to equip the ships which he had chosen, and especially to refit the *Victory,* which was once more to bear his flag. Before he left London he called at his upholsterer's, where the coffin which Captain Hallowell had given him was deposited, and desired that its history might be engraven upon the lid, saying, it was highly probable he might want it on his return. He seemed, indeed, to have been impressed with an expectation that he should fall in the battle. In a letter to his brother, written immediately after his return, he had said : " We must not talk of Sir Robert Calder's battle. I might not have done so much with my small force. If I had fallen in with them, you might probably have been a lord be-

---

* "Songs of Trafalgar."

fore I wished, for I know they meant to make a dead set at the *Victory.*" Nelson had once regarded the prospect of death with gloomy satisfaction; it was when he anticipated the upbraidings of his wife and the displeasure of his venerable father. The state of his feelings now was expressed in his private journal in these words: " Friday night (Sept. 13th), at half-past ten, I drove from dear, dear Merton, where I left all (*a*) which I hold dear in this world, to go to serve my king and country. May the great God whom I adore enable me to fulfil the expectations of my country ! And if it is His good pleasure that I should return, my thanks will never cease being offered up to the throne of His mercy. If it is His good providence to cut short my days upon earth, I bow with the greatest submission ; relying that He will protect those so dear to me whom I may leave behind ! His will be done. Amen ! Amen ! Amen ! "

5. Early on the following morning he reached Portsmouth, and having despatched his business on shore, endeavoured to elude the populace by taking a byeway to the beach, but a crowd collected in his train, pressing forward to obtain sight of his face ; many were in tears, and many knelt down before him and blessed him as they passed. England has had many heroes, but (*b*) never one who so entirely possessed the love of his fellow-countrymen as Nelson. All men knew that his heart was as humane as it was fearless ; that there was not in his nature the slightest alloy of selfishness or cupidity, but that with perfect and entire devotion he served his country (*c*) with all his heart, and with all his soul, and with all his strength ; and therefore they loved him as truly and as fervently as he loved England. They pressed upon the parapet to gaze after him when his barge pushed off, and he was returning their cheers by waving his hat. The sentinels who endeavoured to prevent them from trespassing upon this ground, were wedged among the crowd, and an officer, who, not very prudently upon

such an occasion, ordered them to drive the people down with their bayonets, was compelled speedily to retreat; for the people would not be debarred from gazing till the last moment upon the hero—the darling hero—of England.

6. He arrived off Cadiz on the 29th of September—his birthday. Fearing that, if the enemy knew his force, they might be deterred from venturing to sea, he kept out of sight of land, desired Collingwood to fire no salute and hoist no colours, and wrote to Gibraltar to request that the force of the fleet might not be inserted there in the "Gazette." His reception in the Mediterranean fleet was as gratifying as the farewell of his countrymen at Portsmouth; the officers, who came on board to welcome him, forgot his rank as commander in their joy at seeing him again. On the day of his arrival Villeneuve received orders to put to sea the first opportunity. Villeneuve, however, hesitated when he heard that Nelson had resumed the command. He called a council of war, and their determination was that it would not be expedient to leave Cadiz unless they had reason to believe themselves stronger by one-third than the British force. In the public measures of this country secrecy is seldom practicable and seldom attempted; here, however, by the precautions of Nelson and the wise measures of the Admiralty, the enemy were for once kept in ignorance; for, as the ships appointed to reinforce the Mediterranean fleet were despatched singly, each as soon as it was ready, their collected number was not stated in the newspapers, and their arrival was not known to the enemy. But the enemy knew that Admiral Louis, with six sail, had been detached for stores and water to Gibraltar. Accident also contributed to make the French admiral doubt whether Nelson himself had actually taken the command. An American, lately arrived from England, maintained that it was impossible, for he had seen him only a few days before in London, and at that time there was no rumour of his going again to sea.

7. The station which Nelson had chosen was some fifty or sixty miles to the west of Cadiz, near Cape St. Mary's At this distance he hoped to decoy the enemy out, while he guarded against the danger of being caught with a westerly wind near Cadiz, and driven within the Straits. The blockade of the port was rigorously enforced, in hopes that the combined fleet might be forced to sea by want. The Danish vessels therefore, which were (a) carrying provisions from the French ports in the bay, under the name of Danish property, to all the little ports from Ayamonte to Algeziras, from whence they were conveyed in coasting boats to Cadiz, were seized. Without this proper exertion of power the blockade would have been rendered nugatory by the advantage thus taken of the neutral flag. The supplies from France were thus effectually cut off. There was now every indication that the enemy would speedily venture out; officers and men were in the highest spirits at the prospect of giving them a decisive blow—such, indeed, as would put an end to (b) all further contest upon the seas. Theatrical amusements were performed every evening in most of the ships, and "God save the King" was the hymn with which the sports concluded. "I verily believe," said Nelson, writing on the 6th of October, "that the country will soon be put to some expense on my account, either a monument or a new pension and honors; for I have not the smallest doubt but that a very few days, almost hours, will put us in battle. The success no man can insure, but for the fighting them, if they can be got at, I pledge myself. The sooner the better; I don't like to have these things upon my mind."

8. At this time he was not without some cause of anxiety; he was in want of frigates—the eyes of the fleet, as he always called them, to the want of which the enemy before were indebted for their escape, and Bonaparte for his arrival in Egypt. He had only twenty-three ships; others were on the way, but they might come too late; and though Nelson never

doubted of victory, mere victory was not what he looked to : he wanted to annihilate the enemy's fleet. The Carthagena squadron might effect a junction with this fleet on the one side, and on the other it was to be expected that a similar attempt would be made by the French from Brest ; in either case a formidable contingency to be apprehended by the blockading force. The Rochefort squadron did push out, and had nearly caught the *Agamemnon* and *L'Aimable* in their way to reinforce the British admiral. Yet Nelson at this time weakened his own fleet. He had the unpleasant task to perform of sending home Sir Robert Calder, whose conduct was to be made the subject of a court-martial in consequence of the general dis- satisfaction which had been felt and expressed at his imperfect victory. Sir Robert Calder and Sir John Orde, Nelson believed to be the only two enemies whom he had ever had in his pro- fession ; and, from that sensitive delicacy which distinguished him, this made him the more scrupulously anxious to show every possible mark of respect and kindness to Sir Robert. He wished to detain him till after the expected action, when the services which he might perform, and the triumphant joy which would be excited, would leave nothing to be apprehended from an inquiry into the previous engagement. Sir Robert, however, whose situation was very painful, did not choose to delay a trial from the result of which he confidently expected a complete justification ; and Nelson, instead of sending him home in a frigate, insisted on his returning in his own ninety- gun ship, ill as such a ship could at that time be spared. Nothing could be more honourable than the feeling by which Nelson was influenced, but at such a crisis it ought not to have been indulged.

9. On the 9th Nelson sent Collingwood what he called in his diary "the Nelson-touch." "I send you," said he, "my plan of attack, as far as a man dare venture to guess at the very uncertain position the enemy may be found in ; but it is to

place you perfectly at ease respecting my intentions, and to give
full scope to your judgment for carrying them into effect. We
can, my dear Coll, have no little jealousies. We have only one
great object in view, that of annihilating our enemies, and
getting a glorious peace for our country. No man has more
confidence in another than I have in you, and no man will
render your services more justice than your very old friend, (a)
Nelson and Bronte." The order of sailing was to be the order
of battle—the fleet in two lines, with an advanced squadron of
eight of the fastest sailing two-deckers. The second in command, having the entire direction of his line, was to break
through the enemy, about the twelfth ship from their rear; (b)
he would lead through the centre, and the advanced squadron
was to cut off three or four ahead of the centre. This plan
was to be adapted to the strength of the enemy, so that they
should always be one-fourth superior to those whom they cut
off. Nelson said that "his admirals and captains, knowing his
precise object to be that of a close and decisive action, would
supply any deficiency of signals, and act accordingly. In case
signals cannot be seen or clearly understood, no captain can do
wrong if he places his ship alongside that of an enemy. One
of the last orders of this admirable man was that the name
and family of every officer, seaman, and marine, who might be
killed or wounded in action, should be as soon as possible returned to him, in order to be transmitted to the chairman of
the patriotic fund, that the case might be taken into consideration for the benefit of the sufferer or his family.

10. About half-past nine in the morning of the 19th the
Mars, being the nearest to the fleet of the ships which formed
the line of communication with the frigates in-shore, repeated
the signal that the enemy were coming out of port. The wind
was at this time very light, with partial breezes, mostly from
the S.S.W. Nelson ordered the signal to be made for a chase
in the south-east quarter. About two the repeating ships

announced that the enemy were at sea. All night the British
fleet continued under all sail, steering to the south-east. At
daybreak they were in the entrance of the Straits, but the
enemy were not in sight. About seven, one of the frigates
made signal that the enemy were bearing north. Upon this
the *Victory* hove to, and shortly afterwards Nelson made sail
again to the northward. In the afternoon the wind blew fresh
from the south-west, and the English began to fear that the foe
might be forced to return to port.

11. A little before sunset, however, Blackwood, in the
Euryalus, telegraphed that they appeared determined to go to
the westward. "And that," said the Admiral in his diary,
"they shall not do, if it is in the power of Nelson and Bronte
to prevent them." Nelson had signified to Blackwood that
he depended upon him to keep sight of the enemy. They were
observed so well that all their motions were made known to
him, and as they wore twice, he inferred that they were aiming
to keep the port of Cadiz open, and would retreat there as soon
as they saw the British fleet; for this reason he was very careful not to approach near enough to be seen by them during the
night. At daybreak the combined fleets were distinctly seen
from the *Victory's* deck, formed in a close line of battle ahead,
on the starboard tack, about twelve miles to leeward, and
standing to the south. Our fleet consisted of twenty-seven
sail of the line and four frigates; theirs of thirty-three and
seven large frigates. Their superiority was greater in size and
weight of metal than in numbers. They had four thousand
troops on board, and the best riflemen that could be procured,
many of them Tyrolese, were dispersed through the ships.
Little did the Tyrolese and little did the Spaniards at that day
imagine what horrors the wicked tyrant whom they served was
preparing for their country.

12. Soon after daylight Nelson came upon deck. The 21st
of October was a festival in his family, because on that day his

uncle, Captain Suckling, in the *Dreadnaught*, with two other
line-of-battle ships, had beaten off a French squadron of four
sail of the line and three frigates.   Nelson, with that sort of
superstition from which few persons are entirely exempt, had
more than once expressed his persuasion that this was to be the
day of his battle also, and he was well pleased at seeing his pre-
diction about to be verified.   The wind was now from the west
—light breezes, with a long heavy swell.   Signal was made to
bear down upon the enemy in two lines, and the fleet set all
sail.   Collingwood, in the *Royal Sovereign*, led the lee line of
thirteen ships; the *Victory* led the weather line of fourteen.
Having seen that all was as it should be, Nelson retired to his
cabin and wrote the following prayer :—

"May the great God whom I worship grant to my country,
and for the benefit of Europe in general, a great and glorious
victory, and may no misconduct in any one tarnish it, and may
humanity after victory be the predominant feature in the British
fleet!   For myself individually, I commit my life to Him that
made me, and may His blessing alight on my endeavours for
serving my country faithfully !   To Him I resign myself, and
the just cause which is entrusted to me to defend.   Amen,
Amen, Amen."

Having thus discharged his devotional duties, he annexed,
in the same diary, the following remarkable writing :—

"*October 21st, 1805.—Then in sight of the combined fleets of
France and Spain, distant about ten miles.*

"Whereas, the eminent services of Emma Hamilton, widow
of the Right Honourable Sir William Hamilton, have been of
the very greatest service to my king and my country, to my
knowledge, without ever receiving any reward from either our
king or country :

"First, that she obtained the King of Spain's letter, in 1796,
to his brother, the King of Naples, acquainting him of his
intention to declare war against England ; from which letter

the Ministry sent out orders to the then Sir John Jervis to strike a stroke, if opportunity offered, against either the arsenals of Spain or her fleets. That neither of these was done is not the fault of Lady Hamilton; the opportunity might have been offered:

"Secondly, the British fleet under my command could never have returned the second time to Egypt had not Lady Hamilton's influence with the Queen of Naples caused letters to be wrote to the governor of Syracuse, that he was to encourage the fleet's being supplied with everything, should they put into any port in Sicily. We put into Syracuse, and received every supply, went to Egypt, and destroyed the French fleet.

"Could I have rewarded these services, I would not now call upon my country; but as that has not been in my power, I leave Emma Lady Hamilton therefore a legacy to my king and country, that they will give her an ample provision to maintain her rank in life.

"I also leave to the beneficence of my country my adopted daughter, Horatia Nelson Thompson; and I desire she will use in future the name of Nelson only.

"These are the only favours I ask of my king and country at this moment when I am going to fight their battle. May God bless my king and country, and all those I hold dear! My relations it is needless to mention; they will of course be amply provided for.

"NELSON AND BRONTE.

"Witness { HENRY BLACKWOOD.
T. M. HARDY."

13. The child of whom this writing speaks was believed to be his daughter, and so indeed he called her the last time he pronounced her name. She was then about five years old, living at Merton under Lady Hamilton's care. The last minutes which Nelson passed at Merton were employed in praying over this child as she lay sleeping. A portrait of Lady

Hamilton hung in his cabin; and no Catholic ever beheld the picture of his patron saint with devouter reverence. The undisguised and romantic passion with which he regarded it amounted almost to superstition; and when the portrait was now taken down, in clearing for action, he desired the men who removed it to "take care of his guardian angel." In this manner he frequently spoke of it, as if he believed there were a virtue in the image. He wore a miniature of her also next his heart.

14. Blackwood went on board the *Victory* about six. He found him in good spirits, but very calm; not in that exhilaration which he had felt upon entering into battle at Aboukir and Copenhagen; he knew that his own life would be particularly aimed at, and seems to have looked for death with almost as sure an expectation as for victory. His whole attention was fixed upon the enemy. They tacked to the northward, and formed their line on the larboard tack; thus bringing the shoals of Trafalgar and St. Pedro under the lee of the British, and keeping the port of Cadiz open for themselves. This was judiciously done; and Nelson, aware of all the advantages which he gave them, made signal to prepare to anchor.

15. Villeneuve was a skilful seaman, worthy of serving a better master and a better cause. His plan of defence was as well conceived and as original as the plan of attack. He formed the fleet in a double line, every alternate ship being about a cable's length to windward of her second ahead and astern. Nelson, certain of a triumphant issue to the day, asked Blackford what he should consider as a victory. That officer answered, that, considering the handsome way in which battle was offered by the enemy, their apparent determination for a fair trial of strength, and the situation of the land, he thought it would be a glorious result if fourteen were captured. He replied, " I shall not be satisfied with less than twenty." Soon afterwards he asked him if he did not think there was a

signal wanting. Captain Blackwood made answer that he thought the (a) whole fleet seemed very clearly to understand what they were about.   These words were scarcely spoken before that signal was made which will be remembered as long as the language or even the memory of England shall endure—Nelson's last signal : "ENGLAND EXPECTS EVERY MAN WILL DO HIS DUTY !" It was received throughout the fleet with a shout of answering acclamation, made sublime by the spirit which it breathed and the feelings which it expressed. "Now," said Lord Nelson, "I can do no more.   We must trust to the great Disposer of all events and the justice of our cause.   I thank God for this great opportunity of doing my duty."

16. He wore that day, as usual, his admiral's frock coat, bearing on the left breast four stars of the different orders with which he was invested.   Ornaments which rendered him so conspicuous a mark for the enemy were beheld with ominous apprehension by his officers.   It was known that there were riflemen on board the French ships, and it could not be doubted but that his life would be particularly aimed at. They communicated their fears to each other, and the surgeon, Mr. Beatty,* spoke to the chaplain, Dr. Scott, and to Mr. Scott, the public secretary, desiring that some person would entreat him to change his dress or cover the stars ; but they knew that such a request would highly displease him. "In honour I gained them," he had said when such a thing had been hinted to him formerly, "and in honour I will die with them."   Mr. Beatty, however, would not have been deterred by any fear of exciting his displeasure from speaking to him himself upon a subject in which the weal of England, as well as the life of Nelson was concerned ; but he was ordered from the deck before he could find an opportunity.   This was a point upon which Nelson's

* In this part of the work I have chiefly been indebted to this gentleman's "Narrative of Lord Nelson's Death," a document as interesting as it is authentic.

officers knew it was hopeless to remonstrate or reason with him ; but both Blackwood and his own captain, Hardy, represented to him how advantageous to the fleet it would be for him to keep out of action as long as possible, and he consented at last to let the *Leviathan*, and the *Temeraire*, which were sailing abreast of the *Victory*, be ordered to pass ahead. Yet even here the (*a*) last infirmity of this noble mind was indulged, for these ships could not pass ahead if the *Victory* continued to carry all her sail ; and so far was Nelson from shortening sail, that it was evident he took pleasure in pressing on, and rendering it impossible for them to obey his own orders. (*b*) A long swell was setting into the Bay of Cadiz. Our ships, crowding all sail, moved majestically before it, with light winds from the south-west. The sun shone on the sails of the enemy, and their well-formed line, with their numerous three-deckers, made an appearance which any other assailants would have thought formidable, but the British sailors only admired the beauty and the splendour of the spectacle, and, in full confidence of winning what they saw, remarked to each other what a fine sight yonder ships would made at Spithead !

17. The French admiral, from the *Bucentaure*, beheld the new manner in which his enemy was advancing—Nelson and Collingwood each leading his line ; and pointing them out to his officers, he is said to have exclaimed that such conduct could not fail to be successful. Yet Villeneuve had made his own dispositions with the utmost skill, and the fleets under his command waited for the attack with perfect coolness. Ten minutes before twelve they opened their fire. Eight or nine of the ships immediately ahead of the *Victory*, and across her bows, fired single guns at her to ascertain whether she was yet within their range. As soon as Nelson perceived that their shot passed over him he desired Blackwood and Captain Prowse, of the *Sirius*, to repair to their respective frigates, and on their way to tell all the captains of the line of battle ships

that he depended on their exertions, and that, if by the prescribed mode of attack they found it impracticable to get into
action immediately, they might adopt whatever they thought
best, provided it led them quickly and closely alongside an
enemy. As they were standing on the front poop, Blackwood
took him by the hand, saying he hoped soon to return and find
him in possession of twenty prizes. He replied, "God bless
you, Blackwood; I shall never see you again."

18. Nelson's column was steered about two points more to
the north than Collingwood's, in order to cut off the enemy's
escape into Cadiz. The lee line, therefore, was first engaged.
"See," cried Nelson, pointing to the *Royal Sovereign*, as she
steered right for the centre of the enemy's line, cut through it
astern of the *Santa Anna*, three-decker, and engaged her at
the muzzle of her guns on the starboard side; "see how that
noble fellow Collingwood carries his ship into action!" Collingwood, delighted at being first in the heat of the fire, and
knowing the feelings of his commander and old friend, turned
to his captain and exclaimed: "Rotherham, what would
Nelson give to be here!" Both these brave officers, perhaps,
at this moment thought of Nelson with gratitude for a circumstance which had occurred on the preceding day. Admiral
Collingwood, with some of the captains, having gone on board
the *Victory* to receive instructions, Nelson inquired of him
where his captain was, and was told in reply that they were
not upon good terms with each other. "Terms!" said Nelson;
"good terms with each other!" Immediately he sent a boat
for Captain Rotherham, led him, as soon as he arrived, to
Collingwood, and saying, "Look, yonder are the enemy!"
bade them shake hands like Englishmen.

19. The enemy continued to fire a gun at a time at the
Victory till they saw that a shot had passed through her main-
topgallant sail; then they opened their broadsides, aiming
chiefly at her rigging, in the hope of disabling her before she

could close on them. Nelson as usual had hoisted several flags, lest one should be shot away. The enemy showed no colours till late in the action, when they began to feel the necessity of having them to strike. For this reason the *Santissima Trinidad*, Nelson's old acquaintance, as he used to call her, was distinguishable only by her four decks, and to the bow of this opponent he ordered the *Victory* to be steered. Meantime an incessant raking fire was kept up upon the *Victory*. The Admiral's secretary was one of the first who fell; he was killed by a cannon shot while conversing with Hardy. Captain Adair, of the marines, with the help of a sailor, endeavoured to remove the body from Nelson's sight, who had a great regard for Mr. Scott, but he anxiously asked, " is that poor Scott that's gone ?" and being informed that it was indeed so, exclaimed, " Poor fellow !" Presently a double-headed shot struck a party of marines who were drawn up on the poop, and killed eight of them, upon which Nelson immediately desired Captain Adair to disperse his men round the ship, that they might not suffer so much from being together. A few minutes afterwards a shot struck the fore-brace bits on the quarter-deck, and passed between Nelson and Hardy, a splinter from the bit tearing off Hardy's buckle and bruising his foot. Both stopped, and looked anxiously at each other : each supposed the other to be wounded. Nelson then smiled, and said : " This is too warm work, Hardy, to last long."

20. The *Victory* had not yet returned a single gun; fifty of her men had been by this time killed or wounded, and her main-topmast, with all her studding-sails and their booms, shot away. Nelson declared that in all his battles he had seen nothing which surpassed the cool courage of his crew on this occasion. At four minutes after twelve she opened her fire from both sides of her deck. It was not possible to break the enemy's line without running on board one of their ships ; Hardy informed him of this, and asked him which he would

prefer. Nelson replied : " Take your choice, Hardy , it does not signify much." The master was ordered to put the helm to port, and the *Victory* ran on board the *Redoubtable* just as her tiller-ropes were shot away. The French ship received her with a broadside, then instantly let down her lower-deck ports for fear of being boarded through them, and never afterwards fired a great gun during the action. Her tops, like those of all the enemy's ships, were filled with riflemen. Nelson never placed musketry in his tops ; he had a strong dislike to the practice, not merely because it endangers setting fire to the sails, but also because it is a murderous sort of warfare, by which individuals may suffer and a commander now and then picked off, but which never can decide the fate of a general engagement.

21. Captain Harvey, in the *Temeraire*, fell on board the *Redoubtable* on the other side ; another enemy was in like manner on board the *Temeraire ;* so that these four ships formed as compact a tier as if they had been moored together, their heads all lying the same way. The lieutenants of the *Victory* seeing this, depressed their guns of the middle and lower decks, and fired with a diminished charge, lest the shot should pass through and injure the *Temeraire ;* and because there was danger that the *Redoubtable* might take fire from the lower deck guns, the muzzles of which touched her side when they were run out, the fireman of each gun stood ready with a bucket of water, which, as soon as the gun was discharged, he dashed into the hole made by the shot. An incessant fire was kept up from the *Victory* from both sides ; her larboard guns playing upon the *Buccentaure* and the huge *Santissima Trinidad.*

22. It had been part of Nelson's prayer that the British fleet might be distinguished by humanity in the victory he expected. Setting an example himself, he twice gave orders to cease firing upon the *Redoubtable*, supposing that she had struck, be-

4

cause her great guns were silent; for, as she carried no flag,
there was no means of instantly ascertaining the fact. From
this ship, which he had thus twice spared, he received his
death. A ball fired from her mizen-top, which in the then situation of the two vessels was not more than fifteen yards from
that part of the deck where he was standing, struck the
epaulette on his left shoulder, about a quarter after one, just
in the heat of action. He fell upon his face, on the spot which
was covered with his poor secretary's blood. Hardy, who was
a few steps from him, turning round, saw three men raising
him up. "They have done for me at last, Hardy!" said he.
"I hope not!" cried Hardy. "Yes," he replied, "my back-
bone is shot through!" Yet even now, not for a moment
losing his presence of mind, he observed as they were carrying
him down the ladder that the tiller-ropes, which had been shot
away, were not yet replaced, and ordered that new ones should
be rove immediately. Then, that he might not be seen by the
crew, he took out his handkerchief and covered his face and his
stars. Had he but concealed these badges of honour from the
enemy, England perhaps would not have had cause to receive
with sorrow the news of the battle of Trafalgar. The cockpit
was crowded with wounded and dying men, over whose bodies
he was with some difficulty conveyed, and laid upon a pallet in
the midshipmen's berth. It was soon perceived, upon examination, that the wound was mortal. This, however, was concealed from all except Captain Hardy, the chaplain, and the
medical attendants. He himself being certain, from the sensation in his back and the gush of blood he felt momently within his breast, that no human care could avail him, insisted that
the surgeon should leave him, and attend to those to whom he
might be useful; "for," said he, "you can do nothing for me."
All that could be done was to fan him with paper, and frequently give him lemonade to alleviate his intense thirst. He
was in great pain, and expressed much anxiety for the event

of the action, which now began to declare itself. As often as a ship struck the crew of the *Victory* hurraed, and at every hurra a visible expression of joy gleamed in the eyes and marked the countenance of the dying hero. But he became impatient to see Captain Hardy, and as that officer, though often sent for, could not leave the deck, Nelson feared that some fatal cause prevented him, and repeatedly cried: "Will no one bring Hardy to me? He must be killed! He is surely dead!" An hour and ten minutes elapsed from the time when Nelson received his wound before Hardy could come to him. They shook hands in silence; Hardy in vain struggling to express the feelings of that most painful and yet sublimest moment. "Well, Hardy," said Nelson, "How goes the day with us?"—"Very well," replied Hardy; "ten ships have struck, but five of the van have tacked, and show an intention to bear down upon the *Victory*. I have called two or three of our fresh ships round, and have no doubt of giving them a drubbing."—"I hope," said Nelson, "none of our ships have struck?" Hardy answered, "There was no fear of that." Then, and not till then, Nelson spoke of himself. "I am a dead man, Hardy," said he: "I am going fast; it will be all over with me soon. Come nearer to me. Let my dear Lady Hamilton have my hair and all other things belonging to me." Hardy observed that he hoped Mr. Beatty could yet hold out some prospect of life. "Oh no!" he replied, "it is impossible; my back is shot through. Beatty will tell you so." Captain Hardy then once more shook hands with him, and with a heart almost bursting hastened on deck.

23. By this time all feeling below the breast was gone; and Nelson, having made the surgeon ascertain this, said to him: "You know I am gone. I know it. I feel something rising in my breast"— putting his hand on his left side—"which tells me so." And upon Beatty's inquiring whether his pain was very great, he replied: "So great that he wished he was

dead.   "Yet," said he in a lower voice, "one would like to live a little longer too!"   And after a few minutes, in the same undertone, he added: "What would become of poor Lady Hamilton if she knew my situation?" Next to his country she occupied his thoughts. Captain Hardy, some fifty minutes after he had left the cockpit, returned, and again taking the hand of his dying friend and commander, congratulated him on having gained a complete victory. How many of the enemy were taken he did not know, as it was impossible to perceive them distinctly ; but fourteen or fifteen at least.   "That's well !" cried Nelson ; "but I bargained for twenty."   And then in a stronger voice he said : "Anchor, Hardy, anchor."   Hardy upon this hinted that Admiral Collingwood would take upon himself the direction of affairs. "Not while I live, Hardy," said the dying Nelson, ineffectually endeavouring to raise himself from the bed ; "Do you anchor." His previous order for preparing to anchor had shown how clearly he foresaw the necessity of this.   Presently, calling Hardy back, he said to him in a low voice : "Don't throw me overboard ;" and he desired that he might be buried by his parents, unless it should please the King to order otherwise. Then reverting to private feelings : "Take care of my dear Lady Hamilton, Hardy ; take care of poor Lady Hamilton. Kiss me, Hardy," said he.   Hardy knelt down and kissed his cheek, and Nelson said : "Now I am satisfied.   Thank God, I I have done my duty !"   Hardy stood over him in silence for a moment or two, then knelt again and kissed his forehead. "Who is that?" said Nelson ; and being informed, he replied : "God bless you, Hardy."   And Hardy then left him forever.

24. Nelson now desired to be turned upon his right side, and said : "I wish I had not left the deck, for I shall soon be gone."   Death was indeed rapidly approaching.   He said to the chaplain : "Doctor, I have *not* been a *great* sinner."   And after a short pause : "Remember that I leave Lady Hamilton

and my daughter Horatia as a legacy to my country." His articulation now became difficult, but he was distinctly heard to say: "Thank God, I have done my duty!" These words he repeatedly pronounced, and they were the last words which he uttered. He expired at thirty minutes after four, three hours and a quarter after he had received his wound.

25. Within a quarter of an hour after Nelson was wounded about fifty of the *Victory's* men fell by the enemy's musketry. (a) They, however, on their part were not idle, and it was not long before there were only two Frenchmen left alive in the mizen-top of the *Redoubtable.* One of them was the man who had given the fatal wound—he did not live to boast of what he had done. An old quartermaster had seen him fire, and easily recognized him because he wore a glazed cocked-hat and a white frock. This quartermaster and two midshipmen, Mr. Collingwood and Mr. Pollard, were the only persons left in the *Victory's* poop; the two midshipmen kept firing at the top, and he supplied them with cartridges. One of the Frenchmen, attempting to make his escape down the rigging, was shot by Mr. Pollard, and fell on the poop. But the old quartermaster, as he cried out "That's he, that's he!" and pointed at the other, who was coming forward to fire again, received a shot in his mouth and fell dead. Both the midshipmen then fired at the same time, and the fellow dropped in the top. When they took possession of the prize they went into the mizen-top and found him dead, with one ball through his head and another through his breast.

26. The *Redoubtable* struck within twenty minutes after the fatal shot had been fired from her. During that time she had been twice on fire—in her forechains and in her forecastle. The French, as they had done in other battles, made use in this of fireballs and other combustibles: implements of destruction which other nations, from a sense of honour and humanity, have laid aside, which add to the sufferings of the

wounded without determining the issue of the combat, which none but the cruel would employ, and which never can be successful against the brave. Once they succeeded in setting fire, from the *Redoubtable*, to some ropes and canvas on the *Victory's* booms. The cry ran through the ship and reached the cockpit, but even this dreadful cry produced no confusion : the men displayed that perfect self-possession in danger by which English seamen are characterized ; they extinguished the flames on board their own ship, and then hastened to extinguish them in the enemy by throwing buckets of water from the gangway. When the *Redoubtable* had struck it was not practicable to board her from the *Victory;* for though the two ships touched, the upper works of both fell in so much that there was a great space between their gangways, and she could not be boarded from the lower or middle decks because her ports were down. Some of our men went to Lieutenant Quilliam and offered to swim under her bows, and get up there, but it was thought unfit to haz rd brave lives in this manner.

27. What our men would have done from gallantry some of the crew of the *Santissima Trinidad* did to save themselves. Unable to stand the tremendous fire of the *Victory,* whose larboard guns played against this great four-decker, and not knowing how else to escape them, nor where else to betake themselves for protection, many of them leapt overboard and swam to the *Victory,* and were actually helped up her sides by the English during the action. The Spaniards began the battle with less vivacity than their unworthy allies, but continued it with greater firmness. The *Argonauta* and *Bahama* were defended till they had each lost about 400 men ; the *San Juan Nepomuceno* lost 350. Often as the superiority of British courage has been proved against France upon the seas, it was never more conspicuous than in this decisive conflict. Five of our ships were engaged muzzle to muzzle with five of the French. In all five the Frenchmen lowered their lower-deck

ports and deserted their guns, while our men continued delib
erately to load and fire till they had made the victory secure.

28. Once, amidst his sufferings, Nelson had expressed a wish
that he were dead ; but immediately the spirit subdued the
pains of death, and he wished to live a little longer—doubtless
then he might hear the completion of the victory which he had
seen so gloriously begun. That consolation, that joy, that
triumph was afforded him. He lived to know that the victory
was decisive, and the last guns which were fired at the flying
enemy were heard a minute or two before he expired. The
ships which were thus flying were four of the enemy's van,
all French, under Rear-Admiral Dumanoir. They had borne
no part in the action; and now, when they were seeking safety
in flight, they fired not only into the *Victory* and *Royal
Sovereign* as they passed, but poured their broadsides into the
Spanish captured ships, and they were seen to back their top
sails for the purpose of firing with more precision. The indignation of the Spanish at this detestable cruelty from their
allies, for whom they had fought so bravely, and so profusely
bled, may well be conceived. It was such that when, two days
after the action, seven of the ships which had escaped
into Cadiz came out, in hopes of retaking some of the disabled
prizes, the prisoners in the *Argonauta* in a body offered their
services to the British prize-master to man the guns against
any of the French ships ; saying, that if a Spanish ship came
alongside they would quietly go below, but they requested that
they might be allowed to fight the French in resentment for
the murderous usage which they had suffered at their hands.
Such was their earnestness, and such the implicit confidence
which could be placed in Spanish honour, that the offer was
accepted, and they were actually stationed at the lower deck
guns. Dumanoir and his squadron were not more fortunate
than the fleet from whose destruction they fled : they fell in
with Sir Richard Strachan, who was cruising for the Rochefort

squadron, and were all taken.   In the better days of France,
if such a crime could then have been committed, it would have
received an exemplary punishment from the French Government ; under Bonaparte it was sure of impunity, and perhaps
might be thought deserving of reward.   But if the Spanish
Court had been independent, it would have become us to have
delivered Dumanoir and his captains up to Spain, that they
might have been brought to trial, and hanged in sight of the
remains of the Spanish fleet.

29. The total British loss in the battle of Trafalgar amounted
to 1,587.   Twenty of the enemy struck ; unhappily, the fleet
did not anchor, as Nelson, almost with his dying breath, had
enjoined.   A gale came on from the south-west : some of the
prizes went down, some went on shore ; one effected its escape
into Cadiz ; others were destroyed ; four only were saved, and
those by the greatest exertions.   The wounded Spaniards were
sent ashore, an assurance being given that they should not
serve till regularly exchanged ; and the Spaniards, with a
generous feeling, which would not perhaps have been found in
any other people, offered the use of their hospitals for our
wounded, pledging the honour of Spain that they should be
carefully attended there.   When the storm, after the action,
drove some of the prizes upon the coast, they declared that the
English, who were thus thrown into their hands, should not be
considered as prisoners of war ; and the Spanish soldiers gave
up their own beds to their shipwrecked enemies.   The Spanish
vice-admiral, Alva, died of his wounds.   Villeneuve was sent
to England, and permitted to return to France.   The French
Government say that he destroyed himself on the way to Paris,
dreading the consequences of a court-martial ; but there is
every reason to believe that the tyrant, who never acknowledged the loss of the battle of Trafalgar, added Villeneuve to the numerous victims of his murderous policy.

30. It is almost superfluous to add that all the honours

which a grateful country could bestow were heaped upon the memory of Nelson. His brother was made an Earl, with a grant of £6,000 a year ; £10,000 were voted to each of his sisters, and £100,000 for the purchase of an estate. A public funeral was decreed, and a public monument. Statues and monuments also were voted by most of our principal cities. The leaden coffin in which he was brought home was cut in pieces, which were distributed as relics of St. Nelson—so the gunner of the *Victory* called them ; and when at his interment his flag was about to be lowered into the grave, the sailors who assisted at the ceremony with one accord rent it in pieces, that each might preserve a fragment while he lived.

31. The death of Nelson was felt in England as something more than a public calamity ; men started at the intelligence and turned pale, as if they had heard of the loss of a dear friend. An object of our admiration and affection, of our pride and of our hopes, was suddenly taken from us ; and it seemed as if we had never till then known how deeply we loved and reverenced him. What the country had lost in its great naval hero—the greatest of our own and (*a*) of all former times —was scarcely taken into the (*b*) account of grief. So perfectly indeed had he performed his part, that the maritime war after the battle of Trafalgar was considered at an end . the fleets of the enemy were not merely defeated, (*c*) but destroyed ; new navies must be built, and a new race of seamen reared for them, before the possibility of their invading our shores could again be contemplated. It was not, therefore, from any selfish reflection upon the magnitude of our loss that we mourned for him ; the general sorrow was of a higher character. The people of England grieved that funeral ceremonies, and public monuments, and posthumous rewards were all (*d*) which they could now bestow upon him whom the King, the Legislature, and the nation would have alike delighted to honour ; whom every tongue would have blessed ; whose presence in

every village through which he might have passed would have
wakened the church bells, have given school-boys a holiday,
have drawn children from their sports to gaze upon him, and
"old men from the chimney corner" to look upon Nelson ere
they died. The victory of Trafalgar was celebrated, indeed,
with the usual forms of rejoicing, but they were without joy;
for such already was the glory of the British navy through
Nelson's surpassing genius, that it scarcely seemed to receive
any addition from the most signal victory that ever was achieved
upon the seas; and the destruction of this mighty fleet, by
which all the maritime schemes of France were totally frustrated, hardly appeared to add to our security or strength, for
while Nelson was living to watch the combined squadrons of
the enemy we felt ourselves as secure as now, when they were
no longer in existence.

32. There was reason to suppose, from the appearances
upon opening the body, that in the course of nature he might
have attained, like his father, to good old age. Yet he cannot
be said to have fallen prematurely whose work was done, nor
ought he to be lamented who died so full of honours and at the
height of human fame. The most triumphant death is that of
the martyr; the most awful is that of the martyred patriot;
the most splendid that of the hero in the hour of victory; and
if the chariot and the horses of fire had been vouchsafed
for Nelson's translation, he could scarcely have departed in
a brighter blaze of glory. He has left us, not indeed his
mantle of inspiration, but a name and an example which are
at this hour inspiring thousands of the youth of England—a
name which is our pride, and an example which will continue
to be our shield and our strength. Thus it is that the spirits
of the great and the wise continue to live and to act after
them, verifying in this sense the language of the old
mythologist:

Τοὶ μὲν δαίμονές εἰσί, Διὸς μεγάλου διὰ βουλὰς
Ἐσθλοὶ, ἐπιχθόνιοι, φύλακες θνητῶν ἀνθρώπων.

NOTES AND EXERCISES.

A SIMPLE prose selection like this Life will require few explanatory notes ; but as the chief object aimed at in prescribing the prose author is the cultivation of a good prose style supplementary remarks and exercises are given, chiefly on the earlier paragraphs, in the hope that the student will be led to give his attention to the principles of prose style in his composition. The principles of sentence construction, though important, have not in these notes received much attention, chief stress being laid on the construction of the paragraphs, on the principle that "if we take care of the paragraphs the composition will take care of itself."

[The marginal figures refer to the paragraphs.]

CHAPTER VII.

1. *a* This is a trifling circumstance to break the sequence of the paragraph with ; but in biography the author is justified in introducing such personal incidents, if interesting, or if they show a leading characteristic in the person.

 b Rearrange the clauses here.

 c That is here emphatic ; put it in the proper place for emphasis.

 d and *e* The pronouns **This** and it are here used very loosely. The meaning may be shown by using [This separation], and [an infatuation which, etc.] and running the two sentences together as far as friends ; beginning the next sentence with "It, however, produced," etc.

 f [had] occasioned.

Remarks.—This paragraph, being the first of the chapter, might have contained some general reference to the subject of the chapter. It is rather the conclusion of chapter vi., and the second paragraph introduces the real subject of this chapter. Short as it is, however, it contains two separate groups of sentences—Nelson's public reception, and his domestic life. Each division is introduced by a general statement, which is followed by particulars under it. Nelson's domestic happiness might have formed a separate paragraph and have contained further details of his domestic habits, which

[95]

would be interesting in the case of so remarkable a man. The paragraph contains some of the peculiarities of Southey's style, such as :

Grouping sentences on several distinct topics.

Heading a group with a general statement, and filling in the explanatory particulars.

No words to indicate the transition from one subject to another ; and the omission of words that indicate the relation of sentences to each other.

His sentences are loose rather than periodic. There is no art shown in arranging the ideas or the words. The thoughts are uttered as they occur to his mind, with an easy fluency, sometimes negligent, but always captivating.

Exercises.—1. The student should test each paragraph by the rule given in iii., above, noting the deviations from the rules, and any circumstances that justify those deviations.

2. Write a summary of Nelson's public career that would serve as a "backward reference" introducing this chapter.

3. Write a paragraph on the difference between history and biography.

4. Write a note on Nelson's character, and the manner in which it has been presented in this Life.

5. Write a criticism of the Life of Nelson as a biography, comparing it with any other noted biography.

6. Write notes showing how far Nelson and Southey may, each in his line, be taken as the product of the age in which they lived.

2. *a* This was on the defeat of Pitt on the Catholic Emancipation Bill.

   b There were formerly three divisions in the navy - the red, the white and the blue—each having an admiral, a vice-admiral and a rear-admiral. The distinction is now abolished. The words "red, white and blue," in the song, refer to these divisions.

   c Sir John Jervis, raised to the Peerage for the battle of St. Vincent (see early chapters). It was from him that Nelson had learned the clever manœuvre by which half of the enemy's line of battle were detached from the rest, and destroyed before the others could come to their aid—a manœuvre that repeatedly baffled the French.

   d The naval rights here meant were those by which England sought to prevent neutral vessels from carrying war material to either belligerent power. The dispute led to the armed neutrality of 1780, in which Russia, France, Spain and America leagued to enforce the doctrine that "free ships made free goods." The dispute on this occasion arose upon the interpretation of "war material," the French insisting that it did not include such articles as timber, hemp, tow, etc., which they needed for their ships. The nations in the League of the north were really banded together in defence of their existence as commercial nations. But England had too much at stake to make nice distinctions, and risked incurring the hostility of these powers. Fortunately she succeeded, and the battle of Trafalgar gave her the commerce of the world.

e It is remarkable that each of the three leagued powers, and their oppo nent, England, was at this time ruled by a King more or less crazy. Paul I., of Russia, was at times a violent lunatic, perpetrating frightful atrocities, till he was finally murdered ; Gustavus Adolphus, of Sweden, was subject to fits of imbecility ; Christian VII., of Denmark, was a hopeless imbecile, and had resigned all power to the Prince Royal, his son ; and George III., of England, was subject to periods of imbecility. The condition of government in Europe, however, was at this time such that the people having sane rulers were worse off than those ruled by imbeciles. The pages of this Life give some glimpses of Bourbon rule in southern rule. We can pardon the strong national sympathy of Southey and Nelson, but we must read between the lines of the biographer's page to discover the historian.

f This somewhat epigrammatic sentence implies that a man with the ordinary weakness of human nature cannot possess absolute power without danger to himself, or perhaps without sin.

g Poor little Denmark was in a pitiable condition. Two giant powers, England and France, were contending for the mastery of the world, one was all powerful on the sea, the other on land. She wished to remained neutral, but her navy was coveted by France and her commerce hated by England. If she favoured England she would have been trampled down by France ; if she favoured France she became liable to punishment from England. To further her commerce and save her country she finally leaned towards France, and was accordingly punished.

Remarks.—This paragraph introduces the subject of the chapter—the Baltic Expedition. It opens in Southey's usual manner, with a general statement, which is followed by a few explanatory sentences without any connectives. The first sentence is not well formed, being too condensed, and containing too much to be lucid. The paragraph closes properly, with a few sentences bringing Nelson prominently before the reader.

Exercise.—As a composition, rewrite the paragraph in your own words, taking the statements in the following order :—Nelson's stay shortened by a new appointment—the Northern League—their navies—the aims of France —the determination of the Addington Cabinet—Nelson's application accepted by his old friend, Earl St. Vincent—but second only, as Parker had already been appointed first—popular disapproval—Nelson's merits · his disappointment.

3. *a* Most of these quotations are taken from Nelson's private letters, for

which Southey has been blamed by other writers, as many of the extracts show some of Nelson's weaknesses ; but undiscriminating hero worship is not the best mode of inculcating the lessons of a great-life. Such expressions as "the devils in the north," would show hat though Nelson had the genius of fighting he was not to be trusted with the chief command of an expedition that was to try conciliation and diplomacy before attacking a neutral power without declaring war.

Remarks.—The paragraph is rather loosely put together. The first sentence has no connection whatever with the rest. The Riou incident is given unusual prominence, but Southey seems to favour that captain.

Exercise.— Fill in the paragraph as follows : Nelson joins early season but favourable admiral timid—but Nelson resolute destination known Danes on *Amazon* - Riou.

4. This also is a rather loose paragraph. It opens well with the central idea in a short sentence ; but the second sentence is defective in not telling who Mr. Vansittart was, or what his sailing had to do with the negotiations. The third sentence has no connection with anything before or after it in the paragraph.

Exercise.—Rewrite the paragraph to the following heads : The start—double aim of expedition—mission of Vansittart (Lord Bexley) - reserve of admiral—chagrin of Nelson--his abilities—if government failed to see them the admiral did not—this proved well for England subsequently—Nelson's opinion of plans of attack as learned from his letters.

5. *a* [Profited, with all activity, of the leisure,] does not sound well. Improve it.

   b As this is taken from a letter written in haste, slight inaccuracies, arising from condensation or confusion of ideas, may be expected. There are several in the last four sentences. Write out the sentences correctly.

6. This paragraph is a continuation of the letter, partly in substance only, and partly by direct quotation. Such expressions as " supposing him," and " supposing them," are not elegant.

Exercise.—Rewrite the letter in direct quotation.

7. *a* This word is a favourite with Southey.

   b The captain of the fleet is an officer corresponding to the adjutant-general in the army. He has general supervision of the fleet, but is in command of no vessel.

   c Under way, is the more usual form.

   d Remodel this phrase.

   e but that ; but is now usually omitted.

Remarks. The Pilots are not the leading subject, and should not have occupied that place. Captain Domett's objections should be preceded by some introductory phrase, such as, " He assured him that."

Exercise.—Write sentences on the following heads, keeping up the proper sequence : Difficulties increased—pilots consulted—their advice—Nelson's impatience—fleet sailed—Domett's objections—Nelson consulted—fleet returns.

8. This paragraph, while censuring delay, really shows the English to be in the wrong. The last incident mentioned is scarcely worthy a place. It might have been placed in a foot note.

9. The first sentence here states an isolated fact, having no connection with the subject of the paragraph, or, indeed, with the expedition. The order of sailing, the real subject of the paragraph, is skilfully withheld till the last, where it gives a picturesque scene.

10. *a* Point of land nearest to, etc.

 b Tycho Brahe, a celebrated Danish astronomer, born 1546. In 1576, Frederick II. built him a large observatory and gave him the island of Huen for life, with a liberal pension. On Frederick's death the pension ceased, and Brahe, after a short residence in Copenhagen, removed to Prague, where he met Kepler, in whom he formed those habits of observation that afterwards made that astronomer famous.

 c "partly, but more frequently " are not usual correlatives.

 d The story of Hamlet is found in the history of Saxo Grammaticus. The Prince has been made famous by Shakespeare. In Elsinore, Hamlet's grave and Ophelia's brook are yet shown to visitors.

 e Matilda, the sister of George III., married Charles VII. That King's stepmother intrigued to have the crown descend to her own son, and laid false accusations against the fidelity of Matilda, which were believed at the time to be true. The queen's supposed accomplices were executed ; she was, at the instance of England, spared, but was exiled to Hanover, where she died.

Remarks.—This is the best paragraph we have yet had. The author, while the fleet is approaching the Sound, paints the magnificent view. His language is picturesque, and in dignified harmony with the subject. The subject itself affords a harmony of scene and incident (see Bain), and the author brings in the associated effect of personal interest by a few well selected incidents. The first sentence gains the effect of contrast, by stating a contrary state of affairs to the subject to be described, which is here introduced in the second sentence. The paragraph is long, and might have been broken where it changes from the political importance of the Sound to the description ; this would leave the picture and its personal interest to form a second paragraph. The plan of description shows us each side of the and, with the islands and water in the middle and Copenhagen as a background in the distance. The student should study this paragraph carefully; it will benefit him to criticize and to imitate the explanatory narrative in the beginning, the description of the scenery, and the taste in the selection of the historical allusions.

11. *a* never [before] had.

    b What is the original form of this expression?

    c Fell [short but] near, etc. The idea intended is that the shot did not reach the vessels.

    d [The English had meant to keep] would be better. Pronouns should refer to subjects of preceding sentences, not to objects; and it is not correct to speak of ships perceiving.

    e [So as to get completely out,] would bring the related words together.

    f [Ineffectual, or harmless.] Innocent conveys a moral sense.

Remarks.—Like the last, this paragraph begins in Macaulay's style, by stating something different from what is about to be described, the real subject being introduced by an adversative "but." The passage is well told, and the paragraph ends with a view of the formidable works to be attacked.

12. The deliberations of the Council of War are not related directly, but what is told gives prominence to Nelson, which is the author's intention.

13. *a* and the Danes considered [the] difficulty [of passing through the channel without them] as, etc.

    b "Day and night" generally implies a succession of days and nights, not one day and night as here.

Remarks.—This paragraph also has the adversative statement at the beginning. It has too much condensation throughout.

14. *a* At the distance of about, etc. The form in the text is unusual. The paragraph again begins with the adversative statement. The narrative gives a description from a traveller's point of view, new difficulties being detected as the fleet approaches. Nelson's part is again given prominence; and the paragraph ends with the rest of the plan arranged at the council.

15. *a* Whole, is here slightly ambiguous; it would be better placed after "displayed itself" [throughout the whole city].

    b "own means of defence," should have as correlative after it [the defence of], the invading, etc.

Remarks.—This description deals with the Danes throughout, and it properly forms a separate paragraph.

16. *a* They, refers to an object and not a subject of the preceding sentence.

    b Them [the English].

    c [of] mind. Southey too frequently omits small words in his sentences.

Remarks.—The first sentence appears to have no connection with the rest of the paragraph. It is introduced on the usual adversative principle, but it is too abrupt. The adversative "but," denoting contrast, would have been more effective than "far more so," which denotes comparison.

Paragraph 17 treats of the pilots, and Hardy's daring feat; 18, of the details of getting into action; and 19, of the beginning of the bombardment in position, each having a distinct subject.

    a This reason for giving the signal is denied by other biographers.

20. *a* [To delay the signal at least till, etc.]

Remarks.—The first sentence is well formed, but it belongs properly to 19. If it had been placed there this paragraph would then be confined to the admiral.

21. The scene now goes back to Nelson, and describes his conduct on reception of the signal. The paragraph ends with an affecting account of the death of Riou, to whom prominence had been purposely given in previous paragraphs.

22. *a* In the *Bellona* and [in] the *Isis*, omit "both."

    b Any [other] single ship.

    c Tremendous, the student will observe, is a favorite word with Southey.

23. The scene now changes to the Danes, but too much prominence is given to the Prince Royal by his position, as subject of the first sentence. There is no sequence in the first three sentences.

Exercise.—Write out sentences on the following heads, keeping up the sequence: The unusual importance of the contest to the Danes—national courage displayed in self defence—Thura—word sent to the Prince Royal, the commander, where he was watching the battle—his conduct--Shroeders—Villenoes.

In paragraphs 24 and 25 the scene is still laid on the Danish side, to show the effect of the battle on them; 26 and 27, treat of Nelson's clever note, the decision of the British to withdraw from their perilous position, and the close of the battle.

28. Here the author, after relating the incidents attending the withdrawal, pictures the scene of havoc. He does not boast or glory over the defeated; his sentiments, calm, dignified and melancholy, are expressed in eloquent language.

29. *a* or [from] supposing, etc.

    b of all. Omit "others." This mistake was frequently made by writers of Southey's time.

Remarks.—In this paragraph, the first two sentences belong to 28. The fourth sentence is a fair sample of Southey's long sentences; it is partly periodic, but on the whole loose. The meaning is perfectly clear.

    Paragraphs 30 and 31 are not well grouped. The transitions are too violent and not well marked.

Exercise.—Write out the two paragraphs on the following heads :

30. The English fleet on the night of the battle. Nelson - next morning. The Zealand—the English fleet next day losses on our side the sorrow of the Danes their occupation—their loss.

31. Negotiations meantime continued –interview necessary—Nelson in Copenhagen —settling preliminaries—the report.

32. In this paragraph events are confused by not following the order of time, and the last remark is too trifling for the close.

Exercise.- Re-write in this order : Grief and sympathy of the Danes— aid sent from all parts—burial of the dead—subscription for relief how collected—medals –monument—painters and writers.

34. *a* [The commissioners separated, or the commission broke up.]

    b What is the history of the word *levee ?*

    Note the abrupt introduction of the terms of the armistice, without any explanation.

35. In many of the circumstances related in this and the 33rd paragraph, though Southey's object was to win our sympathy for Nelson, we can see that he was eccentric, petulent and undignified. The reply in the next paragraph redounds more to the honour of the Danes than of the English.

Exercises.—(1) Write an account of the bombardment of Copenhagen in three paragraphs : 1. The causes, and the measures taken ; 2. The sailing of the fleet and its arrival at Copenhagen ; 3. The battle. (2) Write a paragraph on each of the heads of this chapter.

CHAPTER VIII.

2. The first three sentences belong to 1; the next three refer to Sir Hyde, and the remainder to Nelson.

3. *a* The Emperor Paul was assassinated by a band of conspirators headed by Count Pahlen, and his son Alexander, a warm friend of England, was immediately proclaimed Emperor.

Remarks.—Down to the word *Elephant* properly belongs to 2.

5. This sentence is set off as a paragraph to emphasize the important statement it contains, but it might have included the first five sentences of 6.

7. *a* This is an ill-constructed sentence ; too much is condensed into few words ; "and" should couple the last clause, with something about the firing, not about the delay, as in the text. Re-write the sentence, bringing out the four ideas it contains.

8. *a* "answer" and "return" are both used with reference to the message from Russia ; which is correct ?

b [Depart] would be a better word here.

c "Repeated" is not the word to use here.

d His anxious wish [to pay] and [to sign].

Remarks.—The first sentence is defective, as the latter clause dislocates the sequence ; the clause belongs in subject to 7, and should be there.

10. *a* Though no second punishment was given the Danes then, the intrigues of France and Russia, to force Denmark into an alliance, led England in 1807 to anticipate them by taking the Danish fleet.

b The French revolutionary party had a large following in every country in Europe, and as all the Powers were determined to restore the Bourbons in France, the French offered to assist the people of every other country in overthrowing their rulers.

c The meaning here is that if generosity restrained the English from hostilities, an apology should be demanded from the Prince Royal.

11. *a* Even than is the usual form, but "than even" is better collocation.

13. *a* What use of "and" is this ?

17. The opening incident here about the French captain belongs to 16, and this paragraph should be confined to Nelson's private letter.

18. *a* Many of the English people sympathized with the French, and the revolutionary spirit was so strong that the government was forced to use great severity in suppressing the manifestation of popular feeling. But the chief cause of joy at the peace of Amiens was no doubt the hope of relief it brought to the poor who had been in a state bordering on starvation while England was shut out by the war from the markets of Europe.

19. *a* Lady Hamilton, the second wife of Sir William Hamilton, the noted antiquarian, was a woman of great beauty and some ability. Her life was remarkable. She was born of humble parents, and spent her youth in domestic service. While a waitress in a tavern she became acquainted with actors, and soon entered on a wild life. As the wife of Sir William Hamilton she lived at Naples, where she gained a complete ascendency over the mind of the Queen, thus gaining much valuable information for Nelson. After Nelson's death she squandered her means, and after being imprisoned for debt retired with Nelson's daughter, Horatia, to Calais, where she died in 1815.

20. *a* The Mayor [had] replied, would put all the verbs in the same tense.

   b "He" is somewhat ambiguous. Nelson now maintained that he had kept his word, etc., would remove the ambiguity. The Lord Mayor's incident is introduced with Southey's usual abruptness; a sentence, showing Nelson's chagrin at the slight, might have preceded the incident.

21. *a* These five battles are mentioned in the early chapters of his life. There can be no doubt about the difficulty, the bravery and the hard fighting alluded to with regard to Copenhagen, but the victory was dubious; the position of the English at the close was critical, and nothing but the extreme anxiety of the Danes for their fleet, which had been removed to the inner channel, saved the English ships from destruction. Another probable reason for witholding these honours was the political necessity of regaining the friendship of the Danes.

23. The last sentence of 22 might have opened this paragraph, as it introduces the subject.

24 *a* As a Peer of the Realm, he would have a seat in the House of Lords. Paragraphs 24, 25, 26 and 27 interrupt the thread of the narrative to show Nelson's relations with the navy. The opening sentence makes a general assertion, which the four paragraphs explain. The subjects are well grouped; 24 treats of the kind interest he took in the welfare of the men; 25 of his gentle mode of discipline; 26 of his professional zeal for the navy, and 27 of his desire to reward merit.

28 *a* The character of Napoleon is still a disputed question in history, but Southey had no doubt about it.

   b Nelson never had any "film" over his eyes. He had never dreamed of pantisocracy, and his "mother hated the French."

Remarks.—Paragraphs 28 and 29 continue the interruption to the narrative; 28 gives us, in a series of thoughtful and well-expressed sentences, the political character of the French, and discusses their immediate aims in the Mediterranean; 29 explains Napoleon's designs on Europe, and the position of Spain.

32. The first five sentences here belong to 31, as this paragraph treats of Nelson's patient watch at Toulon.

33. *a* Spain was in the position in which Denmark had been between France and England; the one robbed her on land and the other at sea. War had not been declared, but such a life and death contest is not a time for nice distinctions.

   b Were never wounded [more] deeply [than] now.

The remaining paragraphs of the chapter tell in spirited language Nelson's celebrated chase after the French fleet. It was a grand achievement, but in doing it Nelson merely fell into the trap set for him by Napoleon, whose grand scheme then was the invasion of England. To do this he wanted the channel free from English vessels. He held an army of 130,000 men, camped on the coast for two years, with an immense number of transportation boats. Everything was ready; the soldiers and horses were even drilled in embarking on the boats till it could be done in one hour. All he wanted was command of the channel for forty-eight hours. To secure this he directed his fleet to sail to America to menace the colonies, and when it had thus drawn Nelson with the British fleet to America, to sail back immediately, collecting all the French and Spanish vessels from the various ports, and thus get command of the channel for a short time. The first part of the scheme succeeded, and the whole, as far as the fleet was concerned, would have done so if Villeneuve had not been frightened by the terrible name of Nelson into disobeying orders.

CHAPTER IX.

1. a At length, at last; which is the proper expression here?
   b See the account of Hotham's battle off Toulon (chapter iii).

2. a Nelson and the English public were of this opinion, but it is not according to facts. The French had orders to sail for Europe the moment they heard of Nelson's arrival at America.
   b Is this the right word here?
   c What connective is omitted between the sentences here?
   d Villeneuve had positive orders to go from Ferrol to the channel, or attempt to do so, even if his whole fleet should be destroyed in the attempt. Napoleon had now waited for two years for his approach, and was looking every day for his fleet; if it were present for only one day, the army would, he thought, be able to cross. His rage was terrible when he learned that the fleet had gone to Cadiz. He ordered Villeneuve to resign immediately and report himself at Paris; it was the receipt of this order that induced Villeneuve to offer battle to Nelson, knowing well that defeat awaited him.

4. a all [That] I hold dear.

5. a [Never another], or better [no other].
   b So entirely possessed, possessed so entirely. What is the difference? Which is correct here?
   c What object is gained by this use of Biblical expressions?

7. a Though the Northern League had been broken up, the disputed point was not relinquished.

b This statement will probably hold true to a greater extent than the
author intended. Owing to the nature of war ships at present, it is
not likely that in the future any great pitched battle will take
place at sea.

8. Note that the real subject of this paragraph begins with "yet" about
the middle of the paragraph.

9. *a* Nelson was proud of the title Bronte, which had been given him by
the King of Naples for his victory of the Nile, and was fond of
using it.

b "He," means Nelson himself. The order of battle here stated was
that employed generally by the English then. Villeneuve manœu-
vred well against it in his battle with Sir Robert Calder, off Ferrol.
But he said of the French: "We have a superannuated system of
naval tactics; we know only how to place ourselves in line, and that
is just what the enemy requires."

15. *a* "Whole fleet" would lead us to expect a singular verb and pronoun. "All the fleet" would be less objectionable as the idea
is plural.

The manœuvres of the two fleets in 14 and   might have been kept
more distinct.

The incidents mentioned purposely make Nelson prominent, and are
such as awaken our admiration for the hero and give a dramatic
interest to his death.

16. *a* What is Milton's form of this expression?

b The paragraph closes well with a picturesque view of the two fleets
approaching each other, but the personal interest at the close is not
in keeping with the scene.

18. As the divisions are getting into position, a few interesting personal
incidents, still referring to Nelson, are cleverly woven into the narrative.

19, 20 and 21 describe the battle, the chief scene being laid on the *victory*
with Nelson.

Paragraphs 22, 23 and 24 relate with touching effect the incidents of
Nelson's wound and death. The unadorned story, interwoven with
Nelson's characteristic remarks, is constructed with remarkable
skill, and is deeply affecting. In the selection and arrangement
of his materials from Nelson's prayer and letter before the battle to
the sad close, Southey shows the skill of an experienced plot con-
structor; 24 confined to his last words, and his death is purposely
short.

25. *a* "They" grammatically refers to the fifty that fell, which is not
the meaning.

This paragraph relates a trifling incident which, however, gratifies our sense of justice by the death of those who had shot down the hero, after he had twice spared them.

28. The close of the battle, and Nelson's knowledge that he died the most splendid of deaths—that of the hero in the hour of victory.

29. This paragraph opens with a few abrupt disconnected sentences. Other accounts relate that it was found impossible to anchor in the open sea with a gale blowing.

30. We read here of nothing given to Lady Hamilton and Horatia—all that Nelson "held dear in this world."

31. *a* "And all former times;" omit "of" to combine both into one statement, he could not be the greatest hero of former times.

b This is an unusual form of this phrase.

c [Were not merely defeated; they were destroyed.] "But" is adversative, not intensive.

d "All which" is used frequently by Southey. Custom now requires "that" after "all."

This paragraph and the closing one give a fine instance of simple, dignified language, used to express the national affection and grief. Paragraph 32 sings a prose elegy on his death. From the second sentence to the end it is a beautiful passage of rhythmical and melodious prose; indeed, it is almost metrical, as is usually the case when prose approaches the lofty feeling of poetry. It is the most artistic passage in the whole life, and is the only instance of the use of figurative language.

.

www.ingramcontent.com/pod-product-compliance
Lightning Source LLC
Chambersburg PA
CBHW021056030726
47496CB00006B/1868